BLESSED HANDS

Stories

BLESSED HANDS

Stories

Frume Halpern

Translated from the Yiddish and with an afterword
by Yermiyahu Ahron Taub

Foreword by Isaac Elchanan Ronch

Frayed Edge Press
Philadelphia, PA

First English-language edition, published by Frayed Edge Press ©2023

Translation of *Gebentshte hent: dertseylungen* by Frume Halpern published with the kind permission of the Frume Halpern estate.

The book was translated with the kind permission of Frume Halpern's grand-sons, Victor M. Linn and Robert Linn.

The original Yiddish version of "A Few Words About Frume Halpern" is copyright by the Estate of Isaac Elchanan Ronch. Grateful acknowledgement to Isaac Elchanan Ronch's son, Judah Ronch, for kind permissions.

Cover design by Adrienne Waterston.

Frayed Edge Press
PO Box 13465
Philadelphia, PA 19101

http://frayededgepress.com

Library of Congress Control Number: 2023940351

Publishers Cataloging-in-Publication Data

Names: Halpern, Frume. Gebentshte hent: dertseylungen. | Taub, Yermiyahu
    Ahron, translator. | Ronch, Isaac Elchanan.
Title: Blessed hands : stories / Frume Halpern ; translated from the Yiddish by
    Yermiyahu Ahron Taub ; preface by Isaac Elchanan Ronch.
Description: Philadelphia, PA : Frayed Edge Press, 2023. | Summary:
    Collection of short stories originally appearing in mid-20th century Yiddish
    newspapers, providing slice-of-life vignettes focused on people from
    marginalized groups in New York City and other locations.
Identifiers: LCCN 2023940351 | ISBN 9781642510492 (pbk.) | ISBN
    9781642510515 (ebook)
Subjects: LCSH: Working class Jews—Fiction. | Immigrants—United
    States—Fiction. | Working class African Americans—Fiction. | People with
    disabilities—Fiction. | New York (N.Y.)—Fiction. | BISAC: FICTION / Jewish.
    | FICTION / Short Stories. | FICTION / City Life.
Classification: LCC PJ5129.H29 G413 2023 | DDC 839.003 H--dc23
LC record available at https://lccn.loc.gov/2023940351

TABLE OF CONTENTS

A Few Words About Frume Halpern

[A Foreword to the Original Yiddish Edition]

Isaac Elchanan Ronch

Like a fastidious jeweler aiming to work with only the most authentic gemstones, so the storyteller searches and hunts for his theme. A delicious jackpot win is a compelling subject.[1] The extraordinary beckons; the captivating, in and of itself, merits depiction.

But what, for example, can be attractive in the figure of a woman selling newspapers at the subway entrance who is, as nature would have it, neither young nor pretty, but instead gray, ordinary, and often exhausted?

Her face is barely visible on the overcast winter mornings; her voice is monotone; her words monosyllabic—paltry material, surely, for an ambitious writer.

Frume Halpern does not feel that way.

She scrutinizes the desolate, the neglected, those condemned by life to be forgotten, and she looks into the souls of ordinary people, into the bodies from which one usually wants to avert one's gaze.

These are her themes, but her sympathy for them is not pitying. She doesn't aim to elicit emotionalism from the kindhearted reader. She treats her characters as one peer would another.

---

1. Possibly an allusion to the classic Yiddish play, *Dos groyse gevins* [*The Big Jackpot/The Big Prize*], by Sholem Aleichem (1859-1916).

1

It is no accident, apparently, that Frume Halpern's first book is called *Blessed Hands*. In her private life, she earns her livelihood with her hands, bringing healing and relief to weakened and anemic limbs.

Though her world is full of grayness, poverty, suffering, and loneliness, she lives by a simple motto: "Laugh—and the world laughs with you; cry, and you remain alone."

As a result, Frume Halpern doesn't have to chase after plots.

We are surrounded at every turn by characters that garner no attention, but who urgently need the spiritual, blessed hands of a Frume Halpern.

Her artistic eye absorbs them into her very being; her writerly talent analyzes them objectively, but they become her own. And they will become, too, the reader's own.

Every human being needs the touch of a friendly hand—and that touch is really the quintessence of Frume Halpern's creation.

> An old mother, a seeming shadow of a human being with a body that looked like parched earth, who had long forgotten the touch of a friendly hand upon her body, sensed the proximity of Soreh's devoted hand and became talkative.

But Frume Halpern doesn't take the same approach to all of her characters. In the same story, her bitter livelihood inflicts upon her the need to lay hands on a "lady who was like a lazy, well-fed cat," something she doesn't find at all pleasing.

> She quickly ran past the doorman, feeling as if she had just done something foolish…

Frume Halpern is as frank and naïve as the protagonists she portrays: the laboring girl, the ordinary housewife, her "Susan Flesher" characters, who embark upon the path of life with a sunny smile only to find themselves forever stuck in congealed poverty.

Just like Frume Halpern herself, who penetrates deeply but does it quietly and gently, so her protagonists never raise their voices. It's not that they make peace with their lot: rather, the author seems to believe that their situations speak for themselves. In the end, it just isn't necessary to hang a sign on a child in shabby tatters that advertises his situation.

And yet, grayness and sadness don't overwhelm Frume Halpern's stories.

"Munye the Shoemaker" approaches Baruch Spinoza in an original, playful way.

There is a folksy humor in a number of these stories. There is a healthy optimism in Beylke, who "piled the entire responsibility for all of the world onto her narrow shoulders."

Sharp, fiery, glowing flashes of lightning make their way through the black-gray clouds. These are the word portraits Frume Halpern creates. They arrive unexpectedly and illuminate everything around them.

Into our literature, Frume Halpern's *Blessed Hands* brings strange and repressed characters whom we've never noticed, even though they live among us. Thanks to her talent, they become close to us, and yes, our very own.

Blessed Hands

Ever since Soreh stood up on her own two feet and became an independent person, her hands had been in constant contact with human bodies. Her fingers caressed their aches in nurturance, fusing with the pain that comes from hard labor. The hands received thanks and blessings from all sorts of mouths and in all sorts of languages. Sometimes, they were blessed with tears, and sometimes—with a smile.

Soreh didn't take pride in how her hands looked—unless she was working with them. Outside of her work, she maintained, they were nothing to flaunt. Her hands weren't feminine enough. Heavy muscles, taut veins, wrinkled skin, broad palms—in other words, hands without any charm whatsoever. But when the hands came into contact with the human body, they were animated with a life of their own. They appeared tender and soulful—with a maternal devotion, with the will to lighten aches and alleviate suffering, with the drive to care for children and elders. The hands extended not just to the ailing organs but all the way to the human soul.

Through her two unlovely, but effective, hands, Soreh also connected often with those who didn't understand her language and couldn't make themselves understood to her. Her hands were her medium, and through them, patients felt her closeness down to the deepest depths of their suffering, ailing limbs. In their eyes, Soreh detected blessing without words. These mute blessings were a form of encouragement to her, a kind of force field—they were the foundation of the love she carried within her throughout these many years for all those who suffered.

Year in, year out—the same. The same people. The fingers know no prejudice. Agony is similar among all sorts of people. When someone is in pain, that "aagh!" has to be torn out. A broken organ is the same broken organ for everyone. And yet, each person contains within themselves a kind of distinctiveness, something that separates them from all others.

Quite often, it seemed to Soreh that not only did she fathom the sick, but they themselves understood her through her hands. They sensed her compassion. They saw how she absorbed their fears into her very being. As a result, the patients brought to Soreh not merely their own wounded lives but also the troubles of their children and their children's children. In this way, she was woven into the lives of all of their families. She saw them around her, as if they were her own blood relatives.

An old mother, a seeming shadow of a human being with a body that looked like parched earth, who had long forgotten the touch of a friendly hand upon her body, sensed the proximity of Soreh's devoted hand and became talkative.

The old woman didn't know how many of her children perished in the gas chambers, but she did know how many of her grandchildren had. When she spoke about them, tears flowed down onto her hands. Those tears mixed with Soreh's tears, and the old woman felt close to her. She blessed and thanked Soreh, and then became a part of Soreh's family.

The old woman reminded Soreh of her own mother, her mother with her own blessed hands. She had been ill for a long time, suffering from staggering pains that allowed her no sleep. Her children were helpless. Soreh, who was some ten years old, wanted so much to help her mother that she ran her child's fingers over her mother's neck. It worked wonders. Her mother dozed off. From that point on, Soreh could always get her mother to fall asleep with her touch. Every time her mother opened her eyes and saw her youngest caressing her hair, she would say, "A blessing on your hands, my child!"

God wanted these same hands to draw their livelihood from touching the human body. Life also wanted Soreh to share the blessings of her hands. For those who most needed her hands, she could only spare a few minutes. The rest of her time she had to give to those who could pay. Still, in those few minutes, she served the neediest with her hands and she did so with great attentiveness.

These old, sick, and broken people were given a written chart with an allotted number of minutes. But for those who purchased her time, there was no chart; they just selected the time slot when it was too early for them to play cards or go shopping.

Those from the lower social strata were not terribly vigilant in their hygiene or particularly well-mannered; they were heavy and awkward in gait and often dull of mind. Still, when you dug deeper, when you brought out what was buried deep within, all that was most essentially human would shine forth, leaving you surprised and feeling small and insignificant in comparison. Over there—among the privileged and polished, the refined—there God had set His hand and shielded them, protecting them from all that was malignant. And yet there, when you scraped off the sheen, a little worm, a small parasite, would crawl out from behind the refined façade.

When Soreh went to her more privileged patients, she had to put on fresh, clean clothes. She had to doll herself up for the lackey who opened the door for her. When she came to the lady of the house, she had to walk on tip-toes. She had to speak quietly, courteously, with submission, as if she were pleading for her very life. The genteel lady was just pure smiles and paid her banal compliments, and Soreh, too, had to smile and pay for the compliments.

The lady always had a lot to say. She usually complained about exhaustion stemming from too much thinking, from worry, from the servants—you didn't even know how much to pay for their wages. Why, they themselves didn't know how much to ask for! And what a hardship—there was nowhere to escape from them. It all wore terribly on her nerves.

The lady stretched herself out like a lazy, well-fed cat and yawned: it was all just too much! It had to stop! They needed to leave her in peace!

When Soreh worked on the lady in the low, soft bed, among all of the satin and silk covers, when she manipulated the soft body with its pampered limbs and listened to the lady's babble, she thought about her own life. Right here, at the house of the person who had purchased her hands and forced her to listen to her silly chatter, Soreh wanted to demand a small piece of life for herself.

Reflecting on her life, Soreh asked herself: What would I be doing if I were at home? More than anything, she would see to it that her children went to bed on time. She longed to cuddle them, to help them fall asleep with a little story—one she longed to tell them but kept postponing because she had no time.

Soreh remembered her unfortunate mother in her impoverished shtetl of long ago. Her mother had sold her own baby's milk. She hired herself out as a wetnurse for the wealthy. She had to let her own child go hungry, while the wealthy child grazed at her breast. She had to give away a mother's love of her own baby to a stranger's child.

Soreh started suddenly from her thoughts. She thought she was waking up from a dream and grew frightened—had she been speaking her thoughts aloud? Could her reflections have been audible? Had her fingers given away what she was thinking? They were like her musical instrument. Through her hands, her feelings were transmitted to others—over there. She could see that in their eyes. These were vibrating tones, mute music!

She reproached herself for the stolen time, and with the intensity and tenderness of the soul, began to pour herself into the realm of her hands—these hands that would surely lead her onto the right path. These lean, humble hands knew only one path— the truth—even toward those who cannot see another person's truth.

In the room, the stillness was blue, silken. The air was saturated with blue apathy. The quiet, musical tick-tock of the wall clock in its crystal frame, which had been hanging for a few generations in this venerable apartment on Park Avenue, harmonized with her breathing and with the rhythm of her fingers as they moved from limb to limb. Soreh's legs trembled slightly when she bent over. The little dog, napping on a padded, satin rocking chair, stretched out and yawned. This was no ordinary little dog. It looked like a clever housewife who knew all too well what's what. Soreh loved dogs, but this creature that looked at her with the eyes of a human being was not to her liking. It seemed to her that the dog was watching her—tracking her every movement— with suspicious eyes. Each time she saw the little dog yawning or sticking out its long, pink tongue, or showing off its small, white teeth and silky fur, Soreh thought, "This is a real fancy dog that loves to flirt!"

When she was finished with her work, it was hard for Soreh to straighten up. But she didn't want the little dog to notice, so Soreh mustered her strength and stood up straight with a gesture, as if casting off a heavy load from herself.

The lady turned to face her. She stretched out her just-massaged body and a delighted smile appeared on her face. Eyes lowered, she gazed upon herself, and as if talking to herself, said, "What blessed hands! What magical hands!"

Soreh quickly put on her coat and hurriedly headed out. She quickly ran past the doorman, feeling as if she had just done something foolish, as if someone had tricked her and she were a bit angry at herself. She quickened her pace, spewing a curse into the air. Then she made her escape, heading for home.

In the Garden of Eden

Basket of merchandise in hand, the elderly Reb Leyzer headed to the market. As he did every morning, he was going to take his place next to the large fruit stand, where he ran his business while seated on a box. It was a Friday, a day for business, and a wet, slick morning. He was in a hurry, and while crossing the wide, noisy street, he failed to see the car that had materialized out of nowhere. Before he had time to look around him, the basket, with all of its merchandise, flew away and the collision catapulted him off to another world.

Suddenly, he felt as if something were being torn from him. Everything ached, especially his right leg, as if it were being pulled out with pliers. He felt that his right leg was lying off somewhere without him. Shortly after, bitter coldness enveloped him and he heard his teeth chattering. Then the cold turned into a heavy heat, a steamy heat, causing him to gasp for breath. He struggled, wanting to free himself from the heat, but he felt the ground disappear from under him. He so wanted to grab hold of something, but he touched only the void, an emptiness. By then, he was swimming in the dark and was astonished to find that he wasn't afraid. His head was light, as if it had been separated from his body, as if the body itself had split into two parts, as if it were sliding further and further away from him. Because of the dark, he didn't know where he was. The darkness was so frightful; it was if the whole world had fallen asleep.

Suddenly, Reb Leyzer felt that something was jerkily raising him up high. Were they carrying—or leading—him? He only sensed that everything was racing as quickly as the clouds and

11

his head—also a cloud—was rotating bizarrely. Now, light; now, darkness. Suddenly, there was a cutting light, as if coming from a thousand lightning-bright lamps. He couldn't bear the bright light and wanted to turn his head, but it was welded to something and he heard a pounding, as if from hammers. It was so loud he could count the beats: Ta! Ta! Ta! Mixed with the pounding were the chimes of silverware, as if preparations for a festive occasion were underway…

Suddenly, a groaning. Who was groaning like that over there? The groaning—agonized, cutting—pieces were being torn from him! He felt like screaming, and he burst into loud tears. The weeping loosened his throat a bit, but he was very hot. The heat was nauseating. He felt like vomiting. He wanted to uncover himself, but he couldn't find his hands. Who hid his hands? His eyes were stuck shut, but he couldn't fall asleep. The pounding in his temples didn't stop.

Soon, it seemed to Reb Leyzer that someone was speaking. The voice was close at hand, near the bed. Several voices were speaking. Something was taken off his face, and it became easier for him to breathe. But the load still pressed down on him, like a thousand-pound weight was lying on top of him. He couldn't feel any of his organs; it was as if he were congealed, as if he had become pure stone.

Reb Leyzer forced his eyes open and found himself in a bright, spacious room. He was lying on a clean, white bed. He looked for his grandchild, who always slept in his bed and was surprised to find that the child was not there. Momentarily, he closed his eyes and then opened them, thinking that something was amiss. How had he ended up in this white room at all? It seemed to him that he was dead, that he was in the Garden of Eden. The bright, white room was a reward from God Blessed Be He for his hard and honest life.

When he remembered his impoverished, overworked days, a sorrow—for himself and all his household—so took hold of him that a choking began in his throat and he sobbed within. He tried to speak but it was hard for him to open his mouth and the words remained stuck between his tongue and gums. He wanted to think, but that, too, he couldn't do. His thoughts flitted away; nothing stopped moving. This heat—it was scorching!

Reb Leyzer opened his eyes, and next to him, he saw a young girl in white, a luminous smile on her face. He became delighted: this was his Sheyndele, after all, who had departed this world so young, not even seventeen years old. He wanted to look at her thoroughly, but she was no longer there. It seemed to him that he saw her, but her face was swimming away somewhere.

Before him spun a cloudy wheel, and in its center—Sheyndele's face. But when he tried to gaze upon it, it vanished. Poof!

Several times, Reb Leyzer felt needles jabbing him. He wasn't sleeping, but neither was he awake. He didn't know if it was day or night; it was as if time stood still. It seemed to him that he was extending his hand and reaching for something or that he was getting up and walking over to "something," but yet he was unable to move.

His "Sheyndele" was very good to him. She washed him, caressed him, brought him food on a tray, fed him as if he were a small child, but she didn't say a word. She merely smiled. He wanted to ask her something, but he forgot how to speak. He did remember the words, but how it was that a word came to emerge—that he forgot. He must come to remember.

Reb Leyzer had to lie on his back, welded to the bed. His right leg, from the toes to just above the belly, was walled in. So Reb Leyzer now lay in his Garden of Eden, staring at the ceiling with glassy eyes.

Reb Leyzer was a man in his seventies who for years—since becoming a widower—had lived with his son, a poor baker's apprentice. Even though he had had few good years in his long life, he still looked younger than he was. He was small, vivacious, and good-natured. He didn't show his age or his poverty. "Years," he said, "aren't a sign of prestige. They aren't anything to put on airs about."

Reb Leyzer was a passionate and devoted father. He was happy that he was able to help out his son. Although his son had pleaded with him to stop running to the market because they were able to make ends meet without his earnings, he wouldn't hear of it.

Reb Leyzer's basket was filled with all sorts of soaps, threads, candles, and shoelaces. He called his basket "my haberdashery business." At his son's house, the old man was none too comfortable. He didn't have his own bed and had to sleep with his six-year-old grandchild, who habitually pulled away the blanket so that Reb Leyzer was left uncovered and gradually found himself freezing. However, he never complained. He didn't want to cause the children any pain. "If you live with your children in close quarters," he claimed, "you have to be content with everything and give thanks to the Lord Above."

Reb Leyzer had lost several children. Several months after the death of their daughter, who departed this world young, his wife's spirit went out like a flame. The girl's death also upset the father terribly, but he consoled himself with his broken life. "Well, as long as I'm still alive…" he said.

When Reb Leyzer was tossed by the car and brought half-dead, half-alive, to the hospital, he was diagnosed as critically ill and placed in a separate room and given a private nurse. There, lying with a shattered skull and in a delirium, he mistook the nurse for his daughter.

After ten days, the patient's condition slowly changed. The cloud around him retreated for a while, and then he looked around with alertness. His dry lips twisted into a smile, even as they trembled like those of a child about to burst into tears. He always knew when the nurse was next to him. His immobile body somehow reacted to her presence. But this happened rarely and only for a few moments, so he lay there, he eyes fixed on the ceiling. It was hard to say what was taking place within his unseeing world.

Over time, the hospital found out that there was no one to pay for the patient. The son was poor and the car that ran him over wasn't insured, so Reb Leyzer was wheeled over to the general ward. They also sent for his son and informed him that he should either take his father home or to the municipal hospital.

Reb Leyzer's exhausted son, several years past thirty, tried to speak to him, wanting to trigger in him any recollection whatsoever. It seemed that the sick man could see his son, but only half clearly, through a cloud that, at those moments, did not want to retreat from him. He nodded his head, gestured with his hands, panted heavily, and after much effort, lifted his head from the pillow and looked at his son and the rows of beds with patients. A new panorama revealed itself to him. He didn't know if he was in the right place. He fell back upon the pillow, closed his eyes, and, once again, found himself in his Garden of Eden.

Neighbors

In the five-story, smoke-blackened, semi-dilapidated tenement house, a lone Jewish family remained. The Black people, who had slowly come to occupy all of the building, seldom glimpsed their Jewish neighbors—an elderly couple who constantly held hands like children. The two looked like they had stumbled into this building where they had lived for several decades. When Black people moved in, the building became alien to them.

Many years ago, when the Sigels first moved here, the broad avenue was still among the most prestigious streets and no one wanted to rent an apartment to a Jew. The Sigels were the first Jews in the building. But as so often happens, the avenue changed its face over time, shedding its more "exalted" residents. In some places, an old tree still remained. The street itself, and the building, screamed in poverty. At one point in time, the street had a substantial number of Jewish residents. But when Black people moved in, the Jews, one by one, began to leave. At first, it was the wealthier ones; later, it was those who had less; and after that, it was anyone who could just find somewhere else to live. Only those who had no other options remained. The Sigels stayed behind and clung to each other, as if afraid that a stranger would break into their domain.

Even back then, when other Jews lived there, the Sigels rarely mingled with their neighbors. They took refuge in their own slice of poverty. When he was young, Mr. Sigel had been a Hebrew teacher. In his advanced years, he earned a living by preparing boys for their bar mitzvah. The Sigels themselves didn't have any children. When the elderly Mr. Sigel passed away, loneliness and fear of her dark-skinned neighbors weighed so heavily on the widow that she became afraid of her own shadow, too frightened to leave the building.

One morning, a Black neighbor, Mary Crawford, knocked on the widow's door. When the old woman, knees knocking and rendered speechless from terror, partially opened the door, she heard a soft voice, devoid of any brashness:

"Is your name Mrs. Sigel? I'm new. I moved here not too long ago…. Don't be angry. The mailman left your letter in my mailbox. At first, I didn't notice your name on the letter."

"Please don't be angry," Mary continued, extending her outstretched hand toward the half-closed door. Her warm voice blunted the widow's terror, and she opened the door wide. In the darkness of the corridor, she couldn't make out a face. The small white envelope flowed together with the whiteness of a row of teeth into a single whiteness. Some kind of bright shadow danced upon the old woman's yellowed hand as it reached for the small envelope. After a moment, Mary's voice echoed in the mournful, melancholy home. "Please come in," beckoned the elderly Mrs. Sigel, envelope in hand, pointing the way. "Come in, have a seat…" she said, leading the way.

Mary followed her. Her gait was heavy; she trudged, tottering from one side to the other, holding onto the wall of the narrow corridor. She said, "My feet are throwing a tantrum. Sometimes, they're good to me and do as I say, and then other times, they get a mind of their own. I might as well stop walking and start rolling on roller skates." She broke into laughter at her own words. Mrs. Sigel, who hadn't smiled at all since her husband's death, was transported by Mary's laughter. Now, both women were laughing. One, loudly, resoundingly; the other—somewhat to herself. They were two complete strangers, whom a small envelope had accidentally brought together and shown that they have something in common.

Mary sat down and pointed to the envelope that Mrs. Sigel was in no hurry to open, and said, "If not for this letter, I wouldn't have gotten out of bed."

Mary was tall and sturdily built. Her face was stout and round, and her skin gleamed as if made from velvet and steamed with a misty dampness. Tenderness beamed from her wide nose and thick lips. Her eyes brimmed with sorrow; underneath them were blue "half-moons." Despite the heaviness of her body, she nevertheless had a kind of lightness that one sensed when coming into contact with her.

In the first few minutes of their encounter, little, shrunken Mrs. Sigel wasn't particularly sure about Mary, but that uncertainty soon dissipated. Mary's presence in the room warmed her to such an extent that she forgot the differences between them and even the reason for her neighbor's visit. She held the envelope in her hand, uncertain whether she had warmly welcomed her black neighbor.

Mary stood up and said, "My name is Mary Crawford, but I'd prefer that you call me 'Mary.' Your name is Sigel so I'll call you 'Mother Sigel.' It's not good, Mother Sigel. They delayed my check again. I was catching my breath, paying off the debts that have accumulated, and suddenly—no more!" She continued, "I have to keep going there, over and over again, explaining to them why I'm not working… If I could work, would I want their checks? Would I be pleading for a few dollars for a mattress? If you could see my mattress, Mother Sigel, patched up, held together with rope. And the doctor in the hospital shouts at me, 'Don't come to me in such shoes. You need to have good shoes!' So I ask him, 'Doctor, where am I supposed to get money for new shoes? What am I—a shoemaker?'"

Despite her words, there was no bitterness on Mary's face. She spoke in a humorous tone, as if she were speaking not about herself, but someone else altogether. The diminutive Mrs. Sigel, who had never poured the bitterness in her heart out to anyone, now saw herself in in Mary's words. She marveled at how the other woman spoke so straightforwardly from her heart.

Mary had entered Mrs. Sigel's apartment with heaviness, but her departure was lighter, as if her difficulties had been lifted from her heart. Mrs. Sigel, too, felt that her heavy, dark-skinned neighbor had brought something that it would be a shame to lose, and that if she were to lose it, she would miss it afterwards.

"We'll see each other again, Mama Sigel. Don't forget me," Mary said as she departed, and Mrs. Sigel felt Mary clasping her with her strong, warm hands. After Mary left, she immediately felt something lacking in her sad home. As a result, when she heard a knock on the door the next time, she knew that it was Mary, and when she entered, Mrs. Sigel was delighted to see her.

The more Mary came over, the more the wall between the two women shriveled and the stronger the knot between them became. Through Mary, Mrs. Sigel looked altogether differently at her Black neighbors in the tenement house, those who up until now had terrified her and kept her at a distance.

Mrs. Sigel no longer felt that strange, angry eyes were staring at her. She remembered the words of her deceased husband. She had once tried to talk him into moving out of the tenement house that was by then full of Black people. He'd said to her, "You're committing a sin. In all this time, not one of them has done you any wrong!" He even said to her, "Jews shouldn't consider themselves superior to Black people." On another occasion, he told her that "Moses Our Teacher had a dark-skinned wife named Zipporah…" Now she remembered his words. Gradually, Mary became her best friend.

Several of Mary's children had died. But she herself remained both a mother and a child. Within herself, she possessed the generosity of a mother, always ready to help out, as well as the tenderness of a child. When Mrs. Sigel could tell from Mary's face that she was not in a good mood, she knew that it wasn't necessarily because of her knees or because her check hadn't arrived.

Mary could laugh in the face of her own needs, and if she were downcast, something else had to be wrong with her.

Only a few of Mary's children were alive, and they had children of their own. She said very little about her children and grandchildren, but from the few words that Mrs. Sigel did hear from Mary's mouth, she gleaned that Mary was aching for her own flesh and blood. Mrs. Sigel envied Mary's pain. She herself had no children of her own; except for her husband, she had suffered on behalf of no one else. So now she envied heavy, dark Mary with the sorrow in her eyes and the warm ease in her voice.

Mary loved to hear the little tales about miracles that Mother Sigel told her—the miracles that happened to the pious Jews. The tales rang true to Mary, and anything connected to the faith of the old woman seemed to her to be shrouded in secrecy. She saw how Mrs. Sigel wore a small Star of David around her neck and was certain that this small object could protect from all troubles...

Mary, who had toiled since childhood, never went to school. It seemed to her that the tiny, shrunken woman lived in good health because she wore this small object around her neck.

It seemed to Mary that her grandchild was struck with a new sickness every day—and still such a young child. The way he coughed—it tore at your heartstrings. His grandmother forgot her own aches and suffered along with the child. Then a thought occurred to her: Maybe she should ask her Jewish neighbor if she would lend her what she wore around her neck? For herself, she wouldn't have asked, but for her grandchild? Yes, she would!

It took a long time before Mary turned to Mrs. Sigel about the matter. "Good Mama Sigel! What is it that you're wearing around your neck? Is it for luck? Does it protect from evil spirits? We also wear little crucifixes, but it's a totally different thing. One of my grandchildren is not well..."

She stopped speaking abruptly; tears choked up her words, and the old woman practically saw the sick child before her very eyes. She sensed a mother's pain in Mary's words and she did really want to find a way to help her out. But how?

Mrs. Sigel thought about it. Mary looked at her, as if the fate of the sick child lay in her hands.

"Why not try?" Mrs. Sigel thought. "But is it permitted? Isn't it a desecration of the holiness? No, it's not a desecration!" Something in the old woman awakened. "If it's holy, it has to be good, good for everyone…" She removed the little golden Star of David from her neck, gave it a kiss, and said, "Here, have this! I'm giving it to you as a present. Give it to the little one. My husband, may he rest in peace, even said that you don't need to believe in such things. But I want your grandchild to get better. I'm handing this item over to you with my best wishes. I've worn it around my neck for such a long time."

Her hands trembling, Mary accepted the small Star of David. In a kind of whisper to herself, and with her eyes full of tears, she said, "God bless you!" and left the apartment.

Susan Flesher

Although it was a weekday morning, the avenue, which cut through the park, was empty and desolate. People went to their workplaces through side streets and took detours to avoid the terrible wind that came howling and whistling from all four sides, tearing away at anything it possibly could. It looked as if all of the trees would be uprooted in the powerful struggle between tree and wind.

It was a gray morning at the end of February, the kind with a dry bite that penetrates the bones. The commuters racing off to work were gripped by the cold and appeared gloomy and angry, ready to blurt out something that would tug and pierce to the point of pain.

The sun, cold and distant, struggled across the tall chimney tops, as if it were debating with itself about whether or not to appear. Heavy clouds soon draped the morning in a kind of darkness that was neither day nor night.

Susan Flesher headed toward the adjacent alley called "Terrace Park." She walked slowly, pushing an old baby carriage filled with broken boxes and wood shavings that would serve as kindling to heat her home. The alley was walled in between tall, five- and six-story buildings and wasn't visible until you got quite close to it. The few small stooped homes with their broken fences gave the alley the appearance of a desolate cemetery.

The early hour and the biting chill notwithstanding, there was no sign of haste in Susan's pace. She was wearing a light summer dress with many ruffles. Over her dress, she wore a short little coat that reached to the waist, and on her feet, sandals that were long past their prime and completely out of fashion. On Susan's head was a bright silk kerchief, charmingly tied with a knot placed in the very center of her forehead, like a flower. She walked straight ahead. Her pace—minute and certain. The movements of her limbs—rhythmic. She held her head slightly high, as if she wanted to make sure that her gaze would be suitably captured by a photographer. There was something like a pose in the whole way she held herself. She pushed the ruined, squeaking carriage with importance, as if she were taking a flamboyant little dog for a walk.

Susan's movements and clothing garnered notice. The carriage did not drive straight. Its wheels—weak, loose on their axles—required Susan's help, and she generously aided them with pushes from her knees. She did this with such dexterity that the old carriage obeyed her. Every now and then, it just groaned from old age. This drew more attention from passersby than Susan wanted.

It was hard to know how old Susan was. Her hair was completely bright—a mix of childish white-blue and white-gray. Her eyes were green-blue with a dark reflection, and her mouth with its full lips was ready for a word and a smile. Although the shadows beneath her eyes could indeed tell of difficult experiences, there was in her gait and in her voice an ease that suited her better than her deliberateness which seemed more like pretense than her true nature.

As she came closer to the alley, ready to turn into it, a middle-aged, elegantly-dressed man suddenly appeared opposite her. The man looked around in all directions as if he might recognize certain things from the past. He noticed her from a distance and decided to keep going, but as soon as Susan spotted him, she stopped the baby carriage, clapped her hands, and called out, "If it isn't my dear old Thomas! … Oh, Tom! Dear young man, where have you come from? And on a morning like this? … Oh, I don't believe my eyes… Who would have expected to see you again?" She placed her hands on his broad, even shoulders and looked into his eyes with the joy of remembrance, continually repeating, "Thomas, Thomas Heisler!"

For a moment, the man stood perplexed, as if he had no idea who had suddenly fallen upon him with such love. But soon her voice stirred something in his memory. His large, serene eyes set in a full, fresh face stared penetratingly into her, and for a few moments, there was fear mixed with wonder in them. Finally, as if returning to himself, he quietly asked, "Can it really be Susan Flesher? That Susan?"

She interrupted him, "Shh, shh! Yes, that one…" And she erupted into a hoarse laughter.

"Oh, Tom, Tom," she said, extending her hand and pointing toward a large, multi-story building on the street: "Right there, Tom—where that building is—that's where your father's beautiful home with the fine garden was."

The wind blew louder, and Susan, now a bit blue from the cold, took hold of the carriage, and said to the man, "Our home there is about to sink, but it's still standing! I'm afraid my kindling supply will freeze… It's time to get going. Would you like to come along, Tom?"

Not waiting for an answer, Susan started on her way. Feeling somewhat agitated, Tom followed her. When she stopped speaking, he pensively said, "Yes, yes, it's strange—I was sure that I wouldn't run into anyone here—in any case, not someone who would remember me from back then … so many years ago …"

He considered her thoroughly and said, "Not the same—and yet, yes, the same. Life really is strange!"

Although they had both spent their childhood years on the very ground where they now stood, Tom didn't really know his way around. Everything had changed so much, and with such thoroughness, that it was hard for him to orient himself and to connect what he was seeing now with what he remembered.

He was his father's only child. His father had owned a brewery, the largest in town, and it, in fact, wasn't far from here. He
remembered how his father once told him that all of the surrounding land belonged to him and gestured with his hand to show his
son, the heir, the vast extent of his holdings. The brewery alone
took up an entire block. As children, he and Susan had played
together in the sand. His father sent Thomas to a private school
while Susan went to a public school. The public school was far
away, and Thomas used to take her along in his handsome wagon,
driven by an affable little horse, which the children used to play
with as if it were their equal. Once elementary school was over,
life split them apart. His wealthy father sent Thomas to study in
another city and Susan began pursuing her childhood dreams of
the stage. Ever since she was seven years old and had made her
mark in a children's production, there had been no dream more
glorious to her than being in the theater.

With her blond locks, dark-blue eyes, and a smile that enchanted young people, it wasn't very hard for her to step into
the temple that had been the foundation of her dreams. For many
years, Susan's lovely face enchanted theater-goers as she played
light roles with sonorous names. Susan surely had been a great
success. Her portraits on theater posters called out and smiled
down onto the town and then beyond to nearby cities. She herself
floated in a sweet trance from all the compliments and everything
that came with them…

Tom's name drew attention, too. He was his father's son, and
his father was popular because of his gobbling-up of pieces of
land in the neighborhood where he had opened the brewery. He
also opened construction offices. The advertisements for "Thomas Heisler Construction" were posted in many places right next to
the posters that blared with Susan's portrait. At that time, young
Thomas (his father was also named Thomas) was far away, and
his father's business barely interested him. He had plenty of mon-

ey, but he wasn't practically inclined and wasted a lot of money at his father's expense.

It had been years since Thomas Heisler, Sr. had died, and by now the name "Susan Flesher" was long forgotten. Without any effort on his part, Thomas, Jr. became the heir to his father's millions. Not having the ambition to helm his father's business, he handed everything over to managers and bankers and they ran the business for him. He knew that the bankers were more cut out for running the business, and so he left everything to his underlings.

When it came time to negotiate the demolition of old houses in the neighborhood to create more space for a certain construction project, Tom had to visit the neighborhood and give his approval. He tried to extricate himself from this particular responsibility, but, in the end, he had to give the final word.

On that stormy morning, Thomas headed out on his mission. He settled into his luxury car and told the chauffeur to drive to the Bronx. At first, he thought he would stay in the car. He would just drive by, taking note of what he needed, and that would be enough. But when the chauffeur drove into the park and Thomas spotted the brook where he and his school friends used to catch goldfish so long ago and the stone that, from a distance, looked like a large elephant, a boyish curiosity lit up his memory and he found himself compelled to get out of the car. He began to walk through the park. Everything now was so different that Thomas quickly forgot his childish sentiments and longings. He never expected to meet someone who would remember him from childhood. That was all so long ago!

Thomas rummaged around in his memory, seeking to remember friends from that distant past, and decided that such searching after the passage of almost forty years ago was pointless. On his travels, he had come into contact with thousands of people, and the faces of the many had to erase the faces of the few. But actually it was at the same time that he had that thought that he lifted his eyes and saw the woman with the carriage filled with wood.

The woman was wearing clothes that gave her an exotic appearance, and both they and the carriage she was pushing looked a tad bizarre and suspicious. He wanted to walk past her. But the woman stood where she was, set her large, joyous eyes on him, and called out his name with such enthusiasm that he immediately became unnerved and afraid. Only after she repeated his name a few times—Tom—Thomas—Tom—did he remember to whom the voice belonged.

Susan—yes. Much remained in that voice, the very voice that he once adored hearing. And it hadn't just been him. Anyone who heard that voice loved to be on the receiving end of its tones. His father sent him to study in another city so that he would be far away from that girl who was the darling of all the boys in the neighborhood. Even when he was home on vacation, his father didn't permit—didn't want—his son to be friendly with this daughter of an impoverished musician.

When Tom was eighteen years old, he came home but didn't interact with the Fleshers. His father had passed away by then, and Susan hovered in the white clouds… Only now did Tom see the distance between them…

Approaching the small house that looked hunchbacked and old, as if it were shivering from the cold, Susan abruptly stopped, as if she wanted to divert Tom's gaze away from her home so it wouldn't feel ashamed before a stranger's eyes. Gesturing with her hand, she pointed the other homes out to him, saying, "Do you see that little old woman there? We're all one family. We set up an association! We all banded together to battle the big landowner who wants to take away our every last possession. 'They need the land' they say, and they want to send us packing with nothing… They say the law is on their side, and that they can evict us from these houses. Well, we'll show them they can't throw us out!"

Susan looked at Thomas, waiting for a response. She was sure he couldn't possibly see the matter any differently than she did.

But his gaze made her suspect that she was kidding herself. And so she added:

"Yes, the law might give them an advantage, but we'll make it hard for them to throw us off the land. We'll put stones in their way…In these homes, there are some sick people and others who lost children in the war."

When Susan glanced over at Thomas, she perceived boredom and indifference in his eyes. Realizing that her chatter scarcely interested him, a red flush flowed across her freezing cheeks. Since it was hard for her to change her tone at this point, Susan childishly blew through her full lips, as if she were angry, and said, "And you, my prince, haven't even offered to bring up my carriage! My, what the years have wrought!"

She laughed raucously. Helping to push the carriage, Tom thought, "You're still performing on the theater stage, Susan Flesher!"

Once inside, they were in a large, half-dark room with few furnishings. A dog with velvety black fur greeted them. The dog stood still, looked at the guest for a while, and then ran to his mistress with that joy that dogs have, as if he hadn't seen her in a long time. Susan calmed him with a few warm caresses on the head, and said, "Let me introduce you. His name is 'Captain.'" With his half-teary and round eyes, Captain contemplated the guest and then retreated.

On a shabby, dark-red sofa sat a ballerina doll. Her long, thin legs hung down slackly. Her red tulle dress occupied a corner of the sofa, and her eyes, practically without pupils, flashed saucily, as if to say: "Hello there, aren't I pretty?"

Susan led Thomas to the sofa and said, "Here, you have a seat with the lady. I'll go warm something up. It won't take long. I have a fine oven." Alone in the room, Thomas looked around, rubbed his eyes, and smiled. Contained in that smile were discombobulation and disorientation. He took in the half-empty room, the crumbling walls, the cracking plaster. In one hand, he held the smiling doll and marveled at how he had stumbled upon this poverty. It occurred to him that Susan fit well in this setting, as if she hadn't ever known anything better.

"Is this, too, some kind of performance?" he asked himself, and then answered his own question: "No." From the way she carried herself, there was no perceptible sign of the dejection that such an impoverished life ought to have had on her.

This entirely unexpected encounter—the surprise of it—sent Thomas into such a tailspin that he found himself consumed by a desire to get away as soon as possible. The air here was heavy and cold. He realized that Susan hadn't asked him to take off his coat. Perhaps she intended for him to leave quickly? "I really don't need to stay," he thought as he stood up. He approached the piano, the only respectable piece of furniture in the room. Through a window, two twisted rays of sunshine spun in a half circle onto a crystal photo frame. It was a full-length photograph of a beautiful lady. She was wearing a dark dress with lace and a train that gathered in folds around her feet. The dress had a low-cut décolletage. An unusual feminine charm resided in the light profile of this blossoming young woman, in the lines of her neck, in her smile. In her hand, she held a fan made of ostrich feathers before her as if it were a mirror she was reflected in, as if it were alive and she wanted to bring it to her lips.

Thomas mechanically walked away and then returned. He squinted as if the rays of light prevented him from having a good look at the photograph. He almost said aloud: "Yes, that's Susan! Years ago, I saw this photo in a New York newspaper. It was 'Susan Flesher' in the role of Oscar Wilde's drama *Lady Windemere's Fan*."[2] He remembered seeing the photograph in Paris,

---

2. Even if Halpern doesn't state that Susan Flesher played the lead or title role in the Wilde play, the strong implication from this sentence (i.e. from not specifying which role) is that she did so. However, several pages later, it seems that she played the role of Mrs. Erlynne, Lady Windermere's mother. Although Halpern does not explicitly state that Susan played both roles (succeeding in the title role and failing as Mrs. Erlynne), the story certainly implies that and works well with that premise.

and he recalled how surprised he had been back then. Goodness, how she's changed!

It was difficult for Thomas to connect the image of the middle-aged woman with her yellowish face, colorless hair, and artificial smile with this photograph. Why wasn't she open with him? Why didn't she tell him she was poor? She had pushed that carriage forward as if it were something to boast about. He took the photograph in his hand, carried it over to the light, and sadly shook his head. "What a transformation!" As soon as he was about to put the photograph back, he heard her easy, light footsteps. He stood opposite her and said: "A fine portrait. I saw it a while back. How long ago did you have it taken?"

For Susan, this encounter with Thomas was a delightful surprise. In recent years, she'd spent most of her time with older folks who differed from her in both age and temperament. Although they were dear to her and although they were united in their common struggle with the bank that hovered over them like a shadow—she often found them tedious. After all, her past was so different from her present. There had been hours when Susan longed for someone with whom she could share. During those hours, even her Captain looked so wrinkled and old. Then she would open her little magical box and remember her mother's tale.

It was a story about a little box that displayed magical powers. All you had to do was close your eyes and say a wish out loud and the little box would perceive your dream and desire. Susan had acquired just such a little box. Whenever she was sad, she'd open the box and summon times past, returning to those full days and floating on their white pathways. After opening her eyes, the "now" wasn't so difficult, and her life on a limited pension didn't seem as tragic.

How this change in her life had happened, Susan probably wouldn't have been able to pinpoint. That is, if she had even been asked. She only remembered that she had once asked herself whether theatergoers, especially the young people, were applauding her art or her beautiful face. The answer was something she came up with herself: "It is your beautiful face, Susan!" At that point, Susan became someone else, someone who either performed in the theater or did nothing!

It hadn't been easy for Susan to climb the ladder of theatrical success. Along the way, she had to make compromises—playing heated, lukewarm, and just-for-the-heck-of-it romances, performing them for the duration of the theatrical run, and then leaving them behind her. Time passed. One year ushered along the next. She played more and less prominent roles, but the fire that lit up the eyes and hearts of the fashionable young folk in the loges remained in the theater, the very place she later fled.

When Susan made her way with great effort to play the role in Oscar Wilde's *Lady Windemere's Fan*, she was close to forty years old. For months, she worked on her craft, mastering and modeling the sensibility of Wilde's mother, but she only reached perfection in one scene. The others weren't sufficiently convincing. In order to be persuasive, she *herself* had to be a mother, to feel like a mother whose conscience weighs heavily with guilt vis-à-vis her child and who wants to redeem something. Susan was not a mother and therefore couldn't get through to it. From all of her hard work the only thing that remained was the photograph with the feather fan in hand—the same photograph that captured Thomas's gaze and held his attention. With this photograph, Susan ended her career in the performing arts. Everything had happened so suddenly. The news of her mother taking sick interrupted her performing.

When Susan returned home, the one which she had previously left to enter the wider world, the home became a divinely blessed corner for her. She felt as if she were shedding chains—golden, shiny chains, to be sure—but nevertheless chains.

Susan took off her rich clothes, and put on a housedress and said to herself, "You're not performing in the theater anymore!"

Susan became a nurse. She held her elderly, ailing mother and felt that helping her had more value than amusing thousands.

It had been several years since Susan had reconnected with real life. From that point on, her dramas, tragedies, and tragi-comedies were not written by someone else, but rather experienced by Susan herself. Her mother died. Her financial savings were depleted. The home she inherited was old, sinking into the earth like an elderly person, like all homes in the neighborhood—impoverished and neglected and sentenced to death, barely clinging to flickering life.

Knowing the situation in which the residents of the small homes found themselves, the wealthy construction companies exploited their need. They themselves set the prices of the houses, not consulting with those who had to uproot themselves from their own ground and go forth in search of a new home to rest their head.

Susan was the first to see clearly the injustice that the bank was perpetrating against the neighbors. She encouraged and roused them to unite against the magnates seeking to drive them from their homes. With her optimism, Susan became the light tower of Park Terrace, a protective figure on whom to lean and find encouragement in times of despair and gloom. She warmed the neighbors' spirits with her piano playing, which brought joy to those who heard it and stirred new powers within her in the process.

As soon as Susan had spotted Thomas, a bizarre joy grew within her. It was the same joy from long ago when she skipped and ran with Tom as they played run-and-catch. He had been so handsome back then! But when the initial minutes of joy and astonishment elapsed and Thomas went silent, something came to a halt within her. She detected an odd stiffness in his eyes. It immediately occurred to her that she might have been mistaken. Perhaps this was someone else altogether who just looked like Thomas? But in his uttering of the words: "Is that really you,

Susan…", in the measured words that emerged so coldly—as if he were taking care not to utter an extraneous word—she sensed an alienation. It seemed that he even pronounced her name with a certain reservation, the way you do with a name when you aren't sure of it… So yes, she did sense an alienation.

Susan now saw before her a man, a giant, trim, with a broad chest. His face—longish. His eyes—dark brown. His hair was the same shiny black it had been in his youth. By all appearances, she assessed, the years did not weigh too heavily upon him.

When she came back into the room, accompanied by the dog, she didn't know how to begin a new conversation with him. She set about starting a fire. In her actions, there was a kind of annoyance, as if she had found something and then lost it again or had competed against someone and been defeated. She was already wondering whether she should have revealed herself to him. Who knew what kind of world he lived in now? His father, the millionaire, had surely left him a large inheritance. Wasn't it possible that he was one of the landowners who were set to demolish these old houses? And then a new thought occurred to her: "If he were, in fact, a millionaire, then he really ought to know how much she loved them, those millionaires!"

Susan approached the mirror. The face reflected back did not please her. It looked as if it were wearing armor. Maybe she should perform some theater for him? Would he understand? She directed her hands over her sallow cheeks, refreshed her lips, smoothed out the flowered kerchief that brought out the color of her eyes, and smiled: "Right now, I'm not doing that badly …"

Susan placed a little cigarette into her mouth, began to whistle a popular, upbeat ditty, and with the quicksilver unpredictability of a young girl, approached Thomas who was still holding her photo in his hand. Looking embarrassed, Tom put the photo back. Susan fixed a pair of cold eyes on him, passionately nursed the cigarette, then blew smoke from her smiling lips and said, "I've never seen your picture. All these years, you were erased from my thoughts. So that's why when I saw you, I showed such shocked joy."

Both sets of eyes now moved. His—cold, searching; hers—contentedly smiling. She quickly broke into laughter, and, as if this passing episode was causing her merriment, she said, "There once was a great Russian writer named Gorky who said, 'You can't ride in the chariots of the past!'" She added, "I don't even want to ride in them!" Thomas didn't have time to respond. She was already heading towards the door. Before long, she added, "At first, I wasn't really sure you were the Thomas of long ago, but it was the uncertainty in your eyes that persuaded me that it was you. Isn't it wonderful? And you, if you would have recognized me, would you have stopped or walked right by me?"

Instead of giving an answer, Thomas looked at her, silently, searching. Both of them now strode to the door without saying anything. Captain came along, underfoot. Susan bent down over the dog, took his face in her hands, and looked lovingly into his eyes. Thomas turned his head to the piano, unable to forget the connection between the two—the woman in the photograph and the other right here with the dog. The same vivaciousness was in both of them.

"A fine dog," he finally said.

"A very loyal friend," Susan said, and then added, "He never leaves my side."

Already at the door, Thomas, as if he were just remembering something, said, "I want to say something about your stubbornness, the way you go against the current. You won't tame the wind, Susan. The law is on their side. Maybe I can help you live somewhere else? And you'll get yourself some additional compensation, too."

Susan retreated from the door. Her face was suffused with redness and an aggravated outrage screamed from her eyes. Thomas understood that she now realized he was part of the group that wanted to clear out the houses… Words spewed from her mouth like fiery coals. Breathlessly, Susan asked, "What law, whose law? And justice, rights? What kind of concept of justice do you have?" For a moment, she was silent, and then she said sharply, "If you knew how much I hated them! I would happily poison them with my hatred!"

Quietly, scarcely hearing his own voice, Thomas said, "Don't get so worked up, Susan. Calm down… I really do need to go!" He lightly pressed her hand and walked down the steps.

Susan looked out at his retreating form. Captain barked at him in a restrained voice: "Woof! Woof!" She warmed her hands, now grown cold, in the dog's fur…

Munye the Shoemaker and
Baruch Spinoza

Munye the shoemaker was still a young man, somewhere in his early thirties. Small, and round. Everything about him was round: his face, his head, his small blue eyes, his thick and close-cropped little beard. Even his black hair that streamed into blueness was also trimmed roundly around his neck and smooth forehead.

Munye was an ordinary, affable person, and although it was difficult for him to provide for his large household, he nevertheless didn't complain to anyone.

A capable and efficient artisan, he discarded nothing. If there were new shoes to make, good! If there weren't, well, old shoes that needed fixing were nothing to sneeze at, either. He hated to complain.

Munye loved his shoemaker shop. There was nothing that appealed to him more. "I was born a shoemaker," he used to joke.

His wife, Dvoyreh, was taller than him by a head. A healthy, quiet, and hardworking woman, Dvoyreh lived in peace with God and people alike. She had only one complaint to God: She had wanted to have girls, but every few years she had a boy—five boys in all! She did have one girl, but she was a half-boy. The girl didn't want to wear skirts; she yearned to wear tzitzit, the ritual tassels worn by males. The five sons were all large and healthy, taking after their mother.

Munye the shoemaker lived in a wooden back-house in a large courtyard. The apartment consisted of one spacious room divided into two by the wall of the oven. The apartment didn't have a vestibule. When you opened the door, you were immediately in a large kitchen with a single window that looked out onto the courtyard. Munye's workshop was set up at the window. The other half of the room was where the entire household slept.

The pounding of the shoemaker's hammer could be heard throughout the courtyard from morning until dusk. No one knew when Munye slept. Before sunrise, he raced to pray with the first morning minyan. When he returned, Dvoyreh had already cooked something hot. He would wolf down the food and sit down to work. Before the Jewish holidays, Munye worked through entire nights. And yet despite all of this toil, Munye's children didn't have much to eat…

When he was working, Munye was invariably cheerful, unless there wasn't enough bread at home. He would often have to work quickly to finish a pair of shoes and deliver them before the children came home from religious school. At such times, he worked in silence. Dvoyreh was then also quiet and a bit sullen. As soon as the shoes were finished, the quietude exploded. Munye stood up, undid his shoemaker's apron, pulled down the visor of his cap, took up the pair of shoes with two fingers, blew off the dust, and dashed out of the apartment.

The poverty in the shoemaker-home wasn't the sort that groaned, and the crowdedness didn't shriek. Everyone who came there felt at home, wanting to stay longer. And if on the table there had been set a half-loaf of rye bread from which the youngsters pulled pieces and placed them in their little mouths, well, then you, too, would be seized by a craving which would tempt you to pinch off a piece of the aromatic bread. And when Dvoyreh set a full bowl of boiled potatoes onto the table, the mouth of the guest would begin to water and he would think that better food than these potatoes simply couldn't be imagined. Dvoyreh's potatoes were always so floury that they used to practically sing out from the bowl.

In Munye's heart, there was a kind of gnawing that he spoke to no one about, not even his own wife... Munye had always been jealous of the study house Jews who could look inside the sacred books. He was nothing more than a shoemaker and, as a result, he was jealous of those scholars. Yes, that is what Munye often thought about himself—that, in the end, he was nothing more than a shoemaker. This was how Munye's perceived himself before a young man from the study house became a regular visitor in his home.

The young man enriched the life of the shoemaker and his wife—and this was no ordinary enrichment. From the young man's own mouth, Munye discovered that he was no less illustrious than the learned men in the study house. Since then, Munye had lost the gnawing feeling that had plagued him.

When Munye brought the young man home for the first time, Dvoyreh marveled at him: He was so young! Practically a child. But when they sat down with him at the table, it seemed to them that they had never had such a guest. The young man quickly attached himself to the family. The boys were glued to his side. He endeared himself thoroughly to them, and Munye's family prevailed upon him to be their regular Sabbath guest.

The young man was around twenty years old. He was tall and slim, with pale cheeks and large, dark eyes. His voice was so pleasant that you just wanted him to keep talking, and he had so much to tell. He never ran out of subject matter—as if it all arose from a bottomless well. So it seemed to the unassuming Dvoyreh.

Did these honest folks remind the young man of his own home? Or was the air in the study house so stuffy that it drove him out? Whatever the case may have been, the young man integrated himself into Munye's family home. He came several times a week and brought a festive atmosphere to the everydayness of the cramped home.

As soon as Dvoyreh saw the young man through the window, she quickly threw herself at the chair, dusting it off with her apron. Knowing that the young man loved to sit near Munye, she dragged his chair to the workshop even before he entered. Munye lit up when the young man came over. The young man, as if reading the shoemaker's excitement, eagerly began to narrate stories of the great Tannaim of yore who demonstrated that only through honest labor can one attain divinity…

When the young man spoke of the importance of work, Munye felt totally uplifted. He thought: "It's true that I'm nothing more than a shoemaker! But I'm just as important as the men in the study house!"

Among those he considered the greatest and holiest to be found in the world, Munye came to include Baruch Spinoza. He was so astonished to learn about the philosopher that he couldn't get his fill of the young man's words. The young man had to repeat—tens of times—Spinoza's conception of God to Munye. When the young man was speaking, Munye put aside the little hammer, looked directly at him, and murmured, "God is not only in Heaven. He is everywhere. He is in us, with us. He is here; he is there. He is in every corner!

"God is not in the Holy Ark. He is in everything that lives and breathes. The good that is in people is the divine!"

As the young man finished telling how Spinoza earned his daily bread with his own hands, Munye felt like standing up from the chair and covering him with kisses. But he was too embarrassed. When the young man left their home, Munye got up from his chair, thrust his hands into his pockets, walked across the kitchen, and said to Dvoyreh:

"Wow, Dvoyreh, that Spinoza really is a great person!"

Comrade Bashe

Bashe was one of the thousands of girls that our city of millions passes over and overlooks. Not young, not beautiful, no one's eye paused upon her. They all walked right past her.

Bashe was rather wide and short. Because of her full cheeks and round forehead, her cheerful brown eyes were barely visible. Her gait was heavy and lateral, as if she preferred to yield the right of way to someone else. Her voice—quiet, lacking in boldness.

Bashe had been in the country for a couple of decades. For almost all of that time, she had been laboring in a workshop, along with several hundred men and women. But she kept her distance there, confining herself to one corner. It wasn't because she hated people—on the contrary, Bashe's heart longed for a bit of human friendship. But it seemed to her that people didn't like her. She believed that she was fated to be one of the forgotten ones. She nursed her grievances against God, asking Him: "Why have You condemned me to a life in which people look right past me?"

When Bashe came to America, she wasn't yet eighteen years old. Along with her heavy body, she brought with her a heavy spirit and a face full of worry. When she entered the workshop for the first time and noted the beautifully made-up girls at the line-machines, she felt utterly ordinary. She felt stiff in contrast to the easy-breezy, flittering girls, and she just wanted to remain unnoticed. She hoped that, over time, she would manage to shake off her worries, cast off her plain attire, and become equal to and, indeed, even catch up with everyone else.

But she never did catch up with anyone. Why was that? Was she too quick? Too slow? She herself didn't know. She just sensed that, aside from her position at the machine, she had no place in the workshop. The women workers continued to greet her, but the men walked right by her. It was as if she were a "thing," not even worth the effort it took to nod one's head.

When someone in the workshop turned to Bashe, she was always ready to do what was asked of her. When a strike broke out in the workshop, she was the first to stand up and walk out. And when the workshop was unionized, Bashe was among the first to pay for her union booklet. She carefully paid the union dues with the same punctuality her devout father had displayed when he paid her brothers' religious school tuition.

But outside of the workshop and the union—in the realm of the social—Bashe was left behind. She didn't go out with anyone, and she wasn't brought along, either. In the early years, this desolation lay heavily and painfully upon her. For hours at a time, she traversed the streets of the Bronx, as if she were lost. Those wintry evenings were as long as exile itself, and when Bashe grew weary of the streets, she would go up to her apartment, and remain between the walls of her dreary little room that looked out onto a narrow courtyard. She would turn off the lights, draw the curtains, rest her head on her hands, and look into the neighbors' windows for a long time until her eyes began to hurt.

In her apartness from other people, Bashe always had the feeling that she was actually taking something away from them. If she came across someone on the steps, she turned her head so that she wouldn't be noticed.

As the years went by, her longing for people lessened. The longer she was alone, the more sprawling was the territory between her and the life surrounding her.

Like thousands of others, Bashe rode in packed train cars, squished between odorous bodies. She kept her lips pursed shut and stayed silent.

And thus, the years passed.

In the workshop, her only friend was the machine; she confided in it all of her melancholy. The machine, she knew, would tell no one. Oftentimes, Bashe would sing a folksy tune to the machine. Her voice was as soft as a child's and didn't reach the ears of others.

One day, Beylke, another girl in the workshop, approached Bashe and offered her a ticket to a lecture. Bashe fixed her eyes upon her and asked:

"Do you mean me? Why me?"

But Beylke lifted her small hand, placed it on Bashe's shoulder, and said:

"Of course, I mean you. Why are you so surprised? The lecture is being given this evening. Come! I guarantee you won't regret it."

Bashe wanted to say something more, but the ticket was lying on top of the machine and Beylke was already busy with someone else.

Beylke was close in age to Bashe, but because of her small body, she looked younger. She was short in stature, light, and had narrow shoulders, a thin neck, and child-sized hands and feet. Her hair was a mix of bright blond and gray. At one time, her eyes had been green; these days—they were blue. When she smiled, they looked like the eyes of a young kitten. She held her head haughtily aloft, cocked a bit to the side. Her step was light, quiet. Her petite feet barely touched the ground. In the large leather hand-bag she invariably carried, she always had a selection of various tickets. She kept all sorts of financial accounts and yet was perennially short of cash—always down to her last pocket change. But she never took it to heart. "I'll stay the same pauper I've always been," she would think to herself.

Beylke had come to America at the same time as Bashe, but her state of being here had assumed a different tempo. With great zest, she eagerly welcomed and took in all that she encountered.

She became a link in the chain that was needed to make life better. This ninety-pound girl piled the entire responsibility for all of the world onto her narrow shoulders.

Communally-minded work was not difficult for Beylke; she always looked for more work. She had been employed in the workshop for just two days when her friendly hands touched Bashe's withdrawn shoulders. With her intuition, she had spotted Bashe and took her under her wing. Like a timely rain that refreshes a dried-out plant, so Beylke refreshed Bashe's life.

Later that day, when Bashe descended from the workshop to the street, Beylke hailed her like an old acquaintance. She took Bashe by the hand and said:

"You know what? We'll go to the lecture together. Let's get something to eat first. Then we'll take a walk and, after that, go to the lecture."

Bashe felt as if she were being ensnared in a net. She wanted to wriggle free, but didn't know how. She had no desire to attend the lecture even though, aside from her machine at work and her old, deaf landlady, she had no one. Still, she couldn't tear herself free from the diminutive Beylke who didn't even wait for her response. She just took Bashe under the arm and steered her straightaway to the automat.

Bashe didn't feel especially comfortable walking with the small, buoyant girl at her side. Her heavy feet stumbled. She was accustomed to walking alone on the street. No one had ever led her by the arm. But every touch of Beylke's hand was delightful, warm. In the automat, Beylke served Bashe herself, as if she were a guest in her own home.

After their meal, both of them went for a walk in the park. Beylke tried to get Bashe to talk, but words didn't emerge smoothly from Bashe's mouth. She wasn't used to speaking and so the words had a hard time finding their way out from between her lips.

Mostly, it was Beylke who spoke. She told Bashe that she had come here alone, without anyone, but that she didn't remember ever feeling lonely. As soon as she entered the workshop, work was there, awaiting her attention. She quickly directed her hands and began swimming, like a fish in water. She was always busy and didn't know herself where the days and weeks went. There were union meetings and gatherings to attend. Well, for that matter, hearing a lecture was vital, too. Besides, we're still human beings, we need to get together from time to time, even though there was no time! Deep in conversation, they reached the auditorium.

The audience in the packed auditorium startled Bashe—and frightened her a bit. At the beginning, she wanted to sneak out of the room without being noticed. But before she could do anything, Beylke had sat them down next to her friends and began to sell tickets for another event.

The lecturer—of average height, dark, with lively eyes—moved back and forth on the stage. He spoke about the role of women in contemporary industry. Bashe really liked his Yiddish, and the content of his talk appealed to her, too. She was so drawn in that she completely forgot that only moments ago she had wanted to leave the auditorium. Now she asked herself: Who and what had barred her path to other people? Who was guilty of this? Perhaps it was she herself. Bashe didn't see any difference between herself and the others in the auditorium. She saw women who were apparently no more beautiful than she was and yet there was no dejection on their faces. For the first time in her life, Bashe understood that up until that point, she had considered herself discarded goods to be concealed. Previously, Bashe had pitied herself; now, she really wanted to pinch herself in anger.

After the lecture, Beylke ran up to Bashe, flushed with excitement, as if she had discovered a treasure.

"Well," she said, "What did I tell you? I knew you would like the lecture. You'll come again!"

Exiting the auditorium, several of Beylke's friends surrounded Bashe, wanting to know how she had liked the lecture. Someone said to her, "Don't be a stranger to us, comrade!"

The word "comrade" warmed Bashe. It was as if her mother had hugged her. The warmth extended all the way to the tips of her fingers, spreading over her entire body. And on her way home, it seemed to her that all of the faces that she had encountered earlier had smiled at her. She heard the words "Comrade, comrade" flowing rhythmically in sync with the clang and clatter of the subway car wheels.

When she came back to herself in her room, Bashe found herself searching for something. She searched for the corner from which a new life was streaming forth. She approached the mirror and looked for new features on her face. She looked for the face of this other Bashe, this "comrade." She spoke to the mirror that she had previously so despised.

"Comrade Bashe!" her heart called out.

"Comrade Bashe!" answered a pair of hungry, dark eyes.

She, He, and the Moon

She knew that waking up and calling out to her husband, who had descended into a delicious sleep, wouldn't help. She knew there wasn't a magic wand in the world that would keep him from the pleasure of sleep. Nevertheless, she nudged him a few times, imploring him:

"Just take a look, what a night! What radiance!" She wasn't expecting a response. So she had to be content, satisfied, with her own voice. Sadness grew within her from moment to moment, expanding with the night, and every limb of her body wept without tears, weeping from an internal pain.

And the moon, with its shrewdness and cold charm, called out softly and surely: "Are there many nights like this?"

The days, too, so similar, each one to the next, choked her with their monotony. Still, the days didn't disturb her as much as the nights. The days faded away on their own, but the nights? They were with her, inside of her. Nights made demands. Not for nothing did gardeners say that the growth of plants depended more on nights than days... She came alive at the very time when everyone around her was sleeping. When her husband and children fell asleep, her twenty-six years awakened within her and demanded their due, demanded a reckoning.

She had arrived here at the age of seventeen. She came from a small shtetl, unprepared to carry the weight of her own life. She had no specialized skills, no friends, and to top it all off, there was a crisis in this new country. As a result, she became so terrified of her own powerlessness that she grabbed the first hand extended to her. Truth be told, there was no great strength in that

particular outstretched hand, but there was enough to provide a
small amount of security. At the time, she didn't think of anything
beyond that. In those crisis years, you had to be content with very
little.

In that hand she sensed a friendship. Soon after she arrived
in her new home, she came across the hungry faces of men out in
the bitter cold without coats, and small children wearing tattered
shoes, their little hands held outstretched into the snowy street.
At that time, she had fallen into a great panic. So when she met
him at a relative's home, in a small room that had a little window
through which you could see a frozen-white sapling in the park,
she felt as if God had sent her a great stroke of fortune.

The sapling offered this assurance: I will be green again when
spring comes. On her eighteenth birthday, she became the mother of a beautiful little boy, and with that, was severed from both
worlds, the old and the new. The totality of her concern—now
focused on the new little soul who only asked for life's most es-
sential necessities—also weighed upon her as heavily as a tow-
ering mountain.

With all of her sensitivity, she protected and sheltered her
child from all sorts of illnesses that crouched in wait for children
who lived their lives in impoverished conditions. In doing so, she
neglected her own life.

By the age of twenty-one, she was already a mother of two.
Her husband didn't earn much, and she remembered her own
childhood when she had lived her days and nights with everything provided for. Recalling that childhood, she regretted that
she had allowed herself to bring children into the world. She now
saw the world and life itself from her own limited perspective.

Only when the children had grown older did she finally find a
free minute for herself. She started reading books, something for
which she previously had no time. The sounds and echoes of the
living world around her—the world that four or five years ago
had sent her into a fit of terror—reached her. These very sounds

lured and enchanted her. She was far from this particular world, and yet its sounds elicited in her bizarre moods and impulses. She longed to caper like a wild pony on the steppe. When she had been busy with her small children, she didn't have any time for these moods. But now, when she was finished with her housework, she remembered how in her childhood she used to build houses in the sand, make pathways, surround the houses with fences, and then abandon it all and run away. This was exactly how she felt now.

Although she still had to give a great deal to the children, she nevertheless sensed that within her very person there dwelled as-yet unfulfilled desires, that the not-yet-lived was struggling to find its way out of her. It had to be tamed, subjugated. She was waiting for something; she had a premonition that something must come, was going to come—today, tomorrow—and needed to be met.

That "something" did come. A neighbor rented a room from them. He was a writer, and she had read one of his books. Although she didn't think very highly of the book, which she thought didn't portray fully realized, true-to-life situations, but rather shadows, silhouettes of them, she nevertheless showed a great deal of respect for this neighbor—he was a writer, after all.

In contrast to her own lonely, introspective self, the writer was a bohemian, an urbane person down to the core. She thought he was involved in realms that had little to do with everyday life, and she wanted to know about them. But she didn't want him to know about her curiosity. Still, with his sharply developed intuition, he sensed her inquisitiveness, and from time to time, he exposed her—just a tiny crack—to the circles in which he moved. These circles consisted of people, individuals of real spirit, but nothing more than just people after all, whom he dismissed with a gesture of the hand: "People and... nothing else!"

However, such people were not "nothing" to her. The manners of this neighbor, his discretion, did not appeal to her. But he did stimulate her imagination, and she grappled thoroughly with his take on things, with his ideas. She believed that he, as a writer, understood it all, that it was as if he looked at things and people through a magnifying glass.

He himself looked at her with half-closed eyes. When he passed close by her, he lowered his eyes, as if he were looking only at himself. His lips tightened, and he went silent. And yet he was pleased when she asked him something. At such moments, he would stop, run his hand over his forehead, and continue talking, saying more than she could absorb. He spoke quietly. His slightly hoarse voice had a certain depth, as if arising from the chest, and she loved to listen to it.

Between them both a kind of cat-and-mouse game took shape. One of them might be looking for the other. But then when they did run into each other, there would surface between them a frostiness that said: Let's steer clear of each other!

It was on that moonlit night when her bedroom was bathed in a silvery brightness, and sleep retreated from her. Then other, similar moonlit nights that had dragged her out of her long-ago bed came to her mind. In the middle of the night, she would sneak out of her room, taking care not to awaken her little sister. Wearing just a nightshirt, she would go out into the courtyard, and situate herself at the gate to gaze at the moon. It seemed to her that that shtetl moon was the most beautiful moon in the world. She believed that this beautiful moon was beckoning her to a beautiful world that was waiting for her somewhere.

But how deceptive life can be! These thoughts—and others like them—came to her mind during this night without sleep. And the longer the hours dragged on, the more awake she became... until she heard his light footsteps. Unexpectedly, she called out to him:

"Would you like to take a walk? This bright moon won't let me close an eye!"

"A walk. Of course! Definitely! Why not?" came back his answer.

There was no surprise in his answer, as if it were something totally understandable. Nimbly as a cat, she slid out of bed, pulled on a light dress, and stood next to him. He looked at her with half-closed eyes for a long time, then took her by both hands, and, without a word, led her down the stairs.

His powerfully warm hands clasped hers with tenderness, but she didn't feel the warmth. The iciness in his tone of voice also pushed her away, so that her heart's pounding moderated and slowed down.

They entered the park. The moon was garlanded by small, scattered clouds, and the park breathed with deep blue. They were both silent. They walked and were silent. They were walking right next to each other, lost in thought. She: she had to build a new life! That very next day! And he? He had a theme all ready to go! A one-acter with the intriguing name: "She, He, and the Moon"! He told her, "Brava! Excellent!" She responded, "It's time to go home now."

"As you wish, my princess!"

She freed herself from his grip and began to run through the park, provocatively calling out: "Catch me!"

He, the older and heavier of the two, didn't even try to run after her...

She waited at the stairs. He asked:

"How did you like the moon?"

For the first time, both pairs of eyes locked in a genuine encounter and smiled...

Christopher, Seated Until the End

Throughout his life—for as long as he could remember—Christopher had been standing on his feet. When he was still a little boy, he was helping out his mother. That was the kind of work you just always had to do.

When he first arrived at the large, twenty-story building, he wasn't yet sixteen years old. For the first two years, he was a messenger boy sent on all of the errands.

It was his mother who got him the job. The first time she sent him off to work, she told him: "A Black person has to be better than good. If you are obedient and follow God, He will be good to you."

Christopher heeded his mother. He walked in the ways of the Lord. After two years of running all over from eight in the morning until ten at night, the building manager called him into his office and said, "Christopher, you're a good Negro! The best I've ever had. I'll teach you how to run the elevator so you'll have an income and your bit of bread will always be taken care of." He dressed up the Black boy in a blue uniform with brass buttons, and after two days, he had already learned this new job.

For nearly thirty years, Christopher wore that blue uniform with the brass buttons. And in fact, he always did have bread; he never went hungry. The members of his household also had a means of support and a roof over their heads. There was just one thing that Christopher never knew: what it meant to sit down and rest. He had to stand on his feet for long hours, and when he got home, he was so exhausted that he fell asleep with his dinner still in his mouth. The first few years were bearable. In the elevator there was a round stool that he could sometimes sit on—but since they'd finished the renovations, there wasn't the slightest trace of anything to rest on, even for a moment, anywhere in the building. Christopher stood and stood until he could barely feel himself standing.

Sometimes, on summer mornings when Christopher raced past the park, he was drawn to the earth, to the fragrant, dewy grasses. He longed to stretch out for a while, to roll around as he used to do when he was a schoolchild. But he couldn't do it. He always just raced to work, contenting himself with tearing out a clump of grass and drawing it up to his nostrils to inhale the delicious moisture, to delight in its grassy scents.

When Christopher's legs became heavy, he said to himself: "You're probably exhausted from standing all these years. You need to take a vacation!" The union gave Christopher one week of vacation per year, but he never used it. Each year, there was always something more pressing. One time, something had to be bought for the house; another time, something for the kids. Christopher sold his vacation time. He was paid double for working that week...

Last year, he had decided that he had to take a vacation during the coming year. His wife persuaded him not to palm off his vacation time. He already felt himself to be in summer relaxation mode. He could sense the sweet serenity, the taste of seven whole days of not having to get up in the morning. He imagined himself lying in bed until midday and later sitting with both feet up on the windowsill, looking out onto the street. But nothing came of that beautiful dream.

Something else unexpected presented itself. Someone wanted to sell a piano on the cheap, and his children wanted the piano so badly. Christopher didn't want to let this opportunity slip away and so he bought the piano for them. He had no regrets. The children's banging on the piano keys gave him great pleasure. They never took piano lessons, but their playing did him a world of good.

Christopher's legs never did get to experience a vacation. They became heavier and heavier, as if they were attaching themselves to the ground, and he had to drag them around with all of his strength. Soon, Christopher had to stay home. His legs ceased functioning for him. Instead of walking, he crawled. It seemed as if he had to detach one leg from his hips, and then he would stop and detach the other. With such arduous effort, he was always having to stop to rest.

Christopher wasn't getting around anymore. He sat on a low chair that stood between the bed and the window. He was always sitting, and when he was asked why he was sitting, he answered: "My feet just don't want to obey me." This was the justification he gave to others. To himself, he thought that if his mother were still alive, she would certainly have another answer. He didn't even begin to know why he was being so severely punished. It seemed like he had walked in the ways of the Lord, that he had guarded himself from sin. He never went to bed without a prayer to the Lord. He accepted everything with love, just as his mother had taught him. His wife, Tessie, was pious, too, even more so than he himself. And their children were also God-fearing. Why was he being punished like this?

Immediately after this misfortune befell her husband, the pious Tessie rushed to the priest, her dear Father. He heard her out and told her to take her husband to a renowned doctor. Since Tessie didn't have any money to pay doctors, she took him to the hospital. The doctors asked Christopher so many questions that his mouth became dry from having to answer them all. With a deep sadness in his eyes, he wanted to say that he had never wished anyone harm, that his life was pure and honorable, just as his mother's had been, but the doctors didn't ask him about his honorability. They asked him the kind of questions whose answers he didn't believe they needed to know at all.

The doctors took notes, filling up pads of paper, and told him to come back in a few days. As long as he could still drag himself around somewhat, Tessie and their youngest son would bring him to the hospital. The boy, tallish and slim, with a shy face and dancing feet, felt insulted by his father's misfortune. The children, like Christopher, had been sure that God would shield them from all evil. They were obedient children, never taking part in the frittering away of time like some of the other boys and girls in Harlem. More than once, friends of Christopher's son had ridiculed him, calling him "Messiah's son." He got into scuffles to defend his father's good name. He loved his father, believed in him. Now he was seized with pain on behalf of his father—pain and shame.

The boy practically had to carry his father into the hospital in his arms. Christopher had pleaded with him, saying that he didn't want to go to the hospital. He couldn't bear how they carried him around like a sack. But the son insisted: He had to go! So the father capitulated—as long as he could still get into the taxi to which the boy carried him. But now he couldn't take a single step, and he had the feeling that he would live out his few remaining years in this way.

Tessie went out to work, and Christopher was left sitting alone at home. He sat alone for entire days, but it didn't bother him. He had never been quick to answer. He always had to mull things over before he said anything. Now he did speak, but to himself. His talk was a single profound lament. Everything cried out in him, in his gut. His tears were frozen in his large, round eyes, and their reddish whites appeared to be veiled by a glassy membrane.

When the boy with the dancing feet came running home from school, he tried to rein in his feet. He didn't want his father to see how his feet could be raised so easily. He approached his father and asked him, "How do you feel, Pop?" Christopher lifted his head, raked his large hand over the bedcover, and said, "All right, son, all right!"

Having said these few words, Christopher lowered his head and looked at his feet—clumsy blocks that they were—as if he were waiting for them to say something, too...

Christopher thought about his mother. She had been a widow. She had worked, toiled in the houses of strangers, and raised four healthy children. Even in advanced old age, his mother still toiled. From her hard-earned money, she saved enough for her funeral and a grave. She never wanted to ask anyone for anything. She couldn't read, but she recited prayers by heart. She taught her children not to ask for anything from God, but to thank Him for the kindness He showed to all living human beings. As Christopher rummaged through the story of his life, he couldn't fathom why God had punished him so. How had he made Him so angry? Perhaps because he had once wanted to rest?

He used to always be standing. Now, he always had to sit—sit until the end. Christopher moistened his lips that were constantly dry. He tried to stand up, holding onto the bed with his hands. But then he fell back into the chair and forlornly said to himself, "Yeah, it sure looks like I'll have to sit until the end. Just keep on sitting until my time comes."

Blume

I dreamed a dream: you came to me just as I'd seen you, many years ago. Wide, puffy, with your short neck and raised shoulders. As always, your dark eyes shone and smiled and were slightly moist. Your blue-black hair—loose, unkempt—fell softly over your sparkling forehead and obstructed your unfocused gaze. Your full, inflated cheeks—flushed now with a fresh redness— and your full lips. In it all lay the discordant affability that forever drew me to you.

How did you come to me, Blume? Did you smile? But your smile, cast in shadow, was ambiguous, the kind that could be interpreted differently at any given moment. It seemed to me that this particular smile was demanding something, and yet at the same time, was saying: "As you have known me, so I have perished. I received nothing from life and gave nothing to life."

Was there some kind of connection between Blume and the unknown soldier? A certain, yet illogical, comparison there was, yes. In my thoughts was an incessant drilling: There was a Blume who struggled all her life. She was a mother who loved her children; she worked from the very beginning of her childhood; with her two hands, she helped move the wheel of time and didn't herself understand all that she had contributed to the world. Blume perished and was mourned by no one, mentioned by no one. It was as if there had never been Blume.

I think: Blume herself would have said: "Who and what am I to be mourned?" In her life, she really demanded so little. She had no time to make demands, no time to remember herself, and yet!—Bontshe the Silent[3] didn't make any demands from life, either, and nevertheless, his soul "reached all the way to the Throne of Honor"!

How like Bontshe the Silent you are, Blume, and just so shall you remain! True, Bontshe was much luckier than you. He was immortalized by an immortalized, and he was fated to die a human death. But you, Blume, are of the eternally overlooked and did not die a human death, but, together with several thousand Jews of your shtetl, were dragged by the wild beast with a human face into the synagogue, where flames devoured everyone.

I therefore do not want to construct a monument for you. You yourself are the monument.

… I see you, Blume, the way I saw you many, many years ago. I see you at the spinning wheel. Your right hand is turning the wheel so quickly that it's difficult to make out where the wheel stops and your hand begins. In its speed, the wheel whistles like the wind. If the work is going well and the thread doesn't break, your eyes are half-closed and your full cheeks blossom as if the sun's rays were shining upon them. If the thread breaks or gets tangled, you open your eyes wide and blink with moist impatience.

I remember the little song you sang when the work was going well:

> Oh, outside, it's raining,
> Outside, a wind's blowing—
> But dear Mama, don't rest in your grave,
> Just come intercede—your child to save!

I remember you from a bit later. By then, you had a little girl next to you, as well as a strong, temperamental cough that didn't leave you alone when you were at work. After you had a cough-

---

3. The title character in the Yiddish writer I. L. Peretz's classic short story, "Bontshe shvayg" ["Bontshe the Silent"] originally published in 1894. Bontshe never speaks up for himself, no matter the indignities and injustice he suffers.

ing fit, you would excuse yourself as if you had hurt someone. Your child, not yet a year old, sat on the ground, surrounded by bundles of wool so that her head wouldn't get bruised if, God forbid, she fell. Your child, so like you—plump, with luminous little eyes, and cheeks like spring buds. The child cast a fresh light all around her. When she was content and playful, your face was as bright as the sun; when the little one was tired and started rubbing her eyes with her chubby hands and then started screaming, your face began to cloud over and you would speak to the child as if she were an adult...

Thus, you spoke, Blume, to the child: "Soon, soon! Darling! Soon, my sweet baby girl! I'm about to get you. I'm finished here." And when the little one wouldn't let herself be pacified and kept screaming at the top of her lungs, you took her onto your lap and calmed her down. And so, with the child in your arms, you continued to spin the wheel, all the while casting an eye at the door to see if the boss was coming. He would be none too pleased that the child was usurping "his time," owed to him by her mother.

I remember: You once told me that your mother died when you were not yet twelve years old. You took your mother's place; you were a mother to the younger children, five orphans. Your father was a wagon driver. He loved the bottle. Your father brought your husband to you from somewhere far away. He was not a bad person—a driver, too. But when your second child was born, he said he missed his parents. He left, and you never saw him again.

I remember, too: You are sitting at the wheel. Fast, fast, you turn the wheel, a clever speed. The small life near you is delighted by your stunts. She claps her little hands, sprays drool from her little mouth, babbles, and shakes back and forth, as if she wants to pursue her mother's hands. Suddenly, the boss materializes. On his face—a fury; on your face—a sallow pallor. He approaches close; he looks as if he will explode like a volcano. But when his eyes encounter the playful eyes of the child, he quickly turns around, and a smile he'd prefer to conceal appears on his face.

For the favor of being allowed to keep the child next to you, you had to pay with more hours of work, with even harder labor. You were afraid of the boss, but you didn't want him to look at the child. You were afraid of the evil eye.

It's strange: I remember you as someone forever smiling. I remember you as forever quick. You worked quickly; you spoke quickly. You never spoke of loneliness to me. I don't know whether, at night, you tossed and turned on your lowly bed, yearning for your husband and praying for his return; or if you cursed, cursed out the hours when he had meddled in your life of sorrow.

In my mind is engraved your home, the place where you lived. Situated behind the city, among the drunkards, your home looked like a hovel. It felt as if evil spirits were lurking everywhere. Between this home and the dark, dusty factory, you counted your young years. On Sabbaths and holidays, you worked extra in order to make up for the time that your boss allowed you to take off on account of your luminous child.

Not for you, Blume, did the skies turn blue and the sun shine; not for you did the stars sparkle and the birds trill; you were cut off from the delights of nature. Your life—a monotone, submerged in gray need.

Poverty and hardship are not always without joy, and yet sad and gray was your life, as if everything showed its sinister side to you. Like Bontshe the Silent of yore, you didn't struggle against your fate, even though you lived in an era that was different from his. Nonetheless, one large part of the world had brightened— even in your day. Were it not for the raging wild beast, life there would have been brighter still…

I was not present at your perishing. You stand before me now, alive—how can I construct a monument—

… And not in the heavens, before the Throne of Honor, not before the golden angels, do I remember you, forgotten Blume. But rather before the people of your kind, before the people of that bygone era.

Thrice Encountered

The first encounter took place when Freydl arrived in New York and began employment in a workshop that made women's clothing. Back then, everything was new and strange to her. The people, the work—everything seemed to be the opposite of what she had imagined. At the time, she could sew a little on a machine, but she had never so much as laid eyes on an electric one.

Her friends had warned her beforehand not to say that she couldn't sew on an electric machine, so she kept it to herself. The lady who hired her was apparently a little suspicious of her. She led Freydl to a machine, unfolded pieces of silk from a package, sat down herself, and began to stitch. She then asked Freydl if she understood what she was doing. Freydl nodded, and the lady smiled and left.

Freydl thought it all looked very simple. What was there to understand? But when she placed her foot on the pedal, the machine exploded like a wild horse and she quickly withdrew her foot, embarrassed and frightened. She thought the girls all around her in the workshop had seen what happened and were laughing at her. But no one was even looking at her; they didn't even turn their heads towards her. Everyone was occupied in their work, and Freydl didn't see a single face looking at her. Freydl struggled with this machine that didn't want to obey, or at least do anything for her. With the pieces of fabric, it didn't go well for her, either—they all looked the same to her; none of it was working out.

She sat there, dejected, not knowing what to do. She hoped someone would notice her and come to her aid, but she searched in vain. She couldn't catch the eye of a single person.

Not far from Freydl's machine—off to the side a bit—stood three machines in the capital "T" shape of the Yiddish diacritical mark komets. Three Jewish girls worked at these machines. One of them, who had a charming head of curly blond hair, drew Freydl's searching gaze. This blonde girl was bent over her machine, her shoulders rhythmically rocking from side to side. With the fingers of her right hand, she moved the piece of cloth, and with those of her left, she kept the machine going. Freydl saw that the work was a game for the blonde girl and that her mouth moved in conversation with the other two. Freydl looked at the threesome and observed how they spoke among themselves with such enjoyment as they worked, and she became even more downcast.

She sat pitifully, not having the faintest idea of what to do. She felt envious of the happy ones, especially the girl with the little head of lovely blond hair. Yes, it seemed to her that the work was a game for the blonde; her mouth was like a little mill that never stopped grinding.

Freydl thought that the girls sitting next to her didn't want to look at her because she was pitiful, a greenhorn.

She compared her own clumsiness to the other girls, and this made her sick. A feeling of jealousy mingled with rage, and a great sense of self-pity enveloped her. If she hadn't been embarrassed, she would have burst into tears. She didn't understand how a person could be so vile that they wouldn't even look at someone who was sitting there and suffering so close to them.

The anger in Freydl grew from minute to minute. She came to an agreement with herself that she absolutely wouldn't continue working in this workshop. She wrapped her head in a scrap of fabric, slowly tried to run the wild machine with one of her feet, and strained to control the mechanism so that it wouldn't explode. In this way, she made it, with great difficulty, to lunchtime. Then she discreetly began to leave the workshop. As Freydl passed the other girls on her way to the door, her ear caught a few words that the blonde was saying: "We're making progress! Surely, you can see how we're progressing!"

"Progress" was an advanced and intellectual word. Freydl decided that these girls were educated. "Who knows?" she wondered, "Maybe she feels guilty for her own role in the girls not taking any notice of me? It was my mistake; I should have turned to them myself! Well, it doesn't matter. I won't be working here, in any case."

Years went by and Freydl would have long forgotten those girls. She had enough muddles of her own and couldn't even think about what was going on around her.

One Saturday afternoon, Freydl heard "Extra! Extra!" shouted on the street. She ran down into the street, bought a Yiddish newspaper, and read its detailed account of the fire that devoured the lives of four hundred young people, most of them girls. Freydl was so upset that she felt as if she were suffocating. Her own life had almost been in danger. In her mind's eye, she kept seeing those girls engulfed by flames. She envisioned them jumping from the windows. She couldn't tear herself away from the newspapers that depicted the details of this cruel tragedy. These terrible scenes plagued her soul and would not let her rest.

In the mornings, she stood at her window, unable to wrest her gaze from the workers walking past her. She lamented on behalf of each working girl on her way to the workshop, carrying a small food package, as if that girl were heading to her own funeral.

In her pain, Freydl didn't know what to do with herself. Her only comfort was her two small children.

Shortly thereafter, Freydl read about a bereavement demonstration—a political funeral—in memory of those who perished in the Triangle fire, and so she went to the demonstration.

It was a gray, cold day. A thin and stinging rain shower drizzled down, starting and stopping, as if it were teasing. Freydl was early to the demonstration, so she hung around in the streets. She wondered why the people milling about there were so indifferent and cold to the tragedy. Some were laughing and making a ruckus, as if nothing had happened. Freydl ran from one street corner to the next until musical notes announced the arrival of an orchestra. By then, she was drained from her dawdling and dead tired from the wet cold. With her last bit of energy, she tore through the crowd, wanting to get close enough to take in the entire expanse of sorrow, to experience it all with her heart and soul.

Through its very presence, the oncoming, marching demonstration was intended to be a funeral for the several hundred victims: children, daughters, brides. Here were parents: mothers and fathers, grandparents who had lost children and grandchildren. Freydl was electrified by the black procession. Heads bent, the people in black dragged their exhausted feet to the rhythm of the sorrowful tones of the funeral march. At the beginning, she felt as if every hair on her head were aching in pain, and she choked up on a cloud of tears until she felt she was suffocating.

Gradually, this procession of grief changed. Young people— their heads held high, tenacity on their faces, and strength in their steps—began to appear.

The flame of their red flags warmed the cold surroundings. The flags fluttered as they reached towards the clouds. The flag signifying unified worker strength appeared to Freydl's eyes like a proudly displayed armored breastplate, shielding everything and everyone.

Three young men carried the flag. In front of the flag-bearers, a young man and two girls walked in a row. One of the girls looked familiar to Freydl; she quickly recognized her. It was her—the blonde girl from the workshop of long ago! The one with the little head of charming curls. She recognized her from the way her shoulders rhythmically rocked, exactly as they had back when she was sitting and sewing at her machine. A profound seriousness was visible on the blonde's face. There was a sense of resolve in her step. To Freydl, it seemed that the words "We're making progress!" were about to be wrenched from the blonde's mouth.

Just as she had in the workshop of long ago, Freydl now felt small and insignificant next to the blonde. It got to the point that Freydl felt sorry for herself. Here she was, standing by herself and contemplating this tragic tableau, and there was this other girl, marching with such determined steps.

More years passed. One Saturday afternoon, Freydl was coming home from work. It was an afternoon in May and Freydl felt light in body and soul. Yes, it was May: spring, warm. Tomorrow was Sunday, and you didn't have to go to work. Soon she would be on her own street; soon her children would be racing to greet her. She walked with measured steps and considered the trees that seemingly just yesterday were naked and raw, and now—such a breadth of green! Shavuot[4] here in the park sang out from each small leaf on a tree. Freydl thought: How good it would be if it could be Shavuot all month.

At the park exit, she noticed a woman sitting on a box. She couldn't see the woman's face, but the head of blond curls reminded her of someone. Yes, it was her! Once again, that same person from the workshop of long ago! The blonde sat with her pointy knees pressed together. She held out spread-out fingers, shielding her eyes against the sun. When she spotted Freydl, she turned around on the box, wanting to say something—but then remained silent when she realized that she was a stranger.

Freydl no longer looked at the park in festive bloom, with its expanse of greenness. She stopped and looked at the blonde for a long time, wanting to convince herself that this really was "that one." She couldn't see on the blonde's face what she had once seen. Staring at the horizon, the blonde sat tensely, as if she were reliving both the distant and the recent past.

---

4. Shavuot (Yiddish: Shvues): the holiday that falls seven weeks after Passover and celebrates the giving of the Torah on Mount Sinai. In the Bible, Shavuot marked the wheat harvest in the Land of Israel.

She expected the blonde to swing her little head of curls and repeat the same words she had once said at the machine, those words that had so engraved themselves in Freydl's memory: "We're making progress!"

Freydl felt that the woman with the stiffened knees sitting on the box was pursuing her—Freydl the pedestrian—as she moved through the world.

In the Stillness of the Night

When Prager arrived at the summer resort, he couldn't figure out what to do with himself. The more people partied, made a ruckus, and laughed, the more unsettled he felt. Afterward, he sat in a rocking chair and calmed down a bit, trying to de-fog his mind from its lack of clarity. Undisturbed by the surrounding din after a wall of deafness had formed a partition between him and those around him, Prager was able to adjust to his small world and re-live the past, both recent and distant.

He wanted to remember. When had this happened? When did they start to speak to him in the factory in a loud voice?

At first, Prager thought they were shouting because he wasn't listening to what they were saying to him. He was thinking about his home; that's where he was in his thoughts. He didn't let it out of his thoughts for a single minute. He constantly saw her pain-filled eyes fixed on him, pleading: "Help me." Although in truth, she definitely wanted to hide her woes from him. But he heard her sitting at the machine. He heard Beylke behind the door, heard her when he was walking up the steps.

When she saw him enter, she would sweep her hair across her forehead with one hand and draw him to her with the other. Her gaunt, small hand was invariably dry and warm.

She had a guarded voice. She spoke with no one else; only to him did she always have something to say. He didn't have to strain to hear her, even though she never spoke above a whisper.

It was his father who lightened her final days for her. Prior to Beylke's illness his father seldom appeared in their house. He was a good father! Who could have imagined that such a small

69

person would have such inner strength? And perhaps Beylke had something within her that no one was able to sidestep? Was it beauty? No. In fact, his father had said this about her: The spotlessness of her soul illuminated her face.

Prager clasped his hands, swayed in the rocking chair, and looked at his large, heavy feet. He had come here to pull himself together and stand on his own two feet. Good friends of his had suggested that he come here. Now, he looked down at his feet and began to believe in them.

Prager thought now about his father. How had it happened that his pious father had blurted out words against God? Hadn't his father always worked to instill in him and Beylke a trust in God? Her eyes as curious as a child's, Beylke always listened more to her father-in-law, with his talk about trust in God, than she did the doctor! And how many times had his father helped her to sleep with his pious prayers?

It happened that morning, after Beylke quietly fell into eternal sleep. Throughout the week of the shiva period, he didn't exchange a single word with his father, as if both were rendered mute by their grief. Only on the morning of the day after the shiva was over did the sun, unsolicited, invade the two windows and laugh at the orphaned state of the room. The emptiness pressed heavily on him.

The door opened, and his father, exhausted and pale, came up to him with outstretched palms, as if he were demanding the payment of a debt that someone owed him. With its light, the sun disrupted the hollowness in the room. The father spoke as if he were ending a debate he had begun some time ago.

He got up close to his son, to make sure that he heard him. He looked into his eyes and said sharply, "My son, don't think there won't come a time when someone with enough power will reach all the way to the Throne of Honor and demand from the Lord of the Universe a kind of accounting for His actions! Someday, such people will come. But it just has to be the right time... From me, my son, you don't have to demand anything. What do I know?" Those last words his father pronounced quietly. With terrified eyes, as if he were afraid of his own words, he left the room.

Compassion for his father now enveloped Prager. He saw him—the gaunt Jew with the benevolent eyes that were always calling out for something.

His father suffered more than he let on. He suffered when he noticed the weakness of his son's hearing, that he was looking at his mouth when he was speaking to him. Prager felt that his father thought of all this as a punishment being out meted out to him, not to his son.

There was a distance between the father and son and yet they were still so close to each other. The father—a Jew who had more to do with the sacred book than with life; the son—a person of action, of work.

The father had faith that the world would be redeemed through the Messiah. For the son, that redemption would come through the working class. Each believed stubbornly in his own principles. And when it came to the double misfortune in his son's life, the father was certain he had sinned in some way against God and that his son was left to deal with the cruel injustice that life dealt him.

When Prager left his empty home, something flared up in his mind. Small, weak, barely noticeable, the flame had nevertheless staked a foothold. Perhaps in the lap of nature—on the land—the density in his ears would dissolve? Perhaps?

The summer place welcomed Prager with luminous generosity. He gazed in wonder at the infinite expanse, sprawling with festive greenery. Prager encountered everything and everyone with surprise, as if he had come from a faraway world. He surrendered himself to the serenity that was as soothing to him as a glass filled with a light nightcap.

From the beginning, Prager tried not to show his ailment to the others, not wanting them to suspect that he didn't know what was happening around him. But that didn't last long. He began to observe in people's faces that, with his lack of hearing, he was irritating to them. And although he himself wasn't really sure that this was, in fact, the case, he still began to distance himself from his surroundings.

Ever since he could remember, he had been involved with people. He'd never been alone. He always felt himself to be a part of a movement. It was difficult for him to detach himself when everything around him was streaming with life. He ran to the far-away greenery, seeking to conjoin with an old tree that greeted him like a loyal, elderly mother. At that moment, it seemed to him that thousands of leaves were rustling overhead for his sake and that he heard their noise. But soon he thought to himself: "It's just a dream!" He looked at the tree, at its roots that spread out like petrified snakes and then started to run up the mountain. He ran into the distance until he was completely exhausted.

This flight from himself lasted a few days. Instead of look-ing for peace in the outdoors, Prager now began to search with-in himself. He discovered sources, reserves, untouched thoughts that began to refresh him, expanding his very self.

These thoughts began to bring up memories from his past. He remembered that, as a fifteen-year-old, he had worked in a store as a messenger boy. Older friends took him into their cir-cle, where they read forbidden books and spoke of freedom and equality for all.

In the city, preparations were underway for May Day. He was entrusted to circulate the printed proclamations. It was two days before the workers' holiday and when it came to this mission, he had no equal. He carried out his task with the utmost speed. When he finished distributing the proclamations, it was already late at night. He headed home happy and, in his imagination, he fantasized that everyone was praising him for his good work.

Suddenly, someone grabbed him by the throat: "*Stoy*!"[5] He saw two gendarmes, heard them ask, "Where'd this scoundrel

---

5. Russian: Stop!

come wandering from so late at night? Spit it out, you—where are you coming from?" He looked dim-wittedly at the gendarmes and didn't say a single word. They beat him hard, dragged him to the city prison, and shoved him into a cell. A real criminal captured!

Prager smiled when he remembered the prison cell. It was three feet wide, with smooth walls seemingly carved from ice and a tiny window up high, practically at the ceiling. He saw that he couldn't reach the window, that there was no way for him to get out of there. It occurred to him that he should make noise. He began to let out blood-curdling screams, but his voice only seemed to come back to him, like an alien call, as if someone were standing behind the wall and shouting after him. This pleased him. What a game!

In the end, they thought he was a crazy boy and kicked him out of the prison…

The people on the terrace began to get ready to leave. From time to time, a sentence comprised of indistinct words drifted over to him. But no more than that. Everything all around had become quiet.

In the stillness of his surroundings, Prager felt very good.

Hello, Butch

Although he identified with this means of livelihood—inherited from his father—for a good few decades now, and although his grandfather on his mother's side was also a butcher, he nevertheless hoped and pleaded with God all his lifelong years—ever since he could remember, really—for an escape from the butchery trade.

Back home in the shtetl, he knew he couldn't crawl out from under the butcher block. There, even if he would have started to do something else, the butcher block would have dragged behind him. Once a butcher, always a butcher! You got branded with the trade, and you carried that brand to the grave. Some in the shtetl did manage to extricate themselves from the trade, but they were never allowed to forget that they had been butchers. The word "butcher" was appended to their names until they died: Shimen the butcher, Berl the butcher, Muni the butcher. Even their children were called Freydl the butcher's daughter or Sheyndl the butcher's daughter, even when their parents, the butchers, were already in the next world. The butchers prayed in a butchery minyan, and when a joyous occasion was held—or a funeral, God forbid—the butchers were called upon to be the most honored guests.

When Rolkin came to the New World, he was certain he wouldn't go anywhere near the butchery trade. "A new country, a new life!" he said to his wife, and she agreed with him. She, too, wanted to be as good as other people. So they started looking. They met with others from their town in the Old World. But they too were butchers, every single one of them! As if deliberately, they all resumed their familiar work. For a while, Moysheh Rolkin struggled in poverty, until he finally had to take up his old trade. With his two powerful hands and his inherited aptitude, he didn't have to work very long for someone else. It wasn't long before Moysheh Rolkin was standing in his own tidy butcher shop. The women came. By nature, Rolkin was cheerful, talkative, unhurried. He showed patience when listening to the women. He got used to being back in his trade. His wife said: "If not for the little worm eating away at him, if not for that yearning he's had his whole life for something he himself can't name, we would manage, with God's help."

Rolkin didn't underestimate himself. He knew he possessed within himself something that lifted him up from the ordinary sort of butcher who constantly had moneymaking on his mind. Rolkin had his own morals, his own standards. He knew how far a person could allow himself to be drawn into the hullaballoo. Money, he thought, is a good thing, to be sure, but you don't have to sell your soul. And the women soon realized that if Rolkin said something was fresh, you could believe him. If he said it was kosher, then it was kosher.

Rolkin used to share his experiences in the American slaughterhouses with his customers. He complained that there was no love lost for him there, that he had difficulties getting meat because he couldn't be fooled by their showing the brand seal but then selling carrion. He knew all about their seals… In the shop, he was believed because his large, slightly red, teary eyes, were childish and truthful. Many of the customers even asked themselves the question: "How did someone like him come to be a butcher?"

When he convinced himself that he was only destined for the butchery trade here in the Golden Land, Rolkin began to pin his hopes on the next generation.

When his son was born, he had no doubt that this newborn soul would be the little white horse that would lead his father to where his heart had been calling him all this time. The little one would tug the bloodied apron away from him, and he, the butcher, would no longer be smelling the odor of slaughtered chickens. He would become a human being—and a butcher no more… Rolkin placed this very hope before the tiny child who squirmed in his strong butcher's hands and who smiled as if he were laughing at his father's talk and dreams.

This was their first and last child. No more children came. Their one-and-only little son, this boy, was short. He took after his mother more than his father. This only son grew slowly, and his parents didn't have anything to brag about.

The years went by. Over time, the butcher's feet became heavy. His cheeks had become inflamed, but his smile was still youthful and hope still glowed in his eyes. It was as if he were saying: "Wait, wait! You'll see. I'll surprise you yet!"

As if to spite his father, the child categorically adored everything to do with the butcher shop. He very much loved to slide down behind the table and run his little hands over the bone chips that wandered behind the butcher block. He snuck into the shop to caress the big slaughter knife and the saw. When he played with other children, he dragged chickens by their feet, just as his father did. Like his father, he, too, gestured with his hands the way a butcher did when showing the customer what fine merchandise he had. The little one even emulated his father's language: he spoke Yiddish.

When their son was still a boy, Rolkin kept pleading with his wife: "Take him away from there. Do you want him to grow up to be a butcher?" The mother did indeed try to drag her child away from the butcher shop, but the little one kicked his feet, absolutely refusing to budge. Seeing how the child was taking him as an example, Rolkin would yank the child from under the shop counter in great anger.

During the Sabbath meals, Rolkin furrowed his brow, looking over at his wife in one direction and at his son in the other. He wanted to say something, but the words remained on his tongue. Rolkin thought to himself: "He's a good boy, but I'm afraid he'll stay in his father's trade." He would shake off these mournful thoughts the way you drive away a lowly fly and then look lovingly at his son's face, all the while thinking: "All right, so you won't embarrass me, son?"

When the women—the customers—would crow about their sons, telling him how fine they were, how great they were doing, what their teacher in the Talmud Torah school was saying about them, or what a fine speech the bar mitzvah boy had mastered, Rolkin would lower his eyes and think: "I have nothing to brag about. No one says anything—good or bad—about my son." And a peculiar gnawing sensation would linger in the butcher's heart. He would have gladly foregone the women's camaraderie if that would mean that they would stop telling him stories about their children.

The neighborhood where Rolkin's butcher shop was located was petit-bourgeois, neither poor nor rich. Workers who had been in the country for a long time—tailors, hat makers, insurance agents who had managed to put a little by for themselves—lived there. They had a little, but nothing like wealth. Their children were professionals such as doctors and lawyers. The mothers kept boasting about their children, speaking of their sharpness, their intelligence. These boasts drilled a path into Rolkin's mind, getting tangled in his thoughts when he went down into the cellar to bring up a side of meat or when he was cutting the meat for the customers. Rolkin wanted to get a word in about his son, too, but he only moved his lips around as if he were poised to say something but then decided to save it for another time. That gnawing sensation would flare up deep within when he thought about his only son. Pain about the child, and himself, engulfed him.

"A good boy, that goes without saying! But an ordinary boy, without any uniqueness. Soon he'll finish public school and have his bar mitzvah, but then what will come of him?"

The Rolkins didn't speak about the boy's bar mitzvah with the neighbors. They didn't mention it all, as if they were ashamed of it. The parents could have organized a fine celebration just like anyone else. They weren't short of cash, praise God, but there was nothing to brag about here. Better to keep quiet.

By the looks of things, the boy was no fool. He often responded quite adroitly to his father, and the butcher had to admit that he was right. For example, on one occasion, the boy said that he, too, wished he could excel academically, distinguish himself in some way, but if it wasn't to be—well then, it wasn't to be. He would be what he would be.

It was a matter of great urgency to Rolkin that his son receive a good education. He had hoped that when his son grew older and saw how his father spent his years in the shop, around the butcher block, he would come to understand that there was no future here. But the years passed. Rolkin grew older. His bankbook grew, too. His legs became heavier, and a sadness pressed on his heart. Now the boy had finished high school. From time to time, he even helped his father with the accounts. The father said to the women: "By all means, let him help, work with the figures, and earn for his own needs. That will help him in college." "Of course, what else? Who doesn't go to college?" the women answered. "If a man like you, Mr. Rolkin, doesn't send his son to college, who will?"

In his mind, Rolkin counted quite a few friends, the people from his home town in the Old Country, who were also butchers. But their children shunned the butcher shops. Some of the children became doctors and lawyers; others took up a business. Only his son was delighted with the butcher shop… If his father would just let him, he would tackle the job with such skill and gusto that sparks would fly!

Rolkin regretfully noticed how his son took a smooth piece of meat up onto the block as if he wanted to make it better and more beautiful. He saw how his son gathered up the dregs and adeptly threw them into a large tin can set up under the shelf. He really did it with such skill, as if he were afraid that his father would hound him and tell him to bring them back...

Every now and then, Rolkin would toss in a word about his son. "My son is getting ready to go to college in a big city," he'd say with feigned modesty, as if it were all par for the course. Yet even as he spoke those words, he felt that it would have been better if he just let his son pick his own vocation, the very trade which had compelled the boy since childhood.

It was difficult for Rolkin to communicate with his American-born son. His son didn't understand his father's longing—his thirst for something different, something higher, something for which he had no name. Perhaps it was what his wife called "the butcher's sickness," or the sadness of not being able to mingle enough with other people? Over there, in the shtetl, he was *"der katsev"*; here, the "butcher." What a name! They shortened it to "Butch." Hello, Butch!

His son couldn't enroll in City College. He didn't have the necessary qualifications. This really depressed his parents. Even Nathan, the son, who believed that learning was an impediment to "becoming a person," was engulfed by their heartache and decided to go away to college in another state.

Nathan didn't know himself what this news meant for his father. Rolkin was not the sort of person who showed his feelings, and although his mind was full of thoughts and desires, he nevertheless couldn't reveal them to another person.

Rolkin left the cuddling and coddling of his only son to the boy's mother. She did enough for the both of them. If his son hadn't decided on his own to go away to college, Rolkin would never have been able to make it up to the boy for pressuring him. That's because something was bothering the father deep in his consciousness: "The apple doesn't fall far from the tree..." Rather than recognize the truth about his son, Rolkin preferred to think that the boy's sudden decision about college was from his own inclination. His deep fear that his son had inherited his own butcher's brain was one that Rolkin silenced, like a secret, even from himself.

One Friday night, before his son's departure, Rolkin was in a good mood. For that Friday, the boy's mother had prepared better, more appealing dishes than usual. Everything looked more festive. The flames of the candles seemingly burned brighter. Before the Grace After Meals, Rolkin rested his head on both hands and began to speak, as if he wanted to end a conversation he had begun earlier:

"My father didn't want his son to be a butcher, either, but he still used to wake me up at dawn to go with him to the slaughterhouse. In the worst cold spells, he would drag me out of bed, curse his livelihood, and constantly appeal to me: 'May you be protected from having to earn your daily bread this way! Do whatever you can—just don't be a butcher!' Well, you can see for yourself how well he protected me!"

Rolkin spoke aimlessly, not expecting a response. But his son, like a grownup, interrupted his talk with a question: "Tell me, Papa, what is it? What's eating you? You know my friend's father is a dentist and doesn't have money to send his son to college. Money is no problem for you. Did it ever occur to you that if I become a dentist, too, then I won't have tuition money for my kids, either? You don't want me to be butcher, but has it occurred to you that a butcher makes better money than a dentist?"

Nathan was pleased that he could now speak with his father as an equal. During this past year, he had grown tall. His face, though still childish in appearance, was nevertheless full of decisiveness. His greenish, not-large eyes smiled. He looked at his father simultaneously with love and irony. The father, starting to doze off a bit, looked at his son through his cupped hands, and thought: "He sure is talking like a perfect adult!" Straining, he answered half-sleepily: "I can assure you, son, that the dentist would never change places with me..."

"You know, son," he continued, "Money really is, as they say, the world, but there are things that money can't buy. Take me, I'm a simple butcher. I'm not chasing after honor. I don't even know how to chase after it. But I'll tell you—however much money I accumulate, they'll always call me a rich *katsev*, or a rich butcher... They'll point at me: 'There goes the rich butcher!' The dentist is greeted with the words: 'Hello, doc!' But to me, they say, "Hello, butch!' Now you tell me, which would you prefer?"

Half in jest, half in earnest, the son answered him, "I don't care."

Those words pained the father, but his exhausted sleepiness put an end to the conversation. "Go to sleep. Go already!" the wife said to her husband. Rolkin still managed to say to his son: "You're quite the smart one, son!"

When their only son left, the parents felt a sadness in the house. It was the first time that the boy's bed had remained untouched, and his seat at the table stood empty. Each of them consoled the other, and Rolkin even compared his son's departure from home to the cozy middle-class families that used to send their children to faraway yeshivas. This gave him a sense of importance; it seemed to him that his customers looked at him in a very different way. But his wife didn't know what to do with herself. She counted the days since their son had left. She wanted to know how their son was faring among strangers. She worried about whether he had a good place to sleep, whether he was eating his meals on time. She thought about it for whole days before she reached the conclusion that her husband was wrong. With her maternal intuition, she sensed that their son had not wanted to go away, that he had done so because of his father. And though, like her husband, she had dreamed, hoped, and asked God that there emerge from her only son something to be proud of, she nevertheless sensed that Rolkin had overreached. You can't turn a child into a doctor or lawyer through force. Everything was up to fate.

Mrs. Rolkin thought that someone else in her husband's place would have been satisfied. They weren't short on income. They had saved a few dollars. Maybe the young man really was right? After all, she herself loved to see the way her husband stood at his work. It seemed to her that she had never seen someone with such golden hands! True, he wasn't what he had once been. Back then, all of the women flirted with him, and even today, there were still some who would have run after him…

These thoughts did not lift the mother's mood. She couldn't tell much from her son's letters. His Yiddish was as good as his father's English, and so writing was difficult for both of them. For the parents, each day stretched out. They were already counting the days to the son's return home for his break.

The semester ended much earlier than the parents had thought. Nathan came home emaciated and pale, as if he hadn't had enough sleep for many nights. Thinking that their son was sick, the parents were frightened. But after Nathan had rested up and slept, Rolkin understood that their son was staying silent for a reason, that he was holding something back. He was keeping secrets of a sort.

A new Friday night arrived. The small flames of the candles flickered, and Rolkin's eyes were probing. Nathan placed his hands on his father's shoulder and smiled, but his smile wasn't completely convincing. He put both of his hands together, the way his father did, trembled, and finally said, "Papa, I tried. I did it for you. But it was all for nothing! A waste of your money, and a waste of time. Papa, the studying doesn't sink into my brain. I'm not going back. Enough!"

Nathan stood up, started to stride across the room, stopping next to his father.

"Be a sport, Dad, I'm a devoted son. What more do you want?"

For a time, Rolkin was silent, and that silence weighed heavily in the room. When he stood up, his eyes were those of a drunkard.

His legs wobbled. Father, mother, and son stood still in middle of the room. Rolkin's wife had great empathy for her husband, wanting to console him with something, but she couldn't find the words. She began to weep quietly. Rolkin heard his wife's weeping and turning to his son, he repeated several times to his son, "Yet again, Butch, now and forever Butch? Hello, Butch. Hello, Butch…"

The Mute Mother

Every corner of the large pauper's courtyard, where the residents mingled like one big family, seethed in turmoil. The commotion gripped both young and old. Women whispered to each other. Men set against each other with fists. Fear filled the children who had been thrust off to the side by their mothers, who didn't want them to know what had happened. At any moment, they expected something inexpressible to descend upon them from somewhere.

The spacious four-sided courtyard was called "The Alley." It had two entrances and more than ten little one-story houses whose floors were at the ground level. On some of the houses hung the faded little signs of shoemakers and tailors. These artisans were meager earners who had to rely on their children or resort to municipal charity. All of the residents felt as if they had been excluded from the better parts of the city. The men had their own minyan—the one for ordinary artisans—and they turned their backs on the fine homeowners near the eastern walls who called the courtyard "the paupers' corner."

Throughout the summer, the doors and windows were open. From all the windows, poverty sang out, and the air reeked of overcrowding and the odors of poor people's food. Oftentimes, the neighbors set up their bedding on the worn-out, long-unused pole wagons standing in the courtyard. The wagons lured the children during the day, and at night, when the residents were restless in their stifling homes, they commandeered the wagons and inhaled the fresh air with all of their might.

Since there wasn't enough room to accommodate everyone on the wagons, the residents hurried to grab a spot. Sleeping under the vast sky was a pleasure, a real delight, and people enjoyed it as much as a good drink.

The cause of the commotion resounding from every corner of the courtyard was something that touched everyone, although none of them was the culprit. The commotion concerned a fifteen-year-old mute girl who, despite having a mother, was considered by all of the courtyard residents to be their own.

The girl had been born to a sick mother. Her father died even before she came into the world. Her mother was so sick that she didn't want to—and indeed couldn't—do anything. She would make short shrift of tending to the "little freak" by providing a bit of warm water, hoping that God would have pity and take it away. The neighbors saw to everything, ensuring that the child was properly raised, in spite of the circumstances. Some contended that a child with the kind of lip she had was auspicious. As a result, all of the women became mothers to the child. Anyone with God in their hearts contributed something. Those who themselves had nothing of their own would knock on the doors of strangers and beg for a bit of baked goods for the pitiable child. The girl was raised on soaked bread and grits and never took sick. That, in and of itself, convinced the neighbor mothers that the child with the cleft lip and the aged little face was surely providential.

The child grew. Her face matured a bit; her small eyes grew larger and assumed a dark shine. Her little body rounded out and she started to walk earlier than the other children. But she lacked language. She didn't speak. No word left her mouth, even though she definitely did have an acute sense of hearing.

No one called her by her name. She was always known as "the mute."

As she grew, everyone in the courtyard bossed her around. She worked for everyone. She was the water carrier and the wood carrier. People outside the courtyard also hired her to do the hardest work for a few groschens. When the mute saw the few coins, she would let out odd shrieks of joy. She worked enthusiastically, using all of her limbs. When she was working, her body reeked with a hot stench. Not well acquainted with money, she knew nonetheless that it had its uses. She hid the few groschens she earned and then gave them to her mother.

The mute felt a love for those who were demonstrably warm towards her. She attached herself to her friends and faithfully watched over them and their property. Tall and slim, she seldom rested. She ran around barefoot or in shoes that someone had donated to her and in a dress that barely stayed on her body. Racing from house to house, she would wait until someone called her in to tell her to do something.

The mute could also get angry and agitated if she felt she was being duped, like when someone gave her a piece of stale bread or an insufficient number of groschens. In her rage, she would roar wildly and begin to flail about with her hands in the person's face, right up to their eyes. She made such scenes only in front of strangers, not people she knew. The mute displayed a very special love for children. As soon as she noticed a child, she couldn't be pried away from it. With children, she herself became a quiet, gentle child. Her black, sharp, slightly shadowed eyes became mild, and her hands moved tremblingly over the child's body. She looked jealously at every hand that touched a child. Then a tender sound, like from a newborn baby, rolled forth from her throat.

The mute developed physically at a young age. Her hips rounded out, and stiff, small breasts blared from her tight, worn dresses. Unease and hunger cried out from her darting eyes, and she couldn't sit still in one place.

She hadn't yet turned fifteen when the eyes of the courtyard residents opened wide in astonishment at the sight of her. At first, no one wanted to believe it, but as her belly began to protrude considerably, the women began to wail quite vociferously.

"Woe is us! What misery has befallen us! Where were our eyes? How could we have let this happen?" With these words, the women greeted each other, as if the calamity had happened to their own child. The men didn't want to stop at just talk. They wanted to do something that would have tangible consequences, like grabbing hold of the culprit and teaching him a lesson or two. They stomped their feet, rolled up their sleeves, and prepared to strike the scoundrel, give him a drubbing. In their great helplessness at not being able to find the culprit, they got into each other's faces...

Days, then weeks, went by, and the ruckus around the mute subsided. She herself had changed. She shuffled over to dark corners and didn't respond to the shouts and the hue and cry of the neighbors with so much as a blink of an eye. She did her work with even more diligence. She veritably blazed, as if she wanted to stop up the mouths of the neighbors with her vigorous hands. The mute's mother also pretended that she didn't see or hear what was happening right there in the courtyard.

Time passed. The months slid away. The mute had become heavy on her feet, and she began to hide in her mother's dark home. She didn't communicate with anyone, didn't entrust the secret of the identity of the father to anyone. Or else she didn't know what fathering meant... But people observed that she did know what a child was. She sensed that she was carrying a living, squirming being inside of her, and she guarded her belly, not allowing anyone to get close. If someone did approach her, she blocked the front of her belly by forming a protective barrier with her hands.

Although she was "everyone's child" and her "misfortune" had caused such a commotion in the courtyard, no one noticed that the mute was nowhere to be seen for a few days. No one supplied her with a childbirth bed or diapers for the baby. On an overcast Passover eve, the mute tossed and turned in frightened spasms on a straw mattress in her mother's bleak home, bellowing, like a cow, to the dark walls. She tore at her dress and her disheveled hair and bit her fingers, but no one responded to her cries. By the time her mother came to her, she heard a quiet sigh, the kind that comes when you catch your breath after experiencing terrible pains. Her mother also heard the squealing of the newborn little soul.

The mute had become a mother. Alone, without a midwife, but with the help and common sense that nature gives every living being, the mute protected her own life and the life of her child.

The courtyard residents still hoped to find the father of the mute's child. They racked their brains, pondering every possibility relentlessly, reviewing this and that, and shadowing every man who showed up in the courtyard. But when they learned that the child was already born, they caught their breath. It was hopeless!

The new mother stayed silent: during the first few days—from weakness; and later—from great happiness, as if she were a child who had been longing for something and finally received it. Her sallow, gaunt face now shone with happiness. She carefully held the child close to her, and there was such a guardedness in her eyes that it frightened away the neighbors. No one dared touch the child. The mute's eyes screamed: "Get away!" She didn't expect anything from anyone—no food, chicken soup, or jelly. There were no pieces of paper with the text of Psalms 121 meant to dispel evil spirits during childbirth, and she apparently had no fear of evil spirits. As long as her breasts were full, she herself was content with a little barley soup and the cup of chicory that her mother brought to her. She only wanted to be left in peace with her child. The child nursed, and there was no limit to the mother's happiness.

The newborn little soul also needed very little. The mother's milk was sweet; her breasts—warm. The baby was quiet, nursing with full, satisfied lips, and sleeping. With a furrowed brow, it looked like an elderly person. When it occasionally let out a scream, it was with a strong voice, not at all like a newborn baby.

The happiness the mute shared with her child didn't last long. Outside meddlers began to howl. The courtyard residents caught their breath and began to make noise again. The commotion moved beyond the confines of the courtyard and reached the surrounding neighborhood. The urban "benefactors" caught wind of the "illegal" child and set out to make themselves heard. A delegation of four ladies descended. Gussied up, perfumed, white gloves on hands, bejeweled earrings. To enter the mute's dark room was something they didn't want—didn't have the courage—to do. So they stood on the threshold—exchanging glances, consulting among themselves—and waited for someone to emerge and lead them inside. The mute was alone in the room and let out a fearful roar every minute or so. The children of the courtyard gathered close to the ladies as if beholding an amazing sight.

Finally, two ladies crossed the threshold and entered. The rancid darkness assaulted them. The ladies clung to each other, not knowing where to place their feet. One of them asked, "Where are we? "*Bozhe moy*!"[6] Another responded with a question: "Isn't it awful?" Sensing the presence of these unwanted guests, the mute roared her dissatisfaction in her wordless language. The ladies registered her protests coming out of the dimness. When the dark cloud parted a bit, they saw a half of the mute, how she was stiffly pressing the child to her. The voice and the eyes of the mute gushed with such rage that the ladies felt that it would be better and safer for them to retreat from her—while there was still time. As they were leaving, the mute accompanied them, bellowing all the while.

The mute intuited that they wanted to rob her of her child. She wouldn't let anyone near the child, not even her mother. The child, she sensed, was her very own, and no one else's. This little soul, with the two lively legs, the tiny, soft fingers, the full, round face—this was hers! And when the child could barely open its eyes and she saw in them a thin, dark stripe, like the small blade of a pocketknife, she felt even then that the stripe was asking her to hold it tight in her arms and never let go.

---

6. Russian: My god!

Meanwhile, a circle formed in the courtyard around the gussied-up ladies. In the beginning, the crowd wasn't sure of itself, not knowing whether they, with their simple language, would be able to make themselves understood to these ladies. But as soon as the first person dared to open her mouth, everyone began to speak. Whoever managed to push their way into the circle threw in a word on behalf of the mute. They contended that the child was theirs. They had all seen to it that she didn't starve from hunger, and, as a result, they were all crushed by the misfortune that had befallen her.

The ladies tried to make sense of the neighbors' contentions. One of the two who had earlier been inside the mute's home wiped her eyes with a thin, scented handkerchief. Finally, one of the ladies turned to the women and said, "Will you help us and persuade the mute to give the child away to an institution?" The women, entirely caught off guard by this proposal, didn't respond. The lady put on a serious face, wanting to show the neighbors that this was a weighty matter, and then launched into something of a speech: "We're all Jews, so we have to see to it that the child is raised as a Jewish child. Nowadays, how can the child be entrusted to such a mother?"

The entire circle was left speechless; it was impossible to get a word out of them. The lady then said in a softer tone, "We'll give you a few days to think it over." After they were finished with their few words, the ladies left the courtyard, taking slow steps. They lifted their feet, as if they didn't want to step in something that wouldn't be so easy to shake off afterward… For a while, the neighbors stayed where they were and looked on after them.

They simply didn't understand what the lady had said to them. Each one was lost in thought and waited for someone else to say something, to come out with a sharp word against the uninvited ladies of influence. Until that point, they had committed their share of racking their brains and eating their hearts out over this calamity. Still, they had taken care of the mute. They had raised her. And now this trouble!

An old bookbinder with sick, red eyes broke the silence. He inserted himself among the group of women, tilted his little beard upwards, and looking off in the direction taken by the departed ladies, shouted out, "We'll ignore them! What are they saying— that we don't know what a Jewish child is? As soon as a Jewish mother bears a child and it nurses on her milk, it is a Jewish child! And then what? We have to circumcise the child; we'll do it without them! What—aren't we Jews?"

Having had his say, he nodded his head and gestured with his hands, like someone saying: "I've done my part!" He then pushed his way out of the circle and vanished.

The women didn't think much of the old man's insights. They maintained that individuals more knowledgeable about Judaism had to be consulted. There was a man who lived in the courtyard who looked like a rabbi. This man collected challahs for the poor on the eve of every Sabbath. He was called "the man with the sack." He kept himself a bit apart from the neighbors, even though he responded to every greeting in a friendly way. "It's to a man like that that we have to turn to for advice," the women said. "After all, he's a man with a good heart; he'll steer us in the right direction."

In fact, the man with the sack soon took the matter into his own hands. Without asking any questions, without any fuss, he promptly assembled a minyan, raised a toast, circumcised the child, and named him Nosn. Afterwards, the man with the sack said: "Friends, you must know that this child is a Jew. You shouldn't think otherwise!"

The man spoke these words in a commanding tone, with an authoritative manner. Everyone sensed that he knew what he was talking about. He would see to it that everything was handled properly.

From that day on, this man was called "Rebbe." The Rebbe commanded everyone's great respect. The mute mother, who didn't trust her child with anyone, clung to the Rebbe with a speechless humility, and with pleading in her eyes and in every movement of her face and hands. Everything in her beseeched: "Love my child!" And when the Rebbe occasionally picked up the child, a wild joy roared from the mute's heart.

If the mute had been a bit better acquainted with the ways of people, she would have known that this man would never become estranged from her child. The man took the child into himself, gave him a place in his heart, and held him there until the last days of his life.

He was middle-aged, with broad, somewhat bent shoulders, a brown beard, and eyes of mixed hue. These were eyes that, at one point, could seem mild and soft, as if saying "People, come here! I love you all!" and at another point, they could appear gloomy, as if saying "People, leave me alone. Leave me in peace!"

This man had buried his one-and-only child who died at the age of three. Since the child's death, his wife hadn't gotten out of bed. The man himself couldn't decide whether God had sent this strange child to him in his old age as a comfort, someone for him to protect, or whether God was punishing him by opening up an old wound that had never healed. He had to dissolve this wound through the life of this lonely creature. He had to forget that this was someone else's child and bring the child to his sick wife so that he would be a comfort to her as well.

When the man opened his home to the mute and her child, the mute beamed with delight. The child also brought joy to the isolated household. Even when the baby cried, his crying was taken as love, as if it were ripping the sadness asunder with its tears. The man declared that as long as he lived, he would share his last bite with the child, and when he was gone, God would provide for him.

The boy grew. He became bigger, healthier. He had his mother's black curls and lively eyes. The mute always looked for something in the child's eyes, and when he began to pronounce words, she would try to imitate him by speaking with her cleft lip. The mute mother roared with a kind of sound which the neighbors swore they could clearly make out as the child's name. Mother and son appeared to understand each other well, to have their own common language.

People couldn't stop marveling at the devotion the man showed to the child. The man and his wife never let the child out of their supervision. People sensed that the mute was proud that such respectable people were showing such a strong love for her child.

When Nosn was three years old, the man started to teach him the Hebrew alphabet. "I'll teach him," the man said, "as if he were my own child." The man educated the child until he reached the age of five. After that, the man left town. He had always been secretive; where exactly he had come from had never been known. And where he was going—well, that wasn't known, either.

People asked after him, searched for him, but no one could tell them his whereabouts. They just knew that prior to his departure, he provided for the child with the Committee, that he kissed him, that he even kissed the mute on her head, and that on one dark morning, his home stood empty and the grieving voice of the mother could be heard.

The Committee was an institution for poor children and orphans. The children learned a trade there. The Committee was supported by the Jewish community, but the children didn't live in the lap of luxury there. Although they were supposed to have soft hearts, the bourgeois Jews from the city nevertheless didn't want the orphans and poor children to be equals to their own children. So they fed the children barley soup and potatoes, leaving them pale and thin, without any childish joy in their faces. They also wore shabby outfits marking them as the children of paupers. A tin badge on their caps further separated them from the other children in town.

The institution was housed in a short, old building in the synagogue courtyard near the market. The windows—low to the ground. In the beginning, the mute guarded the windows like a loyal dog. She would sit with her feet behind her and her head to the window pane, and rumble something. Later, she contented herself with the minutes that the child was at home with her. Nosn loved his mother no less than she did him. He clung to her and described to her in great detail everything that was causing him distress. As he got older, his love for his mother did not diminish.

The years passed. The mute got older. Just as she had in her childhood, she still raced from home to home. Her mother had long since died. The neighbors still kept an eye out for her, afraid that what had happened before could be repeated…

Then, a commotion began in the city. Rumors circulated that there would soon be a work stoppage. Not a hand was to be lifted! There was also talk of the workers gathering in the forests, that people from the larger cities would be coming down here and delivering speeches to the weavers and tanners. Others reported that the bakers were going to stop baking bread. There would be a strike, just like in the iron factory in the nearby big city.

In the courtyard, several young people moved with a secretive air about them, pretending not to know what was being said. Clever smiles accompanied their words, but the neighbors sought out and found something unusual in the young people's eyes: a kind of waiting, a tense, suspenseful joy. Sixteen-year-old Nosn caressed his mother's disheveled curls with both of his hands and said to her, "You'll see, Mama, you'll see!" He wanted his mother to understand everything. The words he spoke were measured. She stared at his lips, imitating him with her mouth, and both of their eyes shone with childish, mischievous searching. The mother's eyes—black, darting; her child's—green-gray, with large, dark eyebrows, and a bit weary.

The event took place earlier than anticipated. In the course of one day, all of the factories and workshops in the city came to a stop. The workers sprang into action as if from a spontaneous signal. The owners didn't know what was happening. The streets were full of workers who didn't speak to anyone. That, too, appeared to be a previously agreed-upon decision. There was one peaceful day, but by the next, the police had already besieged the city. No two people were allowed to stop and talk to each other. The police and the Cossacks on horseback slashed mercilessly with leather whips. They made anyone who so much as came within reach feel the taste of the lash. As a result of the Cossacks' brutality, people stayed home. The courtyard trembled.

The courtyard was located between the factory and the military barracks. Throughout the day, the stamping of the horses and the jingle-jangle of the Cossacks' spurs could be heard. The elderly hid in their houses. Young people ran wherever they could in order to get some news from the street. Those who went to work hadn't come home for nights. Parents got through their days wringing their hands and trembling in terror. The mute raced from one house to the other, trying to find out what was happening. She sensed that something terrifying was hanging over her child's head. It had been a few days since she'd seen him. She did her utmost to run from the courtyard into the street, but people restrained her. She even went so far as to throw punches at those who were blocking her path.

After three days, which felt to the residents like years, they learned that the workers had lost. Their leaders were thrown into prison, and many were beaten and dragged to the hospital.

It was quiet again in the city—the quiet that follows a funeral. It seemed as if everyone's strength had suddenly been depleted. They had to stop and wait until they could return to their former selves.

Several weeks passed. In the free evenings, Nosn once again clung to his mother. He was gaunt, silent, and smiled like a child. With worry in her eyes, the mute inquired about everything she couldn't grasp. But in her probing eyes, there was also a joy that he was here, that he was her child.

It was a Saturday evening. There were few people on the street. Only here and there, a Jew, burdened by heavy thought, could be seen walking. In the windows, cloudy flames were lit; a gnawing gloom hung in the air. Suddenly, voices poured out from somewhere, the stamping of tens of pairs of feet, heavy steps, as if they wanted to smash something with every step. The police descended on the courtyard as if they had grown out of its shadows. They blocked both exits so that no one would be able to slip away. The neighbors, stunned, clung to each other, as if they had agreed earlier that it had to be this way. The police turned the houses—and the entire courtyard—upside down. Under the dark sky, the people wondered: "What could they possibly find here?"

Soon, the officer in charge and a few of his men turned on the people, shouting for them to hand over Nosn from his hiding place right then and there. They also asked about the man with the sack. It took a while for the neighbors to comprehend what was wanted of them. They didn't understand what this villain wanted with Nosn, the mute's son. And how should they know where the man with sack was? It had been years since they'd laid eyes on him. Everyone quietly agreed to answer: "We don't know anything." The police who stormed the courtyard with such explosive force had to retreat with nothing to show for their efforts.

That same night, Nosn, together with the other journeymen in the clothing factory, were arrested. For a time, the city wondered who could have given up the names of those young people. They learned the secret: Mendl, a Hasid, proprietor of a dry goods store, signed a denunciation declaring that all of the young people were rebels. Another man, who years ago had been a Talmud teacher at Mendl's home, reappeared once again and became the absolute leader of the rebellion.

The mothers of the worker-sons broke the window panes of the informer's house. Every time Mendl passed by, they spit at him. But their sons were sent in a procession of prisoners under escort far, far away—to Siberia. The victim from the courtyard was Nosn. The mood in the courtyard was akin to the Ninth of Av.[7] The mute's pain knew no bounds. From day to day, her condition worsened.

For the first few days after Nosn went missing, she raced around and peered at every passerby with dazed eyes. Fury screamed from her very being. With her wild appearance, unkempt hair, and unwashed person, she terrified everyone. Afterwards, she rolled herself up into a ball, not eating, not drinking, but only roaring, as if a heavy load were pressing down upon her.

One dark evening, a young girl appeared on a neighbor's threshold and asked about the mute. Then, an older Jew with a small gray, clipped beard. The neighbor woman immediately brought in the mute. When the man started speaking, the woman could tell from his voice that it was the man with the sack, the Rebbe.

The mute beheld this man and squirmed with joy. She tugged at the man's sleeves, at his lapel, as if she were expecting her son to emerge from there. The man caressed her head and said, "I've brought you regards from Nosn. He doesn't want you to cry. He will return. But you have to wait for that time to come. Don't cry!" He spoke to her as if he were speaking to his own child. "Wait, wait!" the neighbor woman repeated after him.

The man left. The mute calmed down, and together with all of the residents of the courtyard, waited for that bright day…

---

7. Ninth of Av: an annual fast day in Judaism, on which a number of disasters in Jewish history occurred, chiefly the destruction of King Solomon's Temple by the Neo-Babylonian Empire and the Second Temple by the Roman Empire in Jerusalem. It is considered the saddest day of the Jewish calendar.

Dead Flowers

Night had not yet retreated. In Fay's room, the darkness was still dense. Wanting to see how late it was, she reached her hand out for the lamp. Why had she awakened? What was the hurry? Today would be a day like all other days. She would get dressed, eat something, look in the mirror, and then take the same long walk to work that she took every day. The route was well-trodden. The houses and stores were familiar to her. As for the faces she'd come across—well, she could recognize those with her eyes closed.

A typical morning, as all other mornings—like those experienced two or ten years ago. As if merged into one, the years barely differentiated themselves. But this morning did distinguish itself in Fay's mind, but only in a certain way—inwardly, as it were, within herself. Outwardly, the day was a day like all previous days.

She herself thought very little about the years. All of her limbs were healthy; her step was lighter than people years younger. She wasn't behind on her work. On the contrary, her work was praised more now than it had ever been. With the years of work came experience. Nevertheless, Fay felt within herself a drive to industriousness, a kind of incitement of self, as if she wanted to demonstrate that she was the same Fay of years ago.

When she came into the office and saw that it was already five minutes into the workday, she reproached herself for her navel-gazing and tardiness. She rushed to remove her outerwear, and before she knew it, four girls and the manager appeared. They marched in a procession that looked as if it had been rehearsed beforehand. The manager, who held a little bouquet of flowers in his hands, had a serious face, although his small eyes were slightly smiling. In a ceremonial manner, he offered her the flowers. And like someone accustomed to such rituals, he said quietly:

"… We here didn't forget to commemorate this date marking the twenty-five years that you've been working for us! This is no small thing. After all, it's a quarter of a century! You've reached the point, my dear Fay, where you start to slide downhill the very moment you get there. You've got to hold onto something with both hands, because the law of nature is…"

With his clean hands, he pointed downwards in the universal gesture of things going south, and then laughed at his own joke.

Fay remained standing, as if partially frozen in place. She felt that in preparing the celebration, invoking the exact day she had started working here, and in "venerating" her, the refined manager had stripped her naked right in front of everyone's faces. She didn't know how to respond or what to do with her hands into which had been plunked the humiliated, semi-unconscious flowers with drooping petals. She glanced over at the four girls, who sensed the sting of the manager's words. She saw compassion for her in their eyes. If little Sylvia hadn't come running up to hug and kiss her with tears in her eyes, who knows how the scene would have ended?

Herr Berg, the manager, was some fifteen years older than Fay. Unlike her, he had become an entirely new person in this country. He had come from Austria. Prior to Hitler, he didn't know he was a Jew. Hitler reminded him of that fact. The Nazis robbed him of all his property, even though he had distinguished himself in World War I and received medals for his military service. If he hadn't been smuggled out in time, he would have experienced the fate of all of his Jewish compatriots.

He was a person of education who had a few titles. His way of life and behavior were in the "German style," an "authentic Aryan." But he was "punished" with a Jewish nose, which somehow didn't harmonize with his bright blue eyes, round, ruddy cheeks, prickly whiskers, and a practically hairless head. Berg remembered a few Yiddish words—vestiges of a great-grandfather from Poland—that had turned up in his family. He seldom used these words, and when he did, they were out of context. He himself didn't know their meaning.

Berg hadn't even been in the country a week when he was hired by the institution. But with his talent for adapting to every circumstance, he oriented himself quickly and won everyone's loyalty. He tried to show that he was rejecting anything connecting him to his former home. He didn't want to speak any German and denied that Germany was once a land of culture, and for a short while, he even expressed that the civilized world had to learn from the Russians. He won the loyalty of his people. In his presence, Fay read the left-wing newspapers and journals, and although there was no time for conversations, she was still sure there were no spying eyes that she needed to watch out for.

However, the idyll didn't last long. One morning, when the press announced in big block letters that Czechoslovakia had become a people's democracy, Herr Berg came to work a changed man. Out with the fine phrases about "looking up to the Russians"! In a matter of a few days, everything that had previously been bright and encouraging turned into a volcano that flooded the entire free world...

This new change in Berg affected the colleagues who worked closely with him. The tone of their conversations with him had to change. It didn't come to engaging in political or ideological discussions, but it did create a change.

Fay, who for the largest part of the day was in the same room as Berg, hoisted a kind of stiffness upon herself. She forced herself to smile, to be more disciplined, and, most importantly, to avoid the smallest clue that she was disgusted by his talk. Berg tried to convince everyone that the Russians were the worst, that you had to distance yourself from them. He spoke with fervor and passion. This caused a kind of partition, a barrier, to form between the two of them—Berg, the manager, and Fay, his co-worker. This irritated him, and he looked for an opportunity to break that barrier. On this morning, he thought he had found the opportunity.

Herr Berg had intended to surprise Fay—to bring flowers for the anniversary of the date she had started working there. At the same time, he wanted to have the satisfaction of letting her know that he knew exactly how old she was, and that when you reached such an age, you start to go downhill.

Herr Berg kept the ceremony a secret from the other workers in the institution. He only told them the day before that they were to present Fay with flowers.

The girls—the female workers—weren't accustomed to such celebrations. No one was particularly happy about revealing age. They knew that the management definitely exploited the older workers in no small measure, paying them less than the newer hires, and as a result, they wanted to keep silent about Fay's anniversary. But they didn't want to go against the manager, especially when it looked as if he wanted to demonstrate his good connection with a co-worker… So the girls had to go through the ceremony, even though they resented it.

After the ceremony, Fay worked with a strange momentum, as if pursued by whips. She avoided everyone's eyes and only answered the manager's questions. With the vehement pace of her work, she wanted to tear through the thoughts springing up in her mind like hands speeding over a clock face, like frightened flies. She was barely able to make it until the end of the workday. His words—that she had worked in the institution for a quarter of a century, that there was no longer anything to look forward to—drilled their way into her mind. Put another way—she had given the best of herself, and for that, he brought her a few little flowers. That was the reward for her years of work completed.

How bizarre it was, she thought. Until today, Fay had felt that, as the years went by, she was accumulating something; but today he conveyed to her in his German manner that everything was "kaput." In her own mind, she responded to him in this way: "You, Herr Berg, are somewhat older than I am, after all. Well then, you're 'kaput,' too."

A cheerful ray of sunshine penetrated the room, saying to her: "Look at me! What does a human being know about time?" Fay stood up against the sun and thought: "Let me just change my clothes, get out of here, and leave this resentment behind me." Her gaze landed on the flowers that seemed to be saying to her: "How are we culpable? Don't shame us. Take us with you!"

She took the flowers from the vase, and felt annoyed that she was holding the flowers in cold hands…

On the street, Fay rejoiced, refreshed. When she stopped before a window, she saw a slim woman and marveled that this morning's events hadn't left any outward impression. She had a hankering to walk so she could think more clearly as she moved. She took a major detour to the park. By the time she reached it, she was exhausted. She sat down on a bench, leaned on the handrail with one hand, and rubbed her half-closed eyes with the other. She felt a strange serenity, but in that serenity, she sensed that a little black creature with a tail, like Mickey Mouse—but with laughing, green little eyes—was spinning right in front of her. She felt that the laughter was becoming unbearable, as if those eyes specifically wanted her to peer into them. Where had she seen those little eyes?—she wanted to remember. Those are his eyes; it was him that she was seeing…

Fay opened her eyes and noticed the flowers on her lap. Just as earlier she had wanted to be alone with her thoughts, now she suddenly felt the urge to be with someone with whom she could share her thoughts. She knew all too well that she would be going back to her furnished room where she would have to set the table

alone. This got her thinking: How long had it been since she prepared a table for two? It felt like it had not been so long ago. Back
then, she had raced home, burdened with packages and flush with
the bliss cast upon her by another. Yes, that was all "in the past."
That bliss had disintegrated.

Fay was not the only one with just one "brief connection" in
her life. The other girls at work also lived in their aloneness. They
hungered and acted as if it didn't bother them; they pretended
that they could do without love. Only one of them—Sylvia, the
youngest—managed to extricate herself from the circle of aloneness.

One of the five women, Sylvia was twenty-six years old. She
was the only American-born among them and the daughter of a
family with means. She was short in stature, and her appearance
didn't attract the attention of men. She received a good education,
but even in college, she didn't garner notice. As a result, she went
to work at the institution for social aid where Fay worked.

But there were those who saw in Sylvia a beauty that didn't
shout, a beauty mirrored in her twists and turns, in her interactions
with people and things. Fay was one of the first to see something
extraordinary in Sylvia. And even though she was older than her,
a friendship and devotion—as between an older and younger
sister—started up between them. Fay had an influence on little
Sylvia, and that influence resulted in wresting Sylvia from her
state of congealment to such an extent that she even surpassed
her guide...

Sylvia's work was the kind that took her out to people with
whom she previously had no contact. She saw poverty for herself
firsthand and she dedicated herself, making help for new immi-
grants her area of specialization.

One afternoon, in a half-darkened corridor on a mission for
the institution, she spotted a young man with a broom in one hand
and a newspaper clipping in another. When the young man raised

his eyes from the paper and noticed Sylvia, he quickly thrust the paper into the pocket of his dark shirt, took the broom in both of his hands, and began to sweep the corridor. Who knows, he thought, maybe she was one of the people who came to see to it that the work got done.

He was one of the "newcomers," one of those whom the Hebrew Immigrant Aid Society had provided a job. He was called Karl, but his name was Kalmen. He was the oldest in a family from a small shtetl in Poland that had landed in China. The family had suffered all sorts of illnesses, but he remained in sound physical and emotional well-being and was also the breadwinner and caregiver for his parents.

Kalmen was a healthy young man, full of life and gusto. He didn't like to speak about his difficult past. Nor did he want anyone to pity him or overtly show him compassion. As a result, it wasn't easy for Sylvia to win his trust. But when the young man approached the girl who looked at him with the sort of eyes for which he had no name, they were like two people who had been searching for a long time and finally found each other. What drew the American-born girl to the foreign young man? That stayed Sylvia's secret...

Before long, Sylvia and Kalmen became a couple. Through Kalmen, Sylvia saw the world fully—in all of its true colors.

A breeze began to stir, reminding Fay that she had been sitting too long in the park. By this time, she had somewhat forgotten the caustic words of the manager. She noticed the dead flowers on the bench, pushed them away, and said to herself: "I'll buy myself some flowers. Tomorrow, I'll tell that Herr Berg he made a mistake. After the first twenty-five years, that's when I'll really start to go uphill—not downhill!" She stood up, went to the first flower shop she saw, and bought herself six fresh red roses.

The next morning, Fay came to work a bit earlier than usual. She didn't rush to change clothes, as she had prepared everything beforehand. She thought about the lively "Good morning!" with which she would greet the manager and the words she intended to say to him.

The clock hands moved forward. Everyone was already in the office. The workday was underway. But he still hadn't arrived.

The telephone rang. Fay picked up the receiver: "What? Herr Berg isn't coming? He's sick? Oh, I'm so sorry. I hope he gets better soon!"

Someone soon announced the news that apparently Herr Berg wouldn't be coming in. He was very sick…

A commotion ensued around her. People spoke to her and asked her questions, but she almost didn't see or hear anything. She felt a peculiar heaviness in her limbs and couldn't move, as if she were afraid that any move she made would give away her terrible secret.

Fay searched, and indeed rummaged, inside herself to find out if she had said something to—or wished something upon—him? "No, no!" she shook her head. She had just thought that he was older than her. Had she committed a sin with her thoughts? She felt a pain—a pain for herself, for him who would no longer be here. She didn't know herself why or for whom she felt such pain. She only knew that just yesterday morning, he spoke to her about her twenty-five years here, and with his hand, had gestured to the ground… And who knows? Perhaps he took dangerously ill at that very moment when she swept aside his flowers with her hand…

She remembered that she had once heard of things like this happening. There were certain plants that soak up a human life into themselves and wither when the time comes… The flowers were dead. Dead flowers.

"Big Boss"

When "Big Boss" took over the management of the institution, he soon made himself felt with his deep pockets and weighty personality. The first ones to whom he showed his authority were the ordinary workers. The workers saw him as an expert and gave him the name "Big Boss."

With the doctors and nurses on staff, he conducted himself with an air of reverence from the beginning, speaking to them with an artificial politeness. Everyone called him "Big Boss" and avoided using his real name, as if the name itself conveyed something unsavory.

Before "Big Boss" assumed the helm, the institution was small and poor, but the atmosphere there was comfortable and decent. But due to financial shortfalls, the doctors had to slightly limit their work. When "Big Boss" came, the institution quickly grew, becoming one of the biggest of its kind.

Although they appreciated the motives of the new philanthropist and acknowledged who he was, what the doctors bent down before were his full pockets. Some did so with lowered heads and flattery, while others employed sweet, hypocritical little smiles. Everyone nodded at him when he spoke, saying "yes" to all of his initiatives.

In fact, the results of "Big Boss"'s work were soon readily apparent. The small institution changed its face, beginning to look like "Big Boss" himself. Large marble and brass panels were hung on the walls. Trees and flowers were planted around the building, and on one lovely morning, a statue of the new manager—of the "Big Boss"—appeared in the corridor.

Where did he come from, this gold giant to whom everyone yielded? Who was he?

"Big Boss" was a Jewish man over sixty. He wore his years with a kind of pride, like medals pinned on his chest. He was six feet tall, with a massive and erect body, broad and strong shoulders, and a sure, measured gait. He held his head haughtily aloft and his chest puffed out, as if he were marching at the head of a parade. His face was a bit wrinkled, but sunny, fresh, and tanned. His ginger-gray hair was as thick as a twenty-year-old young man's. His eyes were white, sharp; the brows were also white. His mouth was somewhat wide. The lower lip trembled slightly, and it was hard to tell whether that was a sign of rage or mildness. "Big Boss" dressed in the latest fashions. In general—elegant, stylish, and mannered. Were it not for his hands, he could be taken for a tidy and refined gentleman. When you looked at his hands, something altogether different was visible. These were hands that told secrets; hands that inspired fear; hands that even if seen just once could never be forgotten.

Wide hands, inflated like bladders, with short, spread apart, slightly bent fingers. On each knuckle, a hill of reddish hair. Nails—like brittle stones. These hands looked as if they were independent creatures in their own right, ones that could certainly hold their own.

People felt somewhat avenged against "Big Boss" when they noticed his hands. They thought that God, who had given him these two hands, had played a trick on him. The hands shouted: "Watch out for me!"

For several decades, "Big Boss" had been a pillar of the leather industry. He had a network of factories across the country, and he stood like an iron wall against organized labor. As long as he was the boss, that wall was not broken. When his property holdings surpassed his ambitions and he had satiated his appetites—a years-long process—he withdrew from business.

A man without a family and with enough energy to spare, he decided to make a grand gesture. After all, the world ought to hear about him. He undertook the financing of an institution that promised him a great deal of honor in exchange for much-needed funding. The factory owner became a philanthropist. The transformation didn't take long. At the outset, he was still somewhat modest, but once he saw his name in the papers, he was transformed into someone else altogether. The press wasn't stingy, either. They devoted entire columns to describing him and his philanthropic generosity and printed photos of him. Now, *here* was really something! This was someone who had given away his hard-earned wealth for such a noble cause...

The publicity strengthened his audacity, and he himself began to believe in his own greatness. He held his head even higher, thrust his chest out further, took over the reins, and mounted the horse. Drawing upon the same zeal previously devoted to the accumulation of wealth, he now went after honor. In this race, he made every effort to use his money to sideline any obstacle that stood in the way of his drive to receive accolades.

There were corners where "Big Boss" had no sway because he didn't really know what was done there. One such corner was the technical-medical department, and because he didn't know much about this area, he tried to disparage it.

All doors were open for "Big Boss." You never knew when he would storm in with his chauffeur, who ran out in front of him to see to it that the door was open. Make way! The "Boss" is coming! He always came running in at unexpected moments.

On one occasion, several doctors had assembled to attend a lecture by a Norwegian professor, a refugee, someone new to the institution. Like the "Big Boss," the professor had also brought wealth to this country. But the "Big Boss" dismissed that wealth with a wave of his hand. The professor's affluence consisted of years of medical experience, research work, and academic books.

That was his world. When the Hitler plague reached his country, the Professor—a Jew who knew little of his own Jewishness—was slightly shaken. But he quickly got back on his feet and resumed working in his area of expertise.

It wasn't long before the professor, like his colleagues in the field, also became a part of the surroundings and began bowing his head before the "Big Boss."

The professor didn't look at all "professorial." He was small, round, nimble. He had childlike, brown eyes and a head without hair. He spoke German and was an excellent teacher and a good speaker. When he started speaking, that little person was no longer seen. In front of the eyes of his audience materialized a man of learning that had no limits, a source of knowledge that could never be depleted. So the doctors sat in amazement, welded with all of their senses to the figure of the lecturer. They committed every word he spoke to memory. One day, in the midst of just such a scene, the door suddenly tore open, as if a storm had just blown in. The chauffeur ran inside, drew himself up to his fullest extent near the wall, and announced: "The "Boss" is coming!" Soon, "Big Boss" marched in, as was his wont, with his head held high, his hands resting on his weighted cane. He didn't greet anyone. Eyes full of contempt, he evaluated those seated in the room. The corners of his mouth tightened in a derisive little smile. The doctors stood, smiling sheepishly, as if they had been caught doing something foolish. The Norwegian professor himself ran toward him and his body was quickly revealed, observable in all its smallness. It was as if he had become diminished in the presence of the "Big Boss." A flush spread over his face and neck. He extended his hand and wanted to say something to the "Big Boss" in English.

However, "Big Boss" was in no hurry to extend his own hand in return. The professor remained there with his hand extended for a few minutes. The expression on the face of "Big Boss" said: "Do you really think I understand even a word of what you're saying to me?" "Big Boss" stood there for a few minutes. His hands moved for the entire time, as if they were carrying on a conversation between themselves. And suddenly, without a word, he turned around and marched out with the same stiffness with which he had earlier entered. The chauffeur, who had been standing the entire time as if glued to the wall, hurried out in front like a well-trained dog.

It was quiet in the auditorium—an embarrassed, crushed silence. Everyone felt as if they had just been slapped by a petty creature. Each was ashamed before his neighbor. The professor gestured with his hand, as if he were swatting away a cloud of smoke. He took a few strides across the room, pulled at the white sleeves of his smock. He promptly sat back down. He ran his hand over his forehead, as if seeking to resume his train of thought that had just been interrupted.

"Big Boss," now in the corridor, strode back and forth, beaming with delight from his own presence. He saw how folks moved aside, bestowing servile honor upon him. He smiled at his success in scaring the "naïve" doctors. When he remembered how flustered they'd been in his presence, he had the urge to laugh. He felt like congratulating himself and saying "Good work!"

Clara and Mary

Exhausted and spent after a long medical examination, Clara was full of gratitude for the cool bed and the refreshment of its recently drawn back linens. Her eyes closed. She lay in a state of non-waking consciousness, pleased that the doctors—and her mother and brother—were no longer there. She was alone, and she felt fortunate to be in this strange bed.

Her coming here had been more her mother's doing than her own. She'd wanted—and tried so hard—to avoid the hospital. But she hadn't been successful. The doctor absolutely insisted that she go in for observation, and she relented. She had already undergone the first examination. They tired her out for hours. There was absolutely no end at all to their probing.

Clara didn't know how long she had been lying in this "world of nothingness" when she felt a hand upon her. She winced, thinking: "A doctor again!" But to her surprise, she saw a smiling nurse who inserted a thermometer and then went to another bed.

Considering now the breadth of the ward, she counted twenty-four beds in all. She was one of twenty-four patients.

Clara thought about what had actually happened to her in the last few hours since she arrived at the hospital. Outwardly, nothing happened, right? She was whole; all of her limbs and senses were intact. And yet, she believed that something *had* happened to her. The proof: She, Clara, was so modest—and yet it was about *her* and in *her* presence that the doctors were talking and arguing. What's more, she saw how, Mary, lying opposite her, didn't take her eyes off her, the new patient, despite the fact that Clara thought she had done her best to avoid Mary's gaze.

Once Clara looked directly at Mary, the latter welcomed her joyfully. Before Clara even had time to smooth her hair down a bit, Mary was standing next to her bed, introducing herself with a warm smile, "My name is Mary. Yours?" And as if not waiting for an answer, Mary bent over and read the board and cheerfully sang out, "Clara! Very pretty! As soon as I saw you, I had a sense that I would like you!"

Mary was a small, thin girl with lively, black eyes that appeared slightly clouded over and tired. Up close, her skin was dark and delicate, but from afar—sickly and old. Mary's hair was black, resolutely frizzy. Her smile was so luminous and genial that Clara immediately felt herself warmed in its glow. With Mary's approach, Clara felt that she found something she had lost many years ago.

Mary, taking hold of Clara's hand which had been resting over her heart, gently asked, "What's wrong with you?" "Oh, who knows? No appetite, and I've lost weight," Clara responded softly. Mary looked at her in surprise and said, "Strange. Very strange! Who's copying whom? Maybe that's what drew me to you the moment you showed up!"

Both girls laughed. Mary wanted to say something else, but a groaning, weeping voice resounded over the ward: "Mary, Mary! Dear, hurry, hurry. I can't wait anymore!"

This came from a gravely-ill woman lying in the last bed by the window. That patient had been here a long time. By now, the nurse and the doctors were used to her calls and didn't rush to her bedside. The patient herself knew she would never regain her health and maintained that those whose illnesses were less serious owed her something, were required to come to her aid when she was struck by unbearable waves of pain. Mary gave this patient much of her time, and the patient clung to the weak girl. This was Mary's third week here, and for a large part of the day, she was up and about on her feet. Whenever anyone saw her going by, they turned to her. As soon as she left, Clara impatiently awaited her return.

When Mary came back, she looked tired and downcast from her struggle with the gravely-ill patient. Clara asked her to lie down on the bed. When lunch was served, both of them looked it over. Each one gestured to the other and said: "Eat! Eat!" But neither Mary nor Clara ate. They only drank coffee, smoked a cigarette, and said: "We'll eat later. Maybe tomorrow. Who knows when?"

Visitors to the ward brought hubbub into the room. Next to each bed stood a small group. The lonely patients who had no visitors of their own felt sorry for themselves and looked out for the smile of a stranger.

Clara's mother exchanged glances with Mary's mother, who spoke quickly and in some kind of foreign language while looking at the Jewish mother as if she were expecting help from her. Clara spoke to her mother in Yiddish. They each spoke quietly, as if they were engaged in an illegal act. They went silent as soon as a nurse appeared. Shortly thereafter, both mothers left the hospital with smiles on their faces but pain in their hearts.

Soon, the doctors entered. They barged in noisily, five or six in a group. Stopping at each bedside, they spoke about the patient's condition. The sick person hung onto the doctors' every word, hoping that their utterances would lead to a recovery. All of the doctors stopped at Clara's bed. One doctor read off of a large notepad to the others. The one who appeared to be the head doctor asked her a few questions, flashed her a smile, and then the doctors proceeded on to Mary.

When the girls discovered that there was no difference in their illnesses, they laughed, even if they felt a heaviness inside. They each looked different than they had before. Mary had undergone all of the lab tests since her arrival, and Clara now had to have them. As a result, both girls were separated through the course of the days.

With hungry eyes, Clara followed Mary's walking among the sick. She said to her new friend, "Oh, if only I could do something for the patients like you, I would feel good!"

"Who says you can't?" Mary responded.

The next day, when the doctor let Clara get out of bed, she quickly put on her bright blue kimono and walked with Mary among the patients.

Clara was almost the same height as Mary, but a bit wider and not as light on her feet. Clara had a longish face and a pointed nose and chin. Her neck—long and thin. Her hair was also frizzy, but not as dark as Mary's. They looked like twins. They went from bed to bed, making themselves useful. Clara would help someone struggle out of bed, and Mary—another. This new work touched and reinvigorated Clara.

The day passed a lot faster than either of them expected. There were no visitors. The sun had gotten stuck somewhere between the tall chimneys. Through the windows, an angry sky peered. The windows were covered with a gray, perspiring net, as if by a melting frost. The gravely-ill woman was quiet. Her stillness, although a respite for her neighbors in nearby beds, nevertheless cast a pall of terror. After supper—just coffee, no food—both girls were tired. Clara immersed herself in a book, and Mary—within her own self. She leafed through her life, turning page after page. Here, she saw herself with her beloved; they were holding hands, walking along the avenue like two carefree children, and making plans. They would live with her mother. Her mother could hardly wait. Although Mary was still so young, her mother wanted her to get married right away. And he—well, that was what he wanted, too.

They both laughed. He said, "Just take a look at her! Now she'll be a mother!" He twirled her around, pushing her away and then grabbing her back, and pressing her so tightly against himself that she gasped for breath. Mary drew some air into herself, opened her eyes, and then closed them again… His hands—so strong, so fine! More than anything else, she loved his eyes. She would have kept looking into them… but on that accursed day, at that accursed moment, she couldn't look into his eyes. He kept averting them. He talked, laughed, but didn't look. Why? Whom should she ask? Once again, she opened her eyes, looked at Clara, wanting to catch her eye. She closed her eyes again. If she could at least know where he perished, where his grave was. Perhaps his handsome head had sunk in the mud somewhere?

Perhaps she'd already lived out the life allotted to her? After all, in their short time together, they had experienced so much happiness. Perhaps he, too, thought the same when he looked upon the luminous world for the last time... Oh, my angel! She remembered: At the beginning, her friends wouldn't leave her side. They comforted her, pointing to those—the others—who experienced the same catastrophe, and yet pulled themselves together. Life must go on, they said. All of them had children by then. Many of her friends who had previously been empathetic went on to abandon her. She didn't miss them, but she was dying from sadness.

And her inability to eat—how would that end? Oh, if she didn't have to cling to life because of her mother... Oh, Mama! From her mother Mary did not want to free herself. She would have to pull herself together.

Having lived for years without friends and having just discovered such intimacy with Mary, Clara now needed her friend. Without Mary, she felt lonely. When Clara saw Mary lying there for such a long time with her eyes closed, she became uneasy in her own bed. There were several moments when Clara wanted to get out of bed and check if Mary were sleeping or just feeling weak, but she restrained herself. "I'll wait a little while," she said to herself. Finally, she did go over to Mary's bed, touched her hand, and said quietly, "You left me alone for two hours. Is something the matter with you?"

Mary opened her eyes. She saw Clara's sallow-pale face and the lips that wanted to smile, but the smile turned into a shiver—

like a child who wants to cry but holds herself back. She extended her hand and said, "Did some thinking, half-napping, and then did some more thinking."

Mary looked at Clara and felt guilty. I shouldn't have left her alone, she thought. "You should've called me!" she said.

"Don't be so serious! When I saw someone lying there lost in thought, I got a little jealous. I wanted to know what you were thinking—may I?"

"Yes, you may know. I want you to know," Mary said.

Clara sat on the edge of Mary's bed, and Mary opened her heart to her, the way a young woman would to a close female friend. She started to tell her of the time when she decided to marry the man who'd been her sweetheart since childhood, and she ended with these words: "Lost everything that was alive in me, with me! An angry wind came and upended everything by force. Such a beautiful, active, bright life hauled off into the faraway swamps somewhere, and then—gone forever. Who knows how and where?"

While she was speaking, Mary looked down at her hands, as if she were reading something there. Having finished, she fixed her eyes, veiled by smoke, on Clara's motionless face. She then gave Clara a cigarette and said, "Shouldn't have revealed so much!"

Clara smoked, looked off into the distance, and soon asked, "And how do you feel now?"

"I feel lonely now. My heart is practically bursting from my longing, but I'm glad that we met here. Look, we have the same sickness—and maybe the same heartaches, too."

And then Mary added: "But you haven't told me anything about yourself. I have a feeling you're not happy, either. Am I right?"

Clara nodded her head: "Yes, you're right. You're very smart, Mary. But there's a difference between us. You, Mary, have had a bit of happiness, but then the Devil came and demolished it.

You lost the one who was most precious to you, and I want you to know that I believe every word you've said. But I lost myself. You look puzzled—don't you get it?"

"I really would like to understand," Mary said, "Be open with me, Clara. Maybe talking about it will bring us even closer together."

Clara hesitated slightly and then said, "It's a long story. I've never told this to anyone. After all these years that have gone by, my tragedy has lost its entire meaning. Today, such a thing couldn't happen at all. Because of one event, I was severed from my whole being. There's no other way to say it. Hear me out, Mary.

"When I was six years old, my little brother contracted a contagious disease. He had to be taken to a hospital. My mother wept, certain she would never see him alive again. Wailing broke out at home. I cried together with everyone else. A doctor telephoned the city hospital, and an ambulance came, bringing a doctor and a nurse.

"The nurse absolutely enchanted me. With her radiant face and kind smile, she breathed new life into our home. The extreme fear retreated, and everyone revived. For my mother, the nurse was like an angel from heaven. Even the sick child wasn't afraid of the stranger all dressed in white. She took the child from his small bed and held him close—like a tender mother, really.

"When she left the house together with the doctor, she said, 'Don't worry, your boy will quickly recover!' Her words calmed everyone. Everyone was sure that words coming from such a person's mouth had to be truthful. It took two weeks for the child to become completely healthy. We never saw the nurse again, but I never could forget her. In my childish imagination, I couldn't picture anyone better or more beautiful.

"When I got older, I found out that it wasn't difficult to become a nurse if that was what you really wanted and if you were a good student. I decided that I had to become a nurse, just like that other one… I was a good student; the teachers were satisfied with me. I finished elementary school at the age of thirteen and a half.

"When I reached high school, times were different. The proverbial belts in our house tightened, and I had to work after class. My abilities were average and so learning didn't come easily to me. Still, I passed from one class to the next.

"Things got worse at home. Mama told me about the hardships, and sitting in class, I had to think about the payments we had to make. I worked for a few hours in the evening, which made studying difficult. But I didn't fall behind. The idea that my studies would carry me to my goal was the driving force behind everything I did.

"I declined the pleasures associated with youth. I hid away from my friends when they went to the movies. The goal of becoming a nurse stood before me."

At this point, Clara's voice became so quiet that it was hard for Mary to make out her words. When Mary saw that Clara was straining herself, she said, "Catch your breath. Take a rest. Drink some water."

Clara drank from the glass of water and said, "I shouldn't have started, but I'll keep going.

"I finished high school no worse than many in my class. Only in mathematics was I one grade point short. The principal was a compassionate person. He didn't want me to stay behind for another semester. He called me in and said, 'I'll let you finish on the condition that you study through the summer and make up that point so you can get your diploma.'

"I wasn't the only one behind in my class, and I decided to go to summer school.

"My father worked for a doctor, a refined man and a family friend. When Papa told the doctor about my keen aspiration to become a nurse, the doctor sent for me and said, 'Forget about the grade point. I'll write a letter on your behalf to an acquaintance of mine, an official in a school, stating that you've finished high school. You don't need anything else.'

"I was overjoyed. The next day, even before the appointed time, I was standing in the corridor and waiting. My waiting came to an end when I saw an astonishingly beautiful lady in a snow-white dress making her way through the door. She fixed her large, snakelike green eyes on me, looked me over from head to toe, and asked, 'What do you want?' I handed her the letter and told her that I had finished River High School and wanted to be a nurse. She considered me once again, and now I saw an undisguised hatred in her green eyes. She knew I was Jewish and was unable to mask her loathing.

"She turned the letter over in her hands and told me to come back in two days. My heart was telling me that this was someone who would place stones in my path. The two days dragged on, feeling more like two years. Barely able to make it through the two days, I went back and waited in the lobby. When she appeared, I already sensed there was nothing left to hope for, that all was lost. Looking at me, she screamed: 'You're a liar! You didn't finish school. Our courses aren't open to liars!'"

Through half-closed eyes, Mary stared intently at Clara's sallow, trembling face. With her cold hands, she caressed Clara's dry, hot hands and muttered to herself, "She ought to burn in hell!" She didn't want Clara to see how pained she was on her behalf. She breathed heavily, holding back her choked-up tears. After a few minutes of silence, the nurse brought both of them their nighttime tablets.

Both girls calmed down a bit. In Mary's eyes, Clara was a martyr, and she wanted to find kind, thoughtful words for her. In Clara she saw her own aloneness. She said, "What a shame we didn't meet earlier. You're tired, Clara. Do you still want to talk?"

"Mary, dear girl," Clara said, "I'm grateful to you. I was shut off within myself for a few years. Do you understand what I'm saying? When I came back home that day, my mother took one look at me and didn't even have to ask what happened. A mother's heart understands everything. She sensed more than I wanted…

"I didn't want to see my school friends. They had been sure I would soon become a nurse. They'd already started jokingly calling me 'the nurse.' I lost my own sense of worth. I began to hate myself, and if the situation at home hadn't been so bad, who knows how it all could have ended!"

Clara looked at her hands, biting her chapped lips. Suddenly, she stood up and then just as quickly sat back down, waiting for Mary to say something to her. And then Mary spoke:

"Even though, like you, I, too, distanced myself from my friends when I lost the best, the one most dear to me, now I feel, after hearing your story, that our greatest mistake was that we isolated ourselves, that we locked away the wrong that was inflicted on us. In my case, I couldn't expect help from anyone when my young life was destroyed. But in your situation, if you'd shared with someone—well, maybe one of your friends would have said the same thing I'd like to say to you after hearing your disappointment. And this is what I want to say to you: Spit at that evil woman! Your fate doesn't depend on her. If she didn't like your Jewish face, try to find others who'll accept you with open arms."

Mary was now speaking louder than usual. The veins in her neck bulged. Clara sensed Mary's exhaustion and stopped her: "Maybe you're right. But understanding is one thing, and experiencing is something else. Not everything can be spoken. I'm far from being a beauty. I sensed that when I was very young. When all the girls had boys running after them, I went unnoticed. And so I pushed myself off to the sidelines and consoled myself with the dream of becoming a nurse and being appreciated as I deserved to be. That would be my happiness. But nothing came of that beautiful dream."

Clara's voice grew quieter, so quiet that she herself didn't hear it. Both were silent. The gravely-ill woman began to weep, and she called out to Mary. So Mary dragged herself out of bed and moved quickly over to the bed next to the window. Clara followed her. When the patient saw the girls next to her, her cry got stuck in her throat. She whimpered and spoke words that were unintelligible to them. The girls stood next to the patient's bed until she fell back to sleep.

Back near Mary's bed, the girls lighted cigarettes and rested, and Mary entreated Clara again, "We're not done, are we?"

"I'm sick of talking about myself, but I'm just about done," Clara said. "Enough!"

But Mary persisted. "Let's not talk about something you can't undo. The question is: What will happen now?"

"Now is sadness, loneliness. Now our mouths won't even open to eat!" Clara responded.

Clara's tone sounded almost jocular. She said: "Do you remember what I just told you—that when I went to school, I worked in the evenings? Well, I worked in a big store. The manager was very pleased with me, and he said I could work for him any time. In my despair, I considered this a stroke of good fortune. He offered me a position, and I've stayed there to this day. How many years? That'll stay a secret...."

"I started as a seller, but it's been years since I've been the 'information bureau.' I have a small room to myself, like a cage, and there I leave behind me my days, weeks, months, and years. I have no friends. My only friends are books. I spend my spare time with them. Clever books!"

"Really, now?" Mary wondered, "Why didn't I think of that? When you're feeling sad and lonely and don't have anyone to share your sadness, you pick up a book. You get away from yourself; you get your mind absorbed in something. And such a thing never occurred to me. Got to try it!"

"For me, a book isn't something to while away the time," Clara said, "For me, a book is an open window through which I look out onto the wide world. It often happens that I don't live my life, but instead live the lives in books. Like now, when I met you and felt your pain as my own. How good it would be if people really had compassion for someone else's suffering, the way we feel the agony of that patient here! Oftentimes, I wax philosophical and think that it's not right that people carry only their own life on their shoulders. But I don't hang onto philosophy for long. The heart is pulled elsewhere. What I'm missing—I don't know. I'm here among the sick and would like to know what the doctors have found out after all of their probing and questions. It's weird that both of us are not getting worse or better."

Clara's voice was very soft and gentle. It was good to hear her speak, Mary thought, and to look at her face that was not unlike that of a delicate, sickly child who was content when she was being heard.

More than once, Mary saw herself in Clara's experiences. Clara had suffered because she was Jewish; Mary—because she was Puerto Rican. Clara was spending her young adulthood in a little room resembling a cage; she, Mary, had barely been able to find her way to a job at a switchboard, unable to get anything else, even though her husband had given his life for this country. The more Clara spoke, the closer Mary felt to her.

The nurse on night duty had long since darkened the light. A little old woman in the next bed coughed loudly, unable to catch her breath. Clara offered her a glass of water and helped her sit up. Mary went off to look for a nurse. In the meantime, another patient fell out of bed. A commotion ensued. When a few nurses appeared, everyone clamored for their attention.

It looked as if the nighttime ward had turned into day. It was a hullaballoo. A young Black girl burst into tears, insisting that she wanted only a professor—no one else but a professor—to be called to her bedside this very minute. A doctor was summoned, and he quietened her.

Tired and sorrowful, the girls slowly managed to reach their beds. No words were spoken. The light was out. Clara and Mary wished they could close their eyes and ears, and maybe their hearts, too…

Mary thought: Why do people have to be separated by factors such as language, religion, and custom when in their hearts and souls they are cut from the same cloth? Where and in what lay the difference? Here was this older girl, also suffering, who had become so close—like her other half! Mary felt that if something were to be placed in their way to separate them, it would be painful for them both. No, Mary thought, as far I'm concerned, that parting won't come. She had become attached to Clara and wouldn't let her go. She would come to her aid, as a sister would.

Clara thought: A little sleep! But sleep didn't come to her. Her eyes were closed, but they still looked over to Mary's bed. They would both receive written forms that would release them from here—and then what? They would go their separate ways to different sections of the city and might not be able to meet again. Oh, no! She didn't even want to allow this thought to enter her mind. Why should they be ripped apart, each left yearning for the other? Why should they become strangers to each other? And if Mary's mother goes to church, and mine to synagogue—well, what of it? We, who don't go to synagogue or church, can be friends. Not "we can"—we must!

Both of them were deep in thought, but sleep and thought cannot be paired together.

At approximately 4:30, Clara was awakened from her state of half-slumber by the noise that the nurses' aides made with their arrival. They made a clattering ruckus with the bowls and little water pitchers they were bringing for the patients. They slammed the vessels down and spoke loudly. They woke the patients up from their little bits of sleep and made the day—already long enough for the patients—even longer.

And it was a noisy day, a day of visitors and doctors. The two mothers met in the elevator. Mary's mother greeted the Jewish mother with a warm smile. She spoke to the older woman and didn't expect a response because she knew that she didn't understand. Still, she spoke; she did so out of politeness.

The doctors didn't approach Mary's bed, but they engaged in an extended discussion next to Clara's. She didn't understand what they were saying, and she felt odd, odder still when a doctor noticed something and everyone burst into laughter. Tears formed in Clara's eyes, and she turned her back against those standing next to her and stayed in that position until the doctors left the ward. She was happy to see her mother, who had been standing at a distance when the doctors had surrounded Clara's bed earlier. Now, her mother asked, "How are you, my child? You look better." She smiled, but Clara could see that her mother was distressed.

Clara knew her mother. She knew that that she wasn't sleeping at night because of her. She felt slightly guilty and tried to distract her mother. She took out a pocket mirror, applied lipstick, rubbed her hair, and said, "As soon as I come home, I'm going to have my hair cut short. I want to look younger. This hairdo makes me look long in the face, so that I look like an old noblewoman."

Her mother smiled, "A noblewoman—oh really? When did you dream that one up? Where did you pick up that word?"

Smiling, Clara answered, "From you, Mama. I picked it up from you."

Mother and daughter exchanged glances, and then each looked probingly at the other for a while.

To her mother, Clara's tone sounded new and upbeat. She wasn't used to hearing her daughter talk this way.

Clara added: "And I'll need to have a new dress. My clothes are like me—out-of-date." She laughed out loud.

As always, Mary's mother spoke a lot—loudly and rapidly. She exchanged glances with the Jewish mother, as if she were asking her if she agreed with what she was saying.

The din from the visitors filled the whole ward. A cluster of people stood next to each bed. They forgot that human beings in pain and agony were lying there. When they left and stillness returned, it felt as if dozens of machines had suddenly come to a halt. From this sudden stillness there was a constriction in the hearts of those who were looking toward the future, yet didn't know what it held.

The gravely-ill woman by the window didn't relinquish her sister's hand. The elderly and sickly sister was despondent until Mary approached and freed her from her sister's grip. The unfortune woman felt that her hours were limited, and she clung to Mary's hand as if she saw her only means of protection in that hand.

The day slowly retreated. A bleak, gray sky peered into the window. The naked trees next to the windows shivered from the cold. A damp fog extended over the panes, completely blocking out the street.

Having unburdened their hearts and laid bare their most intimate feelings, both girls felt the need for silence. Both wanted to digest what they'd taken in.

After supper, which, as before, consisted of two cups of coffee and a cigarette for dessert, they lay down and rested after the noisy day. Mary lay with her eyes closed and tried to imagine herself in Clara's situation—her joyless girlhood, her life without love, never having what every young girl's soul wants a taste of when she matures, ripens. She empathized with Clara, because she knew what longing meant. She felt pain on behalf of her newfound friend—so much pain that she didn't want her friend to notice...

Clara thought about Mary and how dreadful it must have been to have had a man in your life so dear to you and then to lose him so terribly, so swiftly. Poor Mary! She must have felt like someone experiencing great happiness, but then a devil came and tore it away, leaving the person alone, lonely, and full of longing—heartbroken. Clara felt such pain for her young friend. She closed her eyes and saw Mary in the arms of a handsome young soldier when suddenly everything dissolved like a white cloud.

Clara awakened, jolted by a scream: "No! No! Get back! Help! Help!"

It was the Black girl who was screaming these words. Soon, everyone was screaming. A terrible scene unfolded before Clara's eyes. The sick patient was in the middle of the room, half naked. Her legs were as thin as a child's. She hadn't been out of bed for many weeks, and now she was standing with one hand under her short shirt, clutching at her body, which was all atremble. Her bizarrely large head with its disheveled hair bobbed up and down. She sang out: "Tsha-tsha-tsha..." It looked like she was about to fall. Quick as a cat, Clara bounded over to her and placed her body in a position to catch her. The disturbed girl kept singing and dancing. Clara said to her: "How beautiful! Really lovely! Come, come. What fine dancing!" There was no nurse on hand. Mary ran over. Both girls got the patient back into bed. She broke into a childish smile and fell asleep singing.

All of the patients were terrified and hysterical. In her fear, the asthmatic Black girl couldn't catch her breath. She choked, struggling with her mouth open and eyes bulging. Her condition was horrifying the patients. The sixteen-year-old girl screamed: "Mama, take me home!" From each bed—a different voice reverberated. When two doctors got to the room, they remained standing in the center, not knowing where to go first. The one who was responsible for the entire tumult lay there peacefully. With her twisted mouth, she smiled and whispered something, words that were incomprehensible. The doctors stood by her bed for a long time, and then they were quiet, their faces turned to the ground, away.

It took some time for the doctors to succeed in getting everyone quiet. The incident shocked Mary. This was the first time she had witnessed death up close, and she felt weak throughout her body. She was cold and brought the covers up over her head. Clara was less affected. Her mind conquered her heart... She thought the patient had been tormenting herself too much, and the sooner the better...

The girls gladly took the sleeping pills that the nurse gave everyone. As she was descending into sleep, Mary argued with and berated someone. She thought of "a point" and struggled to make it, but found herself choking on words she wanted to scream out but couldn't...

In the morning, Mary recounted to Clara her dream and then added: "Your quick action last night convinced me that you were born to work in a hospital and not a little cage. It's not too late, you know." Clara didn't respond. She looked calm and tired.

The bed by the window was devoid of both patient and linen. The old woman next to Clara's bed appeared terrified, and didn't take her eyes from that corner, as if she were afraid that its former occupant would suddenly appear, dancing, before her. Without speaking, she begged the girls not to leave her alone.

After the commotion of the night, the morning—as if awaiting something—began. A pale, clear sky looked through the large windows. Still at some distance, the sun approached slowly, promising a lovely day.

There was no groaning or coughing, as if everyone's pain had gone to sleep. Pietro, the young man hired to sweep under the beds, sang in a quiet monotone, and his song resounded like a prayer.

Both girls, pallid but well-rested, looked at the doctor. They sensed that today they would be released. The doctor—young, tall, with a stooped back, small quick eyes, and a very soft, melodious voice—entered noisily. He stopped near Mary's bed, leafed through a thick notebook, counted something, and finally asked, "Do you want to go home, Mary?"

Mary answered with a question: "Do you still have to ask?"

"Good, you're going home today. But I'm advising you not to spend too much time alone. Seek out the company of others. Goodbye."

He approached Clara slowly. He sat on her bed like a close friend or relative, and said, "I think there's no reason for you to stay here any longer. If you want to, you will get well!" And then he repeated, "If you want to!" He continued: "You have to eat; you can't live without food. But you also need to have fun. A person is born to be *with* life, not *outside of* life, you know. I do believe you understand. You're going home. Goodbye."

Although the doctor spoke to each of them in a different way, both girls understood what he was saying.

The Punishment

It had been three days since Miss Murray had moved into the Saint Paul Home, and although no one had obligated her to come here, she knew quite well where she was headed. She was pleased she had the small sum of money to buy the new apartment she needed after leaving the hospital. When she left her job at the hospital, where she'd been employed for many years, a door closed behind her. There could be no talk—no consideration even—of going back. And yet, she couldn't get comfortable in this home. She was unable to adjust to the quiet all around her.

Actually, Miss Murray should have been content in the home. Throughout her life, she had strived to be among her own kind. But her discontent arose from two factors. First, she had arrived a bit too early. In fact, she wasn't much younger in age than the home's other residents, but she still felt herself to be different from these old folks. She had a desire to have herself be heard and loved it when there was a commotion around her. She was a wild bird that always needed prey, someone to pierce with her sharp beak. Well, things being what they were, she would somehow get used to living here. But the biggest problem was that this home of all places—with the name Saint Paul—was located in a Jewish neighborhood. She considered this to be a punishment from God. It was not something she bargained for.

Hatred of Jews was chronic for Miss Murray. She herself couldn't remember when this disease first manifested itself in her. In the Catholic school for nurses where she'd studied, the Sister Superior would tell the students that a nurse was not permitted to differentiate between patients, that she had to love each one as her own child. Nevertheless, Miss Murray didn't heed the Elder Sister's precept. As soon as she started working in a hospital where there were Jewish patients, those patients sensed the chill radiating from the nurse with the crucifix at her throat. The longer she worked at the hospital, the more hatred she showed toward Jews. True, Miss Murray didn't have to work in a hospital with Jews at all. She could easily have found plenty of hospitals without Jews. But the issue was that in the hospitals without Jews, she felt restrained. There, she didn't have anyone upon whom to take out her emotions. She needed to have someone as an object of her hatred. She had to have someone to insult, someone to torment with her words. There was also another reason why she worked among Jews. Simply put, it was profitable. She had a special technique to extract tips from Jewish patients. When she found out that a Jewish patient was getting ready to leave the hospital, her upper lip and cheeks would tighten as if in a smile and she would start to call the patient—the very one whom she had just yesterday cursed out—by the sweet name of "Honey" and give him advice on how to take care of himself during recuperation. In return, she would receive a small envelope.

For her consistent hatred, Miss Murray eventually paid. As long as she was young and able to do the work of two, no one took the accusations levelled against her seriously. But when she grew older, when her legs became heavier and her body bloated—and she no longer had anything to boast about, they showed her the door for this behavior. Even the little crucifix, which she invariably wore at her throat as a protector, didn't help. One time, she insulted a patient, not knowing that the patient was the sort who did not tolerate insults. As a result, a commotion ensued, and Miss Murray was presented with two "either-or" options: Either she could beg forgiveness and promise that this would never happen again or she could pack her bags and go!

During the course of her many years of practice, she had, in fact, experienced both of these options. But like a cat, she would just shake the past off and begin anew. With the passing years, she became increasingly tense and pathological in her hatred. But she didn't lose her ability to remain on the lookout, keeping her eyes and ears peeled for potential sources for tips. When she sensed that her "throne" was wobbling, she figured that the "Jewish tips" would prove useful to her in her old age by allowing her to provide a home for herself among her own kind. She did, in fact, go to that home earlier than she expected.

In the hospital, she led an isolated existence. Of the company of men—out of the question. The other nurses, too, held themselves apart from her. Even her Catholic sisters—the girls with whom she got on her knees before the altar—never invited her to their homes for a cup of tea. Miss Murray was never up for being anyone's friend. As a result, when misfortune struck, no one went out of their way to help her. When that misfortune came in the form of a heart attack, she was just another patient taking up a bed in the hospital—and no more.

She sat in the garden that surrounded the "home" for the elderly, remembering how painful it had been to be reduced to offering smiles to sick Jews and calling them sweet names when her heart was actually filled with hate. She remembered that oftentimes she simply had to bite her lip in rage at them. But they—the Jews—could tell. They could see it on her face. When she turned her head, she felt as if people were sticking their tongues out at her behind her back. Miss Murray closed her eyes, and it seemed to her that someone was sticking out their tongue at her, mocking and teasing her: "Aha! You hated the Jews and loved their money? Well, so there you have it! In your old age, you have to be in a Jewish neighborhood, whether you like it or not."

Miss Murray stood up from the bench, wanting to shake off this nightmare that she had just experienced. She took a few steps and then froze in astonishment. She spotted before her a white figure—so white that it momentarily blinded her. It was the statue of the saint. He was standing with his hands outstretched as if he were beckoning to passersby. Miss Murray knew that this was a holy martyr who risked his life on behalf of Christ, let himself be tortured because of him, but she had no desire to approach the holy statue. She turned away from it and went into the garden where several seniors were seated on sparsely distributed benches and dozing in the sun that was in the process of setting. The sunset reminded the four-story building and the garden, with its symmetrically pruned border hedges, that night was fast approaching.

Miss Murray sat back down on a bench. Her heart was heavy. The pious, calcified stillness didn't harmonize all that well with the dynamic energy of the surroundings that thrummed with life. Wives pushed children's strollers, carried bags of groceries, and raced home where their husbands were waiting for a meal. Miss Murray's heart gravitated beyond the picket fences. She thought: "I could have stayed among the vigorous for another good few years. What am I doing here with these sleepyheads?" And then: "Maybe I'm paying for my big mouth. Why didn't I keep quiet, after so many years of being with the devils!"

The little old people were getting up from the benches. Miss Murray watched how they moved, taking steps with difficulty. Some of them were even unable to walk slowly, and almost all of them walked with canes. Unless she, too, started to trudge, they would think she had the strength to help others. She absolutely didn't want that to happen. She'd done enough helping!

The clock chimed six. It was now time for the elderly to go to chapel. The Sisters assembled to provide spiritual guidance. They marched in pairs—quietly, their heads bowed—past the statue of Saint Paul standing at the entrance. Miss Murray couldn't decide if she should also attend the service. She decided she would go later. Once again, she sat back down although she'd already been sitting here longer than she wanted.

Her thoughts wandered back to her previous place, the one before here. She saw herself in the hospital, how she had raced among the patients in the long corridors. She was exhausted, filled with fury at the Jewish patients who were the only ones to make demands: Serve them! Fifteen beds and all of them occupied. One bed had just been emptied. Her assistants, the Blacks, were "uppity." You weren't allowed to say a word to them! And when it was time to go, they weren't at all concerned that there was still work to be done. They said to her, "If you want to, go ahead and work! Not me, I'm done!" That made her even angrier. And now here they were bringing her another patient—a Black, in fact. Miss Murray ran to the telephone, pleaded for help to be sent. She wouldn't touch the "n****r"!

The Black girl heard her cursing but didn't know the reason. She was too sick. She asked why no one had been sent. Miss Murray had to deal with her herself, but her hands were none too friendly. She was seething. Her face burned, and wanting to curse someone out, she took her revenge on the Black girl. She didn't know what she said to the Black patient. Probably nothing very pleasant. She only remembered that all of the patients—especially the Jewish ones—were beside themselves. The next morning, when she came to her bed, the Black girl didn't want to answer her. Miss Murray took a look at her contemptuously and said, "What? Look at you putting on airs, n****r!" And then something happened! All of the patients screamed simultaneously, demanding that Miss Murray leave the ward. She didn't want to pay it any mind and continued on with her work. But soon magazines, slippers, and fruit rinds were flying at her. The hurling of these objects was accompanied by screams of "Out!"

Miss Murray fled the ward and screamed that the Blacks and the Jews wanted to kill her! She soon felt as if she were suffocating. She thought she was going to pass out, and she was seized by a bizarre chill…

When she came to, she found herself in a bed. She was lying there alone. No one came to her. Only when she called out for one did a nurse come and treat her with professionalism. No one showed her any sign of friendship. After two days, she was strong enough to work. She was notified that she could no longer work in this hospital. She would also not be receiving a letter of reference.

The house doctor gave her some friendly advice, suggesting that she go into a home. That recommendation had brought her here.

A light bulb went off in Miss Murray's mind: Could it be that the doctor knew that the home was located in a Jewish neighborhood? Miss Murray quickly swatted away that idea—the way you'd swat at an annoying fly. No! That couldn't even be considered. The doctor was a good Catholic. It wasn't the doctor who had banished her here. It was simply a punishment from God.

Goodbye, Cleopatra

Twenty-five-year-old, slightly clumsy Pietro was captivated by the magnificent marvel: building-construction machinery. Ever since he could remember, he had loved construction. He was strangely drawn to anything being built. He would think: "If only I hadn't run away from home when I was thirteen years old; if only I had heeded my father, as other children did theirs, I would surely be a master builder now, like those builders over there— because when it comes to understanding these things, I understand more than they do."

Pietro stood in amazement at the marvelous sight on the street corner where a new building was being constructed. This was exactly how he had stood at the original digging up of the construction site. He felt as if he were a part of the enterprise; it all really was a marvel to him, a surprise, as if he himself were a newborn.

As long as Pietro had a few dollars saved up in his pocket and didn't have to work, he could be found near the construction site for the entire day. He stood and watched from afar as the sounds clattered and reverberated through his mind. But since the few dollars had run out, making it necessary for him to look for work, he had to take leave of the "marvel" for now.

When Pietro left, the process of erecting the steel beams for the building's skeleton had just started. By the time he returned, he observed a different scene before him. Other sounds from other machines now wafted over to his ears. The bricklayers were standing on the scaffolding and laying the bricks. Pietro looked over at the laid-out rows of bricks and a joy arose within him. He sat down on the grass and followed the movements of the bricklayers. He counted the bricks that the workers' hands had so nimbly, skillfully, laid. He followed them with his entire being, with all of his senses, and he sensed that something was growing in his heart, that he himself was also growing.

Oh, how Pietro envied them, the builders of those walls! At the same time, he thought: "Couldn't I stand together with them and lay the bricks? They would surely sing beneath my hands!" He looked at his large hands, plucked a few blades of grass, and felt that his fingers were getting dull. They craved work. Pietro was sorry he didn't have anyone with whom he could share his enthusiasm over the newly-built structure. It didn't bother him that people looked at him as if he were a little crazy. No, he wasn't asking anyone what they thought, and what he thought didn't need to concern them. All that he wanted to know was this: Why were people walking by, indifferent to the building? Why did they see nothing?

When the workers went home for the day, leaving only the building site's guard behind them, Pietro got up close to a part of completed wall and caressed the bricks. How pleasant their coolness felt to him! Approaching the wall wasn't that easy for him. He had to crawl over piles of sand, tubs of mortar, and pits of clay. But it was well worth it. The pleasure was so great that it stayed with him for a long time. He savored it as if he'd swallowed a delicious bite: such smooth bricks, like the body of a child!

For a few weeks, Pietro delighted in the building. His eyes didn't miss the most minute development in the building. Amid the wheezing and bellowing of the brick-lifting machines and the meticulous work of the bricklayers, the building grew with a rhythmic speed. Pietro's heart rejoiced at every sign of progress, the way a mother's heart rejoices at every new baby tooth in her child's mouth.

One day in the beginning of May, the morning outside lavished gifts. A tree turned green at the window. Unexpectedly, a bird with a red beak and blue belly flew up from somewhere. Pietro soon forgot that his pocket was nearing empty, that it was time to go to work.

Pietro was not a skilled worker so he couldn't be picky about jobs. But he set for himself two conditions from which he never deviated. First, the work had to be outside in the fresh air. And second, it had to be the sort of work that required no instruction. He hated it when people taught him, and that's all there was to it!

Pietro took the newspaper in hand, and looked for the page with the "Help Wanted" ads; if he liked the work and committed himself to it, the job would be good. He had a good eye and was sure of himself. He never kidded himself.

With his appearance and clothing, Pietro did look a little curious. When he walked by while holding his hands in the pockets of his baggy pants, people stared at him. They appraised his lined jacket that was folded casually over his shoulder. His dark shirt was unbuttoned, even during a frost. On his head, he wore a small cap that didn't obstruct his frizzy, longish-clipped, bright-brown hair. His face was invariably sunburnt, and although his facial features were heavy, there was something gentle, almost feminine, about his mouth.

Pietro really loved little children. Wherever he went, children gathered around him. When he came to his place, a gang of children soon surrounded him. He showed them tricks with a string, taught them how to project shadows of animals with your hands, and then demonstrated how you could lift your forehead up and down and wiggle your ears. He only did this when adults weren't on hand. If an adult appeared on the scene, he got up: Oh, no! Anyone but an adult!

He didn't have any close relatives, so he acquired his own kinships. The people whom he carried around in his mind didn't know this. More than once, Pietro was engaged to a girl in his imagination. He only selected those girls that were to his liking. He pursued them, admiring their very beautiful faces, the ways

they walked, their gazes. He never relinquished the hope of finding the kind of girl who would make him happy, for example, one
like those he saw in the movies.

Pietro also loved to contemplate the little books he read. Oftentimes, he tried to remember the title of a book that had brought
such light to his soul, but he wasn't always successful. He may
not have remembered the book's title, but its content—that he
didn't need to remember. It was enough that he felt and experienced the book. When you sensed something, he contended,
it was as if you understood it. Pietro loved to buy books, used
books that didn't cost very much.

For several months, Pietro was busy at work and didn't have
time to see his "marvel." In the meantime, the new building had
been growing without his supervision. He didn't let the building
out of his mind throughout the entire time. He named the building "Cleopatra," and his "Cleopatra" always stood before him
in his mind's eye. In his imagination, he saw the building grow,
and the thought that he would soon see her finished, fully grown
and mature, made him happy and uplifted, as if "Cleopatra" were
his very own. Impatiently, he waited for the day when he could
return to the new building. When he was finally able to go, he
started racing to the site with a celebratory feeling in his heart, the
way you run to greet a sweetheart from whom you've been separated for a long time. He had even shaved and washed himself
specially for the occasion.

But once on the way to the site, he made it a point to walk
slowly. Why hurry when everything was standing in place? He
remembered a little tree that he had once planted. He was then
around seven years old. He was afraid that it would get trampled
so he placed a circle of stones around the base of the tree and
inserted a little white flag in the earth. The flag was visible from
a distance. The little tree grew bigger. Oh, how he would have
loved to gaze upon that little tree at this moment. He thought
that when he went home, he would see a fully grown tree. But

instead, he found nothing. It was as if it had been obliterated. What a world!

"Here it is! Right here! That's it! Just look at how everything has changed, even the street is unrecognizable. What a world!" Like a true Cleopatra, the new, twelve-story building stood there reaching all the way to the sky. What a beauty! And so quickly? Now that's what you call building! Even the sidewalk was finished. Trees had been planted all around. And such grandeur, such expanse! But why was he standing here like a fool and gaping in awe? It was time to go inside.

Pietro removed his hands from his pockets, crossed the street, and stopped to consider the building up close. With hundreds of windows, the building looked out onto the neighborhood's old, embarrassed little houses. These houses looked like they were ashamed and hiding in the shadow of their affluent neighbor.

It was already late in the afternoon. From the west, flames danced like tongues of fire on the windowpanes of the higher floors, leaping from pane to pane in mad movements. The colors changed with frightful speed. It seemed to Pietro that tongues of fire were kissing the windowpanes. He patted down his disheveled mop of hair and snuck into the open door of the large, semi-dark corridor. His vision started spinning from the crystal chandeliers and the gilded wallpaper. The corridor was so vast that Pietro felt lost in it. He stood for a few minutes and smiled until he noticed a little man standing next to him, looking him over. Was it possible that the little man had been there since he entered the building, Pietro wondered.

The little man—tidy, with smoothly-combed hair—asked him, "Whom are you looking for here?"

A bit disoriented, Pietro burst into a smile and said, "I'm no stranger here. I'd like to go up to the roof. I never imagined the building would be so tall. From such a height, you can surely see all of New York. I'm heading up!"

The little person, who was now looking at him with suspicion, moved slightly to the side, as if he wanted to make sure of something. Pietro didn't see any stairs. He took step after step. A door opened. He was flooded with light. From the door emerged several well-dressed men. They were speaking to each other and didn't look at the other two in the corridor.

When the elevator door closed, the little person said: "Mister, you're in a building that isn't for people like you. There's no roof. You can't go up there. This is a building for the rich. What do you mean you want to go up there?" With derision in his eyes, the small person pointed to a sentry box in the corner: "You have to announce yourself there first!"

Pietro barely understood what the little person was getting at. He didn't understand what he was saying about the rich, about having "to announce yourself." Pietro had never had anything to do with the rich. The bosses he worked for were modest folk, as he himself was. He'd only seen rich people in the movies. So "his Cleopatra" was rich!

"Penthouse, shmenthouse!" Pietro thought as resentment seized him and he felt an urge to spit into the corridor. He restrained himself until he exited onto the street. He walked quickly, taking heavy steps with his large feet. After several strides, he turned around and shouted loudly so the penthouses would hear: "Goodbye, Cleopatra! Goodbye!"

The Fate of a Strand of Hair

If hair could talk, it would surely show us a heart full of tragic experiences. Like Mendele's mare,[8] it would become a symbolic portrait representing a certain time period, or certain character types. But hair cannot talk!

Back then, oh so long ago, when the hair didn't yet have years to count, when it had just begun to feel the joy of a cool breeze, the warmth of the precious sun, or the chilly prick of a few drops of water—at that time, when the hair, without any desire on its part, allowed itself to be caressed by every hand—its color was golden-brown. In its appearance, it evoked honey. During that golden time, no conflicts were etched into the hair's memory. But since then, the hair had changed a great deal.

When the hair would feel that it had to assert itself against powerful forces, it began to strengthen itself, becoming thick, stubborn—a tousled forest! Beneath a comb or a brush, the hair revolted, resisting surrender. Its color was by then no longer bright gold; it shimmered between chestnut-brown and copper-red.

Who can know if a strand of hair weeps? Who can know if a strand of hair feels? Does a strand of hair perceive pain the way a person does? But the garden shears surely wept when it cut down entire shrubs. They wept the way a saw weeps when it cuts down a young tree.

Years passed. Times changed. The hair obtained a new face.

---

8. "In *Di Kliatshe* (The Mare, 1873), a powerful satire, Mendele allegorically depicts the Jew as a despised beast of burden, suffering as the world's scapegoat. Yet this abused animal has dignity and a moral superiority that demands justice rather than mercy from its tormentors." Payson R. Stevens, "Mendele Mokher Seforim," *My Jewish Learning*, https://www.myjewishlearning.com/article/mendele-mokher-seforim/.

Although it would have seemed that the hair would no longer dazzle with multi-coloredness after having been cut, the way it had before, the opposite, in fact, happened. Like grass after mowing, the hair began to grow again. And with even greater delicacy, appeal, and joy, those new colors played against the sun. In the evenings, when the sun set and a mist steamed the hair with moisture, the soft, satiny hair flirted with the ebbing day.

Then, out of nowhere, hostile winds brought forth a plague onto the hair. It was a merciless plague that burned hair from the head. Our hair was among the victims. The hair really did wage a fierce struggle, not wanting to surrender. Thanks to its youthful strength, it did succeed in the end in saving the root. Of the charmingly beautiful hair, this remained: a small, dark dot that needed to grow anew.

Whether this was because the head, which the hair illuminated, was, by this point, older or whether it was due to something else—the hair once again came into the bright world in another physiognomy, both in color and in character: a new hair, seemingly not at all concerned with that other, its once golden-brown predecessor.

Quietly, as if embarrassed, without caprices, the hair with a dark, almost black, color occupied a spot. It once again became the crown of the head—a crown without pretensions.

Winters and summers arrived and departed. Bouts of chill presented themselves, and the hair didn't dodge the chill. Like a gray hyphen, the chill snuck into the hair. At the initial sighting, the hair thought: "Ah, a guest who's lost his way." Such things happen, yes, even to thoroughly young hair. But it soon became clear that this wasn't just a stray guest, but rather one who had come to stay—forever. The grayness extended itself slowly, but with certainty, higher and higher, until the hair didn't even recognize itself.

Quietly, unassumingly, with slow steps, the grayness spread. The hair gazed at its own mixture of gray and black with delight.

It compared itself to the cool, mild evenings that heralded the serenity of approaching nights.

At the same time, however, the hair felt weaker, less anchored, and although no one had given the hair lessons of any kind, it began to look for something to cling to. In the beginning, that something was a black coat.

… In a semi-darkened train car, the hair snuggled up to and warmed itself on a lady's coat sleeve. There, it dreamed of serenity. But when the lady noticed the long, silver hair on herself, she bit her lips in displeasure, and after quickly pulling off her glove, she also pulled off the hair. She looked around to see if anyone was watching and hastily shook it off.

A young man of eighteen or so years—youthful in appearance, with full, red lips and a longish nose—was sitting and reading a newspaper. The young man looked drowsy. His eyes closed frequently and then opened back up, accompanied by a jerk of his head, as if he were repelling a fly. He spotted the long, bright hair on his knee and smiled the way a child does. With two fingers, he carefully lifted the hair up to his eyes and examined it, as if he were trying to remember from where and whom it came. The boy was hardly well acquainted with hair colors. He liked the color blond. He wanted to have hair from a blonde. He kept moving the hair from one hand to another, as if taking its measure. He didn't know what to do with the hair. He started looking for something in his vest pocket, but at that moment, the hair fell out of his hand. Suddenly, the conductor called out the station's name. The boy made for the exit, and the hair was left alone on the half-empty bench.

The hair was fated for one more sliver of hope. So once again it tried its luck.

An older man, his head bare, sat down on the bench, and the hair, having no other choice, set itself up on the old man's jacket lapel.

The old man sat contentedly, both of his hands resting on a thick cane. He dozed off. When the train jerked forcefully, he opened his eyes as if trying to remember where he was. He spotted the hair on his lapel and smiled broadly. He didn't immediately take the hair down, but shook in joyful surprise. On his face appeared an expression that said: "So you're really here, huh?"

Done smiling and shaking, he grasped the hair with two fingers and scrutinized it for a while with a new expression on his face. Suddenly displeased, he began to flick his fingers. His lips trembled. It looked as if he were getting ready to shout out: "You, so and so! Make yourself scarce!"

He flicked the hair off his fingers and crushed it with his feet.

It's a safe bet that the hair would not be embarking on any more journeys.

Was that the end? The beginning? Who knows.

Click-Clack

The broad, noisy avenue rejoiced, preparing for the celebration of a national holiday. It was a late Saturday afternoon, a hot day. Later on, the heat subsided. A cool breeze wafted, and the crowd, decked out in bright clothes, lent the sidewalks a carnival-like appearance. The women, in multi-colored dresses, gravitated toward the businesses that had dressed up their displays in honor of the holiday. The dressed mannequins in the shop windows looked as if they were strollers among the crowd.

The people appeared refreshed, renewed, and liberated from the heat. Any signs of worry seemed to have vanished from their faces. Some were hurrying; others were walking slowly, as if they wanted to demonstrate their festive mood.

Click-clack! People looked around—it was difficult to find the source of the peculiar, not very loud sound. No one knew whether the click-clack sound had just become audible in the din or whether it had been going on for a long time but just hadn't been detected until now.

Click-clack… click-clack!

The street rejoiced. The street was in full swing. Life shouted out from every step. Here, a young couple was stepping out on the town. She—around seventeen, a spoiled, coddled child with a lovely, shining face. She wore a light, bright-yellow sundress and looked like a little yellow flower. He—a bit older, darker, with a few sprouts on his upper lip.

They were holding hands, the flower sundress swaying from the light breeze and the rhythm of her gait. When suddenly: Click-clack! The girl started forcefully, stopped, tore herself from the

147

boy, and called out: "Oh, God! God!" She covered her eyes with her childish hands and shook in terror.

The boy stopped and looked around: Click-clack! He spotted a little hanging table. On the table—small bows of red, white, and blue. He noticed that a bow was being raised to him, but he couldn't figure out how the bow was being lifted. He had to run to his girlfriend. He was her protector, after all.

"You're still acting like a kid! Why'd you get so scared?" he asked, taking her by the hand. He tried to smile, even though his soft lips were trembling slightly. She snuggled up close to him and said, "I want to go home! I don't want to go to the movies!"

"Don't be a baby," he said, looking into her face.

They walked quickly, and when they reached the corner of the street, they both stopped, as if their feet had agreed on this course of action. They turned around and, once again, heard the sharp, monotonous "Click-clack! Click-clack!"

By this point, it was nighttime and the street was flooded with the glow of fiery electric advertisements, dancing lines of light, and the dazzling theater marquees. And people, people, so many people in the world! But the click-clack, a bit drawn-out as if tired, pursued the waves of people and light. The people couldn't at all see who was standing in shadow next to a dimly-lit window. There was only a small table illuminated there, and in the semi-darkness, shimmering above the table were two metal objects that didn't speak but instead screamed out that eerie sound: "Click-clack!"

Two boys walked by. One of them, around ten years old; the other, still a child. They saw and heard this great wonder and abruptly stopped: "Oh, gee!" The younger one jumped over to the person with the strange gadgets. "Oh, gee!" The little one scrutinized him from top down and bottom up. When he saw that the little man didn't move, he called out to the bigger boy who had moved off to the side and was staring with frightened eyes.

"Is that a real man?" he asked.

The bigger boy pulled him away and ran to the other side of the street to get a better perspective on this weird thing. "Click-clack! Click-clack!" the little one imitated it and laughed out loud... The street sang! The street played! From the stores came the sounds of gramophones, a concert on a high floor. Radios from cars. Everything sang. Everything played and made a ruckus about something: "Click-clack, click-clack!"

A middle-aged woman walked by. She was deep in thought, but the click-clack startled her from her thoughts. She jolted. The sound was close, but she couldn't see its source. For a moment, she stood in place. She saw how people were reaching into their pockets, taking out coins, placing them on a small table, and running quickly away. Very few people stretched out a hand to take the bow that the "clickers" were holding ready for them.

Her eyes wide open, the woman, an ordinary Jewish mother, stood in the same place, looked at the little person, and said to herself, "Oh, no! My God!" But she couldn't leave. Her legs wouldn't move. If she were to stay in place, she thought, she could draw people's attention. So, with a heaviness in her legs, she trudged to the entrance of the pharmacy where the small person was standing. The large, three-sided window looking out onto the avenue and the side street helped the woman scrutinize the scene thoroughly and think things over. Her eyes, seized with pain, stared intently at the little man's artificial hands that tapped with clocklike precision.

A raising, a click, a release, and—click. The small table hanging on the little man's neck was no more than two feet. It had four corners. His elbows were resting on the table; gleaming down from the elbows were aluminum tubes, like trumpets, wide above and at the end—narrower. In a small box between the tubes—bows. Red, white, and blue, and when the tube descended, a little mouth opened at the tip. The mouth stuck out a little tongue, and the little tongued lifted up the bow and offered it to the passerby...

Apparently, quite a long procedure, but long live civilization! It happened so quickly. Click—up; clack—down, and the little box with the bows got emptier. The hill of coins—taller. Few passersby stopped to consider the person behind the tubes: click-clack. They looked around and threw in a dime. Some didn't even stop to take the bow. They eased their own conscience with the coin. What good did it do to look?

The Jewish mother stood by the window for an hour, or even more. The previously festive and pleasant mood had vanished by this point. As she stood there, she was engulfed by a kind of self-torment. She tried to scrutinize the face of the small person. But his face was like a shadow, and even the shadow was artificial, fabricated. She saw that he was very young. His shoulders were narrow; his head—small, and the military cap that had once belonged to a soldier was pulled so low down that his forehead was not visible.

She noticed that his cheeks were very dark and shriveled as if he didn't have a single tooth in his mouth. His lips could barely be seen; they were either shrunken or clenched. She looked and her heart went out to him. At the very least, she wanted to offer him a caress, to show him that she was deeply distressed on his behalf, but she didn't have the courage to approach him.

It was getting darker. There was more noise on the street. Young people were passing by, singing, laughing. The woman felt that while he was standing there with the little table suspended from his neck, the life which remained within him should have screamed, wept… should have cursed! Should have, should have! But—for the first time, she caught a glimpse of the man's little eyes, and they—his eyes—said nothing… My God! The eyes looked like the gleaming eyes of a fake little bear, a teddy bear.

She stepped closer to the display and didn't believe her eyes. She had seen many wounded soldiers returning from both world wars, people without feet, people with empty sleeves. The heart protected itself, became hardened against all horrors, but as for why this small person, this click-clack here and now, had seized her with such horror, that she didn't know.

The woman stood and looked on with awkward helplessness. As she looked, it seemed to her that she had found an answer to her great shock: yes, this person had been altered. He had surrendered his soul to the metal hands and had himself become a piece of metal.

She thought that perhaps it only seemed to her that the eyes of this war-invalid were expressionless. It was possible that it was her own imagination—click-clack! But no! She didn't see a soul in these eyes. The metal tubes had replaced all feelings.

Click-clack… click-clack! The box was empty. The small person shuffled home. The woman, the mother, followed him for a small part of the way, wanting to make sure he knew the way. He turned onto a dark side-alley.

Another Route

Mark didn't tell anyone that, in a short time frame—two to three months—he'd undergone an experience that both ignited and extinguished something in him. Although the encounter etched a wound in his boyish memory, he didn't regret what he went through. Now, he felt like someone with experience. To be sure, he paid for this encounter, but it was worth it. He now knew his place, and he would no longer seek the company of those who weren't on his path. He was taking his father's route.

Now, Mark felt more mature and grown and older than he was three months ago.

It all started one morning, when Mark was standing, packed in tightly with all of the other passengers, on a crowded bus. His eye came upon two beautiful girls. He'd never seen such beauties! Theirs was no ordinary beauty; a luminosity shone from them. When the bus got less crowded, Mark repositioned himself so he could get a better view of the girls. He so enjoyed looking at them; it was as if he were gazing on a garden of beautiful flowers. Their bright clothes, their clean, white hands with the pointed red nails, the watches on their wrists, even the books they carried—all were wondrous to him. He looked at the girls thirstily until he had to disembark and head down into the subway. He decided he had to run into them again. It wouldn't be that easy for him, but you had to try your luck.

Mark didn't understand what sort of spell the girls had lured him into, and the girls had no idea that not far from them stood a young man warming himself in the radiance they were casting around themselves… The girls chatted and laughed, telling each

other how they spent yesterday evening and what they were going to do tonight. Their little mouths didn't stop grinding, and
that grinding had a charm all its own. A sweetness dripped from
their mouths. The girls exuded freshness, the scents of a fresh
morning. Mark was drawn into that morning, and there, he forgot
himself.

Mark saw that the girls were younger than him. They were
students; that is, they were still going to school. If he would have
had the opportunity, he himself would still be going to school. He
only finished elementary school, although his mother had hoped
that he, her eldest son, would be a lawyer or an engineer. But
misfortune struck Mark's father. He cut two fingers off his right
hand, and the doctors were barely able to save the three remaining fingers. The family had to get by on a small pension, and
Mark had to learn a trade. He was admitted to a course in an in-
dustrial school. He quickly finished it and hired himself out as an
assistant in a factory where machines were repaired.

Although not yet a mechanic, Mark's hands were already
black and his fingernails were encrusted with dirt. He rode to
work wearing a dark shirt and heavy, canvas pants. He carried
himself like someone earning his own living. He took long
strides, holding a package of food under his arm and his hands in
his pockets. Despite the childlike appearance of his face, exhaustion was already observable beneath his eyes. He had become an
adult too soon. In his bones, the boy was still there, and that boy
often didn't want to give in to the adult. As a result, Mark was
kind of what you would call "neither-here-nor-there." He wanted
to work. It didn't bother him that he had become the wage earner.
On the contrary, since he'd started cashing his own hard-earned
paycheck, he looked at himself with more respect. Every Mon-
day, he would give his small envelope to his mother, gesturing
like his father. He looked at his mother's face, devoured her loyal
gaze, and offered her a few words of comfort as a supplement to
the envelope.

"Don't worry, Mom, I'll still study. I'm still young. I know a lot of people who studied at night and became great," he said.

Nevertheless, the boy inside him demanded something. He felt as if he had been ripped out of a warm bed in the middle of a sweet, peaceful sleep. The transformation had taken place abruptly. It wasn't just that Mark exchanged the classroom for the factory; he had torn himself away from his sixteen-year-old life and had to leap up over a hill that you typically climb at a slow pace.

When he became a worker, Mark changed his way of speaking and thinking. He also distanced himself from those who, up to that point, had been his friends. The boys began to speak to him as if he were a stranger, as if he had suddenly become someone else, as if he were ten years older than them. The boy in Mark still longed for his friends, but he himself felt like a stranger to them.

Among the workers, Mark didn't feel quite at home, either, although they treated him as one of their own. The workers knew his father, and they could tell that he was cut from the same stock. But to Mark, it felt as if the workers were too indulgent of him, that he was being given something he didn't deserve. It was somewhat difficult for him to digest their benevolence, as if he were swallowing something that was too soft.

At home, Mark was the big brother. His three younger brothers considered him omniscient. They asked him all of their questions, and, as a result, he, the know-it-all, had to act like an adult. To his father, he had to show a happy face. Mark didn't want his father to think that he had snatched him away from his childhood. But he didn't feel right with his mother, precisely because she was the closest to him. His mother kept staring at him, and it seemed to him that she was sifting through every word he said to her.

Still, Mark was very young, and as a sixteen-year-old youth with the drive to advance in life, he tore through the obstacles and cast aside the adversities.

In the morning, Mark left the house with a long stride. With the dose of bass that had set up shop in his young voice, he called out "Goodbye!" When he closed the door behind him, he started to sing aloud a ditty and ran down the steps. When he reached the street, his eyes searched the morning for something. His heart sensed that he was embarking on a day that wasn't his, and he longed for yesterday, gone so quickly.

Mark was not a new passenger on the bus. He had grown up on the street and knew the young people well, but because he was getting up so early, the passengers were alien to him. Previously, when going to school, he had his school friends around him. Now, he was surrounded by older people who cast a heaviness upon him. But ever since he saw the two girls in the corner, everything changed. Because of these girls in the corner, the bus ride had become quite pleasant. The crowded bus did not make him sullen. On the contrary, he preferred it because he could see the girls better without their noticing him—so he looked to his heart's content.

For Mark, the encounter with the girls created a connection that replaced the amorphous longing for his yesterdays. It was a wobbly, thin connection. Mark was well aware that any day now he could lose them. In the sixteen-year-old's mind spun a daring, terrifying, and at the same time, relentless idea: he would try to get to know the girls. How he would go about doing this was something he didn't yet know. He in his worker's clothes, and they—so bright and attractive! But the "how" Mark put off for later.

While they lasted, these were good days for Mark. When he saw the girls, he was in a good mood, but when he didn't see them, his days were turned upside down and everything slipped from his hands. He could barely wait to get home in anticipation of the next morning…

One morning, Mark saw two boys who looked to be the same age as the two girls sitting next to them. The boys, too, carried books. They were smartly and tidily dressed and interacted with the girls as if they were all longtime acquaintances. They sat close to them, speaking quietly. As always, the girls shone. They were smiling so continuously that Mark felt that they were teasing him. He looked at the girls, at the boys, and at his black hands, and with a sharp pain in his throat, he slid further from them. That day, he didn't feel well—a headache. He was angry at himself, angry that he allowed a few skirts to get into his head, as if he were a blockhead, as if he didn't have any other worries. But hope still smoldered in his heart. He was sixteen years old, after all.

Days, weeks, passed. It was mid-winter. The students joyfully welcomed the season's ten-day vacation. They made plans for all kinds of fun activities. This was the time for young people to live it up! For Mark, those ten days were perhaps the emptiest of his young life. He rode to work, half-asleep, gloomy. At work, he didn't open his mouth. The older folks looked at him uneasily; the younger ones teased him, pelting him with jokes about him having crawled off into a swamp. One of them whispered secretively into his ears: "You're in love, old bachelor!" Mark felt his face grow heated, and he didn't know how to turn away from those eyes that crawled beneath his skin.

The next day—this was after the new year—Mark got up, feeling renewed. He left home earlier than usual and went to the bus as if he were headed to meet up with a long-lost friend. In his longing for the girls, Mark felt that the girls were aware of his feelings. As soon as he had climbed into the bus, he ran into them. He was closer to them than he had ever been. Mark couldn't hold back his joy and he broke into a smile. His eyes danced playfully. The girls with the glowing faces exchanged glances, assessed him from head to toe with surprised eyes, turned around, and then both of them burst into hoarse laughter.

The smile, frozen on Mark's face, transformed itself into a dopey one. His feet began to stumble; his hands rummaged for something in his pockets. For some time, he stood there and didn't move. Suddenly, as if bitten by something, he spun his head around to the girls and noticed two other girls cozying up to them, all of them laughing. The bus stopped. Mark was startled to find himself standing on the sidewalk in an unfamiliar neighborhood.

Various feelings swirled inside him. He cursed in embarrassment. Rage wanted to erupt from his choked-up throat. He didn't understand what had propelled the girls to laugh so coarsely at him. He felt an urge to give himself a whipping.

In the midst of this brew of feelings, a small golden crucifix appeared in his mind's eye, momentarily dazzling him. He remembered that a golden crucifix had dangled on a golden chain around one of the girl's necks, and that clarified everything to him.

Mark bent down, picked up a small rock from the ground, threw it in the direction of the bus, and grumbled to himself: "You have to take another route."

Three Apples, Rolling

Several times now, Susan had ridden up and down on the elevator to the sixth floor to ring the doorbell of Madam Lush's apartment. From the very first time she pressed the bell, she knew there wouldn't be a response, that she would be losing half a day's work. Susan was well aware that the ringing was in vain because she was fifteen minutes late and Madam Lush wouldn't have waited for her. Still, she kept taking the elevator. Up and down. Not knowing what to do with herself, Susan stood at the apartment door and kept ringing. She pressed the bell with one finger, and the longer the ringing lasted, the bolder and stronger the pressure she applied—until she could hear the jangle of the bell behind the door. Finally, she removed her finger and stood there, worried. Feeling a heaviness in her heart, Susan railed against herself: "You Black fool! You know you're standing here for nothing. It's high time you get it into your head that that posh lady wouldn't make Pete, that dog of hers, wait for you! Not even if there were ten of you!"

Once Susan was back on the first floor, she went to stand at the entrance. A spark of hope that Madam would soon return still flickered within her. She found a dark corner near the door, hoping to avoid the gaze of the starched doorman.

As she stood, she was surprised that she hadn't realized until now how beautiful the lobby was. Such spaciousness... Several families could live in it. A large, airy quadrangular room with plush benches against the walls, marble tables, and Chinese lamps in the corners. The stillness exuded a dark warmth. People were coming and going; the door opened and closed. And yet there was no noise at all. Quiet reigned. The ornate lobby elicited respect in the people who came into the building. The muted warmth made Susan feel sleepy. She appreciated the dreamy stillness and lost her desire to step out onto the bright, cold street.

Susan was around thirty-five years old. She was large and heavy. Her shoulders and hips were enormous, but her step was light. She carried her heavy body with ease and playfulness. Although Susan was a good worker and had childlike, calm eyes and a vulnerable, feminine face, it was hard for her to get work because of her massive body. As a result, she couldn't be too picky and had to take whatever presented itself.

She'd been working for Madam Lush for quite a long time. She worked half a day three times a week. Madam was a wealthy, disturbed, and capricious woman, but Susan dealt patiently with her. Madam had a cardinal rule: Susan had to be at her apartment at eight o'clock on the dot. If she came earlier, she wouldn't open the door for her. If she came a few minutes later, she had locked the door and gone for a stroll with the dog.

If Susan hadn't been punished with such a heavy body, she would have left Madam long ago. But with such a lack of options! What was she supposed to do when the refined ladies trembled and were genuinely afraid that they would have to feed her too much.

"I'm a cursed Black woman!" Susan fretted. "Now I've gone and lost half a day's work all because I wanted an apple! No one short of God Himself put a test right there in front of me. Those apples tempted me like they were casting a spell! And if it wasn't God, but the Devil—well then, his work was all for nothing. This time, he didn't get what he wanted. I didn't break my promise. I didn't take the apples, but I lost a half a day's work just for wanting them."

Susan stood in the corner in a state of self-introspection. She wanted to convince herself of the purity of her intention. Like all other mornings, she had gotten up today at six o'clock. She recited her daily prayers, prepared food, drank a cup of coffee, and in the middle of chewing, left the house, not wanting to wake up her child. As soon as she opened her eyes, her daughter had something to say. Who had time for her? My poor girl! She was always alone. As soon as she saw her mother, she wanted to speak. It was a bit of a hike to the subway, and the ride itself took a whole hour.

When Susan got out of the subway, she felt as if the Devil himself were pushing her to walk down a side street where there was a large fruit market. As if deliberately to tempt her, a young man happened to be standing and pouring apples from a sack into a box at just that moment. So fresh, so fragrant, only just picked from the tree. It seemed to her that she had never seen such apples. Their fragrance filled the entire street; you could practically hear the knocking of the seeds—a sign of ripeness.

And she did so love apples!

The box filled up, started to overflow, and the apples scattered onto the sidewalk. Three apples started to roll straight toward her feet, coming so close that she was in danger of trampling them. Two apples rolled together, and the other, larger one, rolled on its own as if it were showing the others the way. On its red cheeks it rolled to her feet so that she had to stand aside. She bit into this larger apple with her eyes and it seemed to her that she could feel the juice squirt. Her mouth watered. The froth from the apple poured over her lips. She bent down and her hand reached out... but something inside her said: "No! Don't you have enough troubles, Black woman? They'll see you and accuse you of stealing. That's all you need!"

She looked around. There was no one there. The young man who poured the apples had his back to her. Her inner sweet tooth badgered her: Just one—pick it up! If you don't, someone else will.

The large, red-cheeked apple winked at her. She bent down again, reached out her hand. Suddenly, out of nowhere, a man appeared and ran right up to her. She straightened up, put her

hand in her pocket, and stood there. In a rush and absorbed in
something else, the man wasn't watching where he was going.
He knocked up against the large Black woman, made a grum-
bling sound of sorts, and left. She kept standing there. The apples
winked as if pleading with her: "Take, just take. They'll trample
us, in any case." Again, she wanted to extend her hand, but she
remembered something that happened to her several years ago.

She had been on her way to work. On the sidewalk was a
clean, fresh pear. Without thinking much about it, she picked up
the pear and bit into it when she heard a shout: "Hey, you! Thief!"
She looked around: a fruit wagon. A fruit merchant was coming after her and cursing her with whatever was popping into his
head, as if she were the real thief!

She threw the pear at his face and fired a few curses of her
own at him. But the insult was so painful that she began to cry.
Then and there, she pledged that she would never give anyone the
opportunity to insult her. Never would her hand touch something
that didn't belong to her.

Susan was certain that God Himself had protected her from
sin today by causing her to remember that earlier incident just
when she was ready to give in to temptation. She gave one last
look at the apples as if asking their forgiveness for leaving them
on the ground, and she left.

But just for the craving, she got her punishment. Susan had
wasted time and lost a half-day's work. Now she would have to
trudge through the streets until one o'clock when it would be time
to go to her afternoon Madam. She couldn't go home. She would
have to give her last few cents for carfare.

Susan sighed loudly, almost forgetting that she was standing
here at the door. "And I thought that today I would make lunch
for my little one!" she said to herself, "I shot myself in the foot! I
had a sudden craving for apples, Black fool that I am!"

Susan thought that if she hadn't been punished with such
a large and heavy body, she wouldn't have had to worry about
work. But what could she do? It was God's gift.

The doorman, who had walked past her three times, approached her, as if he wanted to remind her that he was there, too—that she wasn't there alone. He bent his head down to hear her, and very quietly, as if he didn't want to awaken anyone, asked: "Are you waiting for someone? Can I help you?"

He spoke politely, but from his tone, Susan got the message: "You've been standing here long enough. Beat it! Get out of here!"

Feeling a shakiness in her body and a bit angry at herself, Susan reluctantly trudged out of the dark, warm, and somnolent lobby onto the bright, cold street.

Faces

In the early autumn morning, movement in the park was quiet, almost secretive. Everything stirred with rhythmic regularity.

The quiet rustling of the trees, the whirlpool of falling leaves that flirted against the sun with their copper-brown, amber-yellow, iridescent colors piled into mounds on the damp ground, like the buzzing of thousands of varieties of butterflies—a sense of secrecy could be felt everywhere. They were all searching for a sunny spot on one of the benches arranged in a row on the long, asphalt pathway stretching from the east side of the park to the west.

On this weekday morning, few people were out and about. Sheila had been seeking out this very sort of stillness. With her back stiffly pressed against the back of the bench, she covered her eyes with both hands. Through the cracks between her fingers, fiery javelins and triangular figures extended themselves. The triangles spread out over an unlimited distance... Sheila wandered around, as if lost, in that distance. She withdrew into herself, reliving all that was long gone but still fresh in her life.

She still saw her David, felt his eyes upon her. She saw how he had boarded the train car. At that time, she didn't doubt for a minute that he would soon return home. In the course of her twenty years, there had never been a cloud overhead. She believed that he, her beloved, would avoid all dangers, that she did not need to worry about him. After all, David was such a capable athlete. Such a good runner. He would extricate himself from all danger. Now, without him, Sheila felt that she was no longer whole. She was torn in two. So, of course, she had thought it wouldn't take long. So too had he assured her.

The evenings were empty. Sundays—even worse. She quickly threw herself into her work. She worked for the Red Cross, in hospitals and clubs. She arranged it so that she wouldn't have to sit at home, where her mother looked at her with uneasy eyes. She was one of a group of girls who tried to stay active so they could get take their minds off their beloveds for a while. Among themselves, they were intimate and open-hearted. For girls who worked in offices or factories, the work among the sick lifted the spirit. It brought them joy to see how the weakened face of a soldier would light up when he was offered a drink of water or when you smoothed out the pillow beneath his head.

When they had a little free time, they read their letters and unburdened themselves. Some of them had gotten married without their parents' knowledge and only wore their wedding rings when they were with each other. Sheila regularly turned her head away when seeing how little Sylvia, practically a child in appearance, caressed and kissed her ring.

When the letters were delayed, the girls didn't say anything. When a few of them received letters and the others didn't, they all stayed silent, not wanting to cause the others pain. So it went until the first rupture that little Sylvia generated in everyone's heart. For several days, Sylvia didn't show up at all. They suspected that something must have happened. When they went to Sylvia's home, she was already in a sanatorium for the mentally ill.

Sylvia was nineteen years old. She was the liveliest and youngest of them all. Born to impoverished parents, her mother had protected Sylvia from all evil. An only child, coddled from an early age, she was destined to come into contact with the cruelties of the world in her youth. Her nerves didn't hold out. Sylvia learned that her husband—her friend from school for as long as she could remember—had been blown to pieces by a mine in his first oceanic journey, and she fell apart.

With one less among them, the girls went about with lowered heads. Sylvia was a portent that the others could expect something similar. They couldn't easily shake off Sylvia's misfortune. A shadow spread out over the heads of the girls. Before they could get used to the empty place once occupied by Sylvia, one and then another dropped out of the group. When one of them experienced a misfortune—such as her groom being wounded or gunned down—she no longer appeared at the hospital, as if she felt she already paid her debt to the world.

Sheila recalled the case of one who'd made a profound impression on her. Her name was Mary, a dear girl. When Mary didn't come to the hospital, they already suspected that she was in the Devil's fist. Sheila loved Mary very much, and she couldn't hold herself back, so went to see her. But Mary didn't let Sheila across the threshold. She came up to her and explained: "Sol came back with his throat shot through, and can now only speak with the help of a tube. It's hard for him to speak; it's a kind of crowing, not a human voice. He's embarrassed, and so I don't want to hurt him."

Gradually, the girls pulled back. Whole days passed when they didn't see each other. The intimacy was shattered, the work fell heavily on them, each one shut herself away for fear of what the next day would bring. Words were superfluous since each felt what the other was thinking. There were those who did have luck. They frequently received letters. They were expecting to see their beloveds when they returned on furlough, but sensing the sadness of the others who hadn't received such news, they took no pleasure from their own good fortune.

Her eyes closed, Sheila thought about how strange it was that she recalled with such precision what happened to this or that girl, each of whom was still so clearly visible to her, and yet she couldn't remember what had happened to her own self when the misfortune had occurred. She didn't even remember where she was at the time. It was as if everything was veiled by a cloud which her vision could not penetrate. She only remembered the dark gaze of her mother. Sheila remembered, too, how her little sister kept hiding from her. Neither her little sister nor the boy she was friends with dared to smile during the brief amount of time they spent in her presence. Sheila held herself at a distance, not wanting to remind the children of death. Sheila felt then—and now—as if the best part of herself, what had helped shape her personhood, had been torn from her, that she was no longer who she was meant to be.

Sheila didn't believe that years had gone by. During those years she did not have a sense of her own self. She only saw herself in the mirror. There, two bluish-black pain-filled eyes looked back at her. The blue half-moons below her eyes made them appear distant and deep. Three thin strands at its center divided her pale forehead in two. She smoothed and caressed the strands, and it seemed to her that she could see her David in the distance of her eyes. He had always loved to look into her eyes—look and look. She once asked him: "Why do you look into my eyes so much?" He answered: "The more I look into them, the more precious they become to me!" Because he loved her face so much, she felt that she must cherish and take good care of it for his sake.

A few lines in a magazine touched a wounded spot within Sheila: "There are a million women in the country who remain alone, because their men did not come back from war!" Since she read those lines, she was gripped by a new sense of pain. She didn't understand why, until that point, she had suffered only for the dead and failed to see the severed lives of a million women, girls, mothers, children. Without love… without ever getting pregnant. Without life. Such cruelty!

Sheila couldn't get that one and those six zeroes out of her mind. She saw the round zeroes filled with feminine faces. Thousands and thousands of faces! Older, middle-aged, young, and really, really young. Faces with anger in their eyes; faces with cold wrath and resentment; faces that appeared neither dead nor alive. She saw her own face. With difficulty, she even recognized the face of her little sister.

Sheila started awake from the nightmare. It was a terrible dream—she wanted to cry out—what a sick turmoil! It all came from what she heard on the radio yesterday: "In three more years, we can expect a new war." She hadn't imagined it. It *was* true. She heard it when she was awake, not when she was asleep.

As if ripping herself from a terrible, diseased sleep, Sheila left the bench. She started walking downhill. She was tired, drained. Her knees buckled, and she had to sit down again on the first bench she spotted.

Mothers with baby strollers appeared. The sun was higher and warmer now. Downhill, where heaven and earth met, a brook reflected the sun. The whiteness bouncing off of the shallow water erased beginning and end.

Sheila gazed thirstily at the surrounding brightness. With maternal warmth, the sun caressed and coddled her long-settled limbs. It seemed to her that through the quiet babbling of the brook's water flow, the sun was whispering into her ear: You're only twenty-six years old, my child. At such a young age, you mustn't fear life. You must not, my child.

Rusty, My Friend

Rusty, my friend, even though you're four-legged and I'm two-legged, we have a lot in common. My affinity for you is profound. It seems to me that I feel you the way I feel myself, that I hold you the way I would hold my own self. Like me, you've been forgotten and sidelined because of your age. You've lost your practical utility to humans, a quality you'd mastered throughout the years. Now, nobody cares about you. Like me, my four-legged friend, you're alone and not attractive to people's eyes, and as for your practical utility to dogs—well, that's also been lost.

I feel you, my friend, and I don't let you out of my mind's eye. Now I see you, my little lump. You've selected a sunny spot of earth on which to curl up and bury your head in a few wet blades of grass, and with sleepy, cloudy eyes, you look dully at your "hims" and "hers" racing after summer butterflies and the cheerful children around them who fill the air with raucous laughter.

No one can compete with you when it comes to sniffing something from a distance or when you get the urge to play with the "she" around whom everyone is now dancing.

Based on your phlegmatic cleaving to the ground, one might presume that their activities don't matter to you; after all, you're not even looking in their direction. But, my friend, I know that's just a show. I sense your internal pain. I see your twitching nose. I see how you flap an ear and give a snort with your shivering nose, and although I can't claim to be an expert in canine psychology, I could swear that you, with the whole of your ungainly body, are now with them, with the young "puppies" that don't even send a friendly sniff your way…

It's already happened several times. There you were lying down in your loneliness, like you were already buried in the ground, when suddenly, as if the earth whispered a secret in your ear, you leaped up, like you did in your youth, and headed off like a whirlwind. Those around you tried to follow your example by running for a bit, but they soon returned, as if they'd decided: *We won't catch him, in any case. Let him run, that old fool.* When you returned like a victor, with a guest, no one even looked at you. Your master didn't even offer you a caress in thanks.

After one such expedition, I notice a flicker of old age in your eyes. This much is apparent: it's all too much for your current capabilities. You flop to the ground, your usual resting-place, utterly spent. Just a moment ago, you detected from quite a distance, with a sense of smell that has yet to let you down, someone from your household, but he doesn't give you what you deserve. It is he, Grazia, who receives the special treats, the kind words, the caresses. It was he who danced around the guest, not you. He is beautiful. No one can resist his black, gleaming pelt with the white spots. The spot at the very center of his forehead adds a world of charm. Now Grazia rejoices in his conquest!

I've gone through the same thing, and so I feel for you. Oh, how I feel for you, Rusty, my friend. I know you're exhausted and that you have pain in your sides from the running you just did; here you are lying in the tumult, with shortness of breath and sleep in your eyes. I feel for you, Rusty, my friend. Forgotten one, like me. I read all your resentments. Right now, I see that you are tired, that you tremble from time to time. Your muzzle rests on your weak front paws, your wide, pendant ears are even with the ground, and your half-open eyes are veiled with a slimy membrane. It's hard to know whether you're asleep. It's already dark. The setting sun sets a slice of sky aflame. A few rays stumble upon your head and make their way through the dark recesses of your dozing brain to illuminate the remembrances and desires there. You glide in the past, my friend. Here too, I feel for you,

Rusty, my friend, because the setting sun has also stirred up for me times past, yet not forgotten... You are still feeling at this moment how and in what way to throw yourself upon your enemy, upon any dog who stands in your way and doesn't let you get anywhere near the female your heart so desires... A burning fury is ignited within you. You let out a wild howl! You give yourself a shake and there you are again lying on the ground. You woke up...

Oh, Rusty, my friend, how well I understand you. Oh, those years, when your legs were even, flexible, nimble, and swift as an arrow released from a bow! Why, your legs ran so quickly that they were invisible. I, too, Rusty, my friend, when I close my eyes, see myself long ago... the only difference is that I sit on a bench and you—on the ground.

Rusty, do you remember those adoring, soft, and loyal hands that we both loved so? Between you and me, Rusty, there was no place for jealousy. I loved to caress your satiny curly fur—fur of a hue that, in the dark, looked like flames, the only-just vanished flames of the setting sun. Your eyes were so human that I often thought you understood a bit too much for a dog... And what a scamp you were! Your ears stood like a young hare's. She and I, both of us loved to play with your ears. No less than me, you were greedy for the caresses of those hands with their magic-fingers.

Remember how those hands caressed you. You wanted to thank them with a kiss, and on the face, no less, right? Remember how she embraced your handsome head in her translucent hands with such tenderness, so as not to cause you any pain. Then your eyes would ask me to come to your aid. Neck outstretched, you would look at me, a little embarrassed. I saw a tear in a corner of one of your eyes.

Ach, ach, Rusty, my friend, how foolish one can be when young and in love! Now, when I speak to you without words, I can say that to you. You know, Rusty, there was a time when I was jealous of you? No, you can't know. More than once, when I spotted her sitting on a bench in the garden, you at her feet, your handsome head on her lap and she playing with your silky fur— oh, was I jealous of you! Oh, how I wanted to be in your place!

Ach, ach, how monstrous the years can be, Rusty, my friend.

You lie in the corner and although you're always drawn to the ground, you turn your head to the slice of moon that leaps out now and then from the heavy, dark clouds as if seeking to free itself from their pressure. But the clouds are rushing off to who knows where. As recently as earlier today, my eyes followed you as those of your kind held sway over the meadows and you were seized by a sudden urge. You hastily got up from your bed, shook the dust from yourself, looked all around, and spotting a white "she" for whom you apparently have a "weakness," made off in her direction as one would to an old friend. But she, although no innocent young thing herself, started barking forcefully as if you wanted to slaughter her. At the sound of her cries, the entire "dog brigade" came running and started barking, and you, poor Rusty, unfortunately had no alternative but to retreat...

The truth is, you left in dignity, albeit with a lowered head; you didn't flee, but walked slowly, step by step, and then returned to your bed.

As it does for myself, so my heart ached for you, Rusty, my four-legged friend. I experienced something similar in my own life. Strange, but when I saw you coming back with sadness and awkwardness in your steps, it seemed to me that I heard your wide, hanging ears weeping over your bitter fate...

... It's midnight. A stripe of light extends from a lamp hanging from a beam, cutting through the dark fog. You, Rusty, are seemingly enveloped in a shadow, but when an edge of the moon reveals itself, your presence on the ground is spotlighted. When one gets close to you, one might think that you are still, like the ground itself upon which you lie, and like the trees near your head. But that is not the case. It's not just the ground that is still, but also the trees that are still. You, Rusty, are very far from still. In your subconscious, something is happening. It's hard to say what. What I do see: your body gives a shiver, a jerk, as if someone had stepped on it, and from your throat—as if you were enraged at someone—a kind of grrr can be heard... Any minute now you will be coming out with a true canine bark. Perhaps you're angry at the moon... and perhaps the moonlight has brought memories of the past back to you? Perhaps the moon has awakened in you a longing for those tender hands—the hands with the magic fingers, for which I, too, yearn, yearn unceasingly?

Of one thing I am sure: despite your awkwardness and your proximity to the earth, you're a dreamer, and that makes me happy. Because you ought to know, Rusty, my friend, that to dream is itself an achievement. And there's something else you ought to know—one can't always dream. A dream, too, has its time...

So dream, Rusty. Dream, my friend!

Goodbye, Honey

Unbidden, the sun broke through the double-ply, heavy silk drapes, landing first on the floor and then onto the very peak of the cornice over the large mirror, before leaping over to the bed. Slivers of sun stole through the narrow cracks of the sleeper's eyes. Longish, fiery little threads playfully tickled her eyelids. She defended herself, turning her head, as if swatting away a fly. The tickling became unbearable so she opened her eyes and then quickly covered them with both hands. By now, the sun had made itself at home, pouring its golden rays into every corner of the large room and greeting her with a bright, delightful morning.

It was still early, only just ten o'clock. Still too early for her to start the day, but by now, she was no longer sleepy but fully awake, as if she had been up for a long time. Strange…

She tossed aside the cover, savored a delicious stretch, and considered herself. She looked in the mirror hanging opposite the bed with a degree of surprise, as if she were asking herself: "Is that really me? Yes, it is me!" Her radiant face was veiled in light shadow, as if she were remembering that she was about to take an unpleasant medication. She cleared her throat, tested her voice, and called out: "Honey! Honey!"… From the other room came the response: "Yes, baby, coming!"

No footsteps could be heard. The floors were laid out with heavy carpets, but the small pieces of furniture quivered. An old man of seventy appeared. He was dressed to go outside. He stood without any assertiveness, waiting for her to call him again. Instead of saying anything, she stretched out a hand. He walked slowly over, holding his head slightly lowered. His yellowish, fleshy, freshly-shaved face looked both a little offended but also guilty. He took a longer stride, bent down, and gave her a kiss on the lips which she offered him. The kiss—hardly a successful effort—left them both in the kind of pose that made it look as if someone had interrupted them. She covered her face with her hands, and he looked at the ground, as if he were suddenly embarrassed in front of her…

She blocked her eyes with her hands and was filled with pity for him. But soon that pity turned into resentment. Where did this old man get the audacity to buy her? Maybe it was he who pitied her? He had it good, after all! He placed a very warm hand on the naked nape of her neck. She brought her hands down from off her face and noticed his slightly embarrassed, slightly pleading eyes. She saw that he was getting ready to tell her something and that there was immense devotion in his gaze. She regretted her bizarre thoughts. She smiled, and his face revived: "Today, we'll go eat at a one-of-a-kind place in America! You hear me, baby—nothing like it in the entire country!"

"You're a good man, Pop," she answered.

He smiled foolishly and wagged his finger: "Anything but 'Pop'! You make me feel old when you call me that."

"Well then, 'honey' it is! Honey, tell the girl to make something to drink, okay?"

"All right, I'm going!"

He turned around with a contrived agility that appeared comical, and once again, she thought that it was a pity. But a pity for whom?

It had been a total of six weeks since she, Molly the hairdresser, became Mrs. Carson. For years and years, she was Molly. Just Molly. No one called her by her last name. It was also the name of her company: Molly's Beauty Salon. It was a small shop, rather than a fancy salon. She herself, Molly, constituted the entire company.

She had been left a young widow with two boys. With the few dollars left over from a small policy, she learned the profession and became a "company" in a run-down neighborhood. Molly worked hard, really hard.

Molly was still young and beautiful. Her beauty was a tremendous asset in the business. The women were convinced that Molly could make them as beautiful as she herself was. They kept paying her compliments. And the more compliments—the more Molly tried to find favor with her beauty. And while beauty can bring a woman great happiness, Molly's own beauty repaid her with insufficient sleep and yet more hard work than she had the strength for.

She was the model for her "company"… She tried each new style out on her own hair, and because her hair was naturally curly and a lustrous shade of brown, she simply enthralled the other women. And yet, for all her charm, she had to work long hours and remained poor. She could never afford a vacation. She didn't dare travel anywhere on her own. Who would take care of the children? As for taking the children with her—well, that would cost too much. She waited for the day when the children would grow up. By the time the children were grown, Molly had invested much of her own charm and strength—and even a good amount of her hopes—in those women's heads, in their hairdos. When the boys finished their studies, she was once again dependent on the labor of her own hands.

The years raced by, and throughout that time, Molly lived with the feeling that she had to grab hold of something before it was too late.

Molly would come home exhausted. Her legs weighed heavily, her bones ached, and the light in her eyes appeared virtually extinguished. Getting up in the morning was becoming harder for her. To the clock she pleaded: "Hold on, don't run so fast…" It seemed to her that she had only just closed her eyes and yet the clock hands had already crept a whole ten minutes ahead.

And so it went—day after day, week after week. No end in sight. Finally, something of a salvation arrived. One son came home and, contemplating his mother with open eyes, observed: "This isn't working out, Mama. You don't have to put your whole life into women's heads. You should be looking out to the years you still have left…" Molly herself had often thought the very same thing: Hurry, hurry, before your life escapes from your grasp and it's too late. But what was to be done?

Molly had heard a lot about Florida. You got younger in Florida! There, a person could slip on a new life. And in particular, hard-up women went to Florida and found themselves "friends" there… not just lovers. There were also older men there who were eager to find a pretty young wife. True, Molly was no longer what she had once been, but she still had quite a bit of allure left within her. And especially with some rest and dressing up… A sun suddenly rose and shone before her. The sea, she—in a stunning bathing suit, men gazing at her with hungry eyes. She had practically forgotten how one dates a gentleman. For a large part of her life since her husband's death she had lived among women. It often seemed to her that those women had deadened within her the feelings, the yearnings, that a woman has for a man.

Molly was already more than forty years old when a new, belated spring emerged before her.

On more than one occasion, the same women who came to her salon told her fervently: "Have you heard of 'so and so'? She landed on a goldmine!" In her heart, Molly didn't compare herself to those "so and so's." What was she, what kind of person was she that she should need to search? Smiling, she thought: I won't put myself on the market for sale. I'm only going to enjoy sunny Florida and catch my breath a little, feel myself again. Let my sons have a beautiful mother, not an emaciated little mare.

It wasn't easy for her to take leave of the business that had helped her raise two children and granted her financial independence. And yet she sensed that she couldn't continue this work much longer. The salon was draining her body and her soul.

When, after a brief respite, Molly browsed through the shops to buy clothes, she felt as if she were doing it for the Molly who hadn't known a moment's rest in years. That habit of modeling, of making herself into an advertisement for her business, followed her. When she finally reached sunny Florida, she was able to see and perceive her true self.

Florida enchanted Molly. So much sun. So much light. And so much time! It was better, more beautiful than even the most exquisite dream.

Could this really be her? Was she the woman with the bright eyes and rested smile visible in the mirror? Molly contrasted how she looked now to how she had looked some time ago. She felt enveloped by a sense of compassion for herself and for others like her who went through their days existing in a life seemingly unlived.

For the first few days on the warm sand of the Miami beaches, Molly felt as if she were in a kind of a trance. The women staying with her in the hotel suspected that she wasn't well. She was somewhat distracted. But when Molly appeared in their midst one lovely day, subdued and yet full of smiles, they quickly welcomed her into their fold. It was there, in fact, among the "good-time women" that she met him…

At first, when they pointed out to Molly the broad-shouldered, heavy-footed Jewish man with the small, white eyes and hanging upper lip that make him look pouting, angry, and ashamed, when they said to her: "Do you see that gentleman? He's available…", she got irked and was prepared to tell the women what she thought about them. She considered them to be mindless, vain busybodies who had nothing to do except engage in malicious gossip. Why did she have to meet them at all? She had actually run away from such women. But she quickly caught herself. She had waited so many years for this vacation, and, in fact, for the central objective—to escape from her poverty. A voice quietly said to her: "Don't give yourself airs. After all, you came here in the hopes of finding something…"

She didn't respond to the women. She pretended that she hadn't heard what they said to her. The next day, when the red sun started to cool and the beach became less crowded, some of the women from the hotel went to play cards or went on dates, and Molly felt bored. What could she do? Play cards? She didn't know how to play. In the midst of her reflections, "he" materialized behind her back. She panicked a bit, as if he had overheard her thoughts. She was ready to tell him that she wasn't lonely at all, that, as a matter of fact, she really had to go somewhere, but he didn't give her a chance to speak. As if it were the most natural thing to do, he invited her to have dinner with him. He looked at her with a kind of hidden joy and said, practically clicking his tongue: "You look splendid!" As he spoke, his round face became rounder. His hands raced in and out of his pockets as if they were looking for new words there.

Molly wasn't the only woman in the restaurant sitting with an old man. Older men were there with women even younger than Molly. The old man knew where to take her. She saw that the old man was a generous spender, had a kind, indulgent smile, and that he was no stranger here in the restaurant. In general, he was quite well-established in Miami. Apparently, he had a profitable business there.

That evening, Molly's escort revealed to her all of his colors—the attractive and the nauseating…

His name was Mr. Carson. He had been a widower for many years. In the Bronx, he owned an entire block's worth of houses. How had he come by such wealth? Well, that was a long story that he proceeded to tell. The owner of a grocery store, he set aside and saved money while living in poverty and doing all the work himself—and she shouldn't think that a grocery store can bring great fortunes. But then God dispatched the war. Using his savings of a few thousand dollars, he started buying houses—buying and selling. During one winter, he bought and sold the same houses three times. How did he learn this trick of the trade? Money has a way of teaching you. Unfortunately, his wife took little pleasure from his wealth. She didn't want to draw stares from respectable folks. She didn't even want to wear the mink coat that he bought her for a sum of twelve hundred dollars. Well—and then what? The Angel of Death came, and one-two—done! And here Mr. Carson's sulky lips trembled. He looked down at his bright, chubby hands, and it seemed to Molly that she saw a tear fall on his white silk shirt. She was touched. It pained him that his wife hadn't taken any pleasure from his wealth—and after all that she'd had to bear before he became rich.

His narration completed, Mr. Carson took her hand and looked at her with his moist eyes. In his gaze was grief and an imploring for pity. His face reminded her of a dog that stands next to the table and waits for someone to throw him scraps. She thought: How many faces a person can put on!

The next day, Mr. Carson was already sitting next to her on the veranda. At this point, he didn't look as awkward as before. He was elegantly dressed. He suggested that she take a walk with him to the ocean and also asked her if she would be willing to eat out with him again. Although Molly was in no hurry to go along, he finally got her to agree. And although he was a bit annoying in his confident presumption of her willingness, she didn't resist. Fine, she'd go out with him.

They were both soon an item of conversation. The wives said: She's no fool, after all! And the men said: An old-timer, eh? And he's snagged himself a real gem of a little lady! What then—when he's got all of Tiffany Street in his pocket, who can compare?

Later, he didn't have to ask. She waited for him. Each day, he surprised her with something better, more beautiful. Wherever they went, unimaginable luxury materialized before her. At first, Mr. Carson opened a small porthole, and then later, an entire door, onto an enchanted world. Jaunts on yachts, concerts, dances. There was a raucousness to it all. One luxury superseded the last, creating a competition between these various comforts and pleasures.

She wasn't bored with him. They were never alone. Molly didn't think about her yesterdays or tomorrows. She forgot about her age. The ocean waves swallowed up the years. She felt a lightness to her very being, as if she were ready to take off in flight…

More days—more weeks—had now been spent in Florida than Molly had planned. She was starting to run out of money, and although the season still wasn't over, the hotel was starting to empty out a little. A cold mockery formed in Molly's mind: What? Are you really going to return home? Back to the women's heads in the salon? A cloud covered her suntanned and rested face.

Mr. Carson also began to get ready to go home. He stood over her, talking like a businessman. He could promise her much joy, he said. He had more money than he could spend. His only son was rich and didn't need any money. He promised her he would treat her like the Queen of Sheba. She would have a beautiful home, a maid, jewelry. At that point, he took out a small package of diamonds. "Here, you see these? I don't want to know your age, and don't you ask me mine…"

Molly looked at his wide face with its double chin. She saw how his lower lip trembled after every word he uttered. She saw that he looked directly at her so as not to miss a single twitch of her face, aiming to grasp everything—like a bargain hunter wanting to make sure he wasn't being cheated.

When she observed that his face had begun to beam since he was interpreting her silence as acquiescence, she turned her head. A pained resentment seized her. He's already rejoicing, she thought to herself, feeling as if little worms were crawling over her body… But it wasn't long before she was asking herself: Back to work? To the heads, to the hairdos, until long into the night? And how much can a person stand hearing about someone else's good fortune and then be barely able to drag herself home in total exhaustion? No. Back to that—no way!

Molly went about her days with two distinct feelings. On the one hand, a sense of salvation: Done with the beauty salon! Done with the feminine heads! This put her in a festive mood. On the other hand: she was afraid that she would become entangled in a net of lies. A gossamer, golden net, but a net nonetheless.

To New York, they returned as husband and wife. Quietly, without any to-do, Molly leaped over the great distance from an insignificant beauty salon in an out-of-the-way alley all the way to Riverside Drive. Now that was truly quite a distance!

Nevertheless, Molly felt that it was he who got the better end of the deal, not she. It was now two months since Molly became Mrs. Carson. Carson had not exaggerated his wealth. In fact, he possessed even more than he claimed during their courtship. But as for his physical presence, there was no deceiving herself about that. He was soft, pathetic. Because of her, he even tried learning to dance the tango. Molly laughed raucously when she saw how the old man tried to master the exotic dance with her.

At home, Mr. Carson, could indulge himself in being quiet for his "baby"—like a snuggly puppy. But when it came to over there—to "his" street—then he became someone else altogether. His walk was different, and so too was his voice, the way he spoke.

Out there, when he spoke with the tenants, the workers, the painters, the plumbers, and the janitors, he held his head high, and his word was law. He left the house with quiet steps, but as soon as he spotted the chauffeur, he was no longer the subdued old man. He was now the Boss.

They had only started living together two months ago, but already the time was dragging slowly, and although she spent little time at home, the days were hollow… Just two months and then what? A sadness, a yearning for something gnawed at her limbs. Her eyes wandered over the spacious room. A sliver of sun toyed with her leg like a mischievous kitten… Was he gone already? It was good that he was out of the house. She wanted to convince herself that he was actually gone from the house. She rang the little bell on the table next to the head of her bed. A young, slim girl entered with a glass of fruit juice. The girl was brown-skinned, with smooth, bluish-black hair and a small, charming face. She walked on her tip-toes, with a swaying in her step. She was neatly starched, as if she had just gotten herself done up for her madam. She offered Molly the glass and looked at her with a sweet smile. Molly envied the girl's ease, her lightness of foot. It seemed to her that the girl was looking at her with mockery in her eyes. She wanted to say something, to show the girl her place, but she said nothing. She told the girl to put the glass on the table and asked her if the boss had left. The girl answered in the affirmative, and Molly nodded her head, a sign to the girl that she could go now. Following the departing girl with her eyes, Molly's mouth was tightly closed and her throat felt irritated.

Madam Carson was peeved that she told the maid to bring the juice to her bed. It seemed to her that the girl had looked at her with a gaze that asked: "When did you become such a noblewoman? Why should I serve you the juice in bed?" Molly felt annoyed at herself and at the girl. But soon she realized that the girl meant nothing by it. It only seemed to her that she had. Molly thought: Being a great lady suits me the way a top hat suits a cat...

She quickly made excuses for herself in her mind: I asked for the glass of juice to find out if he was already gone. I can't bear the way he looks at me... Once again, she couldn't get the girl out of her thoughts. Tomorrow, the day after, the day after that. She would need to meet the girl's eyes, her bizarre gaze. She would send her away. Today, in fact!

The telephone rang. "Hello, hello, honey? You coming soon? Yes, yes, I'm almost done! Goodbye, honey!"

Yes, thought Molly, the girl had to be sent away. She couldn't do it herself, but he—he would do it for her. Goodbye, honey...

They Came to See Each Other

Pauline sat in the waiting room, in her usual spot on a bench that was the last from the door to the waiting room and the first near the entrance to the instruction room. When Pauline entered and found someone sitting there, that person would stand up because he knew that this spot belonged to her. Pauline would sit down in her place; she found her way there based on the time that it took her to go from the door until she reached that seat.

A group of women seated around her marveled at how nimbly her fingers worked. She was working on a small frame covered with a silken net, and over the net raced long, steel needles that flashed like fireflies in her kinetic fingers. Fast, fast raced the needles, their tips dipping as if underwater, swimming back up, raising the tips, as if awaiting the barely-perceptible movement of Pauline's fingers. Up and down, up and down, and a tiny bump the size of a green pea emerged. One after another, one after another. And behold, the peas were gathered into a small bundle, and a living bud was visible to the onlookers!

And once again, the needles raced and raced and now here at hand, a green leaf was visible. One leaf, two, a third, and the pale, pink bud was garlanded with three fresh green leaves.

The women pressed their shoulders together, looking at each other, and one said: "Just look at those fingers! Each finger looks like a small, magical person." They slid closer to Pauline, who felt everyone's eyes on her and her heart warmed in the process. She moistened her lips, drew her cheeks in, and the dimple on her square chin became deeper. The women asked her: "Where'd you learn how to do such beautiful work?" She blushed and quietly

187

responded: "Oh, this isn't even the best I can do. I've already had my work shown in an exhibition!"

Pauline's companion approached. She had overheard and seen the admiration expressed to Pauline. She knew how much happiness this brought her, and like a mother, she was pleased with this small amount of gladness and the drop of kindness extended to her.

Pauline herself didn't know her actual age. She was tall and had broad shoulders. She walked straight, with a slow, measured gait as if she were walking on a narrow path. She held her head slightly askance, as if she were looking for something on the ceiling. Her hair was dark brown and smooth, with the gentle softness characteristic of a young child's. She had a wide mouth with thick lips and wore heavy, dark glasses. On one shoulder, she invariably carried the work handbag from which she almost never parted. The handbag hung on a leather strap. In the same hand, she always held a thin walking stick. She placed her other hand on her companion, or, as she called her, "my guide."

Frieda, Pauline's companion, was a middle-aged woman with an energetic gait, a dark face, and kind, alert bright-gray eyes. Frieda was more than a companion for blind Pauline. In a short time period, Pauline had become a part of Frieda's life. Although Frieda had a life of her own that included a good and a faithful husband, she functioned as Pauline's connection with the lively, seeing world. Of her own free will, Frieda took upon herself an all-consuming duty which occupied all her thoughts. Oftentimes, she thought: "Without me, what would Pauline do?"

They first met by accident; perhaps their connection would last forever.

Frieda's husband, Mendl, was a laborer—the sort of laborer who wasn't able to achieve anything beyond a subsistence livelihood. His work was basic, unskilled. It was the kind of work that could be done by any other pair of hands. By now, Mendl was a man of advanced years. He came to America during a difficult

time of crisis and suffered so much. After going hungry, freezing, and wandering into free nighttime homeless shelters, he was
forever terrified and dejected. When, after much effort, Mendl
managed to get a job that provided him with bread, a roof over his
head, and an intact pair of shoes, he was delighted. But he never
stopped looking back to the past, to those days of hunger that had
seeped so deeply into his bones, and as a result, he was never able
to free himself from his terror.

A person of small ambition, Mendl was content with what he
had. His focus was on his wife, his kindhearted, dear Frieda. His
greatest ambition was for Frieda to not have to toil in a workshop.
He prevailed in this, and that made him happy.

There were times when Frieda earning a few dollars would
have come in handy, helping to pay the rent or buy a new suit. But
they didn't suffer too much privation. In the slack times, they had
folks from whom they could borrow. Still, Frieda longed to earn
money of her own. She knew that, with her own hands, she could
quickly learn a trade, but since Mendl said no to that, well then,
no it was. She thought to herself: "If my being at home makes
him happier, so be it."

One day, she read the following classified ad in the newspaper: "Seeking a woman to guide a blind girl to the school for the
blind and back several times a week." The ad stirred something
in Frieda's heart. She had enough time on her hands, and here
was this person with the misfortune of blindness. Before she told
Mendl and before she knew whether he would consent to her
going to the blind girl, Frieda found herself suffused with a profound empathy for her. She could hardly wait for Mendl to come
back from work. After he finished eating, Frieda slid him the
newspaper and looked over at him. She wanted to see what sort
of impression this newspaper item would make on him. Mendl
read it slowly, not grasping what his wife had in mind. But when
he saw her looking at him with pleading eyes, he understood.

"Well, do you want to hire yourself out to guide this blind girl?" he asked.

"It's not a matter of hiring myself out," she answered. "I want to be helpful to a poor, unfortunate child. The money isn't important. I won't do it when you're at home, just when you're at work. It won't make any difference to you, in any case, whether I'm home or somewhere else, will it?"

Their eyes met, and both of them simultaneously thought: "We don't have any children of our own..."

Mendl stood up from the chair and walked across the room. "Maybe the poor girl is destined to experience something a little positive. Go, go, go!"

At that time, Pauline was fifteen or sixteen years old. Not long before, she had been placed in a school for instructing the blind. She was sent there from a home for blind children. Her blindness stemmed from a severe case of scarlet fever, and she suffered from other illnesses.

Pauline barely remembered her past. But from time to time a distant image would surface in her memory. She was a little girl. Their home was brightly lit. She was playing with her toys. Suddenly, she tumbled down. Her mother picked her up, tucked her into her little bed, and bent down to give her a kiss. She remembered her mother's hot cheeks, her voice. But her mother's face she could barely remember. Often—in her dreams—she perceived her mother's hands... felt her mother caressing her. Her mother's hands were warm and soft. She also sensed her mother's breath on her face; she heard her mother calling her: "Pesele!" When she awakened, her mother's voice still echoed in her ears. No one, except her mother, had ever called her "Pesele."

Pauline didn't know when her mother died. She only knew that when she had first gotten sick, she had both a father and a mother. She didn't remember her father at all.

Pauline had two brothers. They were both busy people involved in a business. Neither her brothers nor their wives gave very much thought to Pauline's sickness. But they helped her however they could. Pauline felt a hollowness, an eternal darkness. Life—an active life—would now never be available to her. A wall of darkness had been erected before her. But nature worked its course. Despite her handicap, something within her matured, struggled against this fate. She could not accept the limitations of the now narrowed world facing her, even though she could not quite clearly articulate what she wanted to achieve.

It was at that time that Frieda arrived. As soon as Frieda crossed the threshold and got set up in the blind girl's home, a longing to take the blind girl in her arms, to press her close, and to speak to her the words a mother would to her own child in that situation were awakened within her. But she deliberately didn't say a word. She stood and squirmed in the presence of Pauline's hoarse, choked-up voice: "Who's there? What do you want?" As if from a hot spring, scalding tears flooded from Frieda's eyes. She took Pauline's hands and covered them with hot kisses. Her kisses spoke louder than words. With understanding and compassion, Frieda won over the lonely girl's loyalty.

Pauline hungered for human warmth, and Frieda responded to that hunger. Frieda herself hadn't known how much warmth she had for others. In Frieda's maternal hands, Pauline revived the way a weakened plant revives with gushing water. Frieda wasn't prepared for the task of looking into the dark chambers of a young life that hovered in a world of eternal nothing. Still, with her healthy senses and strong will, she found ways to bring light into the days that Pauline could not see. Taking Pauline into her life, Frieda shared her own experiences in a way that allowed Pauline to follow everything in her mind, as if she knew everything, as if she had seeing eyes.

Mendl, Frieda's husband, was a partner in the enterprise. He asked Frieda to bring Pauline home. When the blind girl visited them for the first time, Mendl dressed up as if he wanted to make a good impression on the guest... Frieda was delighted by her husband's hospitality. When Mendl noticed Pauline standing in the middle of the room waiting for someone to guide her to a seat, he turned pale and his lower lip trembled. He stood off at a distance and didn't dare touch her. Gradually, he became accustomed to the blind girl and, from time to time, even guided her home.

Pauline came to love Mendl's hands. Such strong hands, such solid hands, such good hands!

Time passed. One year after another. Pauline became a skillful knitter and embroiderer. With Frieda's help, she was able to attend the school for the blind twice a week.

One day, something out of the blue happened to Pauline. She was sitting by herself in the waiting room; Frieda wasn't there. She was working. The knitting needles raced. The work grew. She was surprised that no one was saying a word. But she sensed that someone was sitting next to her. A sense of unease befell her. By now, she was accustomed to the admirers who would gather around her. She was quite used to hearing their observations being made in her presence. She moved in her seat and said to herself, practically without speaking aloud: "Why isn't anyone saying anything?"

"Do you want something? What can I do for you?" a voice quickly responded.

"Who's there?" asked a somewhat embarrassed Pauline.

"I'm here."

"And who are you?"

"I'm waiting for someone to pick me up."

She stood up without knowing why. She felt as if someone had pushed her off the bench. It was apparent to her that someone right next to her was teasing her and that the voice belonged to a man.

"Where's Frieda? Why isn't she coming?" she asked in a pallid voice.

"Who's Frieda?" the masculine voice asked.

She sensed that she was standing next to the man who was speaking to her and that she might collapse on him. "Frieda is my guide, my companion, my friend. My Frieda!" she said, choking on her tears.

"Oh, oh! A companion, a guide! So you're also like me... That is, just like me, you're... You can't see anything? Really nothing?"

He stretched out both arms toward her, touching her jacket, searching for her hand, and finding it. And then in a different tone, he said, "Don't be afraid! There's nothing to be afraid of!" She sat back down, her heart pounding. Her fear had departed and it now seemed to her that she could hear devotion in his voice. It was the way her brother spoke to her when he was in a good mood. So this man was also like her—blind. Strange, very strange.

Should she ask him his name? She really ought to wait for Frieda to come before doing that. But she couldn't sit there in silence. She had to say something. She wanted him to speak and keep on speaking, to hear the voice that was similar to her brother's when he was in a good mood. She turned around on the bench several times, as if trying to attract his attention. It seemed a shame to her that he couldn't see the lovely fruits of her labor. She started her work, but her hands didn't race as they previously had. She covered the frame and asked him: "And when are they coming to fetch you?"

"A car that's gathering us all together is coming for me. We're coming from several different places," he responded.

Pauline didn't understand. "And why did you come here?" she asked.

"I have to see a doctor," he answered. "Something's wrong with my leg."

Frieda, who'd been delayed, raced in. In the half-empty corridor, she saw the stranger sitting next to Pauline. Feeling guilty, she quickly asked the stranger whether something had happened to Pauline. She didn't immediately suspect that this person to whom she was speaking was blind. He sat with a large leather pouch on his knees. In one hand, he held a cigarette, and in the other, matches that he kept striking. Hearing Frieda's steps next to him, he turned his head in her direction. It seemed to her that he, too, was bracing himself to ask something. Like Pauline, he was wearing dark glasses, and still Frieda didn't realize that he was blind.

Pauline launched into a long stream of words. She spoke quickly. Her face was enflamed; her lips were moist. One minute, she was complaining; the next, she was pleased with the encounter. She tugged on Frieda's sleeve and asked: "How do you like him? He has a warm hand, like your husband. I felt it when he helped me sit down. His voice is like my brother Nathan's. Have you heard Nathan speak when he's not angry? Talk to him, Frieda, talk. I'm telling you. You'll hear…" The mouth of the blind girl ground on, non-stop, like a mill. When Frieda finally said to her: "It's time for us to go home, my child," Pauline responded: "Ask him, Frieda, ask him his name. Ask him also if he'll be here when we come back." Frieda asked him, and he said that his name was Frank. He offered her a printed card with his name on it. He also said that he would come here again. He had to! We'd *see* each other again!

Frieda came home agitated from the encounter. She could hardly wait for Mendl. Frieda was more worldly, well-informed than Mendl, but when an impasse was reached or when something needed to be disentangled, her husband had to be the one who had the last word. He was a man, after all.

When Mendl finished eating and smoking his pipe and was preparing to doze off, Frieda set the problem before him. Like a wild horse, the girl had jolted from the harness. She had had to promise Pauline that she would soon meet the young man who sat next to her again. And so she was asking: What was to be done? After all, Pauline was like her own child to her—not *like* her own child, but, in fact, her own child. The girl was so seared into her heart, so rooted into her soul. What should they do? Who knew who this strange man was? She understood that Pauline was also a living human being, a person with a soul, with the feelings of a woman. How could she dissuade her from such a thing? Well, what did he, Mendl, think? Was it reasonable to bring the two blind people together? Perhaps they were destined to be together? *Bashert*. Who could say?

Mendl considered the matter thoroughly. He swayed back and forth as if he had to deliver a ruling on a difficult Jewish legal question. Then he advised that they wait a little while before taking action. They had to be given time. What was it that Frieda herself said—she was no more than a living human being. She, Pauline, wasn't married, and, after all, you see: There came a time for everything.

After discussing the matter, husband and wife went to bed in a lighter mood. The next day, Frieda tried to speak with Pauline about various things, but Pauline kept interrupting her. She just wanted to know how *he* looked. She also wanted Frieda's opinion as to whether their both being blind didn't actually provide a favorable opportunity for the two of them to start a friendship. A sighted person wouldn't want to be her friend, but she was so eager to have a friend. There, in her school, there were blind males, but they were apparently very young. If she were to try to make friends with the young ones, she would always remain alone.

Throughout the entire time that Pauline was speaking, Frieda felt as if something were stuck in her throat, biting and pinching her. She looked at Pauline with pain in her eyes, looking so long that Pauline sensed it. Inexorably, Pauline felt her face turning warm from Frieda's stare. While parting, Frieda firmly squeezed Pauline's hands.

His real name was not Frank, but Fayvl. He had come here as a lonely young boy. He trudged around for two years until he reached Canada and, from there, he went on to America. This was the year before the start of the First World War. His entry into the country wasn't entirely "kosher," and so he was advised to enlist in the army and become a citizen that way.

He arrived fresh and healthy, with the drive to make a big splash. The few people from his hometown in the Old Country who wanted to help him had huge problems of their own. Fayvl became a soldier and was called Frank Cooper. Before he could even get used to his new name, he was on a ship. He had no idea where he was being sent. After eighteen months on the battlefield, he was wounded. At the time, it seemed to him that the wound under his ear was not serious. In fact, he suffered tremendous pain, but the misfortune which eventually struck him—that he wasn't expecting.

In the hospital, he noticed that they fussed over him too much. He asked the head doctor who looked at him with a pained expression on his face. The doctor, a young Jewish man, hesitated briefly and then said: "I have bad news for you. Your optical nerve is damaged. You can expect to be blind." He conveyed this news and quickly left his bedside.

At the time, Frank felt as if everything around him was filled with smoke. He didn't see any color other than smoke.

It took two years for him to become completely blind. Gradually, the cloud over his eyes became thicker, denser, closer. He knew that he had to take advantage of every light-filled moment, that his days as a participant in that light-filled world were numbered. He learned the Braille system and how to type on a typewriter. He learned how to fix electric lights, and until recently, he could still sense the sun's rays. This gave him much joy. He so did not want to say goodbye to the numbered rays of sunshine, but the time did come. One day, he felt a flush on his face and then—darkness! It was exactly as the doctor had predicted to him.

By this point, Frank was middle-aged. He was tall, slender, and lean as a skeleton. His hair was dark. He had a full mouth of teeth, and a smile that could enchant women. He had seen few of them in his youth and had even less pleasure from them.

But he wasn't depressed. He said that if he didn't come down with a chronic medical problem to counter his overall health, he could still accomplish a great deal. He didn't feel helpless, and he maintained that he could see more than one would imagine a blind person could.

He thought seriously about getting in touch with Pauline. Until now, he hadn't thought he would share his life with someone. But he felt that with Pauline he would be the one who would do the seeing. He had gathered light within himself that he would share with her. The pension that he received was not large but he could always earn a little more on the side.

He dressed elegantly when he was out and about, loved the fresh air, and read everything he could get in Braille. He read three languages. He said to Frieda: "Don't you think that through me Pauline will also see something? Why shouldn't she share with me the bit that I've had the good fortune to learn? A blind person can also be allowed to have something to live for!"

When he spoke, he looked serious, although from time to time, he smiled so that it seemed that he wanted to know what sort of impression he was making on his listener.

The couple began to get together twice a week. Pauline revived. All of her limbs expressed this animation. She kept asking Frieda: "Does he really love me? Do you see it? How do you see it?" From these questions she transitioned into statements and responses: "He's really a lot older than me. He told me so himself. But from his voice, he doesn't seem that old..." She then asked: "Frieda, is your husband also older than you?"

In Pauline's isolated world, just a few people predominated, and from these few flowed the streams of the lively world that, in her mind, took on forms and colors that she wanted to transmit in words. Because of the shortcomings in her ability to express herself verbally, her words sounded childish. Frank's world was different, quite different. In contrast to Pauline, Frank seemed as if he had only just been separated from normal life. But through her, through Pauline, he would connect back to that life and get her, Pauline, to see through his unseeing eyes. When he spoke with her, he led her through a world of colors. He drew from the world and shared with her.

The color in her cheeks changed. Now, her cheeks were enflamed with a fiery redness and now they were extended with a grayish pallor. She clung to his hands as if wanting to be sure that he wouldn't allow himself to be driven away from her. She communicated her mute fear to Frank through her hands. He sensed her childlike helplessness. He felt that she was seeking protection through him, and he pressed her hands with a tenderness that had accumulated in him through the years. It was good to feel that someone needed him, that he wasn't living in vain. He truly felt how necessary he was for the blind girl…

Frieda was as happy as a devoted mother, and Mendl felt like an in-law. She was, after all, their own child! Did they have anyone who was closer to them? But the main thing was that this entire occurrence was a miracle to them. Despite everything, Pauline and Frank came to see each other—and that was enough.

The Reincarnation of a Baby Carriage

On a lovely June morning, a doorman in a blue uniform with silver buttons wheeled a baby carriage out of a brand-new house, accompanied by a nursemaid.

The street—Central Park West—was already lively and abuzz, but when passersby caught sight of the carriage, their fast pace slowed. They'd never seen such a splendid baby carriage.

"Have you ever seen such a thing?" a Black woman asked her friend.

"I haven't and neither have my grandparents," the friend responded. They peered up close, then stepped back and considered the carriage from afar, and said: "When they get really crazy, they don't know what to do with their money!"

The nursemaid felt very distinguished. Everyone was looking at her carriage and smiling at her as if it were her invention. The truth was that she was a bit alarmed when she first spotted this "invention." If she had been asked, she would certainly have persuaded the young mother not to order "such a looker" that shouted holy terror with its appearance, burning your eyes with the reality of its distinctiveness.

The nursemaid was never alone. Invariably, someone would approach the carriage, tap on the wood, admire the wheels, the bedding, the expensive lace that adorned the little pillow, and the cover that had come all the way from Italy.

A peep from the newborn chick. The nursemaid was delighted that she could now turn her back to the gawkers. The little soul—pink, transparent—appeared so small amidst the over-the-top finery that it could barely be seen. It turned its tiny head, moved its mouth, but didn't want to open an eye. It probably wanted a drink of milk. You'll get it soon!

The nursemaid removed a little bottle from her handbag and brought the small rubber nipple to the child's tiny mouth, but the little one was impatient. Into its little mouth was thrust a fist— pink and small, like a young onion.

The sidewalk was wide and tidy. The building—white, smooth marble; with mirrors and plush in the lobby; servants in their livery uniforms; and the starched, neat nursemaid. It was a tableau as cold as ice.

മാരു

It was a pleasant end-of-June morning. People were rushing to the subway. The park was full of people. The well-know "par-kies," as if famished for some rays, inhaled the warmth through open mouths and smiled approvingly at the sun. A young woman, looking for a place on a bench, approached. The sitters all asked in unison, "What is it?" and someone answered, "What do you mean—'what'? It's a baby carriage!"

The woman pushing the carriage felt everyone's eyes on her as if they were piercing her. She would gladly have left, but she knew she couldn't hide from those stares. And wherever she'd go, she'd find onlookers. What should she do? She noticed a big rock. Maybe there? She headed off in that direction. The disgust-ed voices of amazement accompanied her. "Some carriage! Did you ever see such a thing? I haven't!" said one. "A new inven-tion! How did such an antique land here, among us 'regular fel-lows'? It's worthy of the Rockefellers!" said another.

These words deprived the mother pushing the swanky car-riage of her peace of mind. And the owner of this antique still had to smile with gratitude to the woman from her hometown in the Old Country who had bequeathed her this treasure.

The woman from her hometown in the Old Country had told her that she would get her a carriage "to which there is no equal," but when people gathered around her, she didn't feel good. She hated showy things that attracted attention, especially when the neighbors knew that she was a new arrival and lived with a sister in three rooms. So where had she gotten such a carriage? But where could she have gotten a different carriage? Her husband was just learning a trade. It was either carry the child in her own hands or stay at home without any fresh air.

How had the woman from her hometown gotten hold of the carriage? She didn't want to go anywhere near that question. She didn't want to know something that would follow her around for the rest of her life.

The woman from her hometown once told her that she knew a woman of means who, in turn, knew someone who was president in a club whose mission was to provide "underprivileged" young mothers with equipment for their newborn, "underprivileged" babies. The young mother didn't even want to think about how someone could consider a newborn child to be "underprivileged." Taking her little son into a "underprivileged" class even before he had tasted the beautiful world—that was not something she would allow!

She approached the large, hill-like stone. No one else was there. She looked around and saw that several women were sitting and playing cards somewhat off in the distance. She was sure no one would recognize her, but she was spotted and, in fact, "taken on by the wagging tongues." She sensed it, even if she didn't hear what they were saying.

"Do you see that carriage? I've never seen such a carriage in my entire life. You've got to have deep pockets for such a carriage!"

"And they didn't get here very long ago. Maybe she brought it with her?"

"What are you saying? Go on now, go. Brought it with her! Really now!"

"Leave it to them, the newbies, the 'refugees.' They've got it all."

Over time, the mother became accustomed to the unwanted stares, and the park sitters too, had had their fill of staring at the carriage. Gradually, they became indifferent to the great wonder. In the meantime, the little boy grew in comfort.

A happy-go-lucky mischief-maker, the little boy didn't have the slightest respect for the pedigreed carriage. As if he sensed that the carriage provided his mother with little pleasure, he applied pressure on it, seeking to strip it of its "looker" status. Mercilessly, he scratched the finish and tore off pieces of the interior decoration. The carriage really was tough, but the child's healthy legs needed space and pushed it apart. So the parents had to exchange the precious carriage for something larger, more open.

ಬಂ಄ಲ

On a mild, warm, and sun-smiling October day, the neighbors in the large tenement house on the corner of Simpson and 167th Street spotted a middle-aged Black woman on the narrow, not-very-clean sidewalk pushing a beautiful baby carriage. It was "our personage." Although by now old and well-used, it still bore enough signs of its healthy origins. It shined the way it used to, as if it wanted to proclaim: "It's still me!"

In the carriage lay a tiny one—a little girl, not yet a month old. The baby had come into the world with difficulty, and the weak, gaunt mother could barely stand on her feet. The baby's father worked outside the city and only came home on weekends. Of course, there could be no talk of buying a carriage for the baby. That's how the carriage moved to Simpson Street. Long-standing, generous friends said: "So there's no money for a new baby carriage? Well, take a look at this 'looker.' As soon as you can just stand on your two feet, you can take it down with the child into the street. And while it's possible that onlookers will cause you quite a bit of grief, it doesn't matter. It's a comfortable carriage, and the child needs fresh air."

So Susan pushed the carriage that looked out of place beside the impoverished tenement houses on Simpson Street.

Simpson Street was a narrow street with old, tall, six-story buildings—dilapidated buildings with dark corridors that hadn't tasted a lick of paint in God knows how long. Susan, the caretaker of the child, was herself a mother of small children. One of her daughters was in the hospital. Her mind was preoccupied, and she felt sad. As she herself was a mother, the baby was more important to her than the carriage. She was anxious about the baby, and she would have liked to infuse her with a bit of her own strength, only she didn't have much strength.

The baby surprised Susan and its own parents. She was only a few weeks old, but "she grows at night," Susan maintained, "like cucumbers in summertime."

The baby's mother regained her health. The baby was now nine months old and, at that point, didn't want to be far from the ground. She no longer wanted to sit in the baby carriage. In short, it was time for the baby carriage to go through a new transformation. To be transformed into what? Oh, well, take a guess!

ଚଗ

There was a large market on Simpson Street. In this market, an elderly Jewish man had been standing for a good number of years with his box of merchandise. The man sold everything from hairpins to men's and women's underwear. The surrounding women called him the "Jewish man with the Talmudic melody" because he was always humming something that sounded like the singsong used when studying the Talmud aloud. The man was a widower and lived at his daughter's place and that was the location of the carriage's new incarnation.

When the man spotted the carriage, his eyes lit up. "A gift from God!" he called out.

The box that provided his livelihood, his "business," was small. The stock was jumbled and difficult to organize. When he was finished with his day, it was challenging for him to pack up the merchandise. "Oh, what good fortune has God ordained for me!" he sighed.

The next day, after the man had received his new "treasure," a gussied-up stand was visible in the corner of the market. There was the baby carriage, and in it, the man's merchandise: men's underwear, women's stockings, colored handkerchiefs, jewelry, beads—anything your heart could possibly desire! Because of the baby carriage, the whole corner acquired a new look. And the man with the Talmudic melody, too, who had always looked wrinkled and dusty, now looked altogether different. He sat next to his stand with a greater degree of dignity, and even his Talmudic melody sounded different.

And the baby carriage in its new incarnation? If it could just speak, at least on the level of Mendele's mare, oh, how it would tell of the various incarnations it had undergone. But like all mutes, it said nothing...

In the Mountains

The house stood far from the highway, amidst the forests that extended over dozens of miles. All around was forest and mountain, trees and mountains. Old, giant trees, like great-grandfathers, only they were not stooped from the accretion of years. Tall and broad were they. Their growth seemingly called forth to the younger, smaller trees: "Look up at us! Catch up to us!"

And those younger, smaller trees extended their branches upward to the heights. They were in no hurry. They had time; eternity was theirs. Each summer—new bloom; each decade—greater strength, a more resilient resistance, wider and deeper roots.

In their tree language, they called to humankind like devoted mothers: "Come under our shade, breathe in our scents! There will be enough for everyone. Enjoy!"

Sometimes the urban dweller united with the tree, listening to its quiet murmur and then smiling absent-mindedly at the people nearby, seeking a closeness, longing for something, yet not knowing what.

The middled-aged and elderly guests sat on yellow and green painted chairs arranged around the hotel. The young people, who could be counted on the fingers, weren't there. They were running around, only showing up when the bell rang. There were only a few younger people sitting here—those who couldn't run around because they were too weak.

Mr. Kantor, a Jewish man close to sixty, never lied about his age. From his appearance it would seem that he had few worries. His face—fresh; his eyes—lively. His shoulders were a bit rounded. He sat and looked at everything and everyone with open eyes.

He had nothing to hide. He was a man who stood on his own two feet. Mr. Kantor was constantly buying and selling houses, and he regularly made a profit. He was—no complaints—well off. If not for the misfortune that had befallen him when his wife suddenly died and left him alone, things would have been going well for him. He had good, successful children. One was a doctor; another—a lawyer. The children had lives of their own. His wife had always been at his side. Now, he was somewhat lost. Oftentimes, he looked around as if she were still nearby.

He wasn't stingy with himself, Mr. Kantor. He could indulge in spending the entire summer here. There was no one to provide for, and he wouldn't be taking the money with him. But unexpectedly, here in this beautiful setting, he felt lonely. There were young women who knew that Kantor had driven here in a good car and so they cast a smile in his direction from time to time. They would have happily accepted if he had invited them to go for a ride. But he knew that it was the car, not him, that they had in mind. If not for his car, they wouldn't even have given him a second glance. Why should they care about an old man?

Although Kantor was healthy and strong, he had no fondness for the young. Among the young, he felt like an old man. So he sat among the elderly, clinging to someone, anyone, so as not to be alone. On the painted chair that he called "the duck" because of its short legs and tall support, he sat and gazed out with his shrewd eyes at the green surroundings.

Around the hotel were several other Jews, a bit younger than him. Seated among them were men who had wives but still longed throughout their life for something. There were also those who yearned for the years when they were young, for a youth that they had seen in someone else's life but never in their own. They were waiting for tomorrow to bring them something new. For these individuals, life had vanished in a hurry. They pursued, threw themselves at, and raced along with the winds of time. Only now, in middle age, here among the mountains and forests, without the din of everyday life, all that had vanished gnawed at them, demanding: "Why did you squander away the years? Did you really think you could gather them back?" Self-pity enveloped them. To keep the sadness at bay, they blended in. They each became one of the multitudes.

Among those seated was a lady whose years were hard to guess. She could have been thirty or, for that matter, sixty. Both ages could have been applicable to hair that was wheat-blond and cheeks that were yellowish-pink and pinkish-yellow. But beneath her chin was a loose bag, and her eyes were tired. Her mostly bare hands and legs were as white as bleached lime. The woman had come here with a specific goal. She wasn't making any secret of the fact that she wanted to meet a decent man… she'd been looking for one for a long time, even before she became a widow…

The woman wore loudly colored clothes. You could spot her a mile away. Her figure was girlish. Her gait—easy and graceful.

She had heard that Mr. Kantor was rich, owned a good car. He did look a bit too chunky for her liking, but can you ever get someone who has it all? This lady couldn't make up her mind whether to keep her distance from him for the time being, wait until he would notice her on his own, and thereby not make herself too conspicuous to him, or stick close to him. Either way, she wasn't the sort of person to keep her distance. She'd been looking for a long time. Many times, she was on the verge of a match, but, for some reason, it always came to nothing…

When Kantor noticed her for the first time, he thought: Quite a little lady! After he learned more about her, he said: "A terrible pity. Poor thing, I feel sorry for her."

Not far away sat another lady, still young by the looks of it— somewhere between thirty-five and forty. Her name was Molly. She kept herself off to the side. Not, God forbid, because she was misanthropic. On the contrary, she loved people. But it annoyed her that they didn't see that she wasn't an ordinary person.

Molly was very much in love with herself. She knew all of her positive attributes, and believed that people lost out a great deal when they bypassed her. She hardly spoke with the other people, believing that she was too deep for them to understand. She hoped that someday her time would come.

There was another woman there whom everyone called "the lady with the gray hair." It seemed to her that she was in complete harmony with everything. She was full of gratitude for the good, cool trees and never lowered her gaze from them. Although her eyes were fastened on the trees, her ears caught the strangers' chatter. And yet she believed that there were no strangers; everyone had become close to her. When you made the effort, when you searched, you could find something familiar, something relatable in every person.

Someone brought "the lady with the gray hair" a newspaper, the *Morgn-frayhayt*. She was delighted. She had been looking for this very newspaper. She took the paper, went off into a cool corner under an old, thick tree so that she could read undisturbed. Her eyes fastened on the picture of a young soldier with a bright smile. Under the picture, the caption stated: Harold Weiss, fallen in battle in Italy, June 4th. She didn't read any further. She couldn't tear her gaze away from the picture of the young Jewish man, whose luminous eyes would no longer gaze upon the world.

Sunken into the picture, she didn't see or hear anything around her. Later, she detected footsteps. A couple with whom she'd become acquainted several days ago approached. The man had come here to heal from an operation.

This couple had two sons who were off in separate corners of the world. They wrote letters to their parents in Yiddish, and the parents were attached to these letters from their children with every fiber of their being. The letters brought the children close to their parents, as if they weren't in some remote corner of the world, but rather, under the same roof with them.

"The lady with the gray hair," although she knew that the couple would see the picture of the fallen Jewish hero for themselves, nevertheless wanted to spare these good people the agony at least for the time being. As a result, she bent over the picture, trying to block it. But this "trick" didn't work. She tried to smile, but her mouth twisted into a grimace, like a child who wants to cry but restrains himself. The father was the first to notice the picture, devouring it with his eyes.

He knew Harold, who was a friend of his sons, Shloymehle and Moyshehle. He remembered Harold when he was still a child. They had been neighbors. The father stood bent over the picture, saying something to himself, but the words didn't come out. They remained stuck in his throat. The mother, who had also spotted the picture, was speechless. All three of them, as if frozen from cold, pressed together in sorrow and were silent. They felt that words were insufficient. They must live through the sorrow in silence, and if they couldn't remain silent, well then, perhaps they ought to scream loud enough to horrify the world.

An Orphaned Synagogue

Every morning, the young Rabbi could be seen walking in a procession from a side street in the company of two old men. The trio made their way to the store where newspapers were sold.

The Rabbi walked in the middle and took pains to stay in stride with the old men. When it occurred to him that he had taken too quick a step, he retreated a bit so that once again he found himself between the old men. On their way back, the young Rabbi read to the old men the news items that were on the front page of the newspaper. The two old men, who weren't as tall as the Rabbi, lifted their heads, swallowing the news with their mouths agape.

The walk to the store for the newspaper was repeated every morning. Among the witnesses to this particular procession were those who smilingly remarked: "The Rebbe and his servants!" Others blessed him: "He should have a long life! People like that don't come around every day."

The old men never switched places. One walked on the right side, and the other on the left. The man on the left was named Falek. He was small, with red eyes and a pointy little beard. He held his elbows pressed into his sides; the lower part of his arms hung loosely and shook. The man on the right side had the somewhat unusual name of "Thompson." His children had picked out this name for him. It was evident that the old man himself was none too pleased with the name. He pronounced his name only by muttering it: *Thompson*! Well then, Thompson—so be it. That's what they wanted; he himself had no say in the matter... He had a round face, lively eyes, and his breathing could be heard from

211

a distance, as if something was sizzling in his throat. He didn't have a beard, only pointy whiskers, and he was secular in appearance.

Situated between the old men, the Rabbi radiated youth and freshness. He appeared to be about thirty-five years old. Even though he was an Orthodox rabbi, he interacted with people in a free, almost secular manner. The only conspicuously rabbinical element in his mode of dress was his black fedora with the two wide creases which he wore in the summer and winter. The fedora added prestige to his bright blue eyes and his small, blond beard.

When he first took the position of rabbi, the neighborhood synagogue was still new. He strove to forge a bond between young and old throughout the synagogue. It's critical to bring together all of Abraham's children under one roof, he said. But it turned out that not only could he not attract the youth, but, during the weekdays, he couldn't even assemble a minyan for prayer services.

The synagogue wasn't lacking for money. In the neighborhood resided several older, wealthy Jews who wanted a beautiful synagogue for the High Holidays. But throughout the entire summer, they were in the mountains, and for all of the winter—in Miami. As a result, the synagogue stood vacant.

The Rabbi used every means at his disposal to engage the youth. He created various attractions for the boys and smiled at their mothers, but as soon as the boys had their bar mitzvah, they fled. They would run past the Rabbi and stare at him with a kind of mockery in their eyes. Their stares made the Rabbi feel abandoned and empty—as abandoned and empty as the synagogue itself.

The two old men, Falek and Thompson, lived with their children. Falek lived with a son, and Thompson with a daughter. Falek's American-born daughter-in-law was friendly and smiling, but she didn't understand her father-in-law's Yiddish. She spoke about him with great respect, but she didn't allocate a room for him. She lived in five rooms with her husband and her two grown children, but she set up the old man's sleeping quarters in the larger and brighter foyer. They bought a divan bed and a lovely, stuffed chair, hung large mirrors on the walls, and placed small tables in the corners. But in the gussied-up foyer, the old man felt crowded, as if he were being suffocated.

When he sometimes wanted to lie down to take a nap, the daughter-in-law said: "Fresh air, Pop! Older folks need fresh air." From this Falek understood that the ladies were gathering to play cards and it would be better if he, the old man, were to sit in the park while they were there. What if the park were cold? Or if it were raining? And how long can a person sit in the park? So the old man would sneak into his foyer on tiptoes so as, God forbid, not to disturb the guests. He would quietly open the door, sit down in a corner of the sofa, and close his eyes so he wouldn't see a small, bundled-up little Falek staring back at him. He'd sit there, consoling himself. He was small and forlorn, but he was also, if you will, a tree with widespread roots in many countries. Roots and branches, dead and living. True, they were now cut off from him, but in the world to come, all of his children and children's children would come together, and the light of their mother, gone from the world so young, would shine upon her entire household.

Thompson's fate was not much better. He lived with a young daughter, his youngest child. She was a kind soul but had a small apartment. She was a teacher, and her husband still attended university. Each morning, the daughter would leave home quite early. Before she left, she cleaned the few rooms, and he, Thompson, was left alone. But what could he possibly do? Bang his head against the wall? He was weak. Although he wasn't an invalid, it had been years since he'd had a job. His hands were dying to do a bit of work, and he didn't know what to do with them in the house, or in the park. And so for both of them—Falek and Thompson—the synagogue was like a gift sent by God Himself.

As long as the Rabbi still carried around his fantastical plans to gather "all of Abraham's children" under the synagogue's wings, he hardly looked at the few old people. He was certain they'd come of their own accord. But when he realized that his dreams were bursting like soap bubbles, he grew closer with the elderly. He didn't have to exert himself to prove to them that the synagogue was their home. They went to the synagogue with the instinct of a bird that senses the moment when it needs to set out on its way.

The two old men revived themselves in the synagogue, and the synagogue revived with them. They had already seen to it that the synagogue had a minyan for prayer services. The Rabbi didn't just make the old men his students, they also became his best friends. Going every morning to buy the newspaper wasn't the extent of it. He read for them, chatted with them about politics, and in the process, there gathered around the trio a group of Jews that absorbed the Rabbi's words with great enthusiasm as if he were studying Torah with them.

This idyll lasted for a time. Several summers and winters passed, and it seemed as if this trio would walk together forever, that always at the same time they would march along the same path.

Age crept up on the two men. They became weaker, more hunched over. The small Falek became even smaller, and Thompson breathed even heavier. The Rabbi had to bend down even more when he spoke to them, and he had to slow down even further in order to adjust to their slow pace.

One morning, Falek didn't come to synagogue. Thompson looked up at the Rabbi with terror in his eyes and heard how the Rabbi was humming some kind of melody and saw how he was looking off somewhere far away…

That night, Falek had trouble sleeping. The night stretched out; the morning was late in coming. Falek tried to get out of bed several times, but his head sank back into the pillow. He wondered why his legs were freezing, why his throat was dry, and why it wasn't getting lighter outside. But then it did seem to him that, yes, the day was dawning. He lifted his head and saw bizarre creatures staring back at him from all of the mirrors. They all looked like they were about to let loose on him... He wanted to scream, but he couldn't release a peep. It was as if his mouth were sealed shut... He shouted with his last bit of strength but he didn't hear his own voice. Fear seized him. He had to get out of bed. He had to call his son! He quickly got up and thudded back down. Back down!

The daughter-in-law wondered why the old man hadn't gotten up yet. By this time, wasn't he always already in the kitchen drinking his tea? She thought that today she had to clean the house as soon as possible. Today, the ladies would be coming for an early card party, and then on to the theater. Perhaps he overslept? She had to go in and see.

She didn't go far. She soon let out a wild scream. "My God! My God!" She burst into sobs. Her tears were genuine.

Later, she said to her friends: "He was a saint. He died as a saint. Poor, poor old man!"

For an entire week, no one saw the Rabbi and Thompson going to get the newspaper. When they did appear, Thompson looked to be a head shorter, and his face was the color of yellow poplar wood. During that week, the Rabbi had also aged. His mouth was stiff, like after a fast. When he walked, his head was turned to the left, in Falek's direction, as if he felt that something was missing on his left side.

The processions of the two men continued a little longer. But in both of their gaits, in their behavior, there was a perceptible quiet. Thompson breathed with even greater difficulty now, and the Rabbi kept searching for a place to keep his left hand.

Although Falek had not been very close to Thompson (he had been no more than a friend to whom one snuggles up while sharing a bench in the park,) and although both had been equally lonely despite their friendship, Falek's death made Thompson feel like a mourner. Even the synagogue now felt somewhat alien to him.

It was late summer. The air—chilly, cloudy. A lethargy gripped Thompson's limbs, and his eyes kept closing. He would have liked to sleep a bit longer if his Seydele would let him tidy up his bed in the morning... What was the problem—didn't he prepare his bed in the evening by himself? But she was a dear child and was afraid that he might overwork himself. She said to him: "You shouldn't bend down; it's not good for your blood pressure!" His blood pressure hardly bothered him at all. And if there was sometimes a pounding in his temples, well, that too was hardly a catastrophe. After all, he was an old man. Oh, these American kids!

For Falek, death had come easily. Such good fortune was not in the cards for Thompson. One afternoon, while making his way to synagogue, he thought he was going to pass out. His mind became disoriented, and he fell. When his daughter came home, she found him lying on the ground. He was paralyzed on one side and had to be taken to the hospital. His end was a slow one...

The next morning, there was no minyan in the synagogue. Those who did come kept looking out of the windows: Perhaps a Jew who would complete the minyan was walking by outside? But no one appeared.

Close to the windows, practically grazing the panes with its branches, three young, slim poplars swayed in an unvaried rhythm...

The Rabbi entered. With a quick glance, he absorbed the mood of the eight Jews assembled, and with a fiery call and the gesture of a captain who senses that his ship is on the verge of sinking, ordered the sexton: "Turn on the lights! Let there be light!"

The sexton turned on the few electric switches, and so much light poured forth from the hanging lamps that it blinded the eyes of the few elderly men and they had to protect their eyes from the light with their hands... The Rabbi said: "There's no minyan? Well, then let's pray as individuals. Friends, pray!"

Without any apparent desire of their own, the men took to their prayer shawls and phylacteries. Soon a humming like a running waterfall sounded. From under this prayer shawl, the Rabbi looked out at the men and it seemed to him that he was viewing faces in death masks, as in a play from ancient times. He closed his eyes and broke out in a chill.

The Rabbi sat for a long time, resting his head on his hands. He didn't see the men leaving the synagogue one by one. A profound, gnawing sadness seized him. He felt his own helplessness. He had not fulfilled his mission. One had to surrender to inevitability. He ached for himself, for his fate. He, the young rabbi, after the death of the two old men, ached and now felt that his building, built on old foundations, was trembling.

Thoughts drilled their way into his brain. In the brightly-lit, decorated synagogue, he felt like someone sitting on a throne performing in a Purim play. He broke into a smile at this comparison... He glanced at his wristwatch, stood up, and as was his wont, said: "It's time to go get the newspaper!"

When he went out onto the street, he stood there, waiting on the two absent men.

His eyes clouded over and his head bent, he began walking along the same route. He took slow steps, as if he were still walking between the two men.

On his way home, with the newspaper opened wide in his hands, the Rabbi changed course, taking a different route...

By My Mother's Sickbed

Don't wake up, Mama, kind Mama. Sleep, sleep a while longer. Let the good angel cradle you under his wings so your gloomy eyes will be spared the need to rummage in the Void and your pounding heart will lull itself into tranquility. Let sleep be a shield that will protect you from the storm winds spreading over us with such terrifying force, as if seeking to obliterate all that lives...

Keep sleeping, tormented Mama. Don't wake up! I, your child, will stand guard over your sickbed with all of my sharpened senses.

As soon as you open your eyes, I'll be ashamed to look into them. I can't bear the mute questions and the probing to which I have no answer. I also cannot protect you as you protected me when you yourself were trampled by the beastly boots. I'm helpless against the sinister clouds moving in from all corners of the world, precipitating darkness, blocking every scrap of sky. If, from time to time, the sun appears, it is distant, chilly, as if— by turning its cold side to us—it begrudges us its favor, a bit of warmth.

So don't wake up, mother-child, darling Mama. Too powerful is the storm, too horrifying the times for people like you. Sleep until the tempest dies down.

I stand by the head of your bed. I see how your eyes twitch from time to time. The nightmares probably don't let you enjoy total rest when you sleep. Oh, how I would like to spare you from those nightmares! I look at the wrinkles on your face and ask you, ask myself: How old are you, Mama? How old am I? And I answer on my own: Jews, after all, always count the years by calamities, misfortunes—in such and such year, they carried out pogroms against us, burned us, turned us to ashes. Oh, how old we are. Terror grabs a hold of you.

But we are immortal, Mama, we are eternity! We are an example through the generations. They marvel at us, they imitate us, they kill us, and still we are here! And if there will be a world, Mama, we too shall be.

As I stand vigilant over you, mother-child, time slides back to a few decades ago… As now, so too then was my room dark; as now, dark gray stains spread from the corners out over the walls. Here I see how you, Mama, cleared the crumbs from the meager third Sabbath meal. By then, there was no Papa. And that time—dark, terrifying. Something had happened; we were waiting for something. Quietly, as if inside yourself, you recited "God of Abraham,"[9] and I was chilled.

It got darker and darker. You sat at the table, your chin leaning on your hands, and your face, your gaze—so distant… I felt strangely forlorn and sat next to the lukewarm oven that had been smoldering since Friday and was now cooling down. I curled up into myself, closed my eyes, and soon something carried me away into an enchanted world… Before my eyes, a bright blue sky with pure-brilliant stars in the millions moved with mighty speed… The stars were kindled, becoming light, and again, stars, and I was happy.

I open my eyes—the stars are gone. I close my eyes, and they're back! I didn't sleep… I didn't want the stars to fly away from me. So I rose—and I was flying with the stars, with the sky…

About airplanes my childish imagination never dreamed. Besides, I had no desire to fly to the clouds like a bird. I was afraid of heights, and here suddenly, I was flying over the clouds. And,

9. "God of Abraham" ("*Got fun Avrom*"): Yiddish prayer recited by women and girls marking the conclusion of the Sabbath while the males are in the synagogue reciting the Mayrev prayer.

in fact, with genuine wings. It seemed to me that I was *seeing* the act of flying… It was such a wonderful feeling! I was flying over houses, over trees, over mountains without any fear whatsoever, as if this were an utterly commonplace event. I didn't feel small in space, without a ground below and without an above.

How long was I flying like this? Who knows—perhaps a minute, perhaps an hour. When I opened my eyes, there was a dense darkness in the room. Mama, I didn't see you at all. You were just a speck opposite me. Not a drop of light from the street penetrated the room.

I don't know whether it was from the cold or from terror, but I didn't feel any of my limbs. I thought that if I weren't completely dead, I was certainly slightly dead.

This was my first trip into the air. From then on, I allowed myself to fly like a bird into the heights, over the clouds, with the stars, and perhaps even higher… True, I could never say to myself: "Fly!" I didn't have a choice. I flew when I was called to flight. All children probably fly. But I'll never forget my first expedition into space. I remember how you, Mama, looked at me with such terror and disbelief. You asked: "Did you hear, my child, that a person can fly like a bird?" As to whether I persuaded you of my flight, that I don't know.

Now, standing by your sickbed and looking at you, mother eternal, mother silent, I understand that you associated my flight with something symbolic. On that melancholy Saturday night, I didn't—and you certainly didn't—think that in a few decades I would be standing by your sickbed remembering all these small things with the greatest precision … the fact that the match in your hand refused to ignite, and that the wick started to go down just at the moment you wanted to bring it up to increase the brightness—all of this together elicited both for you and me something mystical, something connected to things outside our consciousness. A bit later, you told me your Messiah story that went well with that light-headed evening.

I remember how you looked: somehow so distant, shadowy. You didn't look at me, as if you wanted to hide from me the terror that was enfolding you. The terror was felt in the air of that remote, destitute shtetl, and it broke through the cracks of the walls into the home and into both of our hearts.

I remember how much certainty there was in your tone: the Messiah, the Redeemer of Our People, would have come long ago if we had earned redemption in the eyes of God. When I asked you how He will come, you gave what now sounds to me like a prophecy. I remember your contemplative words: "When the goblet of human suffering fills up to the rim, Messiah the son of Joseph will appear at first. He will inspire terror. Messiah the son of Joseph will appear like an eagle with two heads and two mouths, ready to swallow people up. With his gaze, he will slay the sinful; like flies will they fall."

To my question as to how He will know who the bad ones were, you answered with a bit of surprise and a bit of anger, saying: "A messenger of God does not have to be told who is bad. He will bring low, destroy. At first, the world will become desolate, and then the true Messiah—Messiah the son of David—will appear." I asked: "If everyone will be dead, why is a Messiah necessary?" And you answered clearly and reflectively: "The good ones, the just ones will endure. God will protect them so that he will have from whom to create a new generation, a moral generation."

Wise words, sleeping mother, correct words…

But you, Mama—don't wake up. Keep sleeping. Keep sleeping. Dear mother, sleep!

In a Convalescent Home

On six small beds lined up three in a row, the people lay in their clothes and shoes. It was afternoon, the hour before naptime. The dark, quadrangular room was submerged in shadows. The air was heavy. It smelled of sweat mixed with the sourness of freshly-washed floor.

The first to interrupt the stillness was Mr. Sonn, who was lying next to the entrance, on the first bed. He couldn't stay calm for long. He felt like going out into the corridor.

Mr. Sonn was a small, gaunt person. He was fair. His head was bare. His neck was thin, and his eyes were set so deep in their sockets that they were barely visible. He had small hands and feet, like a woman. Only his voice was strong, resounding, like a young man in his twenties. It was hard to know how such a small man had come by such an energetic, booming voice. Mr. Sonn rarely spoke with those around him. His voice only rang out when the nurse came to his bed. The nurse—the only woman—who brought with her a feeling of freshness, like a spring breeze, spoke to him in Hebrew. When the two of them started speaking, it was as if the gloom retreated from the room, leaving it brightened.

For many years, Mr. Sonn had been a teacher in a Hebrew school for higher education. Now in his seventies, he was slightly deaf. Moreover, he had all sorts of illnesses that came with advanced age. Here, in the "home," several of his former students sustained him. The nurse called him "Teacher" and treated him with great tenderness. When she sat down next to him, the old man was in seventh heaven. He still hoped to get his life back and

spoke with the nurse about his plans. She listened to him patiently, nodding her head, but he couldn't read anything from her face.
His eyesight wasn't sharp enough.

After rest hour one day, the "Teacher" found himself sitting
on the chair next to his bed. He held his small, feminine hands
on his knees, and his mouth said something that no one understood. He looked at the door, hesitating between going out or
waiting… A loud banging could be heard. The small bed started
to dance. He looked around, got up, supported himself with both
hands holding onto the headboard, and waited for the banging to
subside. He had been here several weeks and couldn't adjust to
the frequent outbreaks of banging which erupted with a loudness
capable of waking the dead. When the room started to shake, Mr.
Sonn dragged the blanket over his face, hiding like a child who
hears thunder, grasping whatever what was at hand, and his small
eyes filled with terror.

On the bed next to Mr. Sonn's lay a man without a name. The
lodgers of the home called him the "Whistle." He was a young
man, around thirty-five years old. Although he was neither deaf
nor mute, his neighbors never heard a word from him. He had
been silent for the entire two weeks he had been here. Everyone
uttered the word "Whistle" quietly and in an undertone suggesting that they wanted to omit it altogether. The whistle jutted out
from the cavity between his two collar bones. It was a white,
metal whistle, as large as a twenty-five-cent piece.

After his initial arrival, the people kept asking: Why does this
person avoid everyone's eye? Why does he always turn his back
to everyone? With his silence, with his constant shuffling around
the walls of the corridor, and with the unease that lay in his thin
hands and feet, he cast a bizarre gloom on everyone. Pained
stares accompanied him. In his tall, slightly stooped figure that
obstructed his protruding cheekbones, in his terrified green-gray
eyes, in his helpless gait that was more running than walking was
something that allowed no one any peace.

A friend of his who had brought him there did talk about him, but not many details were discovered.

He was a victim of Hitler. A Nazi murderer had kicked him with his boots and stood on top of him with both feet until he tore his larynx in two. He lost so much blood that other survivors later marveled at his strength, at the fact that he was still alive. A deathly yellowness blanketed his face. He was one of the heroes who had led a vanguard of resistance in that region. He never spoke of those dark days. The whistle at his throat spoke for him. He pressed the whistle with two fingers, and there emerged a voice that, if not clearly intelligible, was better than muteness. In the beginning, he completely avoided looking at people. Later on, he calmed down a bit. It seemed possible that after a certain amount of time he would allow himself to be drawn back into the circle of humanity.

Throughout the entire time his friend was talking about him, he sat with his back to everyone. Every now and then, he lifted his head, and with pain in his eyes, mutely pleaded: Enough already!

He was light on his feet. He didn't sit in one place. Even when everyone else was sleeping, he was up and about. When the weather was beautiful, he could be found in the courtyard. He spun around on his long legs, with his hands in his pockets and looking very much like a kind of human golem.[10]

During the day, nothing was heard from him. But at night, when the murmuring quieted down, the room was filled with his whistle's wheezing. It was the wheezing of someone just before the throes of death. Often, he himself would awaken from his wheezing. He would feel horrified and a little guilty in front of the others, wanting to jump down from the bed and run. He'd see how the small, good-natured eyes of his neighbor were looking over at him, and he would remain lying there tensely, saying

10. Golem: an animated anthropomorphic being in Jewish folklore created entirely of inanimate matter (usually clay or mud) and brought to life by magic; dummy.

to himself: "Just don't fall asleep. Don't fall asleep!" When he did manage to stay awake, he would be transported to his hellish yesterdays, and gripping the mattress, say to himself: "Don't fall asleep!"

On the third bed sat a broad-shouldered Jewish man in his seventies. He wore a dark shirt and, on his head, a yarmulke. His head was heavy and round. His full face, with its trimmed little beard, was still dark, and his voice rose healthily from his chest. If anyone wondered what a man like that was doing in the rest home, all they had to do was see how the man stood up and dragged his right foot while the left one lagged, and they had their answer. The man was talkative. He got things off his chest. After rest hour, a heaviness settled on his heart. When that heaviness came over him, well, you could protest, but it wouldn't do you any good. Once, he dragged his heavy knees and spoke to his neighbor across the way: "Do you hear, neighbor, there's an expression—you get used to your troubles, and you don't want to let go of them. I, you see, would have said goodbye to my troubles without a copeck of profit. I would gladly say goodbye to the dear tranquility of our home. This very minute I would get away from here; oh, I would give up the rancid smell, the noise and the clatter—all these good things!"

His neighbor asked him listlessly: "So then why don't you actually leave? After all, don't you have a home?" Thinking over what he had said, this neighbor continued: "Indeed, this is not a home of your own, but if you're so sick of it here—well, you've got to choose one or the other, don't you?"

The heavy man looked at his neighbor. He lowered his head as if he were speaking to his knee. "I committed a grave sin against her, my daughter-in-law. I'm guilty of my pension being small! If you speak to her, she'll tell you that money ruins a person, that the rich person doesn't believe the pauper. But when I told her that she herself would have treated me better if I had more money, she then lit into a rage and started screaming at me, claiming that if I'd been a union man, I'd have saved myself the need to depend upon children without means. This is how she speaks to someone who has been hit by misfortune, and *she's* the one who's angry…"

The heavy old man stood up with difficulty, grabbed his cane hanging on the side of his chair, and trudged out of the room.

The neighbor to whom the invalid had been speaking was the fourth of the six. He was a Jew who never let his heavy prayerbook out of his hands. In appearance, he was tidy and lively. He didn't have a beard, but he didn't let his yarmulke off his head. This man had not entirely detached from "the world outside the home." He engaged in a little business here. For all of his working life, he'd been a jewelry peddler. In the home, too, he did business out of habit. He had a kind of double personality, this fellow. In the bed and in the room, he was a God-fearing man. He had a pious face. He spoke quietly, was absorbed in himself, his prayerbook, and his trembling hands. When he wasn't looking in the prayerbook, he was looking intently at his hands, as if he were reproving them, had complaints against them, or was begging them not to fail him, not to embarrass him. But as soon as the man donned his business clothes, he was transformed. The old shirt, with its stiff cuffs and collar, lent his face an odd hardness, a pompousness. The small black tie, the threadbare jacket, the fedora soaked from many a downpour—all of it combined to make the pious little man with the thick prayerbook and the trembling hands look like a ruin.

He carried his "stock" in his breast pocket. Here could be found bridal gifts to disburse. Oftentimes, he felt for these bits of leftovers from the good years. When he marched out of the room with even steps and his head held high, five pairs of hungry eyes looked on after him.

The fifth of these local residents, who was in no hurry to leave the bed after rest hour, was a Jewish man who wanted to be noticed as little as possible. He was middle-aged, quite dark, and heavy. His large, bulging eyes exuded horror. He was always clinging to something, as if seeking protection. When he was sitting or standing, he held on not just with both hands but with his entire body. Even when he was lying in bed, he cleaved onto its sides, onto the mattress, onto whatever was available. When a truck rushed by and the building shook a little, the man's hands, feet, and even his cheeks trembled.

He, too, was a victim of the Nazis. A native of Hungary, he couldn't make himself understood to anyone. He knew a few words of the Holy Tongue. He was left utterly alone in the world. All of his relatives had been burned. He had brought a small amount of money with him, giving it to the "home" to ensure that he had a roof over his head. To any question posed to him, he responded with the old Hebrew adage: "*Gam zu le-tovah*," meaning "This, too, is for the good."[11]

When he sat on the edge of the bed, his unlively legs hung down, and he held onto the bedframe with his hands. He was large, heavy of body, and he breathed heavily, too. He looked like someone who had just come from combat and was resting. When you approached him, you beheld a living portrait of darkness, loneliness, fear, and brokenness.

From what sort of dark corners of his foggy mind he brought out those few Hebrew words "*Gam zu le-tovah*," only God Himself knew.

The last one to get out of bed and interrupt the rest hour was the sixth and youngest resident of the room. In comparison with the other five, he was still a boy. And, in fact, that is what the nurse called him: "Boy!" He was young, not yet twenty-five years old. And yet in the "home," he was seen as one of the veteran patients. He had come here, the way one imagines, for only a few weeks, to heal from a sickness, to get back his strength. But his

11. "*Gam zu le-tovah*" (Hebrew): "This, too, is for the good", an adage attributed to the Tannaitic sage, Nahum Ish Gamzu, the teacher of Rabbi Akiva. To any misfortune, Nahum invariably replied, "*Gam zu le-tovah*" and thus his moniker became "Nahum Ish Gamzu" (Nahum the Gamzu Man).

strength began to ebb from him slowly, drop by drop. His name was Gdalyeh. Still worse than Gdalyeh's drawn-out illness was his indifference, his despair. He felt like someone who'd been torn away from life and who no longer had the slightest faith that he would ever get to return to it.

Gdalyeh was as tall and slim as a young poplar. His light, disheveled mop of hair illuminated the grayness that hung over the room like a thin cloud. His face was pinched—the cheekbones protruded—and his dark brown eyes looked lustrous on his yellow, bloodless skin. But his full lips were juicy, and as if mockingly, they smiled, thereby creating the illusion of the bloom of youth. Although he was six feet tall and used to have well-coordinated limbs, his apathy and neglect disrupted the cooperation between his long legs, and his arms hung down indifferently. A sense of helplessness screamed from his long, bony fingers. Gdalyeh lay on his bed, emaciated, pale, but still mobile. When he got out of bed, he was no longer a young man—but rather a pathetic creature, one lump of pain. Gdalyeh was repulsed by his own body, and he wanted to hide it from strange eyes. But he didn't make the slightest effort to use his mental powers to strengthen his physical capabilities.

Gdalyeh's bed was near the window. He turned his head to convince himself that there was no one there. Then he slid out of bed and strode awkwardly to the window. He stood and stood until his legs began to get collapse. Then he pulled his chair close to the window and weakly eased himself onto it.

The room looked empty and deserted. By the first bed, which was near the entrance, the "Teacher's" small skullcap gleamed whitely in the dim light. A sadness radiated from the empty beds. Gdalyeh then sat on the window sill and pressed his head against the heated piece of windowpane ablaze from the glare of the setting sun. The mature poplars next to the window extended high above the building. Between their outspread branches, small, white clouds that looked like winged fans peered forth. Around the very tops of the trees, thousands of swallows circled, as if in a carnival. Like trained soldiers, the swallows flew in snake-like formations. They were making droning sounds and a racket, as if getting ready for a show.

Feeling morose, Gdalyeh followed the noisy life going on high above his head and thought: "How beautiful, how luminous is the world!" He lifted up his head, wanting to follow the cloud-fans. He looked intensely and didn't notice that he was sudden-ly transported to five years ago… The semester at that time had been difficult, but for him it was still splendid. He had received a scholarship, a free trip to Europe, and things were going so well for him that he was in seventh heaven. And his parents! Joy shone from their faces. This was a big deal. After all, with extraordinary effort, they'd achieved a bit of happiness.

When was this? All of five years ago. But for him, it seemed like it had been decades since he'd been ripped from the world of the living. How had it begun? Well, he came home with heavy bundles of work that he had to complete in the fixed number of days before his trip. He was somewhat tired. His mother looked at him suspiciously.

"Gdalyeh, what's happening with you?" she asked. "Why is your face burning?" No surprise, his mother looked too deeply into things and inevitably found something. And yet, he *was* feel-ing warm; his head—heavy. Well, of what importance was a little warmth of body and a heaviness in the head when you felt as if you had wings and were set to go across the world? Nevertheless, out of regard for his mother, he went to lie down for a while. As soon as he was in bed, he felt as if all of his limbs were yielding to him and that all was easy and good. It was as if he were being carried on a wave with his face to the sky, his hands and legs out-stretched, and yes, all was easy and good… He slept for a long time, the kind of sleep that cast a pall of fear on the waking, a sleep that stretched out, draining, like a parasite, the marrow from the bones, the blood from the veins.

At times, the sleep was dreamless, as if he were completely freed from himself, and at other times, the sleep was a struggle to present something, to cast something off himself, to tear something out of himself and escape. He was exhausted from his dreams and bathed in sweat. After the sweat invariably came chills, and after that, sleep without dreams.

The din of several passing cargo transport wagons interrupted Gdalyeh's thoughts. The clatter crashed turbulently into the room. The walls shook; the metal objects clinked. The "Teacher" stuck his head between the pillows, and Gdalyeh held onto the window sill, closed his eyes, and again tried to link back together his fractured thoughts.

The doctors said that the rheumatic fever he had when he was three years old was now recurring. And now, of all times, just when he was on the brink of flying his very highest.

He went from hospital to hospital and from sanatorium to sanatorium until he ended up here. Gdalyeh tried hard to hold his outstretched hand evenly, but his hand fell down. He almost said out loud: "And the doctors still say I'm healthy, that I have to see to it that I make myself useful. What a bad joke!"

Once again, he extended his neck toward the treetops. The birds were no more. The branches moved peacefully, talking things over with each other in their language, and it seemed to Gdalyeh that the branches were laughing at people's helplessness. A fury arose within him, and with his knees trembling, he took hold of the edges of the window. A scream coming from deep within him tore a path out. What a terrible, destructive power rules over people! Where does this power originate? From whom shall justice be demanded, and where is justice? For whose sin was he paying? He asked and knew that he would receive no answer because there was no answer. Gdalyeh wept. His ashamed hands and legs wept. His twenty-three years wept.

He opened his weak arms, lowering his head onto the window sill. His bright curls scattered. The sill was hard and mute…

The nurse came in on tiptoes. She approached Gdalyeh and, seeing him sitting there seemingly frozen, she looked upon the gentle bend of his almost childlike neck. He responded to her with a smiling gaze. In that smile was joy, the joy of a lost child when he spots a familiar face. The nurse—Miss Gold—sat down on the window sill opposite him and, again, both of their eyes met. His eyes—dark, with a feverish shine; hers—green-gray, all pupils, probing, and filled with a certain amount of reproach.

He said: "It's good to see you here, Miss Gold. I have fallen into a mood where everything seems hopeless." He took her hands and tried to press them firmly, but his hands were weak. So he looked at her, flustered. "I didn't mean to do that, Miss Gold, didn't mean to do that…" he said. Miss Gold freed her hands from his. She looked at her wristwatch, slid closer to him, and said: "I have a little time now for us to talk. So hear me out, Gdalyeh. I can sense that you know that I want what's best for you. I felt your awareness of that in your handshake. That alone is a positive sign. I know that you're not content. Still, you should know, my boy, that your recovery depends on you alone. Only you can help yourself. You just have to use your intelligence. True, you're very sick, but time has been good to you, as have the doctors and your relatives. And now you have to do your part. You have to make the biggest contribution."

"We know each other," Miss Gold continued. "We've talked a lot. I know your beautiful head is full of thoughts, ideas." And here she ran her fingers through his long, soft hair. "But within you, everything has fallen asleep. Now, it's your responsibility to wake it up."

She was silent for a while and then said: "Just give it some thought. Such wide horizons open up for someone of your caliber who loves learning. If a person has a goal in life, then life is worth all of the sacrifices. Just take me as an example. I've already told you that for nine months, I was a slave in a concentration camp. I weighed eighty pounds and had to work eighteen hours a day.

What sustained me? Along with thousands of others like me, I was sustained by a superhuman lust for life and a will to outlast *them*! The drive for revenge kept all of those thousands alive."

She concluded: "Well, I've told you what was on my mind. Now I want to hear what you have to say. Has what I've said prompted any reaction? Promise me you'll take a walk in the morning."

Gdalyeh didn't respond. From his eyes, the nurse could see that he was searching for an answer in his mind or that he was trying to remember something. And yet she felt that her words had awakened a sleepy corner of his mind. She broke into a smile.

She left. In the darkness, Gdalyeh observed the rhythmic movement of her white dress. His neighbors appeared at their beds. The room was draped in dense gloom.

Once again, Gdalyeh turned his head up toward the trees, searching for a pure slice of heaven. Finding it, he rejoiced. He thought that if Miss Gold were still standing here, he would show her the blueness between the branches. Perhaps that would be his answer...

The Last Breakfast

The train was scheduled to leave at noon, but mother and son were already up and about at sunrise. Elizabeth, the mother, had slept very little that night. The departure of her fourteen-year-old son, Ted, had been thoroughly planned and pre-arranged weeks before, but for all that time, she hadn't wanted to think about it. She said to herself: "I'm doing it for his own good. Something has to be made of him, and you've got to know that it's one of the two—you can't make an omelet and still keep your eggs." That's also what her brother, Klaro, said to her.

Elizabeth trusted her brother just as she trusted Teddy's own father when he was alive. Klaro was a thoughtful man who had no children of his own. His garage brought in enough income for a family of ten, not just three. Perhaps someday, if Teddy wanted, he would acquire more education through night classes and, with effort, achieve something.

Soon after Teddy's father died, Elizabeth's brother invited Teddy to live with him. But she didn't have the heart to separate from her child. What did she have left other than her child? How could you send away such a small child? He wasn't even four years old.

Elizabeth went to work in a washery, and kind Susie, who had the heart of an angel, looked after the child. The little one lacked for nothing. Elizabeth really did work hard—very hard, in fact—but she had someone to come home to. The child was her comfort. He grew, and if she had had to pray to God Himself for a son, she couldn't have wished for a better one.

Fourteen years passed. Where were those fourteen years of hers? Here they were! She stood half-dressed in middle of the room and looked at her Teddy. He was continuing to pack. My goodness, look at what had accumulated in his drawer! Tons of trinkets. She didn't take her eyes off him. She kept noticing things about him, as if he had just arrived for a visit. She was struck by his resemblance to Abe Lincoln. The things that came to her mind! That was something Susie said to her—that Teddy had the look of Abe: his height, his long face, high forehead and widow's peak hairline—even the nose was the same. But Teddy's lips were more attractive than Abe's. He had his father's lips, and even his voice was beginning to sound like his father's, too.

How he distinguished himself with his readings aloud in his graduation class! Not for nothing did Susie say, "If he didn't have our skin, he'd grow up to be a senator… Nothing less than a senator!" Well, as for me, Elizabeth thought, I would settle for a little less.

Having packed and then secured his boyish possessions with strong twine, Teddy whistled some kind of sad melody and looked down at the floor as if he were trying to make sure he hadn't forgotten anything. His childish but quite serious eyes also followed every one of his mother's steps, as if he were seeing her thin, almost skeletal legs for the first time. Suddenly, he lifted his head, approached his mother with a smile, and said, "It looks like everything's ready. What do you think, Momsy?"

The delicious smell of bacon wafted over to his nostrils. Elizabeth was preoccupied with her kitchen work. She turned her face to her son, and he noticed a strange expression there. As if with forced cheer, she said: "I'm making a festive breakfast! A last breakfast." She took back the word "last" and corrected herself with "A real honest-to-goodness festive breakfast!" She didn't look at him, but gesturing with her head, said, "Look, son, fresh rolls, just the way you love them. Everything's all ready. Sit down at the table." And once again, those same words escaped from her mouth: "The last meal." And she found herself shaken up by her own words.

Teddy looked at his mother, his eyes questioning, filled with pain. Her use of the words "the last" made no impact on him. He didn't understand why she was so agitated. Together, they ate the delicacies in shared indifference. Ted made several attempts to say something, but the words didn't come out smoothly. Overly-lofty phrases spun around in his mouth. In front of his mother, he was ashamed to verbalize these book words, so instead he contented himself with looking at her and smiling. He tapped on her long, heavy fingers, as if he wanted to tap out a specific melody, and hummed along, "Mom, Mom, Momsy…"

It was also hard for Elizabeth to speak, but she had to convey a message to him. She knew he was no fool and would know how to control his tongue, and yet her heart was heavy. And so she warned him:

"My son, dear boy, promise me—see to it—that you control yourself… There, in the city where you're going, we Black people stick in the craw of white people, understand? Here, we're in a big city, and if we're not welcome neighbors, well, we're not too conspicuous. But there—where you're going—things are different. I don't want to scare you. You're going to be staying with a smart uncle. He'll see to everything for you. I just want you to promise me that you'll be as quiet as water and won't look where you're not supposed to. You promise?"

Teddy had never heard his mother speak this way. His eyes clouded over. He became apprehensive. Maybe he shouldn't be going at all? Maybe he shouldn't leave his Momsy? And Cora—but Elizabeth didn't let his reflections go on for too long. She set his suitcases down in the middle of the room, felt the zippers and was satisfied with their condition. She then started to fuss over her son. She straightened the small tie that Teddy was wearing for just the second time. Susie had given him the tie as a graduation present. She considered his shoelaces and decided to give him another a pair—you never knew when these would tear. She noticed that one of his buttons was loose so she got a needle and thread and began to sew it on more securely.

Elizabeth was sitting on a low chair, absorbed in sewing on the button. She felt that the closeness she shared with her son was about to be severed. With all of her senses, she took in her child, as if she wanted to swallow him. She didn't rush, but instead, slowly extended the needle that had lost its way. One stitch, then another... Teddy placed a hand atop his mother's head, played with her curls, and jokingly said: "Momsy, in that time, you could've sewn a sole onto a shoe." Elizabeth felt as though she were losing her bearings. She tore the thread in two and proceeded to hug her son with all of her might. Then she pushed him from her and said, "All right, I'm ready!"

Teddy loved his Momsy. He could never get too much of her mothering. Even though she was always busy, mother and son were drawn to discussing the small and large events of their days with each other. But now, in these precious minutes, both of their hearts were uncommunicative. Teddy really wanted to tell his mother that Cora ran away from him yesterday, not wanting to say goodbye. He wanted to ask his mother whether she thought Cora would be looking out to him from the window when he left, but he said nothing. Enough already! He couldn't bear the sight of his mother's tear-filled eyes anymore.

Maybe it was time for him to say that he wanted to stay with his Momsy... but what kind of man would he be if he did such a thing? No, no, he was his mother's only son. She was getting older and weaker. But staying here with her wouldn't do either of them any good. Uncle Klaro knew what he was doing.

Neighbors came to say goodbye. The mother was ready. She got dressed up in her Sunday best and a beautiful little white hat. It occurred to Teddy that his mother had a strange look in her eyes. He had never seen her looking the way she did now. Their dog, Skippy, sensed that something was happening, and as if he were angry that he hadn't been let in on the secret, he circled around Teddy and Elizabeth with a strange whining sound. He lifted up his head with questioning eyes toward Teddy. Then, jumping up and down, he wouldn't be calmed until Teddy hugged and pressed him close, pacifying him the way you do a crying child.

Their mouths agape, two girls wearing starched dresses, their hair in stiff little braids, offered Teddy a package wrapped in red-gold paper. Their mother pushed them forward and said: "Say goodbye to Teddy, kids." The girls lowered their heads, gave him the package, and quickly ran from the home.

The gardener drove up in his car. He honked the horn three times. Teddy took the larger of the bags; his mother—the smaller. Both of them left the house without any fanfare. A quiet, sad procession descended the stairs. Skippy followed them, not making a sound. Several neighbors looked out of their windows and shouted: "Goodbye!" Teddy looked for Cora at the window, but he didn't see her. His heart felt heavy. No, she wasn't there. He imagined her lying in bed, her head snuggled into the pillow, crying...

In the car, Elizabeth kept Teddy close to her. She thought the trip to the train station would extend for a long period of time and that she would still be able to speak with her son, but the old car practically carried them on wings. There it was! They had arrived at the station, and the train was waiting for them. A gleaming, shiny, ominous, and noisy train. And the throngs—it was as if the whole city was gathered here. Elizabeth was disconcerted, uncertain as to which train car she should settle her son into. Teddy managed on his own. He threw the bags up onto the high steps, jumped back down and held his mother by the hand. Skippy wanted to climb up, too, and when he was held back, he started barking. And then the conductor called out: "All aboard!"

Mother and child embraced and quickly kissed. Elizabeth kissed him on the eyes and the neck. A terrifying whistle sounded, and everything started to shake. By then, she was back on the platform. The train moved... Everything happened with such speed, in such a hurry—a flurry all taking place in the course of a single minute.

The dog scolded and raced after the departing train. Elizabeth looked for Teddy's face among the many faces pressed against the windowpanes. Someone—the kind gardener who drove them to the train station—took her by the hand.

This was Teddy's first ride on such a large train. When, after a few momentary, slow starts, the train took off with a roar, he shook as if he were leaping down from a great height. He was seized by vertigo, and he felt lightheaded and dizzy. He thought he needed to hold onto something so he wouldn't fall down. He didn't fall. He sat next to other passengers, all of them adults, smiling; some of them were quite cheerful. He felt light. As he looked out the window next to his seat, new worlds flitted by before his eyes. Enchanted houses—tiny, colorful—whirled in a dance, along with the mountains and trees. His fourteen-year-old's imagination burst into full play. He had the feeling that he was riding to a dazzling light located over there. *There*—where the train was racing toward—and here he was racing alongside, aboard the train.

Teddy thought about his mother, not with sadness, but with a feeling of commitment. He imagined himself arriving at his uncle's place, and soon thereafter, he'd write his mother a long letter. To Cora, he'd send pretty picture postcards that he'd seen in shops... He untied the bag of sandwiches his mother had prepared with such care, and his throat choked up. He saw the frozen figure of his mother—how she had stood near the steps of the train as it began to move—as if she were standing by the altar ready to fall to her knees. A female passenger noticed that Teddy was daydreaming. So she tapped his knee and, pointing to the bag, said: "Be a man, boy, be a man!"

The woman's words didn't cheer Teddy up. They had the opposite effect, in fact. He choked up on his outpouring of tears. He tied the bag back up, and stared into the darkness of the train car.

Elizabeth returned from the train station to their empty home, feeling as if her feet were freezing. She couldn't feel the actual steps she was taking. Her head still pounded, and she still felt light-headed. Ta-ta-ta! It was unbearable—her head felt as if it were going to fly off into pieces! "Skippy, dear dog, my friend, come here to me. Why are you crying?" Skippy wept in his canine way, and begged her to offer at least a word of comfort. He and she—partners in yearning...

The next day, Elizabeth went to work. She berated herself for not behaving in a manner befitting a woman who had led such a difficult life. After all, she had sent him away for a worthy goal. She still believed that her son would have a better future living with her brother than he would staying with her. She really did have to get a hold of herself. She tried to think less about her Teddy. A few days would go by, and he would write her the first letter. Then she would completely calm down and be able to restrain her nerves in the workplace.

The gnawing in her heart did not subside. But she appeared to be at peace and even smiled: "Oh, to finally get to see that first letter. Is a mother's heart always worried for no reason?—No, not for no reason!"

It was a Sunday morning, four days after she accompanied her Ted with such a heavy heart, and yet with faith that he was going to a new, better life. The day was set to be sunny, bright. One of those mornings that brings joy to yearning hearts...

Elizabeth lay in bed longer than she did on her workdays. She didn't have to prepare breakfast for her child. She looked out the window. The street was inundated with little ones. Elizabeth knew all of the children born on her block. It seemed as if she knew them even before they were born. She found herself drawn to the children. Perhaps she ought to call them into her house? It would be nice to have a home full of little children. No, there was work to be done—but wait, what was this? Why was Jean running that way? Why were they running straight to her from all of the other houses? What did it mean? Everyone—the whole neighborhood—dear God!

A crowd burst into her home without even ringing the door-bell. Wringing her hands and sobbing bitterly, Jean fell upon her neck. She couldn't speak. As she sobbed, she pointed to another woman holding a newspaper. Large, black, incomprehensible letters. Although no one said what the black letters meant, Elizabeth nevertheless sensed that something terrible had happened to her child. Her feet gave way. She fell to the floor, her teeth clenched, her eyelids clenched. The house was filled with people and lament. Children and mothers wept.

The young parson—his face yellow, his lips blue—entered the house. He got down on his knees, touched Elizabeth's head, and pleaded for help in getting her into bed. For a while, he stood there, his eyes fastened on the floor. Eventually, he took a newspaper from his pocket and as his voice choked up with tears, he read:

"Yesterday, in middle of the night, two white, respectable citizens—brothers—broke into a boy's room in the home of the colored garage-man. Against the hue-and-cry of the man, his wife, and all of the nearby neighbors, they bound the boy's hands and feet and dragged him into the forest. There, they tortured the poor child and threw him into the adjacent river. The two white brothers accused Teddy of whistling at their wives when they were walking past the veranda where the boy was rocking on a chair. The boy had arrived a few days earlier to stay with his uncle, the black garage-man… No one was arrested, even though everyone saw the murder…"

The parson's voice plummeted. His last words were barely audible. His stature had somehow become diminished. His head lowered to the floor. The unearthly howling of the mother, thrown into convulsions, tore through the congealed stillness. The parson tried to calm her. He firmly pressed her hands and temples and then he covered her, but Elizabeth had glided into other realms. He tried to speak, but his voice wouldn't obey him. After a few minutes of silence, his voice, ringing out like an echo, could be heard: "Daughter, hear my voice! My child! I speak to you the words of God. He, God alone, will punish them! The guilty ones will pay for the spilled blood! Yes, they will pay!"

Elizabeth remained quiet for a while. She looked at the parson with darkened eyes. He couldn't bear her dark gaze, so he got down on his knees and let out a heartrending cry.

Everything and everyone wept. The house, the women, the children, the street itself. Many, many streets wept...

Dog Blood

The guest who had come to meet the Shtroms was beside himself. Out of politeness, he restrained himself from hurling curse words at his friends with whom he had wandered during the Holocaust years until he finally managed to reach these shores. He thought to himself: How is this actually possible? They'd suffered together, struggled, lived like persecuted wild animals. And so how could a person even think this way? Something must have turned upside down in their minds. He never expected anything like this. Instead of kissing the hand that welcomed him like a decent human being, instead of blessing the country that gave him a roof over his head, Shtrom was nursing grievances about being dragged here.

The Shtroms—husband and wife—were past middle age. Their appearances were still marked by their past suffering, which screamed out without words. Shtrom, a heavy, short man, had a burned-away eyebrow and unhealed cuts on his face. From time to time, he said something. His wife seemed to be completely mute. For her, speaking was a great effort. To whatever her husband said, she nodded in agreement. She scarcely benefited from the milk and honey that dripped here from the trees. She had the face of a skeleton and eyes that seemed large and shimmering. People wondered how she still managed to stay alive.

Simkheh Shtrom answered the guest's claims:

"Who can enjoy all of the good things here if the ground is alien and empty? There, everything was my own! I see you smiling. No doubt you're thinking—some 'my own'! Those blood-soaked fields! I know what you're thinking. But I want you to know that those blood-soaked fields, those trees, even the weeds on the grave knolls are my own and precious to me. When have Jews ever fled from the graves of their own flesh and blood? And if the dead were killed and burned, aren't their graves still graves? We should've stayed there, where our remains are…"

He gestured with his head in the direction of his wife and said, "She—definitely! Do you really think that our being dragged all this way here was a salvation? It makes no difference that she sits on a chair and I drag myself around. We are there! There, we kept our eyes to the ground. Each grain of sand, each pebble reminded us of something. But here? There's nothing to look at. The wealth here is flagrant, making you want to run away, run to the graves." And then he added, "And you ought to know, my friend, that in the places where Jews did stay, a Jewish way of life will take root. It's already happening! If we had stayed there, we would have yet found a consolation for our spilled blood. We would have had revenge and comfort. But here, they begrudge our feeling good about life there, even from a distance. They paint a dark picture of everything as if their life depended on poisoning it to the best of their ability."

Although he was not speaking very loudly, Shtrom spoke in a strained voice. His wife was looking at him with her frozen face, as if she were waiting for something.

Considerably younger than the Shtroms, the guest, a small, emaciated individual with prominent cheekbones, didn't take his right hand out of his pocket. With his left, he picked at his neck, as if he were trying to demonstrate that although he was engrossed in his own thoughts, he still heard what was being said to him. Shtrom approached him and said, "Maybe you'd like to know what I think about your philanthropists and their millions? I believe their amassed property is coming out of their ears. And so they've started to fear that they'll have to account someday for their silence when the earth was rising over there beneath the boots of the drunken Nazis, and the dead were stirring…"

Shtrom's face was a fiery red. He felt his breast pocket, took out a small, old, leather pouch, looked over at his wife, and placed it back in his pocket. He smoothed out his threadbare jacket and then said in a softer voice: "Don't be angry at me. Maybe I shouldn't have brought all that up. I know we both bear deep wounds. We're both victims. But you're younger. The two of us—she and I—won't be reinventing ourselves. Neither I, with the dog blood that I carry in my entrails; nor she, with her skeletal face."

The guest winced. Shtrom smiled strangely. He continued: "And didn't we eat rats back then? A dog's flesh would have been a holiday meal for us. Hunger was quieted with whatever was available. And you think these people here can, or will, heal our souls? I don't believe them. I still remember how I called out to them—I won't do it anymore!"

The guest, his face now darkened, turned in his chair. He tried to say something but couldn't find the right words. Instead, he fussed with his hand inside his pocket and extricated a pack of crumpled cigarettes and a small box of matches. But when it came to lighting a match for smoking, his fingers somehow didn't work. Shtrom helped him. The guest greedily swallowed the smoke, looked down at the ground, and said:

"You see these hands—what wouldn't I be able to do if it weren't for their condition? And if I'd have stayed there, would the graves have done me much good? You're angry with the American Jewish benefactors because they were deaf to our desperate cries for help. Well, I ask: Where was God? Why don't you hold any grievances against Him?" He spoke very quickly, as if he were afraid of being interrupted.

"Nonsense! If you'll forgive my saying so, nonsense, empty talk!"

Shtrom moved slightly away from his guest, wanting to see him better. Becoming heated, he continued, "Was it God who approached me with the choice of going to Israel or to America?

Surely not. I'm not saying that everything they do has no value. All I'm saying is that if only they would accomplish good with what they've accumulated. Nothing more than that. It is impermissible to hide the truth. The truth is that we were wrong to flee. We shouldn't have dragged ourselves here! Believe me, if people only knew about the love and determination of the survivors who remained there and are helping to rebuild the country. The country that is now free for every citizen! Not just they—but the graves of the perished, as well—are secure and protected. I'm ashamed before my slain mother who weeps from her grave…"

Shtrom stopped near his wife, who was sitting and looking with expressionless eyes off to the side. He looked at her for a while and then turned to the guest and said, "Oh, how we screamed, raised an alarm, but their minds were impenetrable. Don't think they're giving away their last penny; they keep plenty!" By this point, his voice was tearing jaggedly from him. Sensing that his wife's mute eyes were pleading with him to calm down, he sat down on the small sofa and, once again, took out the old, worn pouch from his breast pocket. His wife's hands reached out, and for the first time throughout the entire encounter, she stammered "No! Don't!" When he put the pouch away, she lowered her weakened eyes.

Suddenly, as if he had forgotten his wife and the guest, Shtrom stood up, ran to the small table by the window, took out the pouch again using both of his hands, and began to set down the photographs one by one. He did so methodically, without rushing, in order, one after the other, in even rows. He counted four generations. He placed the young together with the young, the old with the old, and he called them by their names and their titles: rabbis, doctors, jurists. From the photographs shone bright, smiling faces of couples in wedding clothes, students with diplomas in their hands, mischievous children's faces with joy and obstinacy in their eyes. Clouds of smoke began to fan out before Shtrom's eyes, clouds of all colors… black, red… He felt ants crawling in his eyes and a ringing in his ears…

With one hand, Shtrom gripped the table, and with the other, beckoned the guest. The guest was in no hurry. He knew what he would see there. His face trembled, as if he were getting ready to stare at a cadaver. Even before the guest reached the table, Shtrom started to sink to the floor…

Everyone was back in their places. The four generations were once again packed away in their pouch in the breast pocket. A chilly and mournful silence reigned in the room. The guest started to get ready to go home. After a long silence, he found his power of speech. As if themselves afraid, his first few, hardly audible words barely cut a path through the dark shadows:

"Lawyers, engineers, rabbis… just because my family is uncultured, without pedigree, just because we were not born into prestigious occupations, just because we were born with big hands and feet, like my grandfathers and my father," he said, looking mechanically at his hanging hand, "do you think my pain is less than yours?"

Shtrom jolted as if he had been savagely bitten. His head and his hands trembled in agitation. "My God! How can a person—a Jew—speak that way? Do you think I care about pedigree and titles? It's the annihilation that's polluted everything. That's what's tormenting me. Manure and dog blood are intermingling in my entrails, and I can't bear it! And do you think that because of their charitable activities, you have to stand before them with bowed head? No, not me! Should I do it because of the dog blood that's in me? Or maybe because of her—that face, those eyes of hers that are constantly searching? I repeat: No! I won't offer them blessings in thanks for this scrap of rotten life. You maintain that if it weren't for them, the survivors wouldn't be in America. I say: Blessed are those who didn't allow themselves to be led astray! They—over there—have already managed to get back on their feet, and we here—what are we? What are we doing here?"

The grayness of the walls spread over their faces. A mournful wind tore ferociously at the loose window frames, and a chill penetrated the three people.

Shtrom stood up and walked to the window with a heavy tread. Between two small houses protruded a thin, trembling, little tree that circled around itself, as if it wanted to twist its way out of there. Shtrom rocked back and forth to the rhythm of the haggard branches that reminded him of human hands he'd once seen reaching up out of mountains of dirt.

The guest bade them good night, but the two Shtroms didn't hear him.

There's No Door

Although the heat was merciless and stinging and the house so scorchingly hot that it rattled and sighed under the heat waves, the three of them not only didn't feel the heat but were enveloped by a freezing cold.

The stillness was tense, congealed. Each of them tried to stay busy with their hands, to keep their minds occupied. Each looked for something in the other, even if they were all in separate rooms...

The first one to blurt something out was the youngest child, six-year-old Bobby. On his face, in his limbs, there was unease, and in his large, dark eyes—fear. He had the feeling that something terrifying—a grave misfortune—was crouching in wait here.

Bobby couldn't look into his aunt's eyes. His kind aunt turned her back to him when she called him. In the meantime, his older brother, Michael, came in, glanced over at the little one, and then went back out. The brother brought a few small cartons of colored chalk, told him to draw something, and acted as if he were busy with something, a matter that he, little Bobby, wouldn't understand.

Bobby had the feeling that he wouldn't be able to stay silent like this for very long. Something was boiling over in his throat. He just needed to finish the picture. He had to finish it!

His hands worked quickly. He daubed, and the colors irritated him, provoking his anger. With his little hands, he tugged at his cheeks, his hair, anything that could be seized. He looked at the elongated, not-high wall that he had drawn, considering its dark, quadrangular little boxes. In one of the boxes, a man's head was clearly visible. The man was wearing round glasses. A bit higher, though not as clear, a woman's head was discernible. Everything was drawn in a childish—but also lively and striking—way. Bobby himself was frightened by his drawing. It cut and tugged at his young heart.

His big brother stopped at the door. His voice filled with weeping, as if he'd committed a grave offense, Bobby lamented: "Just look, Michael—there's no door! Oh no, I didn't make a door…"

Michael ran away, and Bobby burst into outright sobs. His sobbing was so distressing, so heartrending that it seemed that the house, everything in it, and the burning sun that singed the earth behind its covered windows, was sobbing alongside him. He kicked and banged his head on the floor. As if arising from a hidden source, the sobbing was transported into all corners of the house.

The aunt, her frozen face trembling from chill, got down on the floor next to Bobby. She caressed him and, her voice choking up, pleaded with the child: "Bobinke, dear boy, my sweet angel, Bobby, my child…"

Her lips moved, but she spoke without words. She placed one hand behind the child's head, and with the other, kept caressing him. With her hand, she sought to pour the deepest pain of her soul into the child, but it wasn't really her sorrows that she wanted to present to him, but rather her solace. She wanted to take into her heart this child who was sobbing so bitterly, who didn't know the terrible crime committed against him… She caressed his silken hair, and he sobbed and sobbed…

After he had cried out all of his pain and all of the terrors he saw in Michael's secretive glances and in his aunt's dumbstruck face, and after having screamed with his last bit of strength, Bobby proceeded to sigh like an adult. Utterly spent, he turned his child's head away, shivered, and fell asleep.

A deep stillness reigned again over the household. Michael's ten-year-old face was lean—emaciated really—like someone twice his age. His lips were stiff, and thin wrinkles lined his forehead. His eyes were set far back into his head, as if he hadn't lifted his head to look upon the bright world in a long time…

All morning long, he hadn't stepped away from the television. Michael wanted to accommodate his aunt and put something in his mouth, but he was feeling a strong resistance to food and found that he couldn't open his mouth. His lips were dry and his throat was sealed shut, unable to release a single word. He wanted to offer his little brother a kind word, but when he saw Bobby's distressed turmoil, he turned around and abruptly left.

Michael could barely take in what was happening onscreen, but he remained seated, stubbornly, trembling, waiting. Waiting…

Bobby slept fitfully. His aunt's hand caressed him. He felt the softness of her fingers. She said to him, "Sweet Bobby, give me a strong kiss! Hug me with both of your arms." He reached out to her, wanting to offer her a kiss, but his kiss hovered in the air. He struggled and heard her words: "My little angel, give me a strong kiss. Strong!"

The child was startled. The aunt jumped up. A choked-up scream sounded from the other room. Michael clenched his hands together into fists, pressed them against his temples so that he wouldn't fall down. He sat bent over the chair and couldn't stand on his feet.

His screams were choked. "It's all over! All over! Over… Doomed!" he shouted. A greenish yellowness poured over the aunt's face. She lifted the boy with her stiff hands, clutching him tightly. He straightened out and looked into her face, as if he were waiting for something else. She lowered her eyes to the floor. Bobby launched quickly into a new bout of weeping, resting his head against her. All three of them wept quietly. All three of them like a single stone knot… like a living gravestone.

On that same hot evening, a fortunate father heard the first cry of his firstborn: "Congratulations! Congratulations! A boy!" On that same hot evening, a couple left on their honeymoon. "Have a good trip!"

And on that same burning-hot evening, two young people, under the tones of exultant music, left the New York harbor with hundreds, thousands of carefree, radiant pleasure-seekers...

And on that burning-hot evening, two young, luminous souls counted the last minutes left for them to live...

Graduation

During the past few weeks, the boys and girls of the graduating class had been far more preoccupied with the preparations for their graduation celebration than with their studies.

The accumulated pent-up energy of graduating students was bursting forth from them. A rowdy joy radiated from the occupant of every chair so that the chairs themselves seemingly radiated along with them. The students danced and carried on—both alone and with each other. Hardly a small matter—graduation! We're not kids anymore; we're now adults! We're just about there! Any minute now!

Like the other students, Thelma had been waiting for this change in status. But as the big day approached, a sense of unease grew within her. It was an unease that she couldn't share with anyone else. Thelma's friend Frieda, her face beaming and her limbs bopping in excitement, approached her and said breathlessly: "My ma is organizing a big party for graduation night. Do you have a date? If not, go and find yourself one right away!" When the other girl left, Thelma's unease ballooned into such anguish that she felt like crying.

Sitting there, looking at her little book, she visualized her parents in her mind's eye. Her mother—old enough to be her grandmother. Puffy, glum, wearing a torn skirt and a kerchief on her head. Her father—a thin man with a small head, sharp, biting eyes, his dried-out arms crossed against his heart. He sits on a padded chair, looking out the window and rocking as if he were mourning someone.

Thelma never did know whether these pugnacious people, always angry about something or other, felt anything for her, their child. She also didn't know if she herself felt anything for them. She thought of herself as being always somehow severed from… she didn't really know from what. Even as a small child, she was clinging to strangers. All a neighbor had to do was give her a caress, and she would latch on to the person like a kitten. In this, she was fortunate. There were always good-hearted strangers to take pity on a neglected child. With one neighbor woman, Thelma practically found herself a home. There were times when she spent an entire day there, only coming home to sleep.

With hungry eyes, Thelma looked on as the kind neighbor woman's children fell upon their father when he came home from work. He was a cheerful, playful man who let the children ride on his shoulders. Their home was always full of laughter. The happy young father didn't begrudge Thelma a pat with his warm hands. How she loved that pat!

The little girl was too young to understand, or ask, why her parents were so angry, sad, and prone to fighting. She warmed herself at the fires of strangers.

The older Thelma got, the more she avoided her own home. Now it occurred to her that she hadn't ever allowed a friend into her own home. Not a single one. Thelma had come up with all kinds of excuses. But the truth was that she was ashamed of her parents, ashamed of their constant arguing.

When Thelma turned ten years old, she had earned enough to buy a dress. Teke, one of the kind neighbors, furnished the money needed. Each week, Teke gave her two dollars. People were told that Thelma was getting this money because she played with the neighbor's little girl while her mother was away, returning to the workshop the work she had brought to do at home. Thelma remembered the first dress she bought with her earnings: a blue dress with little white squares. Teke went with her to buy the dress. Thelma's mother saw her smile for the first time.

She recalled other events. The skeins coiled around her childhood years were beginning to unravel. When she got older, she
often racked her brain trying to fathom whose sin it was that had
resulted in her being punished with such a home. From some
deep, concealed, hitherto-undiscovered corner she unearthed a
feeling that was new to her: compassion.

Thelma didn't know anything about that feeling. She didn't
know that she had arrived in the world unwanted. She came at a
time when her helpless parents themselves didn't know how to
hold their lives together or how to split apart... or how to loos-
en the foolish, perhaps criminal, knot in which they sought, like
blind people, to save themselves.

By the time she got married, Thelma's mother, "Reyzl the
Lucky One"—as her compatriots from her home country called
her—was already middle-aged. "The Lucky One" was neither
beautiful nor gifted. She never could keep up with the big-city
hustle and bustle. She often suffered from a bit of hunger. The
landlady, in whose home she lived, found a wedding match
for her, a widower who had his own apartment. The man was
a mattress maker. He didn't have any children—or money, for
that matter. He barely earned enough to eke out a living. Well,
a home, somewhere to rest her head, would she have that? Why
should she become an old maid when she herself was unable to
do anything well?

"Reyzl the Lucky One" didn't look into whom she was mar-
rying. At that time, he was out of a job and waiting for work to
present itself. So she contented herself with the home and the old
pieces of furniture. But before work could materialize, he took
sick. As soon as the few dollars that had been saved were depleted, war came to the household. By this point, Reyzl understood
all too well the sort of bargain she had made. For the first few
weeks, she helped him make frequent visits to the doctors without any money. But soon she began to pity herself, nursing grievances against him for her "dark fortune." "Why did you deceive

me?" she asked angrily. He, too, had grievances of his own. "So that's how you care for your husband? You married my bank-book?" The arguments escalated into outright hatred.

His illness continued. It was the kind of prolonged illness that ages you. The life of the couple was one unending squabble.

Yet something held the two of them together. As the Russian expression says: "*Klin klinom vikhivayut*."[12] The phlegmatic, helpless Reyzl who, throughout her entire life, had held herself on the sidelines in fear of the wider world, nevertheless found a sliver of a foundation in this broken man. He had connections of a sort. He was a patient, and God was a father. There were, thank God, organizations, charitable federations! Reyzl was left with an impoverished life. Still, it was better than nothing.

Arguing, sometimes quietly, sometimes loudly, in the very midst of each of them making the other's life miserable, nature played a practical joke on them... Neither Reyzl nor her husband, who was just skin and bones, barely able to drag himself around, could believe it! That is—until the child began to kick. Prior to that, they had shouted: "No, no, and no!"

Reyzl kicked herself in frustration. And as for her husband—his small, green eyes danced around, as if they wanted to tear themselves free from their sockets... Like an unwanted pest, Thelma arrived in the world.

In the clean hospital cradle until she was ten days old, Thelma's fresh, round face shone. She kept looking to put something in her mouth. When the child was prepared to be sent home, she was stamped with the label of "underprivileged child."

A neighbor brought home the mother and the baby, who was wearing donated baby clothing and wrapped in an old blanket. Instead of a joyous father, they found a sullen, frightened little man who, having apparently lost his power of speech, didn't emit a peep. He remained seated, resting with one hand on his cane and

---

12. Literally, "They use a wedge to knock out a wedge." Meaning: Fight fire with fire, like cures like, or one nail drives out another.

the other placed on his heart, as if he feared the little soul would settle scores with him for his sins. He curled up and spoke into his broken, embarrassed shadow: "Serves you right!" The unfatherly father searched for a bit of feeling toward the little soul, and pity for himself and the child seized him, especially when he heard her crying with the voice of a little kitten. Her crying made him try to get up. He wanted to flee, commit suicide. But he couldn't get out of the chair and so he wept into it. How bitter was his life, how burdened he was! No one wanted to so much as glance at him. He would stay forgotten. She, his wife, treated him like a dog. Now she would most certainly let him die sick.

"Reyzl the Lucky One"—weak, without skills of her own—moved through her days with a heaviness in her legs, and her eyes, full of sorrow, bulging over her sallow cheeks, looked lost, ashamed. She couldn't take on the obligations of being a mother. She couldn't quite accept this new reality. The child hadn't changed her situation at all. As before, she blamed her husband for all of the troubles. She was so weak that she didn't have the strength to scream.

With an apparent defiance and to everyone's astonishment, the mite of a child, cared for by a neighbor, shone her light out into the hostile world from the bundle of old clothes. She had a round, pink head, full cheeks, and a big appetite. When she wasn't offered the bottle as quickly as she wanted, she shoved a little fist into her mouth and smacked her lips so loudly that it could be heard all the way from the other room.

Two days after mother and child came home from the hospital, a middle-aged woman in a white dress and a blue coat entered. Her tread was so sturdy that the whole room shook when she walked. The woman brought with her a fresh breeze and a healthy smell. She sat down on the first chair she saw, opened a folder, cast a pair of gray-green eyes on the frightened couple and—as if she wanted to convince herself that she was in the right place—

she once again looked at a sheet of paper crammed with writing. She went towards the old carriage that smelled of something sour and unwashed bedding. She took a look at the child and, in the tone of a police officer, asked: "Do you want the child to be taken away?"

Hearing those words, Reyzl's sallow face darkened. The father's hands started to shake convulsively. He gripped the windowsill with both hands and shifted out of the chair. He wanted to resist this strong woman, but he stumbled, lost his balance, and fell back into the chair. The woman dropped her police officer's tone. Her eyes softened. She took the baby from her rags with maternal hands and began washing her with some hot water and soap. She gave the frightened Reyzl her first lesson in bathing a child.

From that day on, Reyzl tended Thelma under the watchful eyes of the trained childcare professionals more out of fear than affection. The child grew by leaps and bounds. She eluded all illnesses. She became the marvel of the so-called Association for the Protection of Underprivileged Children.

Ever preoccupied with their squabbling, tenderness was utterly alien to the parents. When they were told that Thelma was a lovely, healthy, and intelligent child, they were delighted. Thelma was a girl with bright blue eyes, a head of golden curls, and a vivid smile. She shone in the hand-me-down dresses she was given. Her skin had a bronze color; her limbs—velvety, rounded. "Like bathed in milk and honey," the neighbors would say.

At a very young age, Thelma began to stand on her own two feet. She was advanced for her years, a good student. Among the crowded tenement buildings on Tiffany Street, poverty was omnipresent. Thelma imbibed it with her mother's milk. All of the children who befriended her were poor. Some had a bit more but were still far from wealthy. Nevertheless, a shadow hung over Thelma's life. Of a child's genuine joy, she knew nothing. A deep seriousness was apparent in her blue eyes. There was a constant searching, a yearning for something for which she herself had no name.

Now, one day before the big event, she was reading a book to study the part she needed to play with a boy in her class. The boy's name was Sima. On graduation day, his mother wouldn't be going to work. She'd be taking Sima to a movie. In her own home, Thelma didn't see a shred of evidence that tomorrow would be different from any other day. Her parents didn't mention their daughter's upcoming graduation, and this pained her greatly.

She thought about what to do. Maybe she shouldn't speak to her parents at all about the graduation? At this thought, her young heart compressed, as if it were going into a cramp. Thelma closed her eyes and was prepared to say to those seated around her: "Pardon me. I'm a bad person. I'm ashamed of my parents." She looked around, thinking that someone had heard her thoughts. About to turn fifteen, Thelma experienced a self-revelation, and this revelation was painful.

With all of her youthful being, she realized that a terrible injustice had been perpetrated against her, and against them. Her parents weren't totally culpable. They were what they were. Thelma spotted Sylvia, who was sitting and looking off into the distance. Sylvia had been raised in a children's home, and there was a constant sadness in her eyes. Perhaps she ought to go over and talk to Sylvia? No, she decided, she wouldn't speak to Sylvia about personal matters. She didn't want to talk about her parents at all.

As if propelled by wings, her friend Frieda nimbly ran up and said: "Thelma, I have a date for you. Get ready. Nine o'clock?"

Before Thelma knew it, Frieda was no longer there, disappearing with a dance of her own.

The next day, Commencement Day, Thelma gave her mother two tickets and said: "Both of you, put on some nice, clean clothes and come. I want to see you there." Her mother, morose as always, wanted to say something but didn't manage to get a word out because Thelma had already sailed forth from the house.

The graduation was held in a large movie house. It was a beautiful day. The sky was devoid of the slightest trace of a cloud; all was bright and peaceful as if nature herself had made everything festive, like a gift from God to the world of the young.

The street around the theater was full of throngs of young people and parents. The youth in bright attire looked like one large multi-hued flower garden, like a single, mobile, exultant, and dazzling garden full of light and color.

Thelma, in a bright blue dress and a white flower in her lustrous hair, looked like a sunflower. She was due to appear onstage with her friends in a one-act play, but she extricated herself from their circle, moved some distance away, and looked off in the direction from which her parents were supposed to arrive.

She was overwhelmed and didn't hear anything being said to her. She didn't know how to welcome her parents here, and so she waited for some kind of miracle that would free her at the last minute from the unpleasant encounter.

The miracle did happen. She spotted them coming. Her heart practically stopped. The couple attracted the attention of the entire audience gathered there.

Wearing her Sabbath best and with her hair elegantly combed, Reyzl looked around like someone utterly lost. She was leading her husband with the proficiency of someone experienced in the ways of guiding an invalid. Thelma's father kept one hand on her mother's shoulder and the other on his cane, trudging with his loose, dangling legs. His small body was angled upwards as if aiming to count the stories of the tall building. They moved very slowly. Quick as a lightning bolt, Thelma made off in their direction. She embraced her mother, and for the first time Thelma could remember, her mother held her tightly in her arms. Without words, the tears of mother and daughter mingled.

Gray Lives

Manye had been selling newspapers in her kiosk for years. The kiosk was under the stairs to the elevator on a street corner near the subway. No one knew when Manye had taken over the little stall from the previous newspaper vendor, and if Manye were to hand over her business to someone else the next day, well, no one would know that, either. No one would miss her, because to the pedestrians who grabbed a newspaper while rushing by, it made no difference who was standing behind the counter.

The street corner was noisy, surrounded by all sorts of shops. Most of the people who raced to the station in the mornings streamed out of the side streets in a constant, rapid flow. Newspaper buyers never stopped. With the few cents ready at hand, they took the newspaper themselves and tossed the change on the extended drop-leaf shelf of the kiosk and ran to the stairs leading to the elevator.

When someone had to get change, the transaction was conducted on auto-pilot, through communication by signs and gestures. The hand extended, the change was placed inside it, the customer gripped it and bolted. The later in the morning it got to be, the sparser the crowd. By nine-thirty in the morning, it was already quiet. It was very seldom that Manye would be there with newspapers past ten o'clock. It was a morning business. In the evening, when the newspaper buyers returned home from work, there was no sign that newspapers had been sold on that spot in the morning.

And so it was—day in, day out; year in, year out.

Manye was never seen outside of the booth. In the summertime, the booth was open. The drop-leaf was all the way down. Then, one half of Manye's massive, unfeminine frame was visible. In the winter, the booth was half-open, and from the sweaters and shawls, a pair of bright, curious eyes, a wide mouth, a set of thick, chapped lips, and a narrow strip of a furrowed brow were visible. Manye's eyes were forever changing. One moment, it seemed as if they were searching for something, and at another, it looked as if they were gazing in disorientation—and then still later, with warmth—at the pedestrians racing past to grab their newspaper.

People thought that Manye and her newspaper booth had fused together as one, that both would be there for all eternity. But such was not the case. Manye had not always been a newspaper vendor. She took to the enterprise because she was isolated. Through the booth, she tethered her lonely existence to the dynamic world that surrounded her.

Manye had been fated to stay at home. She was the only child born to sickly parents and had to be their caregiver. Her parents perpetually kept her under the shadow of their fear of death. As a result, Manye neglected her own life.

Manye was not beautiful. God had not bestowed feminine charm upon her. She wasn't destined to have years of bloom, when even unbeautiful women have that certain springlike appeal. Those years were given to others—those more fortunate—but not to her, not to Manye.

In the meantime, the years flew by. Her parents died, and Manye was left on her own. As an eighteen-year-old girl, she began working in a large factory. She was the private secretary of a volatile manager. She got used to working with the unwell man, serving him loyally as if he had taken the place of her parents.

Living alone, one thing remained to her: the job. She divided her life between home and work. Then the scrap of good fortune of having someone make use of her time was also destroyed. Not that long after she was orphaned, the manager took gravely ill and left the factory. The owners replaced Manye with a pretty young girl.

Her own life—that is, living for herself and on behalf of herself—was something Manye didn't have and didn't want to have. And so, when she left the factory position, she lost everything. There was nothing for her to live for.

She looked for another job, writing and responding to letters in the process. She didn't deny her age. By then, she was thirty years old, but she looked older. Tall, wide, with skin of a grayish color, and sagging, jowly cheeks, she was taken for someone in her fifties. When they read her letters, Manye observed a veiled derision in their eyes. She invariably received the same answer: "We'll let you know." Only they never did let Manye know.

Arriving home, feeling sick at heart and insulted, Manye would look in the mirror and say to herself: "They don't want me! I'm too old!" But how can a person live alone? She loved people, even if she wasn't pleasing to very many of them. Manye came up with a way out. With her savings of a few hundred dollars, she bought the newspaper kiosk and hitched herself to it. The kiosk took the place of a full social life. It was a source of sustenance for her body and soul. She didn't ask for much; her needs were modest. She was content with her earnings, and even more satisfied with that other aspect of her business: the one that allowed her, unbidden and unseen, to connect with the rapid stream of customers. In her mind, she brought everyone close to her, sharing with them in her thoughts and offering a devotion that hadn't been asked of her since her parents died.

Manye stood in her kiosk with open eyes and an open heart, gazing at and *through* all of her customers. In a matter of a few seconds, her eye grasped: one female customer, a young, cheerful girl. Singing aloud, well-rested. She grabbed the newspaper and started to run lightly and playfully on the steps to the elevator. Manye smiled along with the girl, and in her chubby hand, the few pennies that the girl left there rested. She clasped the pennies as if to preserve the joy from the girl that remained with her.

And now a tired, pale customer, with an anxious face, was going past her. She took a newspaper with indifference; it was all the same to her which newspaper it was. Manye's heart became heavy. She would have liked to ask the customer: "What happened?" She looked on at the woman, or rather the girl, until the latter's feet landed on the stairs, and she thought: "Perhaps someone close to her is sick. Poor thing, a pity!" This woman, or girl, left Manye emotionally overcome. She couldn't get her out of her mind very easily, at least not until another buyer, with an even worse appearance, or the opposite, one with a cheerful face, showed up and washed the face of the previous customer out of her mind.

Although Manye made no exceptions and incorporated everyone into the circle of her thoughts, men were nevertheless the first and last to occupy her mind. It was probably because more men went to work and bought newspapers. Whatever the reason, more men raced past Manye's line of vision than women, and although they were in a hurry, it seemed to Manye that they were catching a bit of a glance of her. Some of them gestured with the corner of an eye or a lift of a bit of lip or an eyebrow twitch. There were others who even offered her a smile. Manye gathered together all of these crumbs, kindled them with feminine longing, and as if illuminated by an artificial light, the emotions of human contact flared up and then died down within her.

This contact, this whiff of masculinity, was like a divine gift. She didn't have to beg anyone for it, just as she didn't have to ask for the bit of sun that came into the corner of her booth on early summer mornings.

When Manye bought the newspaper booth, her hair was still reddish-blonde. As the years passed, her hair began to turn gray. She reacted to this grayness with fear. She reacted to her whole life as best she could—she patched it up a bit and wanted it to stay that way. But gray hair was a sign of old age and she was terrified of old age. Previously, Manye had almost never looked in the mirror. She had the impression that the mirror was a kind of an exaggerating mocker. Now, she kept looking in the mirror and her heart was full of pleading to the cold piece of glass. She gazed, searching for and then counting the gray hairs. She found a way to comfort herself: It will take some time. Perhaps the grayness would remain at the temples, and that wasn't so ugly. On the contrary, it appeared to soften her face. Her eyes, too, became milder in the reflection that the grayness cast upon them from the temple-corners.

Manye adjusted her dreams, and matched the men that she saw near her kiosk to her own age. She looked at the older men with sidelong glances, not directly seeking their gaze. But with the young men, she felt as if she were from another, earlier world.

The years passed. The customers changed a few times. Others came. Manye's circle did not diminish, it only became larger. But now, whenever Manye went over the list of her self-accepted soul-sustainers in her mind, she only saw men with gray hair. The gray-haired ones had pushed out the others. She herself was now entirely gray. She had practically forgotten the natural color of her hair. Now she even thought that the gray color better suited her.

The gray-haired men were also more suitable to her than the earlier ones. They weren't as stingy with a glance as the others had been, and although they, too, were in a rush, their rush was of another sort. There was time in their rush. They didn't really look at her per se, either, but when they did manage a glance, Manye saw her own yearning reflected in their eyes.

It seemed to Manye that she had always lived in a world of grayness. She didn't understand why the grayness had previously frightened her. Grayness led to something which couldn't be avoided. Since there was, there had to be, and there would be grayness and maturity, well then, she, Manye was no exception. After all, she did not exist outside of time. Time was with her, with her grayness, with tomorrow. With many gray tomorrows.

Grandma Reyze Seeks Advice

… My dear, kind, precious one! I'm sure you have a good Jewish heart. I know you'll believe me. I know that when you look at me, you feel my sufferings. I beg you, my light, give me advice. God will reward you for it. How can I be rescued from the years that stick to me like a nuisance?

How much longer, dear God? What should I do with my superfluous years? After all, I'm like a ruin that's about to collapse but just refuses to do it.

… The world has been turned upside down. The earth has taken away millions of young people. Only I, a woman satiated with years, remain untouched. So I'd like to ask you something, my darling. Tell me, as God is dear to you, how should I tear myself loose from this miserable life? When I don't want any more years… I've had enough. You look at me, I notice, and surely think: Poor thing, this old lady isn't all there! And you'd be right. What else could it be—that I am, in fact, all there? Who, at my age and with the good life I've lived, wouldn't be senile?

There are enough people with troubles. But nobody's troubles can match mine. I'm as full of travails as a pomegranate is with seeds. And it's too much for a single creature with one life. God has allotted me a portion that would be enough for six. God knows I've hauled around my pack of troubles and stayed silent. But when does it end? I'd like just a word from you. You'd earn a share in The World to Come. How, my precious one, can I free myself? I only want to close my eyes and nothing more… To whom should I speak? You already know about my bitter life. I've already told you that of my thirteen children, I was, in the end, left with five, those who stayed in Poland. But now—only God knows what has become of them. As to my children here in America, they all died in the best years of their lives. They were felled like trees. With my own eyes, I had to watch how young fathers of children, mothers of young children were laid in the ground. Why? What for?

I see that you're biting your lip, poor thing. Someone else's misfortune pains you. So what do you think? Can an old wreck like me endure all this?

If I could at least bear this anguish on my own in silence, I would say: God is just, and His verdict is just! But given that my sufferings don't let me sit still during the day or lie still at night and given that I torment others with my laments, those who listen to me truly do deserve heartfelt pity.

I'm no longer a mother, you understand. "Mother" is a word I've already forgotten, buried it in the graves with my children. I've been a grandmother and great-grandmother for years and years. Grandma Reyze—that's what everyone calls me, even strangers. It even seems to me that I was born a grandmother.

I don't want to commit a sin with these words, but what else can God expect from me? If I were a saintly woman, I would say that God was sending Job's tribulations to me because He wants to test me. But who am I? It goes without saying that I'm nothing more than an ordinary old Jewish woman.

When my eyes still served me and I saw the radiant world before me, I thought: However nasty things get, God's world is still beautiful. But now that my eyes can no longer absorb light, and that hearing, too, is difficult for me, all I can do is focus on my travails. You know what I'm going to say to you? I fear that my children's unlived years have crept into me and insist on clinging to me. I, Grandma Reyze, am almost dead. If you'd see my arms, my legs, you'd agree with me. Have you actually seen my fingers? They're like crooked rafters; my body is like dried-out clay. Everything within me yearns for the earth, but God's ears are barred to me.

Will you believe me? I cover every speck of my body so my grandchild won't look at it. I don't do this out of shame, but because I don't want to cause her pain. It's enough that she sees how I practically crawl on all fours...

I don't want her to witness death happening right before her very eyes. She is a mother of four children and has her own share of problems. God didn't neglect her, either. Her two brilliant sons went off to serve. No one sees her pained heart, except me with my half-blind eyes. For days on end, she runs around—here, she gathers money for packages; here, she helps sew for—the good God Himself knows for whom. When I tell her, "Feygele, you're going to collapse!" she responds, "Dear Grandma, my sons are working for me." What can I answer her?

However much I try not to pester her, she unfortunately has enough to put up with from me. No matter how much I plead with her to put me in an old age home, she won't hear of it. She gets angry at me and stays silent. I know that when she's silent, it's because she's in great pain. She says nothing. But I know that she's thinking: Grandma Reyze's barely hanging on. Let her finish out her last days in her own bed.

When God saps a person in her elder years of her strength, makes her a piece of dried-out clay, He also needed to stop up the mind. But He didn't do that. The scrap of life lives in me and eats at me like a worm. I suffer for my flesh-and-blood rotting young in the earth, and I suffer for the living.

You say: It won't always be this way! May God grant you the strength to wait and live to see a better world. I don't want to anymore. For me, it's enough. I've suffered my share. I'd close my eyes in contentment if I believed as you believe. You, my dear, are blessed by God.

Aside from my grandchild, you're the only person to whom I reveal my bitter heart. To tell you the absolute truth, since my grandchild's sons have left home, I don't feel that I can complain to her. I want you to believe me when I say that it's not just any ordinary madness of an old, silly Jewish woman that causes me, for no particular reason, to come to you with such dark words and cast a pall of melancholy over you. On more than one occasion, crawling to you on my aching feet, I turned back as soon I reached your door.

I want to tell you something. If you laugh, well, there's laughter in all suffering. There's laughter and pain in anything a person can come up with.

All my life I knew—I even knew it as a child—that when a corpse is carried out of the house, you're not allowed to lay your ear against the threshold because the soul of the dead person hangs around the threshold and mourns the body. It's forbidden for any human eye or ear to perceive this lament. They say that if someone positions his ear against the threshold, he has to die soon thereafter because God doesn't want to reveal the soul to the living.

Since I seek death and it eludes me, I thought: Let God do with me what He will. For me, Hell is not a frightening place. I'm already in Hell here on earth. So when a neighbor died, I somehow slipped in and hid in the corner. The house was full of people. No one looked at me. But when everyone left to follow the coffin, I stretched myself out over the threshold. People thought I fell so they lifted me up… And as you see, I ended up the fool. I didn't die…

So now I've come to you. Since you've put in so much effort into somehow helping me, I thought that the best thing you can do for me is to help me free myself from life. You'd rather help me live? You say that there is no such thing as being too late for death? Thank you, my dear, thank you, but don't help me. I'll find a way, I'll… Be well. Farewell!

Snowballs

With unbridled joy, the young people set out to greet the first snow. It arrived with all of the fullness and brightness of a surprise during the night and continued into a festive Saturday morning. The snow came with a Saturday sun that flooded the children's hearts and limbs with an exuberant strength, with a noisiness that tore from them like a storm, like a fit of excitement. With its dazzling whiteness and soft shine, the snow covered everything the eye could absorb. Everything appeared renewed, refreshed. The surrounding streets were unrecognizable.

Children lying on their stomachs on sleds and toboggans slid along, rolling with their legs pointed upward, and their clamor filled the air. Snowballs, whizzing by right and left, hit faces, eyes, and noses, and crumbled amid dizzying joy.

On that morning, in her cart positioned near the window of her father's shop, Leyeh stood, beaming, refreshed. Her freezing cheeks, now warming up from the cold, were dark red. Her hair had wriggled its way out of her knitted hat, appearing silver against the sun. Her hands worked nimbly as if they were trying to make up for lost time. They worked nonstop, aiming to seize the opportunity. These two hands knew that such a morning seldom came back.

Leyeh was a twelve-year-old girl. Her father had a small shop where he made and sold cigars. He made the cigars at the window while he kept an eye on Leyeh.

When people went by the store, especially during the summer, Leyeh could always be seen sitting on a low cart that looked like a chair. Sometimes, she held a small book in her hand, and at other times, a jump rope. While sitting, she played with the rope, flinging it as if she wanted to lasso someone with it.

The neighbors knew why Leyeh always sat by her father's window. Leyeh couldn't get out of the cart by herself. Although she wore braces on both of her legs, she still depended on her father. When she wanted to get up, her father had to put aside his work and come over to help her. Even when she had gotten herself upright with her father's help, she couldn't walk without two crutches.

Leyeh would sit and wait in case a girl who wasn't tall would come by and want to jump rope. Leyeh would turn the rope and the girl would jump over it.

Leyeh was her parents' first child. She was a radiant child, with golden curls and dark brown eyes. Her body—as if made from soft velvet. She brought much joy into their not-wealthy household, and all the neighbors in the building—around thirty residents—were delighted with the child. Her mother could not have wished for a greater joy than this golden treasure.

When Leyeh turned two and a half years old, children's paralysis sucked the life out of both of her legs like a venomous snake. She remained lying in her child's bed like a piece of clay, and it was hard to believe that this was the same child. Just a few days ago, the girl had filled the house with her innocent laughter and chatter.

In addition to the child becoming unrecognizable, her parents had aged in a matter of days. The father had to tend to earning their bit of bread and so, sitting at his work, he quite often didn't hear or see at all what was going on around him. With the child in her arms, the mother trudged from doctor to doctor until her own and the family's meager savings of a few dollars were drained. When there was no longer any more money for doctors, the mother proceeded to trudge with the child to the hospitals. There began a flurry of consultations with several doctors who prescribed various courses of action. One doctor recommended that they operate right away; another said to wait. The mother didn't know whom to follow, and she didn't sleep at night. As time went by, there were no signs of improvement.

They tried all of the new "correctives" but without any results. Her illness and helplessness notwithstanding, Leyeh shone like the sun. She was the darling of the doctors and nurses, but everyone's efforts to get the child up and about on her own feet were in vain.

Time did as time does. Several years passed. Leyeh's mother gave birth to another girl and could no longer devote all of her time to the sick girl. When Leyeh's little sister was still tiny, Leyeh played with her as if she were a doll, marveling at every move and jerk and was as delighted as her mother with the baby's every smile and little facial expression. But as the little one grew and ran around into every nook and cranny of the home and as the mother forgot herself and kissed the little one on her hands and feet, something stuck in Leyeh's craw, and her mouth restrained itself from trembling. The bigger and more beautiful her little sister grew, the sadder Leyeh's face became.

Anger set in the corners of Leyeh's vivid child's eyes. Her nose dropped a little. A furrow of annoyance made its way onto her bright forehead, stealing away a part of her childhood. Only the thick, blond locks remained like loyal guards, garlanding her face like a sunflower.

When Leyeh was younger, all of the children on the street always gathered around her cart and played with her. They would make her the child who needed to be served, or when they were playing school, into a student. Leyeh was almost never bored. But when she and her playmates reached school age, Leyeh got lonely. A teacher would come to her house for a few hours a day, but for the rest of the time, she found herself alone.

Later, Leyeh enrolled in school. Every morning, a bus would come to take Leyeh to school. On the bus were other helpless children like Leyeh. A child is—a child... So she found a way to escape her constraints… Children don't think about tomorrow, and on the road, an upbeat mood reigned. They sang, laughed, and threw at each other whatever was at hand. One child infected another with laughter so much that even children who weren't participating in the game joined in the laughter. But when Leyeh returned home, she was back in her lonely world. She followed the jumping, laughing children with her eyes. She tried to imitate them with all her might, but hers were not real, perceptible movements. From time to time, Leyeh would ask her mother: "When will I be able to walk?" After a while, she didn't ask. She saw how her mother turned her head and started to speak about something else. By that, Leyeh understood that her mother didn't really have an answer.

During the summers, Leyeh felt her worst. The summer was when the children scattered, racing around in the parks. Many children left the city entirely. Then, she was left alone and forlorn. The isolation weighed heavily on her, and she grew sick of her books. She, too, could have gone to the park, but it was hard for her to get across the street. And besides, the park was a bit far. So she had to sit next to the shop and look on as her father rocked back and forth over the tobacco leaves. Sometimes, she had an impulse to laugh at her father, but he was so worried, so pale that in the end she just didn't have the heart to laugh at him. She would have embraced him, kissed his wrinkled cheeks were he to run out right now to see her…

It did happen that a girl or a boy Leyeh knew would speed by on roller skates. They waved cheerfully, and she responded with equal cheer. But this was a rare occurrence. She was glad when it rained and she didn't have to sit out on the street to please her mother. She preferred to be alone. She didn't want anyone to see how lonely she was.

Winter was altogether different. Leyeh didn't have to be out on the street as much during the winter. She had a lot of homework from school and had little time to be jealous of the other children. In the winter, she could also be on somewhat equal footing with the others. This was when there was a snowstorm, as happened on that morning.

Leyeh's father's shop was located on a street corner that was empty on all three sides. When there was a storm, whole mountains of snow piled up and you couldn't get to the shop. This hurt his livelihood. But for Leyeh, it was a holiday eagerly anticipated months in advance. When a thick snow fell during the night, each minute was precious to Leyeh. She couldn't wait for her mother to help her go down. Her heart pounded in advance at the thought that today she had the opportunity to be what she was, what she wanted to be, to show what she was capable of.

Leyeh had nimble, skillful hands. Her sight extended far and directly ahead. She stood up on her ironclad legs in the middle of a mountain of snow. Her eyes were shining, and her cheeks were ablaze from the fiery cold… She stood firmly in place and threw with the agility of a cat. The children who wanted to compete with her got a drubbing. Before anyone else could throw a single snowball, Leyeh had already thrown ten. Leyeh's joy was immense. She preferred to hurl snowballs at the boys. At a boy—now that was really something. If one of her snowballs hit a boy at whom she was somehow peeved, joy arose in her every gesture and movement, in every toss of her head and shrug of her shoulder. Her loud laughter resounded in the snowy air, and her mother got choked up with tears and turned her head so Leyeh wouldn't see.

When one of Leyeh's snowballs would hit a mischievous boy who then wanted to play a prank on her, he'd sneak up from behind and grab her hands or cover her eyes with his hands. At that moment—as soon as Leyeh felt the touch—a warmth would reach all the way to her barely sentient legs. The warmth poured magically from top down and from below upwards. Leyeh would have liked the warmth to last a long time, without stopping, or failing that, for it to be constantly repeated…

In order for it to be repeated, Leyeh had to keep throwing and succeed in hitting the target—the boy she wanted—with her snowballs. If only this snow would keep falling and falling and never stop. But winter is so short…

Miniatures

In the Hospital

It was almost quiet in the large, twenty-four-bed ward. Here, a quiet murmur; in the corner, a groan, a low cough. But because of the size of the room, someone entering the room had the impression that the largest share of the patients was napping or resting in the afternoon hour.

Still, something shouted out above the general stillness. A sound reached the ear that was neither a human voice nor a groan nor crying, and yet it wouldn't permit peace of mind. The voice was so penetrating in its quiet that you were sure that a young child was at death's door, that these were the final, flickering sounds of a soul bidding farewell to the body…

If you kept walking, you would enter the other half of the ward, and here the sounds were quite distinct.

In the farthest corner of the room, the half-dead body of an old woman lay behind a partition. Her face was yellowish; her eyes—closed, and from her half-closed mouth a moving, heart-rending lament-song wept its way forth.

She sang out her lament with the tenderness of a young mother who had just lost her only child. With care, poignance, and clarity, she gave voice to her grief: "Little child, darling little girl, don't go. Don't leave me alone."

So it went—repeatedly. Next to her bed stood one of her daughters, a middle-aged woman with a troubled face. The daughter was pleased when there was someone off to the side with whom she could share her vast sorrow. She recounted: "Until we brought her to the hospital, we thought she would at least open her eyes, at least recognize her children. But, as you see, it's now the third day that she's been mourning her first child who died when she was two years old. My mother never forgot that child. She used to mention her whenever she had the opportunity…"

The daughter caressed the still-living hand and the face of the sick woman. But there was no sign of a response. She was nothing more than the body from which the life force was ebbing away.

Here was. Here lived, worked, spoke, laughed and suddenly—something tore—and then was no more…

What remained in her turned back almost half a century—and she was lying over the little body of her dying firstborn child, calling out: "Little child, darling little girl, don't leave me alone!"

But from where, from what buried source came such a stirring, heartrending, almost melodic lament-song? However still it was, the lament in its depth had drilled a path far into the human soul…

Who was capable of conveying this?

Standing at the sick bed, memories of such a lament-song swam up to my consciousness. Yes, I had heard these sounds before. I'd heard them from a great artist of the Habima Theater. Only an artist of that caliber, with such depth of soul, was capable of bringing it out—the artist Hanna Rovina.

What psychologist can drill into the surviving cells of the unhappy patient? And where can you find the words to serve as consolation for the daughter?

The Last Slice

There, by the window, the old man was complaining. Truth be told, he was complaining to himself, since the neighbor to whom he was speaking was lying all curled up and trying to keep in check the distress that, as he had explained it, hadn't subsided since they'd given him the trial injection.

The patient was speaking to himself: This coughing will drive me out of my mind! An itch in the throat, a choking—how to find the strength to bear it? Once the choking seizes you, you might as well jump out of your own skin.

His neighbor lifted a small, white head, looked at him with sympathy, then turned with his face to the wall and said, "Take something in your mouth, even a bit of water can also help a little." The cougher, pleased that his neighbor had heard him, indulged in a bit of self-pity: "Yes, take something! Sure, when the cough is light, then yes, 'a bit of water can also help a little,' but when the cough is ripping and biting you, you feel like shoving a broom down your throat…

"You say take something, whatever it might be. I do, in fact, take something. I've found that a small slice of orange helps a little. My wife brought me a large orange today—big and juicy. She won't be here for three whole days. How long will one orange last? So I divided the orange into slices. When it gets so bad that water doesn't help, I take one orange slice. I guard it as if it were the most precious medicine. Now the bag with the slices has almost run out; there is barely one slice left…"

The patient choked and choked, coughed and coughed. His neighbor approached. He saw how the shaking cougher, his body contorted, extended a trembling hand to the little table, took what was, in fact, the last slice of orange, and tried to bring it to his mouth. Just then he burst into such a powerful fit of coughing that the last slice slipped out of his mouth! He sat there, open-mouthed. Looking down at the floor where the orange slice lay, he broke into a big grin. He grumbled ironically: "Oh God, there's no end to cruelty!"

A Few Words from the Author

This book brings together a considerable number of my stories that were published in the last few decades in the *Morgn-frayhayt* [*Morning Freedom*], and in recent years, in the *Zamlungen* [*Collections*].

This book appears with the help of comrades and friends, who on their own initiative, took upon themselves the arduous burden of generating funding for the book. The members of the book committee, some of whom are distinguished writers, were relentless, and with great insistence, touching devotion, and love for the Yiddish literary word, saw to it that these stories would appear between the covers of a book.

It is only thanks to them that the dozens of human lives, with all of their sorrows, who previously only dozed among yellowed old papers, are receiving their redress in the form of this book. I hope the members of the committee will reap their reward from their conscientious, invaluable work.

Was all of the effort worth it? Do these stories make a contribution to Yiddish letters? Of course, it is the reader who will be the final judge.

For the writer, for the storyteller herself, this book opened new, vivid horizons that even eclipsed the familiar beauty of her own milieu which includes dear friends, men and women.

It is my hope that the light of the characters portrayed here accompany all of these dear friends and comrades on their path in life.

The same thanks are extended to all of those who made a financial contribution. To all, my grateful recognition!

—Frume Halpern. January, 1963

283

Frume Halpern on My Mind, in My Body: Notes from the Plague

(Toward an Afterword)

Yermiyahu Ahron Taub

I feel Frume Halpern's writing—her linking of particular words—in my skin, deep within my aching body, all the way to the remotest pores of my being. Cloaked in anxiety and dread, stumbling through the pandemic sphere, the strings of my mask(s) slicing into the tender skin behind my ears, its front pressing down onto the ridge of my nose leaving welts in its wake, Halpern returns to me. Not that she or her characters ever left me since I first encountered her work. I think sometimes of Prager ("In the Stillness of the Night") as he moves along an arc of memory and a devastating series of losses: his beloved, his connection to the world of movement, all the way to the original moment of loss of his personal freedom, and then loops back to the here and now, to his loss of hearing.

And I think of my mother—her body afflicted with agony, those many trips to doctors and hospitals that dominated so much of her later life. I remember those consultations with the men in white—their conferring, murmuring as they do in "Clara and Mary," the "neutral" inflections that my youthful self tried so hard to interpret as optimistic, how I leaned into hope only to have it dashed. I remember the lilt in the "How are we today?", the professional optimism, the kindness of a nurse so like and so unlike Miss Gold ("In the Convalescent Home") modified for a later time period. Perhaps as the result of her medical studies and work in the Bronx Hospital, Halpern understood and captured well those consultations, those appraisals and diagnoses, their power and possibility to transform a life's path.

The reality of a global pandemic—with its seemingly relentless death and trauma—was more than a backdrop to my translation work. As the mounting numbers of the dead flashed onto the television screen, as basic preventative public health measures became sites of battle in the culture wars, as the stories of those who died appeared with less and less frequency, the pandemic, too, became a part of the project itself. During this hellish time, I navigated anxiety, fear, and isolation as I absorbed Halpern's vision. Her probing depictions of the body and its fragility, vulnerability, and perils seemed particularly suited to the moment. This, too, must be known, foregrounded rather presumed.

As suggested by the book's title, Frume Halpern wrote powerfully and often about people who worked with their hands—not simply the proletariat in the strictest Marxist sense, but also about a massage therapist ("Blessed Hands") as she herself was, a shoemaker ("Munye the Shoemaker and Baruch Spinoza"), a butcher ("Hello, Butch"), and a beautician ("Goodbye, Honey"), to name but a few. Halpern's protagonists live close to or at the edge of financial security or social propriety. Their life stories feel like postcards from the precipice of the class struggle, pulsating with angst. The weight of capitalism presses down upon them ... even if it never quite defeats them.

Even the more financially "successful" of these characters feel uneasy, insecure. Moysheh Rolkin, who has achieved financial stability with an income surpassing that of a dentist, is saddled by the opprobrium of being a butcher, a trade he tried in vain to leave behind when he came to the New World. He's desperate for his son, Nathan, to escape his own fate, but life—and Nathan—have other plans. Molly, who had poured her energy and the best years of her life into the hairdos of women, finds herself adrift, depleted, despite taking a grim pride in having worked all of these years independently on her own terms and despite her beauty. Vulnerable, too, after her sons have finished their schooling. When Molly goes to sunny Florida to rejuvenate herself, she gets drawn into a relationship with a much older man and tastes a ghastly privilege and power ... and a deeper kind of existential emptiness.

The lives of Halpern's characters come alive with telling details, plausible scenarios, penetrating observations, and perhaps most of all, authorial empathy. Her "ordinary people" never feel "ordinary" to the reader, but rather fresh and altogether original. Through her artful interweaving of the "back stories" into the present day central narrative arc, Halpern's portraits feel realized, somehow complete. We feel that we have gained access to their interior worlds. Pietro ("Goodbye, Cleopatra") feels spiritually alive when contemplating a new building being built by others. If only he had followed the edicts of his father, he, too, might have become a master builder. In his imagination, he pursues girls, becoming engaged on more than one occasion. Pietro never despairs of finding the right girl, the one who will allow him to experience true happiness as he's seen onscreen at the movies. In the here and now, he sensually caresses the bricks, marveling at each new development in the construction, at how the light of the setting sun dances off the windows. He even goes so far as to name it after the Egyptian queen. Yet paradoxically, if not surprisingly, when Pietro gains entry to the building, he experiences the ultimate exclusion.

Halpern was concerned with the body and its connection to the soul, to the world around us, to the world beyond us. Perhaps drawing upon her experience of working in a hospital, she wrote penetratingly about the ill and the vulnerable and their indeterminate status in the interstitial, nether world of the public ward—the twilit zone of those whose health conditions have placed them in a state of limbo. These twin foci of body and spirit, or rather the interconnectedness between the two, is established at the outset in the title of the collection and the title story which begins the collection. In "Blessed Hands," the hands of the narrator allow her to connect to her clients in multiple ways, with unexpected results. Halpern writes: "Quite often, it seemed to Soreh that not only did she fathom the sick, but they themselves understood her through her hands. They sensed her compassion. They saw how she absorbed their fears into her very being." In contrast to today's medical dictum that insists on building and maintaining boundaries between medical professional and patient, Soreh insists on removing them altogether. Set in what appears to be the psychiatric ward of a public hospital, the young title characters of "Clara and Mary," each suffering from a trauma that threatens to overwhelm them, are essentially starving themselves to death. Yet they manage to forge a deep, presumably lasting friendship across cultural difference. And with the help of the hospital's staff, their story comes to a hopeful conclusion. The hospital, then, becomes the site of both personal and social healing as Clara and Mary overcome the barriers between communities and the heartbreak within themselves. Long before anorexia nervosa became widely known to the mainstream public, Halpern was portraying the roots and devastating effects of the disease and pointing toward the possibility of a remedy.

Even when not the central producers of work for her protagonists, hands appear regularly in her stories. In "They Came to See Each Other," those gathered in the waiting room marvel at the dexterity of blind Pauline's hands with her needlework. Frieda "took Pauline's hands and covered them with hot kisses. Her kisses spoke louder than words." Pauline's hands become the site to receive Frieda's love, the initial conduit for the expression of that love. About Frieda's husband, Mendl, we are told that "His work was basic, unskilled. It was the kind of work that could be done by any other pair of hands." But later, we learn of the importance of those hands: "Pauline came to love Mendl's hands. Such strong hands, such solid hands, such good hands!" One patient in "In a Convalescent Home" never lets his heavy prayerbook from the grip of his hands. Along with his prayerbook and his own self, those trembling hands become objects of his own meditation. "When he wasn't looking in the prayerbook, he was looking intently at his hands, as if he were reproving them, had complaints against them, or was begging them not to fail him, not to embarrass him." Only when he dons his business clothes are his body and very self thoroughly transformed.

In a number of Halpern's stories, the fragility of consciousness—the sense of life itself hovering—is charged with extraordinary emotional impact. After being hit by a car, Reb Leyzer ("In the Garden of Eden") floats between life and death in the hospital. He imagines that he's in the Garden of Eden where he can see his daughter Sheyndele, gone from him so young. Only every time he reaches for her, she disappears. In his fevered mind, Reb Leyzer imagines that "the bright, white room was a reward from God Blessed Be He for his hard and honest life." In this story, the body is felt to be severed, or severing from him. Reb Leyzer "felt that his right leg was lying off somewhere without him." And then later: "His head was light, as if it had been separated from his body, as if the body itself had split into two parts, as if it were sliding further and further away from him." Halpern brilliantly captures Reb Leyzer's "Garden of Eden," a floating between worlds, adrift between light and sound, the soul in limbo.

And yet for all of the struggle—the grayness of the lives depicted—there's a delicacy here, an appreciation of nature. In two stories, nature's power is juxtaposed against war, or rather the horror and devastation that war leaves in its wake. In the magical opening passage of "In the Mountains," a conversation is envisioned between generations of trees. The older trees call out to the younger ones, daring them to catch up to them. Secure in their youth, the young are in no rush to heed that call. Before transitioning to the central action of the story, Halpern paints a transitional interlude in which the trees call out to humans in their "tree language," to human movements and desires. In the end, nature cannot shield the vacationers. The idyll is shattered. Nature figures briefly but prominently in "Faces," as well, framing Sheila's meditations on her own personal loss and then on the sheer vastness of war's brutality and senselessness.

The single women in this book deserve special mention. Halpern excelled in her portrayals of women living (almost) alone, on the edge—women once considered "beautiful," women never considered conventionally "beautiful." In a number of these stories, the names of these women are also the titles of their stories. Susan Flesher comes across childhood friend Thomas Heisler in a chance street encounter. With her successful stage career as a leading lady long behind her, Susan has declined physically and financially in recent years. Her world has shrunk, appears to be closing in. Thomas, a still well-preserved scion of a brewery magnate, struggles to reconcile the photo taken from Susan's theater days to the woman standing before her now. He is both repelled by and drawn to her in her current condition. Even in her apparent "decline," there is a spiritedness about Susan. The cart she pushes along, her dress, her movements exude a theatricality that remind Thomas of Susan's long-ago career. When it becomes clear that their paths have led them to a conflict zone in which they both have high stakes, they pirouette around their shared histories and hover antagonistically in a troubled present. In the opening lines of her story, we learn that "Bashe was one of the thousands of girls that our city of millions passes over and overlooks. Not young, not beautiful, no one's eye paused upon her. They all walked right past her." Halpern fights against that utter absence of attention as she charts the transformation from Bashe to Comrade Bashe. This is a gentle story of coming of political age, or coming into political awareness. At its center, again, is

the friendship of two young women. It is through Beylke's seeing and befriending her that Bashe re-envisions a different future.
Her mother gone young and her father taken to the bottle, Blume
has to care for her orphaned siblings. Years later, she gets to bring
her child to work, under the ever-vigilant eye of her boss. For
the "privilege" of bringing her child to work, Blume pays dearly.
In "The Mute Mother," one of the most extraordinary stories in
this extraordinary collection—one that should surely become a
part of the Jewish short story canon—the title character survives
through her own pluck and the support of the residents in her
courtyard. We never learn the name she is given at birth; she is
simply known as the mute. When she is found to be pregnant, the
residents are shocked. How could this have happened? And under
their watch? How her fate—and that of her child—intersect with
larger social and political forces makes for a harrowing, gripping
reading experience. The story has an eerie folkloric feel, as if
the stories we heard as children about the Jewish saints and the
lamed-vovniks have now been pointedly enlarged, extended to
include characters formerly beyond the pale.

African-American characters, themes, and motifs were not
unusual in the writings of progressive or leftist Yiddish poets and
authors committed to the struggle against racism, and *Blessed
Hands* is no exception. Indeed, as American Jewish historian
Tony Michels has argued, the Communist Party, in particular,
advocated for Black-white unity and Black-Jewish unity. The
Socialist Party was anti-racist, but it was not focused on Black
culture. Communists enthusiastically celebrated Black culture
in the 1930s and 1940s and framed a new era on this subject.[13]
This framing provides a backdrop to understanding *Blessed
Hands*. Here too, the plight of African-Americans seems central
to Halpern's vision and artistic enterprise. "Neighbors" is a poi-
gnant portrait of cross-cultural amity in which an elderly Jewish

---

13. Amelia M. Glaser, Tony Michels, and Alyssa Quint, "Yiddish and Social Justice," (Zoom virtual program, Yiddish Book Center, December 16, 2021).

woman overcomes fear to befriend an African-American neighbor. As just the third story of the collection, it helps sets the tone of empathy and inclusion that will predominate. After a lifetime of all-abiding faith, Christopher comes to question God's ways when he is forced to remain "seated until the end." In "The Punishment" Halpern takes us far into the psyche of a character with deeply-held racist and anti-Jewish beliefs. The scalpel is cool and if the story's overall tone cannot be called "sympathetic," there is certainly a commitment to authorial understanding, to presenting a life as it was lived. A chance appearance of apples on the street in "Three Apples, Rolling" set in motion a series of events that threatens Susan's livelihood. Halpern portrays the anxiety seemingly etched into Susan's body as she futilely seeks entry to the apartment of her employer, one Madam Lush (!). Here, the racism may be less "overt," but it is certainly no less palpable. Fear of racist reprisal and the constriction of opportunity in a racist society create an atmosphere of dread and fear. "The Last Breakfast" opens with a mother, Elizabeth, sharing a meal with her son, Teddy, before his departure to a place of what she hopes will be greater opportunity. The scene is skillfully set. The textures of the food being prepared, the larger meaning of small rituals such as packing are expertly drawn. Even at the outset, the effects of racism are all too present. Elizabeth's friend Susie wonders if Teddy might have been a senator given his oratorical skills had it not been for his skin color. Elizabeth fears that at his new destination Teddy will be more conspicuous. By the story's end, we learn Elizabeth's fears were fully justified. With the Christian theme of martyrdom evoked in its title—and it is no coincidence that it is the Parson who comes to present the news and provide consolation—"The Last Breakfast" is a haunting portrait of love and intimacy in an atmosphere of impending doom and the devastating effects of racism on a family and a community. Halpern presents the histories, realities and fates of her African-American characters with empathy, balancing their private lives with the larger social forces. Rather than being token slices of diversity, these stories are richly drawn offerings—central to Halpern's authorial commitment to the marginalized in the world around her and thus in the book itself.

The overall feel of *Blessed Hands* can conjure the classics of proletarian literature. Readers will surely notice that there are pro-Soviet references in several stories even if the words "communist" and "Soviet Union" do not appear anywhere. And yet juxtaposed against the support of revolutionary movements and ideals is an awareness of the cruelty of the world and all that keeps people apart, truncated, lost, adrift, lonely. Even as it charts her political coming of age, the ending of "Comrade Bashe" is ambivalent, ambiguous. Bashe ends up before a mirror alone; the words "Comrade Bashe!" echo back to her from the mirror. There is hope here, to be sure, but also uncertainty, and hardly glib triumphalism. In "Thrice Encountered," Freydl comes across a co-worker at a political funeral procession for those who perished in the Triangle Shirtwaist Factory fire. The tableau moves from despair and mourning to fiery resistance. And yet Freydl feels herself to be inadequate in relation to her co-worker whom she spots among the marchers. Freydl never joins the procession. When Freydl encounters the co-worker later in life, she has the uneasy sensation that this person is following her, watching her as she moves through life. Fay ("Dead Flowers") finds herself at odds with her boss, on different sides of an international political divide and furious at him for drawing attention to her age in the workplace. By the story's end, she finds herself questioning her own opinion of and actions around him. For Halpern, then, the question of social change remains fraught. She is clearly interested in characters that are unsettled, who find themselves impeded by obstacles whose power is not readily overcome. It's never quite clear whether justice will prevail.

Throughout the book, flights of fancy, a heightened sense of the bizarre, and a deep connection to Yiddish literature and Jewish tradition are on display. "Click-Clack" takes an almost gothic horror feel in its look at a wounded veteran returned from war. In "The Fate of a Strand of Hair," for example, Halpern creates an affecting parable on aging and decline. In "The Reincarnation of a Baby Carriage," Halpern explores the journey of an intimate, cherished object, the vehicle for someone new to the world—as it tumbles down the social ladder. In those latter two stories the objects are compared to the "grandfather" of Yiddish literature Mendele Mokher Sefarim's mute mare. Blume is compared to Isaac Leib Peretz's Bontshe Shvayg. "The Orphaned Synagogue" provides a sympathetic portrait of a young Orthodox rabbi struggling to keep a synagogue going even as the congregants decline in number. He befriends two elderly members of the congregation, taking them on their walks. They become a familiar—if unlikely—sight in the neighborhood. Halpern takes us beyond this unusual image into the lives of the elderly gentlemen and the young rabbi and the fragile threads that bind them. Many of her stories defy easy categorization altogether.

Halpern was a master of the story genre—internal dialogue toward an other, soliloquy, missive, prose poem—in which an unnamed narrator speaks directly to the central character, creating an extraordinary degree of emotional intimacy between them both—and the reader experiencing that connection. In the aforementioned "Blume," the narrator speaks directly to the title character—"a mother who loved her children; she worked from the very beginning of her childhood; with her two hands, she helped move the wheel of time and didn't herself understand all that she had contributed to the world." The narrator's precise relationship to Blume is never specified, even as the latter is remembered in various stages of her life of "monotone, submerged in gray need." Early in the story, Blume is compared to the unknown soldier and, as noted above, to Bontshe Shvayg who at least was immor-

talized. Underlying that comparison is the premise that the story
"Blume" is necessarily a form of memorialization. Throughout
the story, the parameters of homage remain elusive. The narrator
both resists interpreting this story as a monument to Blume and
yet by the story's end seems all too aware of that inevitability.
That interplay between memorialization, and obscurity and erasure render "Blume" a monument of a new kind, both extraor-
dinarily intimate and eerily unresolved. In "Rusty, My Friend,"
the narrator finds strange kinship with a dog through their shared
object of affection, thereby giving new, unexpected meaning to
the expression "man's best friend." The story "By My Mother's
Sickbed" presents a kind of reverse lullaby—here the child urges
the mother to sleep, to not—perhaps ever—awaken. The narrator seeks to protect the mother from the terrible reality of the
world as the narrator's first flight decades before from that reality
is recalled. Undergirding that flight is the understanding that the
mother was unable to protect the narrator so many years before—
and now—from the world. The story underscores the limits of pa-
rental power within the parent-child dyad when the context is terror and upheaval and becomes a meditation on Jewish history and
suffering—and survival and endurance too. Even as the mother
is urged to sleep, the narrator takes to heart the mother's belief
that "The good ones, the just ones will endure." In a mere four
pages, Halpern creates a spine-chilling mood that hovers between
polarities: the here-and-now and the immediate past in the lives
of the characters, the immediate and distant pasts, the dark rooms
of reality and flight into freedom and space. For all its brevity, the
story feels so complete, so primal. As if it's always been there, as
if it had to be there. Here.

Frume Halpern's work appeared in and was highly lauded in
communist Yiddish publications both during her lifetime and after it. As she noted in her author's note to *Blessed Hands*, her
stories first appeared in the *Morgn-frayhayt* [*Morning Freedom*]
and the *Zamlungen* [*Collections*]. A group of Halpern's friends

and advocates came together to assemble the stories into book form. The chairperson of the book committee was Isaac Elchanan Ronch who wrote the book's introduction, and one of the finance committee members was Bella Goldworth, herself a well-known Yiddish writer on proletarian themes. One, among many, of the individual supporters of the book was Nora H. Linn, Halpern's daughter. The book's publisher was IKUF (also Ykuf, acronym for *Yidisher kultur farband* [Yiddisher Cultural Organization]) farlag which was founded in 1937 and provided a home for the poets and writers grouped around the journal *Proletpen*, which was under the editorship of the *Morgn-frayhayt*'s editor, M. Olgin. These writers later gathered around the journals *Yidishe kultur* and *Zamlungen*.

Significantly, Frume Halpern's name appears in several articles in those journals. In a *Morgn-frayhayt* article marking the offerings of the fourth issue of *Zamlungen*, N. Bukhvald highlights Halpern's contribution "In a Convalescent Home." Bukhvald noted how in her style of psychological depth she created an atmosphere at the story's outset in just a few lines—"a magnificent beginning." He called her "a genuine talent of substantial caliber." But he did note that "the story does not end; it stops."[14] In a lengthy, balanced review of a newly published anthology entitled "*Amerike in Yidishn vort*" ["*America in Yiddish Letters*"] compiled by Nachman Mayzel, Itshe Goldberg reflects on the challenges of as well as the potential pitfalls in compiling such a work. Goldberg contends: "Compiling an anthology is, in no way, a mechanical, automatic compilation. The selection of materials is usually determined by the compilers' literary and social inclinations and interests. However objective he tries to be, what is turned out is tinged by his personality and the ideational and social passions that dominate him. The result is an active co-creation between the anthologist and the work that is evident both

---

14. Bukhvald, N. "*Dertseylungen un eseyen in dem fertn numer 'Zamlungen'*" ["Stories and Essays in the Fourth Issue of *Collections*"]. *Morgn-frayhayt* [*Morning Freedom*], Sunday, February 20, 1955: 11.

in the material he selects and in the material he discards in the process of compiling the work."[15] Goldberg notes that this particular anthology not only highlights Jewish life, but also "the life of America of which we became a part. Tens of literary examples bear witness to the fact that each pain of America became our pain, each joy of hers—our joy. Each wrongdoing of hers—a wrongdoing committed against us. Haymarket in 1886 became our pain, even though not one of those who perished was a Jew. The struggles and suffering of coalminers were ours, even though there probably wasn't a single Jewish coalminer in America. The lives and suffering of Negroes became our cause because America became our cause."[16] The anthology's broad inclusivity that encompassed non-Jewish protagonists, and indeed African-American ones, was critical to Yiddish writers of the left and, of course, reflected Halpern's own approach. Some five pages later, Goldberg asks: "How can it be that writers such as Sh. Dayksl, M. Bornshteyn, D. Keshir, Borekh Miler, Frume Halpern and a number of other writers are missing from the anthology? The tone and theme of the entire anthology would naturally have been enriched if Yiddish word-artists who, with their entire essence, rooted themselves in the progressive Yiddish culture of America had not been omitted or overlooked?"[17] It is significant that Goldberg considered Halpern to be one of the writers whose words would have enriched the anthology. In his drawing attention to Halpern and other writers, then, Goldberg performs an act of restoration of his own.

Isaac Elchanan Ronch highlighted one of Halpern's stories, "An Encounter," in his review of a new issue of *Zamlungen*, noting: "It is a shame that Frume is so seldom seen in printed columns. She always has something to say, moreover not about the unusual but about the most ordinary, and that is not the easiest

---

15. Itshe Goldberg, *"Amerike in yidishn vort"* ["America in Yiddish letters"], *Zamlungen [Collections]*, no. 8 (Winter 1956): 49.

16. Ibid, 52.

17. Ibid, 57.

thing for a storyteller to do." The story explores how two concentration camp survivors come to pour their hearts out to each other
in a chance encounter.[18]

In a wide-ranging article entitled *"Der gayst un gang fun der
moderner Yidisher literatur"* [The Spirit and Sweep of Modern
Yiddish Literature"] marking the one hundredth anniversary
of Mendele Mokher Sefarim's *"Dos kleyne mentshele"* in *Kol
mevaser* [*The Herald*] (1864), Ber Green argues that the essen-
tial thrust of that literature—from the classic writers, Mendele
Mokher Sefarim, Sholem Aleichem, and Isaac Leib Peretz on
down—was and largely always has been with the people. Writes
Green: "There is no racism, hatred, enmity among ethnic groups
in our literature. Since our classic writers and continuing to this
day, in the course of a full hundred years, the flag of our Yiddish
literature has carried the ardent slogan, the message, the resounding exhortation: humanism. Secularism, humanity, fraternity, democracy, with a face towards the people, deeply rooted in the
people, living with their problems, struggling against want and
against the roots of want—these are the foundational tendencies,
the main streams of our new Yiddish literature."[19] Following
this introductory outline, Green proceeds to sketch out succes-
sive generations of Yiddish literature, citing principal concerns,
publications, and figures. Reaching up to what was his present
day, Green discusses writers who were concerned with "America,
factory life, social struggles (against hunger and unemployment,
against racism and anti-Semitism, against reaction). Included in
that list of writers here are Rontsh, Green himself, and Frume
Halpern.[20] Like Goldberg, Green saw Halpern as a crucial voice
in the course of Yiddish literature.

---

18. Ronch, Isaac Elchanan. "Vos dertseyln unz di zamlungen: vegn der proze in
numer 22 'Zamlungen'" [What the Collections Tell Us: On the Prose in Number 22 of
the Collections"]. *Morgn-frayhayt* [Morninig Freedom], Sunday, March 16, 1961: 11.

19. Ber Green, *"Der gayst un gang fun der moderner Yidisher literatur"* ["The
Spirit and Sweep of Modern Yiddish Literature]," *Yidishe kultur*, volume XXVI, no. 6
(June-July 1964): 1.

20. Ibid, 5.

What's striking about Green's analysis to a contemporary reader is that the concerns of writers on the left are not situated outside of or in opposition to the mainstream of Yiddish literature but rather as directly within that mainstream. In the view of Green and possibly the editorial board of *Yidishe Kultur*, Frume Halpern is herself the literary descendant and heir of the classic Yiddish writers. And in many ways, given the references to that literature that pepper her stories, one could argue that Halpern saw herself that way, as well. What Green's broad sketch does not capture are the ways in which Halpern's writing resists easy categorization. In her unceasing exploration of human suffering, Halpern does not offer facile answers or solutions to the ills that plague her characters and their worlds. The revolutionary potential of Halpern's writing lies not in an embrace of communist messianism, however ardently that may have been maintained by her literary champions and perhaps even by the author herself, but rather in the ability of its protagonists to make sense of what life has dealt them, to find meaning and connection in an often harsh, brutal world.

Frume Halpern's book was enthusiastically feted upon its release. On the evening of Saturday, April 13, 1963, a celebration was held in the IKUF center to honor the book. More than one hundred people were in attendance. Bella Goldworth, the evening's host; Sh. Dayksel, vice-president of Frume Halpern's book committee; David Seltzer representing the IKUF Writers' Union; Borekh Miler, secretary of the book committee; Y. Fisherman representing the Yiddish Culture and Aid Organization of which Halpern was a member; and Rose Aronoff representing the IKUF City Committee all gave greetings. Avraham Yehoshu'a Bik gave a short appreciation of the book, highlighting Halpern's method of presenting her protagonists "in a quiet manner with a heartfelt approach vis-a-vis the poor and lonely." The stage artist Menashe Oppenheim read excerpts from the book as well as other pieces. Also in attendance were Ber Green, Sam Liptzin, Shloyme Vaserman, and Sh. Budin. The article noted that a second celebration was to be held on the evening of Friday, May 10 in the Sholem Aleichem House organized by the Morris Rosenfeld reading circle and the Yiddish Culture and Aid Organization.[21]

In a review of the book upon its release, Avraham Yehoshu'a Bik noted that "Frume Halpern is a quiet writer-storyteller... She does not chase after the big, tangled themes. Her people are ordinary, modest and struggle with their fate and don't make much big tragedies or dramas out of their life problems." He noted that it "is quiet in her stories ... so quiet that every gesture and movement of a character has an echo." Bik compared her to the Yiddish writers Reyzen, Opatoshu, and Glasman and contrasted the poeticism and lyricism of her descriptions of nature with the prosaic nature of her characters' speech.[22]

Halpern was remembered and honored after her death. A memorial meeting in honor of Frume Halpern was held at 6:30 on the evening of Thursday, March 3, 1966 at the IKUF Center, 189 Second Avenue, New York. The memorial was arranged by the Yiddish Writers Union. Those scheduled to speak about Halpern were Ber Green, Sarah Kindman, Shloymeh Vaserman, Bella Goldworth, Borekh Miler, Y. Fisherman, and Berl Kvalvaser. The meeting was also arranged by the Yiddish Culture and Aid Organization.[23]

In the year following her death, the aforementioned Ber Green penned a lengthy and deeply moving homage to Frume Halpern that preceded the republication of her story "Neighbors." Green's text is worth quoting at some length:

---

21. "*Ayndruksfule fayerung le-koved dershaynung fun Frume Halpern's bukh*" ["Impressive Celebration in Honor of the Release of Frume Halpern's Book"], *Morgn-frayhayt* [*Morning Freedom*], Sunday, April 21, 1963: 13.

22. Bik, Avraham Yehoshu'a. "*Shtile dertseylungen vegn poshete mentshn*" ["Quiet Stories About Ordinary People"]. *Morgn-frayhayt* [*Morning Freedom*], Sunday, May 12, 1963: 10.

23. "*Frume Halpern ondenk-miting hayntikn donershtog*" [Frume Halpern's Memorial Meeting]. *Morgn-frayhayt* [*Morning Freedom*], March 2, 1966: 8.

Quietly and modestly did the writer Frume Halpern walk among us. A woman of the people, a workshop worker, a longtime nurse in a hospital. A person with progressive ideas. An activist in her fraternal club, an active member of the Yiddish Writers Union of IKUF, a colleague at the *Morgn-frayhayt* and *Zamlungen.*

A daughter of Jewish poverty, she maintained throughout her life a deep understanding of and sympathy for poor people, the rejected, the insulted, the abused, those whom life—"society"—had set aside "*ke-oni be-pesah,*" like a beggar at the door...[24]

...

Just as in her life so in her writing, in her stories, was Frume Halpern a nurse, a healer. With her friendly, dedicated, and blessed hands did the *nurse* Frume Halpern bring ease and encouragement to the sick and suffering in the hospital. With those same friendly, dedicated, and blessed hands did the writer Frume Halpern bring healing, solace, and hope to the poor people in her stories—the victims of privation and brutality, those made to feel shame, the stolen-from, those robbed of light and warmth, a kind word, a place in our society.

The frank, devout, talented, and progressive Yiddish writer, Frume Halpern, who deeply knew the tastes of need and penury, clasped to herself these folks of hers—the protagonists of her stories—like a mother and a sister and gave them her love and tenderness. She healed their wounds. She gave them courage—and language. And if they were lacking language, then she, the creator of these real-life heroes, became their speech provider, their defender, their interpreter, their spokesperson, the advocate for their rights.[25]

Green noted that there were "warm sparks of Avrom Reyzen the great man of mercy" in several of Halpern's stories and then proceeded to summarize and evaluate some of the stories. He ended with the following: "A figure such as Frume Halpern, who came to this world with "blessed hands" to help heal "wounded lives" became dear to the hearts of her readers, co-workers, and colleagues. Such a figure remains unforgettable."[26]

---

24. Ber Green, "*Frume Halpern—un ire dertseylung [afn fritsaytikn toyt fun der talentfuler shrayberin*" ["Frume Halpern—and Her Stories [Upon the Premature Death of the Talented Writer"], *Yidishe kultur* 28, no. 3 (March 1966): 35.

25. Ibid, 36.

26. Ibid, 36.

A *Morgn-frayhayt* article written by Y. Fisherman published some fifteen years after her death sheds light on Halpern's life and legacy. Fisherman wrote:

> For a great part of her life, Frume Halpern was devoted to progressive movements. The literary fraternal club in the Bronx of which she was a prominent member, felt very proud that this beloved and talented writer was one of them and shared their philosophy and dreams.
>
> Frume was a gentle soul, generous, sensitive, and shy. Her club wanted to dedicate an evening to her writings. She objected vigorously; however, she did not prevail and the evening took place. She was highly praised by her friends and colleagues, but could not see what the fuss was about.[27]

Toward the end of the article Fisherman offers critical information about the end of Halpern's life. He writes: "Several years before she died, she began to lose her eyesight. To her this was the greatest tragedy. In her despair she thought of suicide. "How will I be able to live not being able to read or write?" Her friends came to her assistance hoping to help her to overcome her depression. They decided to publish a book of her stories. Miraculously, this helped. On being told that her book would be published she was temporarily revitalized. Her eyes improved and she once again was back at the typewriter and with her beloved books."[28]

The biographical information I've managed to gather about Frume Halpern is meager and even some of that is necessarily provisional. How many times in reading "A Few Words from the Author" did I wish that she had stated the year and place of her birth! Frume Tarloff (also Tarloffsky, Tarlowska, Tarlowsky, etc.) was born in 1881-1888(?)[29] presumably in (or near?) Bial-

---

27. Fisherman, Y. "Frume Halpern," trans. Nora Linn and Immanuel Klein, *Morgn-frayhayt* [*Morning Freedom*], November 1980: 1. My thanks to Robert Linn and Judith Linn who sent me this typescript translation.

28. Ibid, 2-3.

29. I have encountered a range of dates of birth for Frume Halpern. The S.S. Prinzess Alice states that Frume was 22 years old. If she was born at the end of the year, it's conceivable that she would have turned 22 at the end of 1903, which could put her year of birth in 1881. A family tree provided by Victor M. Linn states 1882. The

ystok. Her father was Yikusiel (Kusil; ca. 1851?-ca. 1920?) and her mother was Rejzel Tarlowska (ca. 1850?-1894). Following Rejzel's death, Yikusiel married Hinde Abrash. Frume's siblings were Nochin (Nathan) Kuszelew Jankelew Tarloff (1872-1944; a tailor), sister Feige Rachel Yolken (1882-1964). Frume's half-sisters (children of Kusiel and Hinde) were Devorah Baron (1896, Bialystok-1941; perished in the Holocaust) and Helen Nechama Stollman (1903, Bialystok-1998, Franklin Township, N.J.). Feige married in 1900 and arrived in the United States in 1905. There is a Fruma Tarlowksi (Tarlowska?) on the ship's "List or Manifest of Alien Passengers for the U.S. Immigration Officer at Port of Arrival" for the S.S. Prinzess Alice, which sailed from Bremen on July 30, 1904 and arrived at the Port of New York on August 9, 1904. She was listed as twenty-two years old, "f" (female), and sgl (single). Her race or people was Hebrew. Her last place of residence was Bialystok prior to the journey, and her destination was New York. She was going to stay with a cousin Davis Greenberg of 492/94 Water Street. According to a Geni.com page, Davis Greenberg was the son of Frume's father's sister, Sara. Frume's husband (partner?) was Isaack Halpern (1881-1947(?)). His 1907 declaration of intention provides a number of facts about Isaack. His occupation was bookkeeper. He was 26 years old, of fair complexion, 5 foot 2 inches tall, 120 lbs. and had blond hair and blue eyes. He was born in Grodno, Russia (now Belarus) on September 27, 1881. He then resided at 1765 Bathgate (?) Avenue. He traveled from Rotterdam on the Ryndau and arrived in the

aforementioned translation of a *Morgn-frayhayt* article by Y. Fisherman about Frume Halpern sent to me by both Judith Linn and Robert Linn has a handwritten 1883 on it. Robert Linn confirmed to me that this is the handwriting of his mother, Nora Linn. Frume Halpern's gravestone has 1885. In a March 18, 2022 email, Susan Gail Igdaloff provided me with a social security application that states that Fanny Tarloffsky Halpern was born on 24 Dec. 1887 in Bialyptok [sic], Soviet Union. That information is also seconded on a Geni.com page that Susan also sent me. Halpern's biographical note in *Arguing with the Storm: Stories by Yiddish Women Writers* (The Feminist Press at CUNY, 2008) has 1888 as her year of birth.

port of New York on February 25, 1905.[30] On his petition for naturalization, Isaack's wife is listed as Fannie. Their two children were Nora, born on January 19, 1906(?) and Vera (Yetta), born on April 18, 1907(?)[31]. On the petition, all are listed as residing at 1883 Crotona Avenue. According to the 1920 census, Frume and Isaack were naturalized in 1914. Years later, Nora married Harry Linn (Grescia Chevlin; 1897-1966), and Vera married David Kaplan (1910-1955?). Nora died in 2006 and Vera in 1995. Nora and Harry's children are Victor M. (1933-) and Robert J. (1937-), and Vera and David's children were Paul David and an infant who died. Paul David married Lore, daughter of Edgar and Joan Price.

Victor Linn's wife, Judith Carol Ernst Linn, recalls being told that Frume was a registered nurse in Bialystok but did not practice nursing in the United States. She took classes in massage therapy and became a certified massage therapist.[32] Judith recalls being told that Nora was quite young when Frume and Isaack split.[33] However, according to the census of 1930, Frume (aged 44 as of last birthday) and Isaack (aged 46 as of last birthday) were living in the same household with their daughter Yetta (aged 22; listed as a nurse). Nora always referred to Isaack's leaving as a divorce. She believed that her parents were mismatched. She described her mother as cold and said her father was warmer than

---

30. The censuses of 1920 and 1930 confirm that Frume's and Isaack's dates of immigration were 1904 and 1905 respectively. However, the census of 1910 has the years of immigration as 1903 and 1904 respectively. The documentary evidence does confirm that Frume and Isaack did not emigrate together, and that Frume arrived one year before Isaack.

31. The years 1906 and 1907 for the births of Nora and Vera are listed on Isaack's Petition for Naturalization. On a Geni.com page that Susan Gail Igdaloff sent me, the years are 1907 and 1908. On Victor M. Linn's family tree, the years are 1907 and 1909 respectively.

32. Judith Linn, "Did Frume Earn a Nursing Degree in the United States, Too?", email, April 1, 2022.

33. According to Halpern's sister Feige's granddaughter, Nancy Abramowitz: "Family lore had it that Itchke met Frume's successor at a communist/socialist meeting. Not sure about Frume-Itchke meeting but I believe it was in Bialystok. They seemed to be of the same political persuasion. Also, I was under the impression theirs was a common law marriage," Nancy Abramowitz, "How Frume and Isaac Met?", email, March 31, 2022.

Frume. Apparently, there was little or no contact between Frume and Isaack following the split. Frume worked in the Bronx Hospital for a long time. She would leave the apartment at 7:30 a.m. and take the bus down the Grand Concourse. She took two buses to reach the hospital. Frume moved into Amalgamated Housing in the Bronx in 1942 or 1943; she had lived elsewhere in the Bronx prior to that. She lived quite close to Nora, and for the first three years of their marriage, to Judith and Victor.

Frume Halpern lived in a small apartment. The living room doubled as a bedroom. In the living room was a desk with a Yiddish typewriter on it, ready for the use. "The typewriter was always out," Judith recalls, "Sometimes there was paper in it, sometimes not. It was a permanent fixture—never put away. Like a lamp." In total, the apartment had a living room, kitchen, and bathroom.

Frume did not speak about her involvement with Yiddish culture to Victor or Judith. In fact, she did not reveal much about herself at all. Judith described her as "friendly but cool ... sober, serious... not effusive, not demonstrative." In fact, Nora said that Judith actually warmed her up; she felt that Frume was warmest to Judith. Judith maintained that she would not have known that on her own. Judith recalls that Nora told her that her mother kissed her twice in her life and that she remembered both times. Nora did not specify what those two times were, and Judith did not have the presence of mind to ask.

Nancy Abramowitz, Frume's sister Feige's granddaughter, recalls that Frume came to visit her grandmother when she had a stroke. Nancy recalls that Frume had a soft face, a funny, squeaky deep voice, and pierced ears. Nancy's grandmother was a homebody; she loved Frume very much. Nancy's mother was very fond of Frume. By the time Nancy was born, her grandmother had moved from a large house to a two-room apartment just two blocks from Nancy's house. Nancy recalls Frume's visiting their house. Nancy was seven years old when her grandmother Feige had a stroke.[34]

Additional memories of family members are instructive in helping us learn or imagine more about Frume Halpern. Victor recalls that when he was four years old, he was admitted to the Hospital of Contagious Diseases on New York's Lower East Side. Frume came down with his parents to visit him. He imagines that his parents must have driven her there. This is Victor's earliest memory of Frume. When he was growing up, Victor went over to spend time with Frume. He had meals with her. According to Victor, "Frume made the best potato latkes in the world."

Judith met Frume when she was eighteen years old. "She shook hands with me," Judith recalls, "She was not at all frivolous or playful. All business, very serious. She carried the world's troubles on her shoulders. She was a very formal woman." When Judith was teaching pre-school, she dropped by to see Frume. They talked about Judith's students. Ordinary chit-chat. Frume was pleased that Judith was working and earning money as a young married woman.

Robert's general impressions of Frume were that she was distant. He rarely saw Frume—once or twice a year—even though she lived across the street. "She didn't talk about herself at all. She was very quiet," Robert remembers, "She cared for us in her own way but she was not terribly outgoing ... I always thought she was a sad person, but I never knew why." The family did see Frume on Hanukah, and Robert confirms that Frume made the best latkes. Interestingly, Nora insisted that Robert learn Jewish history and Yiddish, and Robert studied with Immanuel (Manny) Klein who gave classes at the Amalgamated. Robert believes that it was Frume who suggested that Robert go to Camp Boiberik, the Yiddish cultural camp founded by Leibush Lehrer in 1913, which he did in 1948.[35] When Robert married a non-Jewish Ital-

34. Abramowitz, Nancy. Interview by translator. Zoom. November 4, 2020.
35. Linn, Robert. Interview by translator. Telephone. February 3, 2021.

ian woman, Frume refused to attend the wedding which was held in a church. This upset Nora greatly.

Communism played a key role in the family. Victor, Judith, or Bob could not confirm whether Frume was a party member or a fellow traveler. Nora and Harry married in 1929. According to Victor, Harry was a member of the Communist party. Nora was certainly not a member; in fact, she was the least political of the group. Nora blamed her mother's distance and lack of warmth on the party. Nora felt neglected by her mother and was always trying to understand why her mother was so distant and unresponsive to her. During 1938-1939, Nora was in psychoanalysis to discuss marital troubles and her unresolved issues with her mother. Nora adored her father who took her to the Museum of Natural History and told her about the constellations, the stars, and the moon. Judith recalls that Nora told her that the family bought a piano but the movers came to take away the piano when the installments were no longer paid. Nora was heartbroken when that happened.

According to Judith, Vera was much closer to Frume than Nora. Victor recalled that Vera was very much a part of the Communist party. Vera's husband David was a machinist in Philadelphia, and the two moved to Los Angeles. Tragically, David died quite young (in 1952?).

Frume was close to Harry, Nora's husband. Harry cared deeply for her, trying to help her see that the road was not as bleak as she saw it. Politically, Harry and Frume were aligned, and Judith and Victor speculate that she was probably more open with him than with Nora. Victor recalls that Harry went to the Soviet Union in 1936 to visit his mother in Dolhinov (now Belarus). It was clear to Harry that things were not going well. The first thing he did upon his return was tear up his party membership card. Harry was 39 when he ended his party affiliation. Victor believes that Harry couldn't pull Frume away from communism.

When she was diagnosed with glaucoma, Frume went into a deep depression. Nora put her in contact with a psychologist at Montefiore Hospital.[36] Nora tried to convince her that medical science had advanced so that there were treatment options. But Frume was convinced that she would go blind. She could not bear the prospect of not being able to read or write. Approximately a year and a half before she died, Frume closed the windows and stuck her head in the oven. A neighbor smelled the gas and alerted Nora, who lived close by. Frume survived. But her second and bloodier attempt resulted in death. Victor recalls that Frume slit her throat. Judith remembers that she stabbed herself in the abdomen. Frume Halpern died on September 24, 1965. Victor said, "The only … self-indulgence you ever saw in my grandmother's life was when she killed herself."[37]

In reading Frume Halpern, today's readers are not encountering an undiscovered writer. As outlined above, Halpern was admired during her day and after it. That admiration has continued into recent times. One story translated by Roz Usiskin and two stories translated by Esther Leven appeared in *Arguing with the Storm: Stories by Yiddish Women Writers* (New York: The Feminist Press at the City University of New York, 2008). Joachim Neugroschel translated "Dog Blood" and included it in *No Star Too Beautiful: A Treasury of Yiddish Stories* (New York: W.W. Norton & Company, 2004). Yet experiencing all of the stories in a single translated volume allows one to see the breadth and depth of the author's concerns. Halpern was a voice, indeed a literary advocate, for the marginalized—not only the poor, but those rendered "other" by illness, handicap, race, not measuring up to conventional standards of beauty, and social opprobrium. Her work takes us into corners we may prefer to avoid. She doesn't let us

---

36. Linn, Victor M. and Judith Linn. Interview by translator. Zoom. January 5, 2021.

37. Linn, Victor M. and Judith Linn. Interview by translator. Zoom. January 31, 2021. Much of the information in the biographical section of the afterword provided by Victor and Judith comes from this second, longer interview.

look away. And when we do look—no, when we really see—what we might have thought was sad or pathetic is actually filled with possibility, wisdom, tenderness, perseverance—the very material of and strategies for life itself.

Blessed Hands insists that we consider the stories within its covers as art—to be aware, yes, of the ideological milieu and presumed political beliefs of their author, to see clearly its few oblique references to the monstrous totalitarian regime that designed and executed one of the major genocidal catastrophes of the twentieth century that murdered millions of people, including some of the leading lights of Yiddish culture, but also not to let those references mar the experience of the book as a whole, and, more generally, to avoid the trap of red-baiting and erasure that remains so prevalent and indeed powerful to this day. This is a delicate, fraught balancing act, to be sure—the holding and cherishing of an illuminated crystal globe held in one's palm as one is balanced on one foot on a trapeze wire above a pack of ravenous wolves. I say "presumed political beliefs" because we simply do not definitively know what Halpern's views were towards the end of her life. In the end, what we have are these stories. And what fine, powerful stories they are. In this, her only book, Frume Halpern made a singular and enduring contribution to Yiddish literature. And it is my hope that these stories will stay with you, the reader, wherever you may be in the world, our ailing, perilous, fragile, tottering world.

Translator's Notes

In an article entitled "Wokeness and the English Language," critic Michael Lewis argues that the term Black is generally believed to have replaced Negro or colored person in 1968 when James Brown proclaimed "Say it loud—I'm Black and I'm proud." Writes Lewis: "Black was a word that in sound and dignity was equivalent to white; even better, it was a word proposed from within the community and not assigned from outside. It was adopted virtually overnight. After that, terms such as Negro and colored, which had previously been the polite alternatives, came to sound out of touch, if not outright offensive."[38] In his article "When Did the Word Negro Become Taboo?" Brian Palmer dates the moment of transition even earlier. He writes that "the turning point came when Stokely Carmichael coined the phrase "black power" at a 1966 rally in Mississippi. Until then Negro was how most black Americans described themselves. But in Carmichael's speeches and in his landmark 1967 book, *Black Power: The Politics of Liberation in America*, he persuasively argued that the term implied black inferiority."[39] In my translation, I decided to use Black rather Negro in most instances for a variety of reasons. According to the *Wikipedia* article on *Negro*: "However, during the late 1950s and early 1960s, the word *Negro* began to be criticized as having been imposed by white people, and having connotations of racial subservience and Uncle Tomism. The term *Black*, in contrast, denoted pride, power, and a rejection of the

38. Michael Lewis, "Wokeness and the English Language," *Commentary*, November 2021, https://www.commentary.org/articles/michael-lewis/wokeness-english-language/.

39. Brian Palmer, "When Did the Word Negro Become Taboo?" *Slate*, January 11, 2010, https://slate.com/news-and-politics/2010/01/how-old-was-harry-reid-when-the-word-negro-became-taboo.html.

past."[40] Thus, this article suggests that the linguistic turn to Black was already underway by the time that *Gebentshte hent* was published. Additionally, I wanted to draw in contemporary readers and felt that "Negro" might make the text feel dated, a historical curiosity, eliciting an inevitable wince or grimace. For example, the *Merriam-Webster Dictionary* defines Negro as "dated, often offensive: a person of Black African ancestry."[41] I also felt that Black might be in better keeping with Frume Halpern's progressive spirit. I realize some readers may consider this decision to be "ahistorical" and ask for their understanding in advance.

In the first paragraph of page 65 in the Yiddish text, I removed the following lines from the translation: "Even the heads of the other workers didn't turn to her. Each was working at a machine that she had never laid eyes on. ("…, *afilu di kep nit oysgedreyt tus ir. Yede is geven mashin hot zi nokh biz dan nit ongezen*"). The sentence simply doesn't work in this paragraph. In fact, the sentiment ("No one was even looking at her; they didn't even turn their heads towards her. ") appears again in the third paragraph of the same page, and it is there that that it actually belongs.

Readers of the original Yiddish text will notice that on page 95, the mute's son is said to have "his mother's black curls and her lively green-gray eyes *("der mames shvartse krayzlekh un ire lebedike grin-groye oygn")*. However, on page 97 of the original Yiddish text, the text states: "The mother's eyes—black, darting; her child's—green-gray… *("Der mames oygn—shvartse, arum-loyfndike, dem kinds—grin-groye…")*. I resolved this apparent contradiction by removing "green-gray" from the first instance and thus that translated sentence reads: "He had his mother's black curls and lively eyes."

In most cases, names of writers (e.g. Mendele Mokher Sefarim, Isaac Leib Peretz, etc.) are given here in the heading forms

40. *Wikipedia*. *"Negro,"* viewed February 20, 2022, https://en.wikipedia.org/wiki/Negro.

41. "Definition of Negro," *Merriam-Webster Dictionary*, viewed April 30, 2022, https://www.merriam-webster.com/dictionary/Negro.

established in the Library of Congress/NACO Authority File and not in systematic ALA/LC or YIVO romanization.

Except for the Y. Fisherman article from the *Morgn-frayhayt* published fifteen years after her death, the translations of articles from the Yiddish press that appear in my afterword are my own.

For any errors and omissions, I ask the reader's forgiveness.

Acknowledgments

My first debt is to Frume Halpern's grandsons Victor M. Linn and Robert Linn and to Victor's wife, Judith Linn, for their unflagging support of my translation project. During telephone calls, Zoom gatherings, and email correspondence, they generously shared their knowledge, memories, and photos of Frume Halpern.

I thank Susan Gail Igdaloff, the great-granddaughter of Nathan Tarloff, Frume Halpern's brother, and Nancy Abramowitz, the granddaughter of Feige Rachel Yolken, Frume Halpern's sister, for providing me with considerable information about the family and meeting with me on a number of occasions to discuss the family history. Their information led me to Lisa Linn, Victor Linn's daughter-in-law who in turn directed me to Victor and Judith Linn.

Thank you to Judah Ronch, son of Isaac Elchanan Ronch, for graciously granting permission to translate and publish his father's introduction to this book. Thank you to David Mazower for connecting me to Judah Ronch.

Norman Buder is my Yiddish guardian angel. With great thoroughness and precision, Norman answered numerous questions regarding challenging Yiddish linguistic concerns and offered vital feedback, suggestions, and helpful insights. Norman presented sage counsel on the textual discrepancies mentioned in the Translator's Notes. Norman's extraordinary erudition has greatly enriched this text, and his enthusiasm about this project and his encouragement mean so much to me.

I am extremely grateful to Elżbieta Pelish for her prompt responses to queries on Russian and Slavic linguistic matters and the eastern European cultural context. Ela's generous and spirited engagement with questions of language and culture continues to animate my translation journey.

A number of gifted library professionals and archivists have aided my research. I thank Leo Greenbaum and Hillel Yadin of the YIVO Institute for Jewish Research for providing scans of bibliographic cards from Ephim H. Jeshurin Collection (RG 451) regarding *Gebentshte hent.* Susan Garfinkel, research specialist, Digital Reference Section, Library of Congress, and Sheree Budge, Reference Librarian, History and Genealogy, Researcher and Reference Services, Library of Congress provided extensive genealogical information and research strategies overall via emails and meetings. Rachel Becker of the Hebraic Section, African and Middle Eastern Division, Library of Congress provided invaluable assistance during my research time there.

Several translation workshops proved most beneficial. DC-ALT workshop facilitator Keith Cohen and participants Nancy Arbuthnot, Laurel Berger, Jack Gatume, Katie King, and Lynn E. Palermo provided insightful comments on thorny translation issues and offered welcoming and supportive fellowship. I thank ALTA workshop facilitator Kareem James Abu-Zeid and participants Addie Leak, Joon-Li Kim, Helena Lipska, Sebastian Schulman, and Nariman Youssef for vital feedback on an excerpt from the manuscript.

I thank Cecile Esther Kuznitz for research procedural insights and help, and for providing photographs of Frume Halpern's tombstone.

I am extremely grateful to Alison M. Lewis, Ph.D. and the entire Frayed Edge Press team for their belief in this book and for so expertly shepherding the manuscript to publication.

Pearl Gluck's wisdom and support were instrumental to me from the very beginning of this project through the publication process. For your faith, friendship, open ear . . . and heart, thank you, dear Pearl.

I would like to thank the colleagues and friends who have nurtured me in so many ways: Angelika Bammer, Andrew W. M. Beierle, Bella Bryks-Klein, Cindy Casey, Ellen Cassedy, Jim Feldman and Natalie Wexler, Allen J. Frank, Michael Gasper, Ken Giese, Reiner Gogolin, Paula Goldberg, Peter Goodman, Ada Gracin, James Hafner, Janice Hamer, Anne Henochowicz, Miriam Isaacs, Kate James, Deborah Kalb, Julia Spicher Kasdorf, Eitan Kensky, Oksana Klebs, Barbara Krasner, Cecile Esther Kuznitz, Amos Lassen, Elizabeth Goll Lerner, Laura Levitt, Ashira Malka, Erin McGonigle, John N. Mitchell, Elżbieta Pelish, Rita Rubenstein, Nancy Sack, Yankl Salant, Paul Edward Schaper, Faye-Ann Schott, Sebastian Schulman, Jeffrey Shandler, Harvey Spiro, Jonathan Sunshine, Michael Swirsky, Phil Tavolacci, Deidre Waxman, Rivka Yerushalmi, and Sarita Zimmerman.

My sincere apologies in advance to anyone whose names I have accidentally omitted in these acknowledgments.

About the Author

Frume Halpern (neé Tarloff, among other forms) was born ca. 1881-1888(?) presumably in (or near) Bialystok (then the Russian Empire, now Poland). It is likely that she immigrated to the United States in 1904, and became a naturalized citizen in 1914. She worked as a massage therapist in the Bronx Hospital, and wrote stories which appeared in Yiddish-language publications such as *Morgn-frayhayt* [*Morning Freedom*] and the *Zamlungen* [*Collections*]. *Gebentshte hent* [*Blessed Hands*], a collection of these stories, is her only book. Halpern died in 1965.

About the Translator

Yermiyahu Ahron Taub is a poet, writer, and Yiddish literary translator. He is the author of two books of fiction, *Beloved Comrades: A Novel in Stories* (2020) and *Prodigal Children in the House of G-d: Stories* (2018), and six volumes of poetry, including *A Mouse Among Tottering Skyscrapers: Selected Yiddish Poems* (2017). Taub's most recent translation from the Yiddish is *Dineh: An Autobiographical Novel* by Ida Maze (2022). Please visit his website at https://yataubdotnet.word-press.com.

Printed in the USA
CPSIA information can be obtained
at www.ICGtesting.com
CBHW070329080324
5091CB00002B/5